Jolly Good Detecting

Jolly Good Detecting

Humor in
English Crime Fiction
of the Golden Age

BRUCE SHAW

McFarland & Company, Inc., Publishers

Jefferson, North Carolina

LIBRARY OF CONGRESS CATALOGUING-IN-PUBLICATION DATA

Shaw, Bruce, 1941–
    Jolly Good Detecting : Humor in English Crime Fiction of
the Golden Age / Bruce Shaw.
      p.   cm.
    Includes bibliographical references and index.

    ISBN 978-0-7864-7886-6
    softcover : acid free paper ∞

    1. Detective and mystery stories, English—History and
criticism.   2. Humor in literature.   I. Title.
PR830.D4S53 2014
823'.0872—dc23   2013043229

BRITISH LIBRARY CATALOGUING DATA ARE AVAILABLE

Front cover: detective and background images (iStockphoto/
Thinkstock); fingerprint © 2013 Shutterstock

Manufactured in the United States of America

McFarland & Company, Inc., Publishers
  Box 611, Jefferson, North Carolina 28640
   www.mcfarlandpub.com

To the memory of
Susan Vos

Contents

Abbreviations

ABC Australian Broadcasting Corporation
COD *Australian Concise Oxford Dictionary*
OED *Oxford English Dictionary*
SBS Special Broadcasting Service (Australia)

Preface and Acknowledgments

This book is an appreciation of selected authors who make extensive use of humor in English detective/crime fiction. Works using humor as an amelioration of the serious have their heyday in the Golden Age of crime writing but they belong also to a paradigmatic tradition recognizable to this day. When I began the project I thought that the field would be conveniently narrow, that very little humor would be found in crime novels. It seemed a contradiction in terms. I was wrong. There is an identifiable lineage or stream of humorous writing in crime fiction that ranges from mild wit to outright farce, burlesque, even slapstick. In my previous book, *The Animal Fable in Science Fiction and Fantasy* (221–222), I planted the seeds of this new project by mentioning the mystery story, melodrama and the crime novel, directions in which my mind was already heading. Personal choice played a large part, often facilitated by moments of serendipity.

A mix of entertainment with instruction is an identifiable tradition in English letters. David Lodge in *Consciousness and the Novel* (163) discusses early works that challenge, disturb and entertain, adding (164):

> In combining elements of comedy, often of a robustly farcical kind, with satirical wit and caricature, in order to explore social reality with an underlying seriousness of purpose, Evelyn Waugh belonged to *a venerable and peculiarly English literary tradition* which we can trace back through Dickens and Thackeray, Smollett, Sterne, and Henry Fielding [163–164, my emphasis].

English crime fiction partakes of this, most obviously because the greater number of its practitioners are raised in the mainstream literary tradition, only that they turned their skills to detective fiction. They are the humorists of the genre, called farceurs by Julian Symons who describes them as belonging to the "Farceur school, of detective novelists" (247). I prefer to call them humorists and the "school" to which they belong as their tradition because their joking is not only through farce but makes use of other modes of humor as well.

Close reading is a venerable tool dating from the 1930s with F. R. Leavis and I. A. Richards. It is defined by M. H. Abrams as "the detailed and subtle analysis of the complex interrelations and *ambiguities* (multiple meanings) of the components within a work" (223, his emphasis). The approach is also called explication — development and clarification of the meaning and implication of an idea or principle (COD) — and includes paying attention to figures of speech and ways by which a tale hangs together in its structure, and the meanings it conveys. But we should not lose sight of character, thought and plot, which provide the context in which the identification of metaphors and their use and meaning in a text otherwise is lost. In the more traditional Australian university departments, a standard approach is first to provide a potted biography of the author under discussion, sometimes to outline the plot, next to move on to character, and then to themes and literary devices that help make it all appear real or at least plausible, where the principle called suspension of disbelief enters in. This is how lectures were presented when I studied English at the University of Western Australia as a first year undergraduate in 1964 and, although my professional work took a different turn, the attractions of that approach stayed with me.

The other part of the procedure is to embed close reading within the form of a review essay. Walter Murdoch defines the essay as "a quiet talk, reflecting the personal likes and dislikes of the author" (103), marked thus by a degree of informality. Abrams notes a distinction between formal and informal essays in which the formal essay, which is comparatively impersonal, discusses a topic with some authority and in an orderly fashion, whereas the informal essay is more loosely constructed and deals with everyday matters (56). Both usages, however, do not claim to be exclusive in and of their selves. Similarly, Chris Baldick says that as "a minor literary form, the essay is more relaxed than the formal academic dissertation" (75).

This overview, then, is a cross between formal and informal as I reflect upon humor balanced between the serious and non-serious, exemplified by a sampling of individual works that I see as primary sources: the novels, novellas and short stories of a particular author, and autobiographical works that are by definition primary because they are personal documents. Biographies, on the other hand, I regard as secondary sources because they are written "second hand" while often relying heavily upon primary sources such as letters and journals. They can be critical or non-critical, balanced or leaning towards hagiography. The same goes for literary criticism: reviews in newspapers, journals and books, as well as commentaries on authors or their works. They are my secondary sources.

The internet is a comparatively new resource that offers material equally as useful as in more conventional print media. In the last fifty years there has been an explosion of knowledge, now more easily disseminated not only by good quality books but also through the World Wide Web. "Googling" has become part of our language. Wikipedia, begun in 2001, improves steadily in quality. I refer to it as I do for more traditional sources in print and manuscript, gauging the authority with which it speaks, including its accuracy, by cross-referencing where possible with other sources. As the publishers of Wikipedia say in their disclaimer: "Wikipedia articles should be used for background information, as a reference for correct terminology and search terms, and as a starting point for further research." In their citations page they add a warning to budding students: "Most educators and professionals do not consider it appropriate to use tertiary sources such as encyclopedias as a sole source for any information — citing an encyclopedia as an important reference in footnotes or bibliographies may result in censure or a failing grade." I cannot agree. In the world of literary criticism where one's opinion may be virtually as good as another's — depending upon the strength of their logic — readers must judge for themselves and in some circumstances an encyclopedia entry may be useful. The warning is not to use Wikipedia and other depositories of knowledge as one's only source.

It is possible to cover the entire *oeuvre* of some authors in my list with confidence. E. C. Bentley wrote two novels (the second co-authored with a friend), a number of short stories, and a ponderous "shocker." A. A. Milne produced essentially one crime/detective novel and, much later in life, a some-what odd juvenile effort (in the two principal dictionary senses of the word "juvenile"). However, John Dickson Carr wrote at least forty-five novels under his own name and many under pseudonyms such as Carter Dickson. John Innes Mackintosh Stewart wrote more than fifty using his pseudonym of Michael Innes. Bruce Montgomery as Edmund Crispin produced ten Gervase Fen detective novels and two collections of short stories, an output that is more approachable. Nancy Spain wrote ten novels. Simon Brett perpetrated eighty-three crime tales. Margery Allingham produced at least forty. Dorothy L. Sayers wrote nineteen Lord Peter Wimsey stories. Ngaio Marsh wrote approximately thirty-two detective novels. Faced with this overabundance, my policy is to take from most of these authors their first novel and one or two others, choosing what might be considered a reasonable sample of their best work. The approach is a little like that of Colin Watson in his influential study *Snobbery with Violence* (1971) in which he takes, as he says, "characteristic samples ... and not neces-sarily the best known or most widely approved" (14).

So this is not intended as an exhaustive study but an introduction into what I consider the best produced by a handful of very capable and enjoyable authors. It is for students such as myself and shall direct my reading down new paths once the project is done as much as it may for the reader. Along the way I shall identify and discuss types of humor and some of its paradigmatic prin-ciples in crime fiction tradition, focused upon the Golden Age.

I am indebted to George Van Ikin for his advice over the years.

Parts of the chapter section on E. C. Bentley subtitled "The Meeting that Comes Once" are published in Geoff Bradley's *CADS: Crime and Detective Stories*, 62, February 2012. It is not a peer-reviewed publication, but it is a substantial and well-organized magazine and I recommend it highly. My thanks to Geoff Bradley for permission to reproduce parts of that essay.

My thanks goes to Bruce Montgomery's biographer Dr. David Whittle, Director of Music at Leicester Grammar School, for clearing up a point about the personal names of Montgomery's widow.

Introduction

At first sight a crime novel does not allow much comfort. The more serious-minded reader is likely to find it intellectually rewarding through the puzzles to be solved before the last page, even if one scans ahead and knows the outcome. Knowing the identity of the murderer does not necessarily detract from the enjoyment of a well-written plot. One reads on or re-reads a novel, for enjoyment in the detail and to see how it is done, or in some instances through pure enjoyment of the style. This is the crime novel many serious readers expect.

Intellectual pleasure in solving a detective mystery is described by Karel Čapek as "the mad, tormenting, voluptuous pleasure of the intellect in solving problems: the passionate need of the brain to crack the hard nuts of problems artfully posed" (106). The sensual images remind me of Roland Barthes's *The Pleasure of the Text* (1990). For less serious-minded readers, however, a crime story is more enjoyable when an element of humor is present. On the animal fable, which often contains amusing situations, David Lodge says, "Part of the pleasure of this kind of fiction is that our intelligence is exercised and flattered by interpreting the allegory" (144). One might say that we experience a broadly similar pleasure when wit, farce or other sorts of geniality lighten a crime story. The interpretation and appreciation of a joke likewise flatters our intelligence.

The pleasure in reading such tales as a problem-solving pastime or for a smile marks a comparatively sharp dichotomy in twentieth-century crime fiction that is recognized by several critics. Leroy Lad Panek in *Watteau's Shepherds* (1979) takes the comic as his principal theme, that is, reading and writing for pleasure. He gets sidetracked, however, because other themes such as puzzle solving or modes of the thriller jostle for equal time, for humor is only one element in crime writing. Panek's first chapter, "Backgrounds and Approaches," contains interesting statements on this thematic splitting-off:

It is significant that the new generation of writers ... all singled out that which was patently false and obtuse and made their people comic, sensitive, intelligent, and at times tender — things which the thriller hero and his bulldog successors could never achieve.... The body in the library may be a cliché today, but in the twenties it was a relief from multiple bodies flopping out of secret passages, shadowy doorways, abandoned houses, and hidden dungeons [13–14].

The point of the title *Watteau's Shepherds* rests in an idea from Robert Graves that the detective story of the Golden Age is comparable to rococo art, as in Watteau's paintings that are, says Panek, "full of comfortable, pretty, mildly exciting amusements which do not inspire sublime emotions or probe the basic mysteries of life," because most readers, worn out in post–World War II England, preferred "a good read" (71). This is not entirely accurate. While the strain of humorist writing has a strong cozy aspect, it is subversive as well, introducing serious issues masked behind diverting laughter. Multiple bodies continue to flop out of hidden rooms and passages, but usually no more than three or four, and there are plenty of unsettling country cottages and mansions populated by a variety of potential victims.

Inversion, overturning, ribaldry and joyous play — that is, the carnivalesque — and the sobering reality of tomorrow just round the corner fit into this pattern. It comes about while at the same time the same works contain themes to make us thoughtful: instructive, unsettling insights, moral issues, people being killed. We like being sobered and shocked by a story, hence the popularity of crime fiction. The shock *is* the entertainment because of its cathartic value. This is why there is a widely held fascination for novels about serial killers that persists from Jack the Ripper to the present day.

Crime fiction takes in the detective or mystery story, the gothic and the thriller. We do not find a lot of humor in Conan Doyle's Sherlock Holmes mysteries, or in Agatha Christie, P.D. James and the others. The hound that haunted the Baskerville family is unlike the enquiring cats Koko and Yum Yum in Lilian Jackson Braun's Jim Quilleran series (1960s on). Nor are amusing elements present in any force in the Gothic genre represented by Mary Shelley's seminal *Frankenstein* and its offspring. Edgar Allan Poe, frequently hailed as the founder of detective/crime writing, as far as I am aware does not employ many humorous images. Pits and pendulums fall short of gaiety. But Panek calls him a joker, that is, a trickster figure for his use of surprise endings and the introduction of principal clues late in the plot (14). All the same, there is a place for levity in crime fiction. It adds to our intellectual pleasure in the reading.

There is, too, melodrama of the kind performed in nineteenth-century stage plays that has a sort of exuberance and usually a moral ending, and is a distant forerunner of the crime mystery in what Panek (55, 57–58) identifies as "sensation fiction." Melodrama and sensation fiction are forerunners of the thriller. Modern love romances or bodice-rippers, including the gothic pulp novels of the 1960s to the mid–1970s, belong to the thriller/mystery strain. Parodies and satires of all these genres abound, one of the functions of which is to instruct us subtly in right behavior, that is, what is approved in our society, while at the same time they challenge the status quo. This can be said of humor in general.

Literary studies of crime fiction became of academic interest from 1941 through the 1950s, and revived in the late 1970s and early 1980s, if we use Chris Baldick's select bibliography of E. C. Bentley's work as a rough guide (Baldick, 1995: xxii). But there was an earlier period, with Dorothy L. Sayers' watershed essay in 1928 discussed below. Howard Haycraft's *Murder for Pleasure* is among the earlier studies, published by Appleton-Century in 1941 and re-published with revisions by Carroll & Graf in 1984. In his foreword to the 1984 edition, Haycraft establishes a double-barrelled theme: that a sort of renaissance (my word) of detective fiction was brought about during the London blitz, with "the appearance of books in the fetid burrows while the bombs rained overhead" (vii), that were read by many down in the air-raid shelters, "the underlying object of the work [being] ... pleasure — for reader and writer alike" (ix). The *raison d'être* of detective-crime tales, then, is "a frankly non-serious, entertainment form of literature which, nevertheless, possesses its own rules and standards, its good and bad examples, and at its best has won the right to respectful consideration on its own merits" (xi–xii).

George Orwell in an essay on "Good Bad Books" (1945) singles out the Sherlock Holmes stories and the *Raffles* tales and by extension the detective/crime stories and thrillers as belonging to this escapist literature (318). Two pages later he mentions works such as *Uncle Tom's Cabin, Dracula* or *King Solomon's Mines*. To explain this, Orwell makes a distinction that: "art is not the same as cerebration" and that such books, although they are "absurd" and not to be taken seriously, have survived alongside the more serious literature and will probably continue to do so (320). Nearly seventy years later we know it to be true. This, it can be argued, is for two reasons, (a) a human need for amusement and excitement, and (b) a human need, though not one possessed by all, for good writing. As Orwell puts it: "there is such a thing as sheer skill, or native grace, which may have more survival value than erudition or intellectual power."

Haycraft (xiii) chooses to represent the authors he discusses "whenever possible at the prime of their careers rather than in the sunset years of life," whereas I follow a different principle. I include the end points of writers' lives because that way we understand more about them as individuals with personal troubles within their social milieux. Haycraft's timeframe is reflected (xv) in his Contents table, dividing the years alternately between the United States and England and sometimes including Continental Europe: "Genesis" (America from 1841), "Development" (nineteenth-century England), "Renaissance" (the obligatory chapter on Sherlock Holmes), a "Romantic Era" from 1890 to 1914 for the two hemispheres, the Continent (France), the Golden Age in England and America (his dates are 1918–1930), and "the Moderns" from 1930 on (to the date of publication). There are eight additional chapters on themes such as "rules of the game" and future trends. His approach is to synopsise each writer's work with a short biographical sketch.

Haycraft's style leans towards pomposity and wordiness but his descriptive material is interesting. One of the most striking things about it is that he makes his commentaries when many important writers are still living — such as Bentley, Allingham, Sayers, Carr, or Innes — and before they have written some of their best (or worst) work. He describes E. C. Bentley as living "quietly and modestly with his wife in Paddington: a large, graying, essentially simple, idealistic, and generous man," clearly before the bombing of their flat and the shattering of their lives (115). Dorothy L. Sayers "lives in rural semi-retirement near her schoolgirl home in East Anglia with her husband" (139). Concerning Margery Allingham: "The Carters live to-day in a Queen Anne country house, where plump, dark-haired Margery Allingham divides her time between writing and village and household activities" (184).

A second period is signposted in Panek's *An Introduction to the Detective Story*, by a revised edition of Julian Symons' *Bloody Murder* (1985) thirteen years after its first publication in 1972, in Penzler and Friedman's popularized *The Crown Crime Companion* (1995), and T. J. Binyon's *Murder Will Out* (1989). The genre became the object of renewed interest more recently with reference works such as Forshaw's *The Rough Guide to Crime Fiction* (2007) and P. D. James's *Talking about Detective Fiction* (2009) which is short at 157 pages and lacks an index (indexes nearly always assist ready-reference) yet as an overview remains a good introduction for the beginning student and seems comparable with the long essay by Dorothy L. Sayers in 1929.

These critical overviews are a mixed bag. Panek's two studies, *Watteau's Shepherds* (1979) and *An Introduction to the Detective Story*, cover the field but they are uneven. *Watteau's Shepherds* deals with the period of the Golden Age from 1914 to 1940 writing "as a lark," but he detours as well into serious themes and motivations (21). It could not be otherwise when trying to make sense of a large field and his difficulty, shared with other critics, is that there are disparate themes to cover. Penzler and Friedman take mysteries as the generic starting point, as in their subtitle *The Top 100 Mystery Novels of All Time*. The volume is essentially sets of lists with commentaries and mini essays contributed by members of the Mystery Writers of America, some of whose books are rated in the list. Out of the "Top 100" (18–19), Dorothy L. Sayers' *Gaudy Night* rates at 18, E. C. Bentley's *Trent's Last Case* at 33, and Edmund Crispin's *The Moving Toyshop* comes in at 72. *Gaudy Night* and *The Moving Toyshop* rank also as

"Cozy/Traditional" (121) and *The Moving Toyshop* as "Humorous" (133). Aside from these, few of the works I review make it to the lists.

Gregory Mcdonald, writing on the basis of his novel *Fletch* (it is number one in the Humorous category), refers in passing to "the refined wit of the ironic" (135). He cites Zangwell's (1864–1926) reference to "real persons with individual humors" perhaps without understanding that humor in the nineteenth-century context has a different usage from that of today and refers to medieval thought about bodily fluids affecting different temperaments such as being "sanguine" or "melancholic" (Baldick, 103). Quotations from Mcdonald's books appear not especially funny to my eyes. They read more like a writer trying to be humorous, a notorious pitfall. This might reflect a difference between Australian-British humor and that of the Americans and so reveals critical bias in myself as an Australian. However, Mcdonald touches upon two important ideas: that "international cultural revolution" took place in the 1960s and 1970s concomitant with a "degree of apprehension regarding profound changes" (136–137). This is another watershed in personal troubles vis-à-vis cultural anxieties.

An explanation that assists our understanding of humor in what otherwise is a serious business includes the truism that writers of crime fiction who make use of humor are reflecting societal fears as well as their own liking for comic situations. Walter Murdoch says in his essay (3) on "The Bloke" that: "The great writer does not originate ideas; he is the spokesman of the age he lives in, taking the ideas that are in the air around him, finding words for them, stamping them with finality." This seems as valid now despite the time of publication (early 1940s), the single gender usage, and my thought that there is no real finality in a genre (humor in crime fiction) if it can be traced to the present day, for obviously it continues. Together with this, ideas among the crime writers nowadays are for the most part not original. As a reworking of older themes, they are comparable to the recasting into the first decade of the golden age of a set of conventions established by E.C. Bentley.

One of P. D. James's insights relates to two themes that influenced my approach to anthropological uses of oral history in a former life and continues in my approach to literary appreciation: "We have to remember that the detective novelists of the thirties had been bred to a standard of ethics and manners in public and private life which today might well be seen as elitist" (136). Personal and public mores are necessarily infused into their writing. As James observes: "I have come to believe that most fiction is autobiographical and some autobiography partly fiction" (124). Yet there are shifts of emphasis and not all fiction reflects necessarily the writer's personal state or vice versa. Says James, "The great international changes of the immediate post-war years largely passed these writers by in their fiction, though not in their lives, as no doubt was artistically understandable" (106).

It is not so clear-cut as James would have it. For Margery Allingham, private troubles, both physical and psychological, remained private. They might, however, be matched against differences in tone between her earlier novels and those written later, when she was often under intense pressure to produce a substantial output in order to earn a living. Her early Alfred Campion novels are more lighthearted than her later work that has a darker tone, yet in James's estimation the later books "are markedly superior to those written earlier both in characterisation and plot" (104). Margery Allingham's biographer Julia Jones writes that Allingham had an "instinctive desire to redress one book's natural imbalance in the next. *More Work for the Undertaker* [1948] had made comedy of social change, *Tiger in the Smoke* [1952] considers individual moral choices in a markedly less genial world" (283). A developmental seriousness of tone is to be found in the work of several other authors. Taking one example, E. C. Bentley's work declined in his later years due to a combination of personal loss (the wartime bombing of his flat, the death of his wife) and heavy drinking, the one contingent upon the other according to Bentley's son Nicolas.

Writers of crime fiction, like those in other genres, reflect the outside world and its troubles or triumphs whether consciously or not and whether they like it or not. In 1948, a date that, broadly speaking, marks a transition from the three decades of the "Golden Age" to the subgenre of the "hard bitten" or noir detective story, Raymond Chandler, cited by Hiney & MacShane, wrote: "it is just possible that the tensions in a novel of murder are the simplest and yet most complete pattern of the tensions in which we live in this generation" (96). It seems one cannot get away from considering together different facets of the private and the public. They cannot easily be dismissed.

Writers in My List

Works of merit in crime fiction where lightheartedness is prominent include E. C. Bentley's *Trent's Last Case* (1913), A. A. Milne's *The Red House Mystery* (1922), Margery Allingham's Albert Campion adventures, John Dickson Carr's Dr. Fell and Sir Henry Merrivale mysteries, Edmund Crispin's (Bruce Montgomery's) Dr. Gervase Fen's crime-solving, and Nancy Spain's satirical romps. These six authors with representative works are my centrepieces. To them I add Dorothy L. Sayers' Lord Peter Wimsey, Michael Innes' Inspector Appleby, Ngaio Marsh's Inspector Alleyn, Leslie Thomas's Dangerous Davies, Colin Watson's Flaxborough Chronicles, Gladys Mitchell's Mrs. Bradley, Caryl Brahms' Adam Quill tales, and Simon Brett's Fethering stories. I do not give them equal space. Other works shade into novels written after the Golden Age, that is, post–World War II to the present in which crime novels, often with an international voice, continue to use elements of humor but within a darker framework. They include the Sicilian Andrea Camilleri's Inspector Montalbano, the Australian Kerry Greenwood's Phryne Fisher mysteries, and Shamini Flint's Inspector Singh tales. Many of the novels have film versions, notably those of Bentley, Allingham, Sayers, Marsh, Thomas, Watson and Camilleri.

Another purpose of this study is to showcase the literary value of almost forgotten works. Several of these authors slipped into obscurity within the last fifty years or more—in particular Allingham, Carr, Crispin and Spain—but recently their best work has found its way into reprints to be read by new generations. This goes a long way towards what defines a classic: a work that continues to entertain generations of readers. We have several themes to explore: (1) a tradition of humor in crime fiction that by definition has a lineage, (2) its application to public (societal) fears and individual anxieties, (3) a set of conventions (a paradigm) largely adhered to as well as subverted intentionally through parody and satire, (4) the finding that several authors who have a place in this lineage slipped into obscurity and are beginning to be rediscovered, and (5) many of the authors in the list produced good work only to fall prey to the usual range of human failings in their later years (depression, alcohol, loss of inspiration), that is, starting well but ending poorly. It was of course not the case with them all.

It appeared at first that a great many of the publications were out of print and often difficult to find through the secondhand booksellers advertised on the Internet. As the project that began in 2009 matured over the next three years, this state of affairs changed rapidly. One of my nice points was to have been that many of the neglected authors be re-published because the quality of their work made it no more than their due. Pleasingly, House of Stratus, Felony & Mayhem Press, Vintage Books, and Rue Morgue Press stole my thunder. With the exception of Nancy Spain, all major authors in my list now have this recognition.

"Crime fiction" is a generic label, meaning that it denotes a broad classificatory field which is neither specific nor special (COD). It takes in genres such as detective fiction, thriller, mystery, romance, gothic, or the comic. These lie somewhere within the strain of crime fiction that Leroy Lad Panek calls a little disparagingly: "the crime novel, the amorphous twentieth century term which embraces any work of fiction about crime, detection, police work" (7). John Dickson Carr's biographer Douglas Greene expresses a similar view when he writes that "the term ... which has recently gained currency [that is, in 1995 when Greene's book was published], is so broad that it is almost useless" (95). Julian Symons makes a similar point when he says that "the most sensible sort of naming is the general one of crime novel or suspense novel (and short story) (13)" and "these rigid classifications don't work in practice" (15). Howard Haycraft is critical likewise, saying that he restricts his study to what he calls a "bona-fide" or "pure" form, the "detective story and its craftsmen," and not mystery or criminology (x). While not perhaps becoming bogged down, Haycraft finds that, all the same, he has to acknowledge certain authors whose works lie "on the border-line between adventure and bona fide detection" (157), namely John Buchan or H. C. McNeile ("Sapper") who we call today writers of thrillers or "shockers"; or to devote pages to A. E. W. Mason's melodramatic thrillers *At the Villa Rose* (1910) and *The House of the Arrow* (1924) that have investigating detectives (72–74). Haycraft's coverage would be incomplete if he did not include such borderline cases.

I find it advisable to be amorphous too because several authors in my list blend together elements from different genres. Margery Allingham, for example, draws upon her early experience in serialized adventure stories, romances and the gothic when she writes the Albert Campion mysteries. Her novels have moments of the thriller and the gothic although they are largely intended as detective stories and are often parodies of such tales. Edmund Crispin and John Dickson Carr use elements of farce and the thriller combined, as in slapstick chase sequences and, especially in Carr's work, touches of the gothic or the supernatural. Writing in 1995, Margaret Maron states that "because modern readers care about more than murder for murder's sake, many novels now play out against a textured backdrop of societal issues and challenge complacent assumptions" (124). This is as true of the Golden Age and its precursors as it is for Maron's day. Interestingly, many of the authors in my list shift from a mix of crime and the comic in early novels to a more serious shaping of their plots in later works. It is a subtle (but sometimes not too subtle) change towards what becomes in the 1940s a full-blown movement towards noir fiction. As well as reflecting the experimental work of these authors, their novels mirror the growing and changing anxieties of the world around them.

Most critics recognize the era between World War I and World War II as the Golden Age for crime fiction. A similar golden age for science fiction and fantasy comes later from 1938 to 1946 (Clute and Nicholls, 506–507) overlapping that of crime writing. The Golden Age tapers off with changes in sentiment and societal fears after the close of World War II, just as it begins with post–World War I disillusion and reconstruction when, in the Western countries at any rate and particularly in England, people turned to different forms of gaiety. "Hard boiled" crime fiction came to the ascendant after World War II, a development in American (United States) crime writing characterized by the novels and short stories of Raymond Chandler and Dashiell Hammett and the noir films they influenced, both American and European. But the genre always had instances of dark humor (irony). Several writers in my list lived through these transitions and adapted accordingly. Moreover, the tradition of farce and other forms of humor continue to the present day albeit in a diluted state.

Humor penetrates present-day crime fiction sufficiently to demonstrate that the theme has not been killed off. For one thing, several seminal works have been rediscovered, if never entirely forgotten, and are frequently republished. Different publishing houses specialize in this variety of forgotten authors. The UK publishers House of Stratus have put out new editions of all E. C. Bentley's major work, including a book of clerihews and the disastrous novel *Elephant's Work*. Similarly, most of Edmund Crispin's Gervase Fen novels and Margery Allingham's books are in reprint under the Felony & Mayhem Press. A. A. Milne was republished in a 2008 Vintage Books edition. Some of John Dickson Carr's work is republished by "crimemasterworks" under the Orion imprint. New editions of Agatha Christie's *oeuvre* come out all the time from HarperCollins, who also reprint Dorothy L. Sayers' Lord Peter Wimsey novels and short stories. Rue Morgue Press in the United States republishes Colin Watson's Flaxborough Chronicles and Sheila Pim's work. There is a considerable book publishing industry for old but not quite forgotten works. But Nancy Spain remains largely neglected and her novels have to be found through second-hand bookshops, a recourse I had to take for John Dickson Carr, too. Television dramas help keep a lot of the work alive.

There are some instrumental works of criticism. One of the best, *Bloody Murder* (1972/1985) by Julian Symons, takes humor as a major theme. In the prologue, Symons says in his poem "The Guilty Party," "The author / Puts down his pen. He has but poisoned in jest. / Stabbed and strangled in jest, destroyed in jest / By unknown means the smiling neuter victim" (11). In his 1984 "Preface to the Revised Edition" Symons wishes to show that "crime stories are not simply entertainments but also literature" (9). On the vexed question of how to classify the genre he takes my view, saying that "the most sensible sort of naming is the general one of crime novel or suspense novel (and short story)" (13).

Laughter

In the study of animal tales in science fiction and fantasy, I survey a number of authorities on laughter, noting that Bakhtin's concept of Carnival, with its adjective the carnivalesque, enriches our understanding by providing complementary insights into such literary modes as satire and parody and their application in social criticism. Rules are relaxed and authority subverted. The carnival of popular medieval festivals that took place immediately after Lenten fasting allowed a relaxation between the traditional social hierarchies so that commoners might poke fun at their lords, kings and clerics without fear of severe reprisals. Robert Darnton acknowledges Bakhtin's study of Rabelais and Carnival: "Mikhail Bakhtin has shown how the laughter of Rabelais expressed a strain of popular culture in which the riotously funny could turn to riot, a carnival culture of sexuality and sedition" (99). Hence Carnival brings with it a temporary relaxation of taboos, the dissolution of inequalities, and the subversion of authority by turning accepted modes of conduct upon their heads. Bakhtin finds value in the "regenerating, creative meaning" of laughter expressed through the carnivalesque (71). Similarly Walter Murdoch when referring to Cervantes writes that "the soul, with its starry splendours and its towering aspirations — the body, with its needs and its greeds and its hurts and its frailties — out of the clash of these comedy is born" (53).

Laughter, then, belongs to the comic that includes humor and wit (Abrams 197–198). Such qualities invite us to see the world afresh and stand in contrast to serious aspects of life. They unsettle and discomfort us, and for this reason, paradoxically, they appeal to us. Narratives that make use of the carnivalesque, satire, parody, and the like are subversive in their intent for they instruct as much as they entertain. Hence crime with comedy becomes a recognized sub-genre in crime fiction. It even has a place on the Internet (see for example *Crimespace* and *Crime Watch*).

On the other hand, Henri Bergson (1859–1941) critiques laughter in largely negative terms (71, 63) as an "absence of feeling" that, he says, "usually accompanies laughter" (63). He implies that laughter involves a suspension of pity and for that reason he disapproves of it. Charles Baudelaire (1821–1867) takes a similar position on "the essence of laughter," observing that the comic is in one instance "barbaric," in another violent, and that it leads us to entertain ideas about our superiority over others (140–161). Voltaire (Francoise-Marie Arouet, 1694–1778) writes about laughter as *both* regenerative and cruel.

Sigmund Freud reiterates one of his key ideas, that "like wit and the comic, humor has in it a *liberating* element. But it has also something fine and elevating [his emphasis]" (215–217), meaning that the ego becomes victorious because "it refuses to be hurt by the arrows of reality or to be compelled to suffer." This is an appeal to the triumph of the "pleasure principle" in the face of adversity. Described as simply as this misses the importance of social elements outside the psychic life of any one individual, but Freud sets the apparent omission right when in a later and more detailed work he refers to "jokes as a social process" (140–158). He also talks about comic contrast in which "the comic is concerned with the ugly in one of its manifestations," such as caricature (10).

In "Pleasure and the Genesis of Jokes" (119–122), the pleasure taken in a joke derives from the bringing together of two or more disparate "circles of ideas" that "short-circuits" the usual train of connected (logical) thought. This relates specifically to play on words. Technical methods that make use of this are similarities of sound, multiple uses, the modification of familiar phrases, and allusions to quotations, all of which appeal to our "rediscovery of what is familiar." Freud cites Aristotle's idea that our joy in recognition lies at the center of our enjoyment of art: "rhymes, alliterations, refrains," the pleasure of remembering and our rediscovery of the familiar. Aristotle (384–322 B.C.) discusses comedy briefly in his *Ethics* (58, 135) and the *Poetics* (9), the latter is fragmentary at two short paragraphs. His translator Malcolm Heath, in a brief commentary, says, "The loss of the extended analysis of comedy which the original *Poetics* probably contained makes it difficult to be sure what Aristotle's view on comedy would have been" (lxii). Heath observes that persons of low social status such as slaves and peasants played central parts in Classical Greek comedy and are referred to as "inferior" not only because of their low status but also for their tendency to behave badly. He cites Aristotle: "comedy aims to evoke laughter," whereas tragedy evokes pity and fear (9). What Aristotle wrote 2,500 years ago is applicable still.

Aristotle's missing book is a central motif in Umberto Eco's masterful novel *The Name of the Rose* (1980/1983), a medieval "detective" investigation into unusual deaths within a Benedictine monastery. It hinges upon the discovery in that community's archives of Aristotle's missing book on comedy and the baleful attempts to suppress its circulation among the monks by one of their number, who coats the pages with a slow-acting poison transferred from print to mouth when the reader wets his tongue in order to turn the pages. Julian Symons (186) calls *The Name of the Rose* an "avant-guarde [*sic*] crime story," and refers to Eco's "elaborate periphrastical [roundabout] jokiness," which is another way of describing wit.

Examples of humor in crime fiction can be arranged along a continuum from buffoonery (slapstick and farce) to innuendo (wit and irony). In my opinion, wit and irony tend more towards seriousness. Abrams (27–29) describes comedy as of four kinds: romantic, satiric, comedy of manners, and farce and high comedy. There is also comic relief (30). It is no simple matter and Abrams' typology (if that is what it is, for the entries in his glossary appear not clearly organized) is not the only one possible. While not attempting a strict hierarchy, laughter may be elicited through wit, irony, satire, farce, parody, burlesque and slapstick.

Parody imitates "serious" writing — the work itself or an author's style — but in a different, more lighthearted vein, what Abrams calls, "a lowly or comically inappropriate subject" (18). Satire aims at making a subject ridiculous by means of derogating it or diminishing it, and is used "as a weapon" against a work, a person or an ideology outside itself (166). Parody can be employed as a weapon in much the same way. The similarity of these two arts to the overturning and ribaldry of Carnival should be no surprise; they belong to the same family of narrative approaches that can express dissidence, resistance, and paradox. They discompose. Baldick defines satire as "a mode of writing that exposes the failings of individuals, institutions, or societies to ridicule and scorn ... 'indirect' satire usually found in plays and novels allows us to draw our own conclusions from the actions of the characters, as for example in the novels of Evelyn Waugh" (198). We can immediately relate this to my opening paragraph citing David Lodge on Waugh's novels within the English comedic tradition. Satire "uses laughter as a weapon," observes Abrams (166), for it frequently has social criticism in its sights, whereas it is sufficient for comedy to bring forth our laughter. Satire and the comic are often blurred in characterization.

Slapstick is the name applied to clowning humor that involves pratfalls, acrobatics and simulated fighting. The "slap stick" is traditionally a wooden affair constructed from two flat laths that make a loud clapping sound when struck together, usually upon some part of a clown's body. It may be impregnated with powder to allow a cloud of the stuff to burst out with each blow. This style of comedy has a long history that goes back to Renaissance times, but some argue for a greater antiquity in Classical Greek drama ("Slapstick"). It became the stock-in-trade of Italian live theater known as the *Commedia dell'arte* that flourished in the sixteenth to seventeenth centuries, in which appear stock characters such as "foolish old men, devious servants, or military officers full of false bravado" ("Commedia dell'arte"). The English Punch and Judy with their club-wielding Punchinello come from this tradition: "The Punch and Judy puppet shows, popular to this day in England, owe their basis to the Pulcinella mask that emerged in Neapolitan versions of the form. In Italy, commedia masks and plots found their way into the *opera buffa* [Italian: comic opera, punning on *buffa* = hood, and *buffo* = comedian] and the plots of Rossini, Verdi, and Puccini" ("Commedia dell'arte").

Burlesque has two general meanings, the first a variety of parody that, as Chris Baldick says "ridicules some serious literary work either by treating its solemn subject in an undignified style ... or by applying its elevated style to a trivial subject" (27). In this definition I see it has a kinship with parody. The second meaning has the more popular sense "of comic entertainment with titillating dances or striptease." The standard example of the first sense is John Gay's *The Beggar's Opera* (1728) parodying Italian opera and itself spawning imitations. The U.S. vaudeville figure of Gypsy Rose Lee is a good example of the second ("comic entertainment with titillating dances"). The two forms come together in one of the best imitations, that of Bertolt Brecht's (1898–1956) *Threepenny Opera* (1928). The German and French film adaptations by G. W. Pabst with the music of Kurt Weill, the German version in 1931, introduce such characters as Mackie Messer ("Mack the Knife") [German: *messer* = knife], Polly Peachum, and assorted ladies of the bar room.

Farce is not far removed from burlesque and slapstick. Baldick's definition includes elements of cruelty and anxiety that are part of the general definition of laughter: "a kind of comedy that inspires hilarity mixed with panic and cruelty in its audience through an increasingly rapid and improbable series of ludicrous confusions, physical disasters, and sexual innuendos among its stock characters" (82). The wild chase scenes in Edmund Crispin's better Dr. Fen novels and in some of John Dickson Carr's Sir Henry Merrivale mysteries are good examples of farce and slapstick.

Wit lies at the other end of the continuum from the tomfoolery of slapstick or farce. Its definition has changed over the last five centuries to apply today "to a brilliant and paradoxical style ... a kind of verbal expression which is brief, deft, and intentionally contrived to produce a shock of comic surprise" (Abrams 197). Baldick describes wit in similar terms, saying: "The usual modern sense of wit ... is one of light cleverness and skill in repartee or the composition of amusing epigrams," like those of Oscar Wilde (242). Writers as diverse as Dorothy L. Sayers and Nancy Spain frequently use quick repartee in dialogue, from the measured and comparatively subtle pronouncements of Lord Peter Wimsey and Harriet Vane to the flamboyant comments of Miriam Birdseye and Natasha DuVivian.

Wit often merges into irony, "in which," says Baldick, "an apparently straightforward statement or event is undermined by its context so as to give it a very different significance ... structural irony in literature involves the use of a naïve or deluded hero or unreliable narrator ... [and] dramatic irony, in which the audience knows more about a character's situation than a character does" (114). Abrams makes the interesting note that the *eiron* in Greek comedy was a character who misled ("dissembled") through understatement: "hiding what is actually the case; not, however, in order to deceive, but to achieve special rhetorical or artistic effects" (91). Richard Holmes writes:

> For Voltaire, the essence of intellectual freedom was wit. Wit — which meant both intelligence and humour — was the primary birthright of man. The freeplay of wit brings enlightenment and also a certain kind of laughter: the laughter that distinguishes man from the beasts. But it is not a simple kind of laughter: it is also close to tears.... Life amuses him and delights him; but it also causes him pain and grief [348].

David Lodge in *The Art of Fiction* finds two "primary sources" for comedy in fiction: situation and style as well as "a combination of surprise ... and conformity to pattern" (110–111). Character (characterization) is important to situation, for "a situation that is comic for one character wouldn't necessarily be so for another." So elements of situation, characterization, style, surprise and pattern are interrelated. Lodge illustrates some of these points in his 1992 introduction (vi) to Kingsley Amis's novel *Lucky Jim* (1954) in which comedy comes from situation, such as in Jim Dixon's attempts to hide from his hostess cigarette burns in his bedclothes, and from the novel's style, too: "full of unexpected reversals and underminings of stock phrases and stock responses, bringing a bracing freshness to the satirical observation of everyday life." Amis, says Lodge, "avoids all the traditional devices of humorous literary prose — jocular periphrasis (circumlocution, euphemism), mock-heroic literary allusion, urbane detachment." What works for this particular subgenre, the campus novel, is just as applicable in the best of the crime/detective novels. In the crime novel, however, we shall find examples of other traditional devices (especially literary allusion) as well as richer veins that undermine the stock devices.

Several types of humor can be found in comedic crime fiction: verbal humor including wordplay that we may call wit such as puns, wisecracks and drollery (Bentley, Allingham, Sayers, Crispin), satire (Innes), parody (Carr), situational humor such as slapstick or ridiculous situations (Carr, Crispin, Thomas), farce (Crispin), and eccentric characters (Allingham, Carr, Crispin, Spain). There is a pattern in the evolution of several writers' work. Early novels are often affable and relaxed, such as those of Edmund Crispin whose *The Case of the Gilded Fly* (1944), *The Moving Toyshop* (1946), *Love Lies Bleeding* (1948), and his last novel *The Glimpses of the Moon* (1977) all climax in slapstick. Wild chase scenes are a situational leitmotif for Crispin. Margery Allingham's *The Crime at Black Dudley* (1929), which introduces her character Albert Campion, similarly is built upon hijinks and ridiculous situations brought about by a bumbling group of young people. John Dickson Carr also reaches heights of slapstick.

Fairy Tales and the Crime Novel

Two traditions come together when considering the animal fable and crime fiction. Comedy may result when a sentient beast engages in detective work. But there are few examples of this. Animals figure in some serious mysteries, as in Poe's "The Murders in the Rue Morgue" where the culprit is an orangutan, a little unfairly as those primates are peaceful vegetarians. One or two mystery tales with animals can be found in science fiction (more in fantasy, dragons and the like). Most recently have appeared Bob Burke's *The Third Pig Detective Agency* (2009) and the series of Chet and Bernie mystery stories of which the first is titled *dog on it* (2008). Humor in these offerings comes a lot from the making of bad, not to say clichéd, puns mediated through the thoughts of an unreliable narrator who perceives events through canine senses. There are as well a substantial number of tales whereby a mystery, usually murder, is solved by the intervention of an animal companion, as in the extensive series of The Cat Who ... novels by Lilian Jackson Braun. The animals in this subgenre, however, are not sentient in that they do not have quasi-human thoughts, nor do they speak although they might miaow suggestively or point a paw in the right direction. But there are plentiful *elements* from the animal fable and the fairy tale in crime fiction.

Maya Slater identifies several related factors in the beast fables of La Fontaine: diversity and duality, pessimism with light-hearted irony, subversion, a variety of layers and shifts in perspective, the intention to both instruct and entertain the reader, moral or cautionary instruction, the use of allegorical characters, the tradition of using animals as characters to emphasize points being made, the use of wit and humor in driving home serious and unsettling points, and the skilled crafting of many a written or spoken tale (vii–xxvii). In his collection of essays titled *In Praise of Newspapers* (1951) Karel Čapek's framework of fairy-tale narrative elements ("Towards a Theory of Fairy-Tales") seems equally good for other genres:

> So the teller of fairy-tales uses all kinds of tricks to slow up the progress of the story; he allows himself detours and deviations, he repeats always three times the theme of obstacles, of questions, or of the tasks, he links up heroic deeds and adventures, he piles one theme on top of another, and he weaves several stories into one action which becomes slightly confused, but at any rate complex and spacious [68].

Čapek might have been writing about crime/detective fiction, for many if not all the stylistic strategies noted for the fairy tale are used to good effect by the best of the crime writers. Symons observes that "the detective story with its closed circle of suspects and its rigid rules had always been a fairy tale, but the point and pleasure of fairy tales is that by exercising the imagination one can believe them to be true. In the post-war world this sort of story changed from a fairy tale to an absurdity (22–23)," this last point flagging the close of the Golden Age.

Karel Čapek in "Holmesiana, or About Detective Stories" writes about motifs in crime fiction as well. This article (1924) is among the first critical discussions of the genre. In a statement that conflates the two ideas of the detective story as literature with a debt to the fairy tale, Čapek says: "A detective story ... is a literary phenomenon just as simple as, for instance, an epic poem or a child's fairy-tale" (102). Čapek outlines characteristic motifs and themes: the criminal motif, the judicial motif, the motif of mystery, the motif of achievement, the theme of the companion, cleverness or wit, the spirit of method, the motif of chance, Bertillonage (from Alphonse Bertillon whose studies in human measurements influenced the pseudo-science of anthropometry), and escape.

A classic uneasy mix between entertainment and the serious rests in the first of these, which Čapek calls the criminal motif (102). On the one hand there is pleasure, laughter, and the like and, on the other hand, a general fascination with crime, brought together in phrases such as "delight in petrifying horror" and the "dreadful disclosure" (103) attendant upon it: "People are not interested in crime merely for its literary appeal but because of its general possibility. They are interested in it as something important and personally close. They are excited by the horrifying realization that it can be done" (103). This is the truism that under certain conditions many of us are capable of committing the crime of murder, but that we have at the same time a strong ethic to see justice prevail (the judicial motif). So when reading about crime we experience "a double pleasure" that makes the story "twice as exciting." To this is added the intellectual pleasure taken in solving puzzles, the motif of mystery (106) allied with that of achievement (108) or adventure:

> A criminal is something like a hero: he is shrouded with romanticism, he is an outcast.... Among all the other human actions a crime is adventurous and epic first of all because it is something of a personal attack by an individual upon society ... and because at the bottom of our hearts we are all dreadful anarchists.

At this point, shifting from motif to theme, Čapek reinforces the old tradition of the cave hunt with that of the fairy tale: "traps, the spotting of traces in the dust and mud ... pursuit, escape, defence, the rounding-up of the victim, close fighting ... detective stories are the most ancient literature" (109). This is akin to the thriller, especially where pursuit, the hunt and fighting are concerned. Looking back to Čapek's judicial motif, "the same critical astuteness finds its place just as well in fairy-stories in the shape of sorcerers' magic and in the expeditions of princes" (105).

Critical astuteness interrelates with two other elements. A summing-up of the preferred qualities for a detective in Čapek's motif of chance suggests "rules of the game" drawn up in lists such as those of Knox and Van Dine and one or two others: "A detective must have luck; he must possess the right disposition; a kind of allégresse [rejoicing], no gloominess, no fatal passions, pleasure in active life, and some sort of freedom of the spirit" (118). Rules like these, themselves satiric, are flouted cheerfully by most crime writers of the Golden Age. See Curtis Evans's recent informative overview of transgressors in his essay on *The Detection Club and Fair Play* (2011).

It seems true, however, that the fictional investigators of the Golden Age (amateur detectives especially) were more cheerful, often witty, and possessed of fewer social blemishes than those depicted after World War II and the rise of noir fiction with its depressed and alcoholic sleuths. Earlier in his essay, Čapek refers to Till Eulenspiegel, the prankster or trickster figure in Germanic folklore responsible for satiric and often misleading communications ("Till Eulenspiegel") but with the attribute of wit. Such a character can be likened to the investigator's companion or sidekick, although wit seems not to be a marked feature of this relationship so much as comic relief. Hence the Watson figure copied and often parodied after the character of Sherlock Holmes' companion and biographer.

By the motif of escape, Čapek appears to be linking the old with the present that itself becomes old, something "we keep adding to ... all the time ... there is so much that as yet has neither been discovered nor thought out so that we can set out on an expedition" (120–121). Expedition equals escape. As well as tradition linking the old with the new, Čapek likes "method":

Let others glorify passions, romantic demons, the beauty of women's eyes, or sunrise, I praise lucidity, context, and order, the strength of the brain which compares, relates, arranges, and binds, the method, this wise companion takes us by the hand through the chaos of facts: and see, they come apart [115].

Walter Murdoch's statement on Charles Dickens's *David Copperfield* (1849–1850) is appropriate. Dickens's work can be said to be "compounded of many elements, including a keen eye for people's little peculiarities of character and speech, an immense experience of life, a clear understanding of human nature, and, above all, a vast generosity and sympathy and pity." This is somewhat idealistic but I think Murdoch's elements can be ranked with those of Čapek: method certainly, the solving of the puzzle and discovery of the criminal as well, but also time for laughter and women's eyes.

Experimentation: Rules of the Game

When enough writers are agreed upon conventions for their genre, key motifs to which those conventions may be attached, and a general as well as an individual style by which they are expressed to best advantage, we may speak of a paradigm which means, put simply, "a set of concepts, etc., *shared by a community of scholars* or scientists" (*Macquarie Dictionary*), the shared concepts helping to define such a community. Similarly, a motif as defined by Baldick is "a situation, incident, idea, image, or character-type that is found in many different literary works, folktales, or myths; or any element of a work that is *elaborated into a more general theme* [emphases mine]" (215–216).

A great many elements go towards defining the subgenre of crime fiction written by the humorists of the Golden Age. But identifying them where humorous writing matters is to identify much the same elements in "serious" puzzle-solving crime fiction, because the consideration of all the clues and final unravelling of the puzzle applies equally well in both streams. It is a question of personal choice among writers. For many, humor has a way of spilling over into the serious writing and subverting it, as in the formulation of so-called rules which writers in crime fiction are encouraged to observe. When some of these lists are devised by humorists such as Monsignor Ronald Knox, it gives the game away. Rules imply a set of conventions to which all writers should adhere, emphasising the customary and therefore "correct" practices by pointing up the incorrect or forbidden ones, and there are good reasons behind this.

Writers of crime/detective fiction attempt to distance themselves from other genres dealing with themes that are very similar if not the same. They seek to make a distinction between their preferred mode and those of the adventure story and the thriller. Remaining faithful to this distinction is not always successful, however, for crime fiction writers of the Golden Age more often than not write thrillers as well and, in a spillover, frequently include elements of the thriller or the adventure tale in their detective novels, often cheerfully and tongue in cheek breaking "rules" laid down by their colleagues.

Questioning and experimentation is nearly always healthy for a discipline, and so it was in the Golden Age. Leroy Lad Panek in *Watteau's Shepherds* includes the category "rules of the game" in his index. He also comments upon A. A. Milne's *The Red House Mystery* (69–70) and adds a useful appendix (200–218) that discusses S. S. Van Dine (Willard Huntington Wright) and alternative plot structures. Knox's "Ten Commandments" (they could in fact be more because points four and six are amenable to subdivision, but that would rule out his neat Biblical framework) and Van Dine's twenty rules are listed respectively in *Wikipedia* under "Golden Age of Detective Fiction" and in the *Gaslight* web site. They are worth paraphrasing.

Knox's "Decalogue": (1) Early in the story the criminal is to be mentioned, but their thoughts should remain closed to the reader; (2) there should be no supernatural occurrences; (3) the writer is allowed one only secret room or passage; (4) there should be (a) no exotic undiscovered poisons put to use, and (b) no item of equipment that demands lengthy scientific description or explanation; (5) Chinamen (and Chinese women?) are not to appear (which might be extended to include other suspicious foreigners, that is, characters exotic to British perceptions); (6) there should be (a) no "accident" (or, I suggest, coincidence), and (b) no inexplicable hunch or intuition on the part of the amateur investigator (but the binary opposition between systematic method and intuition is frequently discussed in crime fiction); (7) the investigating detective should not be the criminal as well (it is not playing fair on the reader); (8) the detective character is obligated to reveal to the reader every clue he or she finds; (9) the thoughts of the so-called Watson character who is sidekick and intellectual foil to the main detective (a) should be freely available to the reader and (b) this character's mental operations should make them a tad dumber than the average reader; lastly, (10) there should be no brothers, especially twins (or sisters?) unless the reader has been prepared for them beforehand.

Several of Van Dine's Rules overlap those of Knox. Van Dine finds about twenty: (1) There must be an equal opportunity with the detective for the reader to unravel the mystery, which means that all clues should be given (Knox's point eight); (2) the reader should not be deceived by tricks and deceptions except insofar as the criminal does this to the detective; (3) a love interest is not required; (4) the detective should not be revealed as the criminal (Knox's point seven); (5) "logical deductions" should solve the case and not coincidence, accidence, or a criminal's confession (Knox's point six); (6) there should always be a detective who investigates and gathers clues; (7) there should always be a murder because the reader is not satisfied unless a corpse is available; (8) the crime must be solved "by strictly naturalistic means" and not through supernatural means such as séances and mind-reading and so on (Knox's point two); (9) there should be only one detective, otherwise the reader will be confused (probably because there is reader identification with the investigator). Margery Allingham broke this rule in her first novel *The Crime at Black Dudley*. (10) The criminal should be known to the reader throughout the story (a little like Knox's point one); (11) the murderer should not be a servant. There is a touch of the English class system here and, perhaps to provide a balance, in at least one parody it is the butler. Servants as henchpersons abound in the thriller. (12) The criminal should be one person only, although they might be allowed an accomplice or two; (13) there should be no secret societies or criminal organizations; (14) there must be a "rational and scientific" means of committing the murder (a little like Knox's point two); (15) the solution of the puzzle must always be there for the reader to find out (a little like Knox's point eight); (16) there should be no long descriptions, literary embellishments or in-depth character analysis, nothing to do with "atmospheric" touches (touches of Knox's point four); (17) the murderer should not be a professional criminal, a bandit or burglar but an ordinary usually unimpeachable character such as a churchman or a philanthropic spinster; (18) there should be no anticlimax such as a suicide or an accident that would "hoodwink the trusting and kind-hearted reader"; (19) motives in detective tales should be personal, relevant to a reader's everyday experience and to some degree an "outlet for his own repressed desires and emotions."

Finally, the twentieth rule is a grab bag of overworked devices best avoided by the serious writer. Matching a cigarette butt with its brand to catch a murderer is jejune. (Or any other similar deduction one thinks would annoy Van Dine, such as gravel on a shoe as evidence that a body has been in a different place from where it was found). Frightening a suspect during a séance is another weak ploy, so too the forging of fingerprints. Establishing an alibi by setting up a dummy is similarly feeble. The dog that does or does not bark has entered the realm of cliché. (It is still used in television crime drama.) Pinning the murder on a twin or a lookalike relative (see Knox's point ten) is also indefensible. Equally appalling are hypodermic syringes, knockout drops, word association tests, and code letters. Even the locked room mystery is highly suspect.

Another set of rules come from a third and perhaps surprising authority, the mainstream literary critic and poet Thomas Stearns Eliot in a review essay published in the *Monthly Criterion* for June 1927, a year before the publication of Van Dine's twenty rules. They are summarized by Curtis Evans in *CADS* magazine and include the following guidelines:

> The story must not rely upon elaborate and incredible disguises [that] must be only occasional.... The character and motives of the criminal should be normal [and the reader must have] a sporting chance to solve the mystery.... The story must not rely upon occult phenomena or ... preposterous discoveries.... Elabo-

rate and bizarre machinery is an irrelevance ... treasures hid in strange places, cyphers and codes [are not to be encouraged].... The detective should be highly intelligent, but not superhuman [4].

On humor in the subgenre, Evans notes that T. S. Eliot did not frown upon its use (4). Indeed Eliot took Knox to task for not being humorous enough, saying that Knox's characters "are as witty as most people succeed in being in real life, but that is not witty enough for a book." Perhaps Eliot thought later that the use of humor ushered in a "human element" — or he may by then have been on a different tack — and that a key principle here is an either/or matter: either to concentrate on human factors or to give greater weight to the puzzle element; but not to attempt both because it was (in Evans's paraphrase) "too great a challenge." Injecting humor into crime fiction is in my opinion a very human element, but this does not exclude the puzzle aspect. Edmund Crispin and John Dickson Carr succeed by writing comparatively long novels, about 95,700 words for Carr's *Night at the Mocking Widow* and a solid 118,000 words in Crispin's *The Glimpses of the Moon*.

Failures to adhere to rules appear in one variation or another among the writers in my list, which is a comparatively restricted cohort of humorists. Such rules are embedded in the oath taken by Detection Club members: "Do you promise that your detectives shall well and truly detect the crimes presented to them using those wits which it may please you to bestow upon them and not placing reliance on nor making use of Divine Revelation, Feminine Intuition, Mumbo Jumbo, Jiggery-Pokery, Coincidence, or Act of God?" ("Detection Club"). To which we have Nancy Spain's amusing comment: "They intone a terrible oath which conjures the members on pain of diminishing sales and returns to stick to the rules of clues and foot-prints" (123). The Detection Club continues to this day.

In fact the rules were relaxed long before the present day. E. C. Bentley, John Dickson Carr, Edmund Crispin, even Dorothy L. Sayers have substantial love interests in their novels. Edmund Crispin in his short stories does not always give us a corpse. The supernatural is a defining element in John Dickson Carr's work, and Dorothy L. Sayers too includes a bogus séance in one of her novels. The servant as villain makes an appearance in a parody by Anthony Shaffer, *Whodunnit*, a play in which the narrator who is the butler turns out to be the murderer as well. Margery Allingham's novels make use of secret societies a great deal. It is a plot element that Edmund Crispin uses at least once, in *The Moving Toyshop*, although the secret society in this instance is somewhat small, a group of avaricious persons attracted by hopes to inherit from an old woman's estate. A hypodermic syringe figures in one of Nancy Spain's stories. Code letters/ciphers appear as plot elements in E. C. Bentley's short story "The Old-Fashioned Apache" (2937) and in Crispin's *The Moving Toyshop*. While we are spared them for the most part, long descriptive paragraphs make an appearance in E. C. Bentley's classic novel *Trent's Last Case* as well as in Crispin's *The Glimpses of the Moon*. Again, Margery Allingham's villains are often professional criminals. Accidental death instead of murder as at first suspected is the outcome of Sheila Pim's novel *Creeping Venom*. The short story featuring Conan Doyle's dog in the night appears first in "Silver Blaze" (1892) and so was a cliché when E. C. Bentley wrote "The Bad Dog" published in 1937. In A. A. Milne's *The Red House Mystery* the protagonists place dummies in their beds and the plot has almost identical brothers. The locked room mystery (also dubbed the impossible crime) may not have been approved by Van Dine, but it was polished to a high degree by John Dickson Carr who made it his own in *The Hollow Man*, and Edmund Crispin follows suit in *The Case of the Gilded Fly*. Secret rooms and passages are well represented, for example in *The Red House Mystery* and *The Crime at Black Dudley*, and Simon Brett's *Murder in the Museum*.

There are a number of logical reasons why the rules of the game are cheerfully violated. First of all many of the Golden Age writers crafted thrillers, adventure stories and melodrama and used elements from those genres in their detective tales such as ciphers, syringes, and secret passages. Secondly, some forbidden elements have an intrinsic appeal to writers who gain pleasure from exploring new twists on the old, and to readers who enjoy reading a fresh version. The locked room idea is clever and seductive. The nighttime dog is a smart piece of observation and deduction that captures the imagination. Many of these writers are paying homage to their predecessors, contemporaries and those longstanding ideas they tinkered with by not only emulating them but also parodying and satirizing them, which is another point where humor enters into crime fiction. A love interest when handled well can add quality to a crime story (women's eyes), and for the same reason there is nothing wrong with long descriptions. It comes back to Umberto Eco's point, too, that in novelistic or filmic art, clichés may be piled so thickly one upon the other that the final product can achieve the standing of a cult. It is fair to say that the locked room mystery in particular achieves a cult-like status. But bringing these elements together, I suggest, has similarly helped to entrench if not create an entire subgenre.

Literary Conventions: Motifs and Style

A great many standard motifs are to be found in both the serious puzzle-solving tales and those of the humorists. The victim is almost universally disliked, which at first widens the range of suspects until various clues eliminate them one by one until the alleged murderer is identified. This element in literature and drama goes back to antiquity and is appropriate for the adventure tale and the thriller as well as crime fiction. Umberto Eco discusses the depiction of villains and anti-heroes in an essay (98–99) on Victor Hugo: "The villain was always ugly, hideous, grotesque, or absurd," referring to such works as *The Hunchback of Notre Dame* (1831) or *The Man Who Laughs* (1869). In some instances, however, the murder victim is innocent and well liked, such as Mavis Trent in *The Glimpses of the Moon*: "a thoroughly nice woman" (84).

Another prominent motif— really a cluster of motifs — involves the setting out of typologies such as those on motives for murder in real life. George Orwell in "Decline of the English Murder" states that "sex was a powerful motive … the desire to gain a secure position in life, or not to forfeit one's social position by some scandal such as a divorce … to get hold of a certain known sum of money such as a legacy or an insurance policy" (346). They are reflected among our writers: madness, jealousy, passion, hatred, lust and anger, financial security (*Cinderella Goes to the Morgue* 52, 55); or "Money, vengeance, security" (*The Moving Toyshop* 124). A different sort of criminal, the black-mailer, might well become a murder victim as in *The Glimpses of the Moon*. Allied to these are such prerequisites as means, motive, and opportunity (*A Bullet in the Ballet* 11) and "Accident, Murder or Suicide?" (*The Fourth Wall* 6). These are procedural questions; in each case investigations follow different paths depending upon whether suicide, accident or murder is involved. In one story, for instance, we find suicide as revenge (*The Hollow Man* 157) as well as the more frequent ruse of murder made to look like suicide.

A key motif in crime fiction is this: that the murderer might have gone undetected were it not for a single mistake on his or her part. The mistake in *The Fourth Wall* is Carter's neglect in not destroying the incriminating blotting paper, as well as leaving his revolver under a bedroom pillow, so allowing one of the two heroines to empty it of its shells. In *Poison for Teacher* there is Brace-wood-Smith's mistake over Natasha's silk scarf. In E. C. Bentley's short story "The Genuine Tabard" it is a fraudster's lack of knowledge about university practices. In *Night at the Mocking Widow* the colonel gives himself away through the bureaucratic style of his poison pen letters when, having achieved his aim, he might as easily have done nothing more.

Associated with this may also be a coincidence that thwarts the murderer's plans, as in *Trent's Last Case* when Cupples intervenes because he believes that Sigsbee Manderson is about to shoot himself. There is an element of coinci-dence in Crispin's *The Case of the Gilded Fly* (56) in the movements of characters after breakfast, and in *The Moving Toyshop* (129) Cadogan and Fen by chance meet a key character in a teashop. These examples violate rule 6 of Monsignor Knox's ten commandments and rule 5 of Van Dine's twenty rules, yet they are relatively minor and in context do not stretch the imagination because an ele-ment of chance works in everyday life just as much, if not more so, than in fic-tion. The rule in both Knox and Van Dine is probably placed in their lists as a timely warning not to go to extremes. For example, Bentley's novel *Elephant's Work* is founded upon an unlikely rail accident and is criticized on that point.

Most writers of the Golden Age stop short at piling up the body count beyond a reasonable limit. In the body of most tales there is usually a second and sometimes a third death. *The Red House Mystery* has one murder, *The Glimpses of the Moon* has three deaths including one before the action of the novel, *Poison for Teacher* likewise has three, also one before the action, and *Mystery Mile* surprisingly has no killings, although a mouse dies and there is an altruistic suicide. Often enough there is a death under mysterious circumstances that takes place before the action of the plot as in *The Skeleton in the Clock, The Glimpses of the Moon, The Moving Toyshop,* and *Poison for Teacher.* A suicide in *Night at the Mocking Widow* qualifies as a mysterious death. John Dickson Carr, Edmund Crispin and Nancy Spain favor these elements.

A subplot is frequently included that may be a criminal activity falling short of murder (e.g., blackmail, poison pen, theft). In the short story such a subject is usually the chief theme, especially in those of Crispin, and murders may not even figure. In some instances in the novels a secondary investigation takes place in tandem with the main puzzle. One example is Carter Dickson's *Night at the Mocking Widow* in which Sir Henry Merrivale deals with a charlatan psychiatrist's domination over a troubled adolescent and her mother. That is the subplot while Sir Henry pursues inquiries about the monolithic carving of the Mocking Widow of the title. Kerry Greenwood's Phryne Fisher regularly solves two mysteries in every novel.

Love interest is another conventional motif that may act as a subplot that might or might not have direct bearing on the investigation. For example, we have Edmund Crispin's young ladies. Like Michael Innes whom he admired and emulated, Crispin tended to idolize heroines such as Sally Carstairs in *The Moving Toyshop*: "She was about twenty-three, tall, with a finely-proportioned, loose-limbed body, naturally golden hair, big candid blue eyes, high cheek bones, and a firmly moulded chin. Her scarlet mouth broke into an impish smile as she called back to someone in the alley-way" (70). Sally is not the kind of girl who faints when physical danger threatens (91). Such heroines often have hopeless admirers such as "Philip Page, who was safe if rather pathetic" (98), while young Cadogan who is the Watson figure alongside Professor Fen succeeds in winning her. Sally Carstairs is important for the plot in *The Moving Toyshop* because she is its damsel in distress. On the other hand, the role of Mabel Manderson in *Trent's Last Case* need not have been as central as Bentley made it. The solving of Sigsbee Manderson's apparent murder could have been accomplished with less attention to Mabel, although it would have made the novel shorter and more humdrum. In the last quarter of the novel the chance meetings between Trent and Mabel and their gradual coming together form a definite subplot.

A controversy over capital punishment is scarcely explored because it is beyond the point. The murderer's final end on the noose is of little importance to the author (and, it is implied, to the reader as well) once the puzzle is solved and the guilty party confronted and apprehended. But here and there some writers consider the implications. Edmund Crispin is notable for this in most of his novels.

Under some circumstances the murderer is allowed to go free, or given an "honourable" way out through suicide instead of the disgrace of execution, or escapes the hangman's noose by coming to a violent end, a stock closure in the thriller. It seems to me that the tendency among writers here to sidestep the unpleasantness of state execution is good negative evidence for their chief interest being the mental pastime and enjoyment in solving a puzzle — trying to guess from the clues how the murder was done and, colloquially, "who done it" — or to keep the reader's attention on the humor of the situations in which various protagonists find themselves. This probably became easier once capital punishment was discontinued in England where "the last executions in the United Kingdom, by hanging, took place in 1964, prior to capital punishment being abolished for murder (in 1969 in Great Britain and in 1973 in Northern Ireland)" ("Capital Punishment in the United Kingdom").

Frequently enough, there are violations of established police procedures such as destroying evidence or moving the body, not always done by the murderer. Beginning with *Trent's Last Case*, Marlowe, who is innocent of the death of Sigsbee Manderson, moves the body and changes its clothes in order to divert suspicion from himself. Jenny Windell in A. A. Milne's *Four Days' Wonder* carefully replaces disturbed objects and wipes them clean of what one imagines is blood. In Nancy Spain's *Poison for Teacher*, the body of Theresa Devaloys is moved. Lord Wutherwood's body is carried from the lift in Ngaio March's *A Surfeit of Lampreys*, but he is still alive at that point. However, the protagonist Roberta Grey in a fit of good housekeeping wipes the victim's blood from the lift wall.

Other motifs include secret rooms and passages, the art of disguise on the part of both criminal and detective, incriminating letters or letters of revelation, the inclusion of dodgy characters who are also non–English (Chinese, Italian, German, Jewish, American), and there may be a touch of the ghost story and the supernatural from the tradition of the horror tale.

The best examples of stylistic conventions from my list include literary allusions, the atmospheric use of weather and scenery (the pathetic fallacy), and the making of lists, the last-named called "The Poetics of Excess" by Umberto Eco (97). The nineteenth-century social critic John Ruskin (1819–1900) coined the expression in his chapter "Of the Pathetic Fallacy" cited by Abrams, who in a footnote says that "the term *pathetic* refers not to something feebly ineffective but to the emotion (pathos) with which a writer invests his descriptions of objects, and of the distortion (fallacy or falsity) that may result" (1331). The phrase "pathetic fallacy" reads better than something like "false emotion" as long as we remember its nineteenth-century meaning. The reader's acceptance of this conceit is a little like Coleridge's concept of the suspension of disbelief (also cited in Abrams 397–398). One answer Ruskin suggests is that we receive some expressions in poetry with pleasure when we find beauty. I think it is not a great step to find such reader satisfaction in prose works as well. When it appears in literature as the pathetic fallacy — "the attribution of human feelings and responses to inanimate things" (COD) — it is one of several stylistic devices to add atmosphere to a situation in the plot.

In the hands of the crime-writing humorists of the Golden Age, this trope can appear at its simplest and most mundane, or it might be spelled out in one or more solid paragraphs with a more intensive elicitation of atmosphere and mood. E. C. Bentley deliberately evokes mood within physical settings, most strikingly in the chapter titled "The Lady in Black" where Trent's cliff-side swimming is described in detail. Not every writer in my list makes such use of this conceit but Nancy Spain does it a lot, as does Simon Brett. I do not think it is an accident that the convention appears among novelists who draw upon the thriller, where mood and atmosphere are primal ingredients to heighten suspense and dramatic tension.

CHAPTER 1

A Crime Fiction Lineage

The short history of contemporary crime fiction spans 170 years, broadly from 1841 with the work of Edgar Allan Poe — see Penzler and Friedman (87) — to the present day if, like many critics, we accept Poe as the founder of the detective mystery story. For convenience I divide the contemporary period into a number of overlapping eras: the nineteenth century, early twentieth century, the Golden Age (1914–1940), World War II noir (1930s–1940s), "cultural revolution" (1960s–1970s), and *fin de siècle* (the late twentieth and early twenty-first centuries). As E. H. Carr says, "The division of history into periods is not a fact, but a necessary hypothesis or tool of thought, valid in so far as it is illuminating, and dependent for its validity on interpretation" (60). This is a comparatively short time period when compared against what came centuries earlier. For before the genres became ever more finely differentiated through the nineteenth century to the present, fledgling forms of spoken and written entertainment with the themes of murder and retribution, like the beast fable to which they are related, go back a very long way. By this metaphor they are generic in that they belong to a genus (a taxonomic group of many species) and consequently have no clear brand name.

Antiquity

The lineage for crime fiction might be said to begin with the collection of Indian beast fables named the *Pancatantra* (c. 300 BC), a Shastra which according to Olivelle is "a treatise on government or political science [whose] literary sources [are] the expert tradition of political science and the folk and literary traditions of story-telling" (x). A tale in the *Pancatantra* titled "The Barber Who Killed the Monks" is classified in Book V as the second of two stories "On Hasty Actions":

Three religious mendicants came and woke him [the barber] up. They said to him: "Tomorrow morning we will come back in this same form.... When you club us to death, we will turn into gold coins, and you should show no mercy in this regard...." [The merchant hires a barber to cut his nails and hair as part of ritual cleansing before feeding the three Brahmins].... The merchant-class man did as he had been instructed, and they became piles of money ... the merchant gave the barber three hundred gold coins as a gratuity and to make him keep the secret. Seeing all that, the barber, because of his lack of judgement ... took a club and waited in readiness. Soon three religious mendicants as a result of their previous actions [bad *karma*] came there to beg for food. The barber bludgeoned them with the club and killed them. But he did not get a pile of money. Soon thereafter the barber was arrested by the officers of the king and impaled [158–159].

The desire for money is a strong motive for murder then as it is now.

The Golden Ass by Lucius Apuleius (c. 158 AD) draws upon Graeco-Roman folktales of metamorphosis (Grant xi–xii). Mikhail Bakhtin (111–112) describes it as "an adventure-everyday novel." Its plot revolves around the hero Lucius whose metamorphosis into an ass forces him to wander the countryside and towns. These wanderings pass Lucius from owner to owner where he witnesses human cruelties. As Douglas Greene (96) remarks: "Many of the episodes in Apuleius' *The Golden Ass* (second century AD) are about crimes and criminals."

The novel must be one of the earliest examples of the picaresque. There is a chapter in which the ass is taken to a bandit's cave where he overhears cautionary tales of robbery and death (56–66). Later the bandits receive rough justice from an ex-soldier of Imperial Rome and vigilantes from the nearby town. Interestingly, Grant (ix) tells us that when Saint Augustine renamed the story *The Golden Ass* (originally it was *The Transformations of Lucius*) he was using "Golden" in the sense of "the adjective that street-corner story-tellers applied to their tales ... to imply ... 'the best of all stories about an ass.'" So the use of the word "golden" in reference to "the best of"—as in the Golden Age of crime writing—goes back to antiquity.

From the medieval period comes an example from Chaucer (c. 1342–1400), "The Prioress's Tale" (169–176), an anti–Semitic poem whose verses tell of the killing of a devout Christian child by a group of Jews who hire a professional killer. The child's throat is cut, but through supernatural intervention he is enabled to sing the *Alma Redemptoris*—a Marian hymn, that is, a hymn or chant to the Virgin Mary — and so reveal the whereabouts of his body. The murderers are identified and condemned to death by the provost, in one definition a medieval counterpart to a head of police (COD). The tale is culturally oriented and politically incorrect by present-day standards (until the standards change). Its chief importance is the introduction of the popular phrase "Murder will out": "Of what avail your villainous intent? / Murder will out, and nothing can prevent" (173).

Contributors to Wikipedia have a slightly different take on the antiquity of crime stories ("Detective fiction"). Whereas I note counterparts of the detective or policeman in vigilantes, officers of the king or a provost, a Wikipedia contributor who is doubtless paraphrasing Dorothy L. Sayers points out that the Old Testament contains tales of cross-examination and that Sophocles' tragedy *Oedipus Rex* involves the use of witnesses. The Wikipedia entry moves on to refer briefly to "Early Arabic detective fiction" in reference to a tale from *One Thousand and One Nights*, "The Three Apples," before jumping centuries forward to Edgar Allan Poe. Also considered are two tales from "Early Chinese detective fiction" from the Song or Tang dynasties that were written up during the Ming and Manchu times. One of these came into English as *Celebrated Cases of Judge Dee* translated by Robert Van Gulik: "who then used the style and characters to write an original Judge Dee series." Van Gulik is mentioned in Symons who calls his work "well-informed pastiche" (212) and in Binyon (125–126) who finds the tales "interesting and well told" (126). Symons notes that "the trick or puzzle element is present in several of the Arabian Nights stories" (27).

Binyon cites "a brilliant short history of the crime story" (1) by Dorothy L. Sayers, in her introduction to the anthology *Great Short Stories of Detection, Mystery and Horror* (1928), in which she includes two tales from the *Apocrypha*, one from Virgil's *Aeneid* and another from Herodotus. Binyon adds that in another seminal essay published in 1946 about "Aristotle on Detective Fiction," Sayers claims tongue in cheek that Aristotle's *Poetics* has detective fiction in mind because of the "perfection of beginning, middle and end" (2). Stories of crime and retribution are present too in the monitory tales of the seventeenth-century *Fables* of Jean de la Fontaine (1621–1695). Leroy Panek in *An Introduction to the Detective Story* sees the beast fable as a more distant medieval precursor of the crime mystery: "There are the clever ruses of the beast fable and the *Fabliau*, the Robin Hood tales, and the murder-will-out stories like Chaucer's 'The Prioress' Tale'" (3).

While not going back as far as I have in identifying main themes, critical studies on the evolution of crime fiction take into account elements that appear in medieval tales and lead on to the development of eighteenth-century mainstream literature. Panek (4–5) draws attention to "the Elizabethan revenge play," the figure of the "rogue hero" in the Renaissance (4), disreputable "eighteenth-century criminal literature" such as Gay's *Beggar's Opera* (1728) and the picaresque novels of Fielding and Defoe. The last-named make use of such stylistic elements as the surprise ending and a "tongue-in-cheek method" (10), "discrete elements of subject and narration." But, as Binyon puts it, "the attempt to trace the genre back to the beginning of time is impossible: although, as we have seen, discrete elements of subject and narration may easily be found, they do not add up to a whole" (4).

The Nineteenth Century

By the nineteenth century tales about misdeeds underwent further refinements and coalesced into new and comparatively distinct genres, principally the gothic as in Mary Shelley's *Frankenstein* (1818) — that is often claimed either directly or indirectly as a forerunner of science fiction and fantasy — the thriller, the adventure tale, and the romance respectively. Panek traces this development through several chapters, beginning with William Godwin's *The Adventures of Caleb Williams* (1794) and Edward Bulwer Lytton's *Pelham: or the Adventures of a Gentleman* (1828), and goes on to discuss in turn Edgar Allan Poe (1809–1849), Charles Dickens (1812–1870), Wilkie Collins (1824–1889), and Émile Gaboriau (1833–1873) [born, however, in 1832 according to the Wikipedia or in 1835 if we follow Chambers (558)].

Gaboriau's protagonist Monsieur Lecoq of *L'Affaire Lerouge* (1866) — the Widow Lerouge/the Lerouge Affair ("Émile Gaboriau") — is a forerunner of the Sherlock Holmes type. Gaboriau is a French writer whose creation is detective Lecoq in such novels as *L'Affaire Lerouge* (1866), *Le Dossier 113* [Document 113] (1867), *Monsieur Lecoq* (1869), *Les Esclaves de Paris* [The Slaves of Paris] (1869) and, with a neat *frisson*, *La Cord au Cou* [The Neck Cord or perhaps Cord at the Neck] (1873) (*Chambers Bibliographical Dictionary* 558).

Acknowledgment to these precursors of the crime novel is *de rigueur* in the critical commentaries. Symons covers much the same ground in his second chapter on Godwin, Vidocq and Poe, and in chapter three on Dickens, Collins, and Gaboriau, as do Panek in *Watteau's Shepherds* (5–9), Julian Symons in *Bloody Murder* (27–63), and T. J. Binyon in *Murder Will Out* (1–8).

Far-reaching social changes in England helped produce these results: urbanization, the invention of police forces (the *Sûreté* in France in 1817, the London Met in 1842), a growing and increasingly literate readership, as Panek observes in his 1987 follow-up study (8–9). The author given a chapter by Panek (shared with Edward Bulwer Lytton) is William Godwin whose wife was Mary Wollstonecraft and daughter Mary Shelley (by Godwin's first wife), and son-in-law Percy Shelley (Wynne-Davies 562, 903–904). Godwin wrote *The Adventures of Caleb Williams* (1794) with the intention of doing: "a series of adventures of flight and pursuit" (cited in Panek 14). He "drew somewhat upon eighteenth century crime literature" (15), in particular the lives of pirates, reflecting the picaresque literature of the previous century. Panek (17) credits Godwin with stumbling upon two stylistic techniques that became important in later detective fiction, that of warning the reader in advance about what had taken place or is about to happen in the plot, and the "presentation of documentary evidence." They were ploys, however, that remained largely undiscovered until Wilkie Collins wrote *The Moonstone* (1868) more than seventy years later in the tradition of sensation literature.

Godwin's concept of "flight and pursuit" became a mainstay of the thriller, as in John Buchan's *The Thirty-Nine Steps* (1915), but it became also a stock ending for many crime/detective novels such as the slapstick chases in Edmund Crispin's Doctor Fen stories or the darker ending of Margery Allingham's *Mystery Mile* (1930). Symons takes this further by noting that Godwin, when following the convention of the time to produce three-volume blockbusters, writes his flight-and-pursuit volume first, although in the order of publication it came third: "This manner of working back from effect to cause, from solution to problem, is the heart of crime literature" (29). When the convention changed to favor single-volume novels, many writers such as E. C. Bentley did their last chapters first.

Panek calls Edgar Allan Poe's "The Murders in the Rue Morgue" (1831) "the first genuine detective story" (24). Karel Čapek as early as 1924 names Poe "father of the modern detective story":

> From the laws of induction, analysis, textual criticism, and logical probability developed a detective method through abstract philosophy while the classical Sherlock Holmes enriched these devices with a terrific arsenal of professional knowledge acquired by scientific expertise and direct observation [114].

Many authorities agree with this assessment although others spend a lot of time passing the accolade on to Conan Doyle. Poe's works are more in the tradition of the sensation writers with their heavy emphasis on the gothic and macabre, but he is hailed for what were in his time original plot devices. As Symons tells us: "Almost every later variation of plot in the detective story can be found in the five short stories he [Poe] wrote which, with a little stretching here and there, can be said to fit within the limits of the form" (34–35).

Symons' disclaimer is significant because Edgar Allan Poe was only one of several writers who laid the groundwork for the evolution of the crime novel. In a sense it does not matter a great deal. It is a little like the inconclusive search for the origins of human customs in anthropology where it is more realistic to say that there is a gradual accretion of elements from a variety of sources, and that some elements are codified by certain writers. Thus one speaks of a lineage with apical ancestors, but a lineage does not stop with such ancestors. It is only that one cannot go back further because the origins are lost in the mists of time and memory.

Panek says that Poe is important for establishing "the conventions of character and the narrative formats that would power detective fiction for the next hundred years" (24). One of these conventions is the use of "close observation and reason" (25) as in Voltaire's novella *Zadig* (1746–1747). When challenged by unbelieving judges over the loss of a valuable horse, Zadig explains:

I noticed some horseshoe tracks. They were all the same distance apart. "That horse," I said to myself, "has a perfect action".... Beneath the trees, which formed a bower some five feet high, I saw some leaves which had recently fallen from the branches, and I deduced that the horse must have touched them, and therefore that he stood fifteen hands high [132–133].

After this explanation Zadig is nearly flogged and sent to Siberia, upon which he decides in future not to be "too clever" in revealing what he sees (133). Poe saw himself as an "investigative reporter" possessing such deductive qualities (Panek 25). Symons observes astutely that "Voltaire's prime concern is not to show the power of reason, but its inadequacy in dealing with all the unreasonable people in the world" (28). An investigator's secrecy in some matters can last until the dénouement of a crime novel, an element that stands in opposition to the principle of allowing all the clues to be present for the reader along with the fictive detectives.

Charles Dickens is acknowledged by Panek (33) on the strength of having written novels with "many of the devices used by later detective writers" in such works as *The Mystery of Edwin Drood* (1870). The other critics, Symons, Binyon, Haycraft, Sayers, and Watson also include Dickens. Panek goes on to say: "All that we need to do is to add the idea of playing with readers' curiosity, and we get detective technique" (37). The creation of suspense (acting upon a reader's curiosity) is a common feature of much other genre writing (romance and thrillers, for example) as well as in so-called mainstream literature. Crime novelists of the Golden Age in particular often moved between genres. John Dickson Carr wrote many historical romances; A. A. Milne specialized in children's tales, plays and poetry and wrote *Chloe Marr* (1946), a major novel of good quality; Edmund Crispin edited several collections of science fiction short stories; Nancy Spain wrote two biographies and three autobiographies. It is fair to say that conventions and narrative tricks from mainstream literature such as that of Dickens permeate crime fiction.

Wilkie Collins (1824–1889) is described in Panek's next chapter as laying down one of the foundation stones of the thriller, at this point identifying it with "sensation fiction" in Collins' use of melodrama and elements from the gothic tradition in *The Moonstone* (1868) and *The Woman in White* (1860). Panek (52, 63) gives a nice snippet of crime writing history: "Collins frequently uses the word "clew" in its original sense — that of a ball of magic thread followed to find the way out of the labyrinth — to explain the development of the action rather than explaining it as the accumulation and use of knowledge."

There are interconnections in all this. Sensation fiction was a reaction to the historical novel, says Panek (55), from which later writers broke by altering the emphasis on the villain (59), and the use in melodrama of "the traditional themes of tragedy and social propriety" (58), not to mention Agatha Christie's "guilty-innocent-guilty technique" (59) first represented in *The Moonstone*.

Other factors that make Collins a forerunner of "the fully-developed detective story" (62) are his emphasis on how a crime impacts upon the personality of the detective (60) — *Trent's Last Case* is a good example — the use of recapitulation (61) and frequently bidding the reader to be attentive (62). These became standard devices. To this can be added Symons' overview of Collins (48) whom he sees as producing mostly melodrama but, for our interest (49) and referring to "The Biter Bit" (1858): "Collins was particularly good at depicting bumptiously self-important characters, and this is one of the few successful comic detective short stories."

In Panek's survey Émile Gaboriau is the last of the strictly Victorian writers who influence crime fiction. (Conan Doyle straddled both the nineteenth and twentieth centuries and Panek gives him a separate chapter). Gaboriau's influences include (a) establishing a "structural pattern" influencing other writers towards the close of the century, (b) rivalry between a (vain) detective and the police force, and (c) statements made on arrest and the use of psychological evidence. Wilkie Collins and Gaboriau together help to establish the characterization of a professional detective safeguarding the innocent. Symons points out that: "The detective's changed character in fiction reflected a change in the nature of society, and his standing as a watchdog against evil was only seriously questioned after sixty years, in the work of Dashiell Hammett and Raymond Chandler" (56).

Just as the rise of the circulating libraries in England brought books more readily into the hands of a growing reading public, so too in France the appearance of *feuilletons* in the newspapers popularized the serialization of crime tales. As Panek says: "Mixed up with the careers of all of these writers and with the history of French crime literature is the rise of popular journalism in France.... Almost all of the major writers of fiction in mid-nineteenth century France ... were *feuilletonists*" (67). The *roman feuilleton* appears to have been a distinctively European invention, the practice by some newspapers to fill the bottom unused section of a page with essays, fiction, or poetry by various authors. In France *feuilletons* were often small newspapers but the practice was not restricted to France. In Czechoslovakia Karel Čapek used the form extensively. His novel *War with the Newts* (1936) was serialized as a *feuilleton* over two years. Thea Holmes (v) notes that Dickens' medium, *The Monthly Magazine* was the equivalent of a *feuilleton*; similarly Arthur Conan Doyle (1859–1930) saw his Sherlock Holmes stories serialized in *The Strand Magazine*.

Conan Doyle was lucky. As Panek says: "Doyle hit the beginning of the rage for the popular illustrated magazine" (78) and he had a good illustrator in Sidney Paget. Conan Doyle began writing a new kind of detective story at a fortuitous point in the technology of publishing. As Symons notes, "the popular periodical, selling at a low price and publishing plenty of fiction and non-fiction which, although always light and mostly trivial, was conceived on a level above that of the penny dreadful and the dime novel" (62). Those earlier forms made their appearance in 1841 with Edward Lloyd's introduction of "books in weekly parts sold at a penny" (43). The serialization of stories in the English papers and magazines paralleled the *roman feuilleton* in Europe.

Conan Doyle saw immense changes in English society, but the form of his Sherlock Holmes tales appears embedded more in the Victorian and Edwardian eras than in the early twentieth century. His work influenced most if not all writers of crime fiction, either in emulation or in reaction, and it is customary to include him in most overviews of the genre. Says Panek: "Doyle directs his detective stories away from disturbing or controversial public topics which might alienate readers" (83). This came together with a strong element of chivalry that "links up directly to the element in the Holmes stories coming from the Victorian schoolboy story and its reincarnation in the popular novels of Stevenson and Haggard" (90) influencing I am sure other thrillers such as those of John Buchan. The detective stories of Conan Doyle's time mostly had the form of the short story and so were light on characterization (Symons 63). As Symons states a few pages later, "Holmes is conceived in outline, with attributes that are really substitutes for characterization — the eagle eye, the misanthropy, the remoteness" (68). This reflected the Victorian zeitgeist.

Panek remarks upon Conan Doyle's use of humor in the Holmes stories "Silver Blaze" and "The Naval Treaty":

> Unlike the majority of detective writers before him Doyle came to realize, by accident or choice, the detective story can profit from a combination of non-serious, comic, and playful with the serious, tragic, and human implications of crime.... This combination is one of the things which enables the genre to be popular [93–94].

But Conan Doyle was careless in his execution, "writing off the top of his head" (Panek 92), and while he "wrote the Holmes tales out of protest against torpid contemporary fiction" (90) so too later writers react to his weakness by, firstly, producing any number of satires, parodies and burlesques on Sherlock Holmes (97) and, more interestingly, being spurred on to do better.

The Edwardian Era and the First World War

Strictly speaking, the Edwardian period ran for less than a decade, 1902–1910, scarcely enough to be called an era, but it is often extended to cover the close of World War I ("Edwardian era"). In a flowery account, Haycraft suggests the Armistice as a major turning point for crime genres: "After 1918, we find a new and distinct cleavage, with the tinseled trappings of romanticism relegated for the most part to the sphere of mystery, and a fresher, sharper detective story making bold and rapid strides on its own stout legs" (112).

When looking at "Turn-of-the-Century Writers" Panek (98, 100) singles out Mary Roberts Rinehart (1876–1926) for her anticipation of "the mature fusion of the comic and serious side of the detective story which flourished during the Golden Age," adding that "the scientific detective story" represented in this period by Gaston Leroux barely lasted beyond the First World War because the Golden Age writers did not take to it, although it is present in science fiction in the works of H. G. Wells. Binyon credits Gaston Leroux and others for devising one of the earliest locked-room mysteries (28). Panek tells us that G. K. Chesterton (1874–1936) from 1911 begins the Father Brown short stories with surprise endings in a "poetic style" evocative of the fairy tale (105). Symons observes that Chesterton sought characteristically to convey "the poetry concealed in city life" while at the same time "he was never able to take anything that he wrote quite seriously" (76–77). Women detectives flourished briefly, usually as "one book phenomena" (Panek 108).

Before discussing the next period, that of the Golden Age, Symons makes two short digressions to note the differing evolution of the short story and the novel. The "Golden Age" of the former, he says (85) began with Conan Doyle's Sherlock Holmes and closed by the Second World War, but the short story as a preferred form began to wane a lot earlier as the novel became increasing popular by the end of the First World War (86). Arguably this dates from the publication in 1913 of E. C. Bentley's *Trent's Last Case* that Symons uses as a type example, but Chesterton should be included here as well.

The Raffles stories of E. W. Hornung first appeared in the late 1890s in *Cassell's Magazine* published as a collection titled *The Amateur Cracksman* in 1899. Three later publications in 1901, 1905, and 1909 bring Hornung into the Edwardian Period. Hornung's stories, says Panek, have charm but also bite (114). Charm, however, is not the same as wit or humor and I do not spend time on Hurnung and his creation. Panek remarks also that "the master criminal and his gang reflect turn-of-the-century anxieties about secret societies," a theme that reappears from time to time during the Golden Age in detective fiction but more prominently in the thrillers. It is with us today. Indeed, secret societies and their like became part of the definition of the thriller (115). What Panek calls the "crook story" (112), closely associated with the thriller, has several sub-varieties (Panek refers to them as "plots") such as the disguise (or mask) tale, the tale of technique (how to crack a safe, for example), tales of escape, and tales of double-crossing (a form I think of the surprise ending). Panek remarks, "All of these plots, additionally, can be colored by the telling, and writers could choose to narrate into their stories vicarious excitement, social satire, burlesque, moral censure, or a combination of these to reach different parts of the readers' appreciation" (112).

Symons states that the gradual decline of the short story and rise of the novel as a preferred form are linked to economic, technological (he says "technical") and social changes (86). One of the effects of the First World War was a shortage of paper together with other scarce commodities. This probably lies behind Panek's note that at this time publishers began accepting books in shorter format (118). To this he adds, "the concept of the tightly constructed novel in high-brow literature suggested new methods and new models for the detective novelists" of the next decade. For example, "narrative trickery" becomes "a standard mark of the detective story in the next generation" (118–119). However, he notes, "wit and comedy" tended to be forgotten as the magazines declined and the regular reappearance of Conan Doyle's Sherlock Holmes distracted the attention of readers from the new work. Panek is not entirely correct, however, for comedy and wit form part of a thematic stream in the two decades of the Golden Age and are carried on beyond that era.

"Best of all stories": The Golden Age

The two decades through the 1920s and 1930s with a little overlapping on either end are generally accepted as the Golden Age in crime fiction. It is a time during which "the best of all stories" were written by a variety of like-minded novelists, many of whom moved within the same circles, bounced ideas off one another, sometimes bounced off one another, and sometimes knew one another intimately. It is also a time when the austerities brought on by World War I became ameliorated to encourage "golden ages of publishing and advertising" as Panek has it: "After World War One, publishers competed with libraries for the expanding reading public by issuing cheap editions of popular books and authors" (120). The general social ferment of post-war life in the 1920s provided an agreeable undercurrent, although this began to change in the 1930s with the economic depression and the rise of Nazism in Germany, until life melted again for the worst with the onset of the Second World War. Most of the authors reviewed in my list belong to this period and just after.

A major test of a novel's success is whether one wants (a) to reread it, and/or (b) to read another novel by the same author. The notion of the literary classic is important enough to have its own definition, as in Chris Baldick's entry, "a work admired ... deemed to have stood the test of time and outlasted changes in critical taste" (57). Susan Sontag notes in one of her 1965 diary entries: "The principal characteristic of a classic is that it's beautiful" (153). Perhaps "beauty" is not the best generalization. It seems to me that, although there are different ways by which we may define beauty, the novels of Margery Allingham, Dorothy L. Sayers, John Dickson Carr, Edmund Crispin and their colleagues in crime have continued appeal for present-day readers for other reasons. The most obvious of these is that they are written to amuse and to raise a laugh as well as to plot a puzzle the reader enjoys solving, a bringing together of serious crime fiction with subversive humor.

The list begins with the detective fiction of E. C. Bentley that by many accounts ushered in the Golden Age. *Trent's Last Case* (1913) led a reaction against the image of the infallible detective as exemplified by Conan Doyle's Sherlock Holmes character and, after a hiatus caused by the First World War, moved such writers as A. A. Milne, Margery Allingham and John Dickson Carr to emulate as well as to parody Bentley's novel. Plot elements and overall structure from *Trent's Last Case* can be recognized in several of those writers' works. E. C. Bentley is one of the first to introduce humorous writing into the crime novel, for which he had a special talent, says Symons (87), and the success of *Trent's Last Case* is due to its being perceived by readers as "light entertainment" (88) than as an "exposure," as Symons puts it, of detective stories. The touch of ambivalence comes from Bentley's intent to counter the infallibility of figures such as Sherlock Holmes by making Philip Trent a fallible detective. As Symons points out, "The line between the comic and the serious in the detective story is a fine one" (87) and, a little later, "Bentley wavered into seriousness against his original intentions" (92). Wavering into seriousness appears to have afflicted many writers for various reasons.

Agatha Christie makes her debut at the beginning of the decade with *The Mysterious Affair at Styles* (1920). The eccentric character of the Belgian detective Hercule Poirot is a comic figure and there is an element of wit in her tales, but there is more of it in the crime novels of Dorothy L. Sayers and Margery Allingham. If we are to look at this study as a lineage in crime writing, then the more affable sort of novel to a significant extent stands apart from the English country cottage form represented by Christie.

Two branches of the lineage in crime fiction I suggest peel off in the 1920s and proceed parallel to each other while meeting at many points: (a) "serious" writing focused upon puzzle solving, and (b) the rise of what Symons calls the farceurs "those writers for whom the business of fictional murder was endlessly amusing" (104). The farceurs were mostly British, he says, adding a trifle snobbishly but I think with some point that American writers at the time were not sufficiently sophisticated and, perhaps more importantly, that England was a safer country to live in, at least for the middle classes. The chief humorists of the Golden Age, then, are E. C. Bentley, A. A. Milne, John Dickson Carr, and Edmund Crispin, with Margery Allingham, Dorothy L. Sayers and Ngaio Marsh a little less prominent where humor is concerned (their strong point is wit), followed in the second half of the era by Edmund Crispin and Nancy Spain. Allingham and Carr, and Michael Innes, too, span both decades and continue well into the post–World War II years.

Arguably, the first half of the Golden Age is a cozy period. There are successful collaborations between writers, the best-known being Manfred B. Lee and Frederic Dannay using the nom de plume of Ellery Queen (Panek 122). The publishers Methuen set up a contest for aspiring detective writers (Panek 121). Standards in plot lines are laid, usually tongue in cheek, with writers such as Monsignor Ronald Knox's codification of ten rules in 1929 ("Golden Age of Detective Fiction"), and S. S. Van Dine's twenty rules in 1928 (Panek 123). The Detection Club is founded in 1928 by Anthony Berkeley Cox according to Panek (122) or in 1930 according to a Wikipedia contributor ("Detection Club"). Its membership includes Margery Allingham, E. C. Bentley, Simon Brett, John Dickson Carr, G. K. Chesterton, Agatha Christie, Edmund Crispin, Ngaio Marsh, A. A. Milne, and Dorothy L. Sayers. This is an experimental time for variations on the theme of the fallible detective, and for trying out various story-telling techniques such as showing different points of view, or producing multiple solutions to a crime puzzle.

In Panek's view, "*Trent's Last Case* began the whole movement and remains one of the most influential golden age books…. A. A. Milne's *The Red House Mystery* established a standard of ease and playfulness which later writers either envied or, like Raymond Chandler, detested" (130); Michael Innes "produced some of the most intricate plots and the zaniest books" (129); detective characters such as "Bentley's Trent, Sayers' Wimsey, Allingham's Campion, Marsh's … Alleyn, and many others use peppy, witty language" (127); "Dorothy L. Sayers did much more to establish the detective story as a semi-legitimate literary form" (128); "Cox demonstrated a bent for acid detective burlesque in his early books" (130); "Carr went on to create some of the most baffling plots, the funniest characters, and the most boffo situations" (130). Motifs such as a bridge or a chess piece, says Panek, come from the genre of the thriller; also, I might add, images of the weather — "it was a dark and stormy night," attributed to Edward Bulwer-Lytton ("Edward Bulwer-Lytton, 1st Baron Lytton") — and the sea, lake or tarn. The detective tales also reflect English snobbery and class-consciousness in their enclosed settings of country house or mansions with servants such as butlers, housekeepers and maids. Predating Panek's 1979 and 1987 studies, Colin Watson, a prominent reviewer who is also a writer of crime stories, makes this his theme in *Snobbery with Violence* (1971), English class snobbery being another facet of the cozy environment of the Golden Age.

Near the close of his chapter, Panek draws attention to similarities between crime fiction of the Golden Age and the stage play in the inclusion of plenty of dialogue as well as humor: "Michael Innes' novels draw extensively, and admittedly, from the patterns of stage farce" (134). The unity of place and time so essential to the theater, as Aristotle saw it, notes Panek, are two other features of the crime novel of this period. The fictional present of a crime novel is usually that of a few days or even hours, comparable to the length of a stage play, and many Golden Age writers in fact contributed to drama. A. A. Milne (as Panek notes) was a playwright who included a crime story in his output:

The Fourth Wall (1928), titled "The Perfect Alibi" in the U. S. John Dickson Carr and his disciple Edmund Crispin were journalists who also wrote radio plays and television scripts as their chief livelihood. The settings reflect their life experiences in the universities as well as in the theater. Anthony Shaffer (1926–2001) wrote *Whodunnit: A Comedy Thriller* (1983) as well as more serious crime drama such as *The Wicker Man* (1979). His novel *The Woman in the Wardrobe — A Lighthearted Detective Story* (1951) is written under the pseudonym of Peter Antony and illustrated by Nicolas Bentley, the son of E. C. Bentley ("Anthony Shaffer"). Unfortunately it is unavailable in the Internet book market.

Nineteen-twenties society in England had its share of socio-cultural anxieties: post–World World I "Roaring Twenties"/"Jazz Age" in the U.S., "Golden Twenties" in Europe stimulated by economic boom, increased urbanization, the rise of extremist political movements such as the Nazi Party in Germany, communism in Russia, and fascism in Italy and Spain, closing with the Wall Street crash in 1929 and harder times in the 1930s. In the 1930s — more or less the second half of the Golden Age — John Dickson Carr and Edmund Crispin join the ranks of the other farceurs with fresh twists of irreverent humor. But changes were taking place. The transition from the 1920s into the 1930s saw life becoming more serious.

As I see it, lesser humorists of the 1920s include Anthony Berkeley Cox (1893–1971), Monsignor Ronald Knox (1888–1957), and A. A. Milne (1882–1956). For instance, Cox, writing as Anthony Berkeley (also as Francis Iles), created the amateur detective Roger Sheringham who, observes Symons: "Like Trent ... was conceived almost as a joke, a caricature of an offensive acquaintance. He was taken seriously by readers, however" (99).

The second half of the Golden Age, then, is characterized by gradual shifts in crime fiction led by writers who start out as humorists but over time lose their ease with the world and become more serious, but "early Allingham, mid-career Innes, and almost total-career Carr display in their detective novels the desire to ladle as much slapstick, wit, and bizarre comedy into their books as they will hold" (Panek 140).

The Second World War changed a lot. In England George Orwell in defending Wodehouse points out that "the upper classes were discredited by their appeasement policy and by the disasters of 1940, and a social-levelling process appeared to be taking place. Patriotism and left-wing sentiments were associated in the popular mind, and numerous able journalists were at work to tie the association tighter" (298). Columnists such as "Cassandra" (Sir William Neil Connor 1909–1967) wrote "demagogic propaganda" and "it was generally felt that the rich were treacherous." Panek says that some writers such as Innes and Christie began to alternate between the thriller and the detective novel, because "the war changed the rules of the game, and master criminals without sane motives loosed mass destruction on humanity." This is a little more pessimistic than merited by later developments (142).

The 1930s indeed marked a turning point from the comfortable cottage mysteries that characterize much of the Golden Age, gaining some inspiration from the American hardboiled detective fiction of Raymond Chandler and Dashiell Hammett that has, incidentally, its own form of noir humor, especially in wise-cracking dialogue, says Haycraft (212–213). In Continental Europe the Belgian writer Georges Simenon (1903–1989) invented the character of Commissaire Maigret and, according to the blurb on the frontispiece of *The Hotel Majestic* (1977), produced over the years "75 novels and 28 stories" (short stories or novellas, I think). Many were published in the 1940s to the 1950s. They are police procedurals and, although the character of Maigret has eccentricities, the "dark realism" of the novels in my opinion does not qualify Simenon as a farceur.

The decade is mostly taken up with the worldwide Great Depression, continued rise of authoritarian governments and outbreak of World War II in 1939. The old flamboyance of the 1920s continues to be expressed through the Art Deco movement. This is a *mise en scène* in the BBC London Weekend Television retrospective dramatizations of *Agatha Christie's Poirot* (1989, 1990). Mainstream literature in the 1930s includes Tolkien's *The Hobbit* (1937), Aldous Huxley's *Brave New World* (1932), Hemingway's *To Have and Have Not* (1937), and Raymond Chandler's *The Big Sleep* (1934). Towards the close of the 1930s, "the pulp fiction magazines began to feature distinctive, gritty adventure heroes that combined elements of hard boiled detective fiction and the fantastic adventures of the earlier pulp novels" ("1930s"). Julian Symons discusses the importance of the Second World War as a turning point," a watershed in the history of the crime story, separating ... the world of reason from that of force" (138).

Post–World War II Humorists

Despite this, the thread of comedy is maintained throughout the crises. Sayers, Allingham and Carr continue writing, joined by two comparative newcomers, Bruce Montgomery, writing under the pseudonym of Edmund Crispin, and Nancy Spain. Crispin was strongly influenced by the detective fiction of John Dickson Carr and, while Symons calls Michael Innes "the finest of the Farceurs" (115), he also names Edmund Crispin as "the last and most charming of the Farceurs" (142). Crispin wrote his first Professor Gervase Fen novel *The Case of the Gilded Fly* in 1944 and his last with that character in 1977, *The Glimpses of the Moon*. Nancy Spain was motivated to try her hand at crime writing after becoming acquainted with Margery Allingham and others through her work as a reviewer. Spain's first Miriam Birdseye and Natasha Nevkorina novel *Poison in Play* was published in 1945; her last, *The Kat Strikes,* in 1955, nine years before her untimely death in a light aircraft accident in 1964. It might be argued that Spain belongs to the next notional time period for the lineage of comedy in crime, that of "Cultural Revolution," because of her iconoclastic influence on social mores.

The thriller remained strong. It has its own lineage that harkens back to the pulp adventure tales of the turn of the century and such school-day reading as the *Boys Own Paper* and the Richard Hannay novels of John Buchan, beginning with *The Thirty-Nine Steps* (1915) and ending with *The Island of Sheep* (1936). They are tales of World War I espionage and international criminal gangs. Panek states, "In Britain, the schoolboy story had a large effect on the development of the adventure story written for adults, but had little impact on the detective story, which always danced around the skirts of regular literature" (145).

This is not convincing. Panek appears to say that the thriller belongs to mainstream literature (adult adventure tales = regular literature?). But if the detective story lies on the fringes (the skirts) of mainstream (regular) literature so too does the thriller. They are both examples of what is today called genre writing. This includes westerns, romances and, more recently, forms of underground writing, called literature in an alternative and less formal use of the term. The second point is that several writers of crime/detective fiction include strong elements of the thriller in their plots, Margery Allingham for example, as well as John Dickson Carr. Social troubles such as war, Prohibition (in America), and economic depression help strengthen the thriller as a form of escapist literature alongside the cozy country house crime. Panek is on firmer ground when he writes that "the hard-boiled story is in large measure the adventure story based on a plot that strings dangerous incidents together. But the hard-boiled story weaves a detective plot into the adventure plot" (158). It is escapist literature all the same. As we shall see, it is evident from the life profiles that most of the detective/crime writers of the Golden Age are conservative figures, which perhaps helps to explain their production of escapist literature.

In this period Somerset Maugham writes on "The Decline and Fall of the Detective Story" (1952). Symons critiques Maugham's essay, saying that it is "on the whole not very original, with its observations that there is little room for humor and none for love interest, and its insistence that 'fine writing is out of place.' All this had been said before" (219). I agree. In my reading of Maugham's commentary I suspect he cribbed a lot from Dorothy L. Sayers' Introduction to her anthology *Great Short Stories of Detection, Mystery and Horror* because he follows relatively closely Sayers' structure and main points. He might also have read Sayers' "Aristotle on Detective Fiction" (1935). But he does not mention Sayers as one of his sources.

To be fair, it can be argued that an overview such as Maugham's covers much the same ground as many others, and Maugham adapts and so produces a shorter, lighter essay than that of Sayers. To me, Maugham's essay is a little careless, certainly relaxed, and a trifle vain. Maugham tells us that he wrote it during the outbreak of the Second World War while living in a yacht that found temporary mooring at the coastal town of Bandol on the French Riviera (76–78). He uses his enforced leisure to write and names his essay from the title of Edward Gibbon's *The Decline and Fall of the Roman Empire*. Largely, Maugham says he draws upon his reading of crime novels. He possessed several and mentions the possibility of exchanging them with others among the Riviera leisure set (78). He mentions Raymond Chandler's *The Simple Art of Murder* (1934). We can take Maugham's essay perhaps in the spirit in which it is intended, as a light overview, laid back, not meant to be scholarly (unlike Dorothy Sayers' detailed critiques). But he is wrong essentially: the detective story does not decline and fall. On the contrary, it evolves over the next decades.

Howard Haycraft has an interesting but flawed thesis based upon the premise that shortly before the outbreak of the Second World War the importing of Agatha Christie's detective novels and Edgar Wallace's thrillers was banned in Italy by its Fascist government, and that a few years later in 1941 similar novels were removed from Germany's bookshops by the Nazi Party (312–313). Haycraft's idea is this:

> The detective story is and always has been essentially a democratic institution; dramatizing, under the bright cloak of entertainment, many of the precious rights and privileges that have set the dwellers in constitutional lands apart from those less fortunate ... safeguarded by known, just, and logical rules ... democracies require and scrutinize evidence.

Haycraft continues with a pro–Democracy polemic. As he notes, he is reflecting the cultural anxieties of the Second World War, during which he is writing. The flaw in Haycraft's thesis is that not many decades later lowercase fascism becomes a major tool of Western administrations. While supporting rhetorically the idea of democracy at home they seek political advantage in the international arena through the use of naked force, the core definition of the ideology of fascism: "Fascism promotes political violence and war, as forms of direct action that create national regeneration, spirit and vitality. Fascists commonly utilize paramilitary organizations for violence against opponents or to overthrow a political system" ("Fascism"). The ideology is often symbolized by the ancient Roman *fasces*, the bundle of sticks with axe blade attached that represents power in unity. The image is ubiquitous in the United States where, for example, the fasces "is a common element in US Army Military Police heraldry" and appears also in the National Guard Bureau insignia ("Fasces").

The 1950s saw a gradual recovery from the Second World War, but this was concomitant with Cold War competitiveness between the Soviet Union and the United States of America. In 1949 George Orwell's dystopian novel *Nineteen Eighty-Four* was published and has wide influence. The big ideologies of Communism and Capitalism divided Western thinking. Technologically, the "space race" began. Politically, in the U.S. Joseph McCarthy pursued the vilification and public inquisition of citizens, including writers and film actors. Militarily, the U.S. entered into the Korean War (1950–1953), and, through such organizations as its Central Intelligence Agency interfered with democratic changes in South American countries because the changes were perceived as reflecting socialist ideologies: "Latin America was the center of covert and overt conflict between the Soviet Union and the United States. Their varying collusion with national, populist, and elitist interests destabilized the region" ("1950s"). The Vietnam War began in 1959. There was a revival of folk music. Dissidence and an accompanying counterculture emerged in both the U.S. and England. By the 1960s came the rise of feminism and the gay rights movement that in the next decade gained ground with other dissident movements. David Lodge makes a sober judgment about the former in relation to Kingsley Amis's *Lucky Jim*: "Is this contrast between the two women sexist? [Christine and Margaret who complicate Jim Dixon's life in the novel]. Of course it is! So was most fiction written by men in the 1950s, or indeed at any other time, judged by 1990s standards of what is Politically Correct" (xvi).

The contents page on *Wikipedia* for the 1970s catches the major social changes of that decade with the rise of four social movements: anti-war protests, environmentalism, feminism and civil rights. They are reflected in several trends in mainstream literature that overlap into crime fiction:

> The early '70s brought a return to old-fashioned storytelling.... Racism remained a key literary subject.... With the rising cost of hard-cover books and the increasing readership of "genre fiction," the paperback became a popular medium. Criminal non-fiction also became a popular topic. Irreverence and satire were common literary elements. The horror genre also emerged ["1970s"].

Ned Polsky refers to the social changes of the sixties and the seventies (particularly in the United States) as the rise and collapse of the "counterculture":

> A population explosion took place with the succeeding generation, the beats of the 1950s, and an even bigger one took place with the arrival of their descendants, the hippies of the 1960s. For a combination of demographic and political reasons — the baby boom following World War II, the unpopularity of the Vietnam War ... the counterculture reached its peak size toward the end of the 1960s; and then it collapsed virtually overnight with the end of America's undeclared war in Vietnam [230].

Panek acknowledges the close of the Golden Age in detective fiction with the Second World War but points out (as I say) that "the patterns survive" as well as there being a growth of noir fiction with an element of wit: "though

World War II affected the development of the Golden Age detective story, and some of the best writers dropped the trade [or died], there was hardly a gap in the line stretching back to E. C. Bentley. New writers stepped in to continue the tradition" (190). But he believes that the new generation of writers do not reach the same level of fame as the older established authors. This remains to be tested. Police novels, "police procedurals," also form part of the more serious writing stream in the decade following World War II, but "contemporary detective writers do copy the golden agers" (191). He goes on to cite Edmund Crispin's "very funny, ironic, and erudite novels" (190), and names several others who contribute to the general line but without the emphasis on humor. As a friend remarked recently: "These crime writers seem to have a nice turn of phrase, and a cynical but well placed understanding of human nature" (personal communication, Basil Lambert).

Others who continue the tradition of the farceurs overviewed by Symons and other critics include Joyce Porter with *Dover One* (1964) and Colin Watson's *Hopjoy Was Here* (1962) that has "some brilliant comedy" (Symons 189). As Symons points out: "Successful comic crime stories, short or long, are rare.... Unfortunately the law of diminishing returns operates most powerfully in relation to comic detectives" (188–189), so that having established a protagonist's quirky or eccentric personality the writer cannot develop the character further, merely repeating the foibles that in later publications tend to lose their novelty. This is a difficulty that I think is experienced by the earlier writers as well, and might help to explain why Allingham and Carr leant towards more sober work in their later careers, complicated by other factors in their lives. Allingham continued writing more in the vein of the thriller, which she had always done; Carr turned to historical romances.

Although Panek mentions Watson briefly (199) in *Watteau's Shepherds* (1979), in his later study of 1987 he unaccountably misses Colin Watson whose first of the Flaxborough Chronicles, *Coffin, Scarcely Used,* appeared in 1958. This is more surprising because Watson's highly engaging general history of English crime writing, *Snobbery with Violence,* came out in 1971, sixteen years before Panek's first study and eight years before his follow-up commentary. Panek does include Watson in his 1987 bibliography. Surprisingly too, Panek and Symons both miss Leslie Thomas whose Dangerous Davies series began in 1976 with his first novel *Dangerous Davies: The Last Detective.* It overlaps Panek's book. Other humorists in the years of "cultural revolution" include H. R. F. Keating's "semi-surrealist" style with his Inspector Ghote stories in the 1960s (Symons 189), and Sheila Pim writing between 1945 and 1964. It seems that some critics fail to acknowledge or give weight to overviews written by other critics. One suspects minor undercurrents of professional jealousy as well as fair criticism. Symons' criticism of Somerset Maugham I think is fair, but the omission of Colin Watson is not easy to explain.

When one writes studies like those of Panek, Symons, Binyon, Haycraft and Watson, it is difficult to forecast who may or may not emerge as a prominent writer in the future, or the advent of a particular theme. Symons in the 1985 edition of *Bloody Murder* sums up: "The development of crime novels, a bag of literary allsorts ranging from comedy to tragedy, from realistic portraits of society to psychological investigation of an individual, together with the flowering of the spy story as a literary form" (234).

Fin de Siècle

One of the most recent critical overviews of crime-cum-detective writing is P. D. James's *Talking About Detective Fiction* (2009). At 159 pages it is more like a monograph than a detailed analysis of the genre and, with its extremely brief "Bibliography and Suggested Reading" (seventeen works listed), stands as a very short springboard into the subject. The references are divided equally between general analyses such as those of Symons and Watson and biographies of select authors such as Margery Allingham, Dorothy L. Sayers, Agatha Christie, and Ngaio Marsh. James's feminist emphasis is reflected in the choices. There are no male writers in her list. In her own right, James is a prolific author of at least eighteen police procedurals — for example, *An Unsuitable Job for a Woman* (1972), *The Black Tower* (1975)— that gives *Talking About Detective Fiction* a cachet of authority, and her commentaries are pertinent.

While it is apt to say that James's dissertation is comparatively slight, she has not been fairly reviewed by one critic who, while writing ostensibly about *Talking About Detective Fiction*, does not really accord the book a hearing. Venero Armanno approaches his subject carelessly, dismissing *Talking About Detective Fiction* as "a series of coolly analytical essays" (21) that read like academic papers (which they might well have been) and missing the point when he says redundantly that the works James discusses "seem, and are, oddly antiquated." Armanno's review is a good example of how genres can become confused in the mind of a critic. He begins by saying how much he likes Stephen King's horror tales and the reviews of novels and films King writes. But detective fiction belongs to a different genre, as Armanno should know, and he really was not focusing on James's contribution at all. Armanno is one of those critics who today want excitement and reader involvement as well as horror and hard-boiled detective fiction. In this respect he reflects one side of the dispute whether or not to use humor in crime stories. This controversy is already taking shape in the latter half of the Golden Age and grows to dominate the post–World War II movement towards noir fiction. If one considers the history of detective/crime fiction, authors of the Golden Age, their precursors and those who come after have to be assessed.

What Armanno calls "antiquated" works are not only the forerunners of present-day crime fiction, they also influence it profoundly through a natural reaction that gives rise to emulation, parody and satire on the one hand, and a greater focus on brutal aspects of crime, on the other hand, that arguably reflect the present-day mood. Although that mood is dark with its police procedurals and obsession with serial killers, and while P. D. James is not a humorist, she acknowledges (146, 157) the importance of humor: "we do not expect popular literature to be great literature, but fiction which provides excitement, mystery *and humour* also ministers to essential human needs" [my emphasis].

CHAPTER 2

The Crime Fiction of E. C. Bentley (1875–1956)

E. C. Bentley, it seems to me, never fully breaks from his cautiously minded and conservative Victorian origins to the freer spirit of the literary golden age that he influenced and through which he lived. The lighthearted and amiable character of his fictional amateur detective Philip Trent may be at war with Bentley's reticence towards women, to give one example, and an attitude towards writing as a chore balanced uneasily against his journalism, revealed in the stiff—not to say Victorian-Edwardian—ramblings of his memoir. As a consequence his output in detective fiction is considerably less than that of his peers, school chums such as G. K. Chesterton and John Buchan, and members of the Detection Club such as Margery Allingham and John Dickson Carr. Yet he influenced two generations of crime writers profoundly. The significance of locating Bentley in place and among close contemporaries is that he was almost literally in the centre of cosmopolitan and literary life.

Edmund Clerihew Bentley was born in 1875 at Shepherd's Bush, a suburb approximately ten kilometers west from central London (Charing Cross, Soho, the West End). In 1890 he attended St. Paul's School in the nearby suburb of Barnes in South West London, beginning at the preparatory school where he met G. K. Chesterton and moving on later to the "big school" (Bentley 47). There is an element of hero-worship in Bentley's memoir of Chesterton: "G.K.C., when I knew him first, was an unusually tall, lanky boy with a serious, even brooding expression that gave way very easily to one of laughing happiness" (46). Chesterton was one of Bentley's lifelong friends.

Bentley studied history at Oxford University, graduating in 1898, followed by law. He left the bar not many years later. In his own words: "I wanted to begin making a living as soon as possible. I also wanted to get married as soon as possible. I was earning a little by my pen week by week, all through my time in Hansell's chambers, and even before that; my evenings were occupied in this way" (141). So in 1901 he married Violet Boileau. They had three children, including Nicolas Bentley who became an artist and collaborated with his father in the production of a book of clerihews.

The clerihew, taken from his middle name, is Bentley's invention. It is a slight verse form that suffers by comparison with the more popular limerick. There were early school-day efforts but it first appeared in book form in 1905 as *Biography for Beginners*: "On one occasion when Browning / Saved a débutante from drowning / She enquired faintly what he meant / By that stuff about good news from Ghent" (*Clerihews Complete* 1951). The "Biography" in the title refers to one of the "rules" for the form that, as Stephen Fry observes, "clerihews be non-metrically written in two couplets, the first of which is to be a proper name and nothing else.... Properly done, they should tell some biographical truth, obvious or otherwise, about their subject, rather than be sheer nonsense.... Clerihews have therefore some utility as biographical mnemonics" (263–264). *Biography for Beginners* is followed by *More Biography* (1929), *Baseless Biographies* (1939), and *Clerihews Complete* (1951). The last-named had three illustrators: Bentley's lifelong friend G. K. Chesterton, Victor Reinganum the Surrealist illustrator (1907–1995), and Bentley's son Nicolas Bentley. E. C. Bentley drew one illustration: "depicting the death of William Rufus in the manner of the Bayeux Tapestry" (158) which was, he wrote, "a servile imitation" of the original work. *The First Clerihews* was published posthumously in 1982 (OUP synopsis 1995; Baldick xxii).

Concurrent with his marriage and substantially impelled by it, E. C. Bentley found work as a leader writer for the *Daily News*, beginning in 1901 and carrying on to 1912 when he changed to a position with another newspaper, the *Daily Telegraph*, where he stayed until 1934. During that long career he contributed to *Punch* magazine and other periodicals. In the 1940s he came out of retirement to rejoin the *Daily Telegraph* as literary critic. During the war years his house was destroyed and as a result Bentley became depressed and turned to drink. He died about ten years later, in 1956 aged eighty-one (OUP synopsis to *Trent's Last Case*).

The Edwardian period lasted from the accession of King Edward VII to the British throne after the death of Queen Victoria in January 1901 and ended with Edward's death in 1910. But the relatively brief period is often extended a further ten years, its close either the sinking of the RMS *Titanic* in 1912 or the onset of the First World War in 1914, the armistice marking the end of the First World War on 11 November 1918, or the *Treaty of Versailles* 28 June 1919.

This short era is characterized as a time during which Victorian severity gradually gave way to a relaxation of social mores. The king surrounded himself with "a fashionable elite" that followed European trends in the arts and commerce. English social history paralleled that of the *Belle Époque* in France and Germany. It is no wonder that E. C. Bentley was a Francophile like many of his social class, as well as those of the aristocracy, with their educational grounding in the Continental European languages (French, German, Italian) and the Greek and Roman classics. Like most times perhaps, the Edwardian period has its contradictions, for although there was a gradual freeing-up in many areas of life, the British class system remained strong. It had been established in the nineteenth century with occupational divisions grown sharper between rich and poor as a result of the Industrial Revolution: "The lower classes, as with earlier periods, were segregated from the aristocratic and mercantile ... and led lives far removed from the relative luxury enjoyed by the other classes" ("Edwardian era"). At the same time there was increasing awareness through the new mass media of social inequities regarding the poor, greater social mobility, women's suffrage, and the rise of socialism.

Edwardian "press barons" have their counterpart in the character of Sir James Molloy in *Trent's Last Case*. Imported Continental music and theater is represented in the Ninth Symphony played by Mabel Manderson on piano (138) and her attendance together with Trent at the opera *Tristan* (117). Changes in leisure and clothing fashions are reflected too in the novel. Trent is depicted as a sportsman, a strong swimmer, and Mabel's "wave of dark brown skirts" suggests a literal freeing up of women's bodies. Women's Edwardian dress, while retaining the flowing lines, narrow waist and accentuated bust, became softer and less restrictive than in the earlier half of the decade with its tight bodices, corsetry and crinolines inherited from the Victorian era. With the onset of the First World War women's clothing fashions changed radically, becoming more functional and austere as many entered the war effort and dress materials became scarcer.

Universal education, the public circulating libraries, and increased flow of book publications begun in the Victorian era gained momentum in Edwardian times. Highbrow and popular literature became more sharply distinguished. P. G. Wodehouse (1881–1975), J. M. Barrie (1860–1937), and Kenneth Grahame (1859–1932) were E. C. Bentley's contemporaries, as were many other authors writing in different genres. Henry Rider Haggard (1856–1925) was producing racy adventure tales such as *King Solomon's Mines* (1885) that led to "penny dreadful" plots and the "ripping yarns" tradition later disseminated in "pulp" literature.

Nicolas Bentley's Critique

Bentley's memoirs *Those Days* came out in 1940 (OUP synopsis 1995; Baldick xxii) when Bentley was sixty-five. Read now, its prose style is informal but Edwardian and mannered, and tends to rambling as memoirs can do. It focuses upon his school days and journalistic career and very little else. The short chapter on the writing and publication of *Trent's Last Case* is useful but there is next to nothing about his family life. His wife and children, for instance, are rarely mentioned. I counted four passing references to his wife, whose name is never given. Bentley could note that the maiden name of Chesterton's mother was French, "like my own wife" (255) without revealing either of the two names, when he and Violet met the Chestertons by chance in Paris (254). On that occasion Bentley took the opportunity to summarize the plot of *Trent's Last Case* to Chesterton. I suspect that the character of Mabel Manderson in *Trent's Last Case* is in large part a depiction, probably idealized, of Violet Boileau. There is a depth of feeling between Bentley's fictional protagonists that has no corresponding reflection in the memoirs.

When reading the memoirs of Edmund Bentley's youngest son Nicolas Bentley, it is interesting to see how many of the patterns distinctive of the father remain in the life and viewpoints of the son. As Nicolas says, he was the youngest of three siblings: "My brother Neil and my sister Betty were just too old for me to join in their games" (17). Compare this against the father's childhood where Edmund Bentley was the eldest of four brothers with whom he had little in common (24). Gilbert Chesterton, who was a close friend of the father, became Nicolas's godfather and someone to whom he could turn as a confidant rather than to his own father (19). Nicolas by his own admission was a solitary child "dissociated" early in life from his parents. Such children in later adult life can be very critical of their parent:

> My father was a complicated man, much more complicated than you would have imagined from his manner, which was shy, although it was open and interested. He was extraordinarily reserved, and yet he was capable of being extremely affectionate. He valued friendship, and yet often seemed deliberately to discourage it.... As I first remember him, he was always a stickler for physical fitness, but gradually he degenerated into a hopeless hypochondriac, and later on in life he began to hit the bottle. I believe one cause was a suspicion — perhaps there was a certain amount of justification for it — of his having been something of a failure (20–21).

Edmund Bentley's withdrawal from life appears to have been gradual, however, for the son can in one breath write that: "he took little or no account of the pressures, social, technological, and even intellectual, that had resulted in the changing and streamlining of this type of fiction.... [H]is interest in contemporary literature, particularly fiction, was extraordinarily meagre" (22); but, sixteen pages later observes to the contrary that "the subjects that preoccupied my father were international politics and the world of books and writers, in particular the craft of detective fiction" (38), in the context of the wife's (Nicolas's mother) complete lack of interest in such topics. What Nicolas Bentley identifies in his father is "a premature slackening of his creative impulse"

(21) so that (for example) Edmund Bentley's friend Warner Allen had to exert "strong pressure" upon him to write in collaboration with Allen *Trent's Own Case* (22). Despite Edmund's reported reluctance the novel was a good one. The real failing came later with the disastrous *Elephant's Work.*

Nicolas Bentley suggests that the underlying cause of his father's malaise was his failure to graduate from Oxford by a first in Greats, achieving only a second (23). This would be a rough equivalent in an Australian university of gaining second-class honors for a Ph.D. instead of first-class. It set Edmund Bentley apart from his contemporaries, at least in his eyes, and caused him to remain, says Nicolas, "on the sidelines throughout his life" (23), symbolized perhaps by his becoming a family tutor on Lake Windermere in July 1895 after taking his final examinations. By contrast, Edmund Bentley's school chums achieved notable academic success. John Buchan (1875–1940)— First Baron Tweedsmuir — studied classics at Brasenose College, Oxford, and in 1897 won the Stanhope essay prize, graduating in 1900 ("John Buchan, 1st Baron Tweedsmuir"). Hilaire Belloc (1870–1953) graduated through Balliol College, Oxford, and gained first-class honors in history ("Hilaire Belloc"). G. K. Chesterton (1874–1936) (*Chambers Biographical Dictionary*) was the exception. He did not complete his literature degree at University College, London, but went instead into journalism like E. C. Bentley and made his mark independently of a university triumph ("G. K. Chesterton"). Arguably, the subsequent careers of these three men outshine that of Edmund Bentley.

Victorian remoteness in personal relationships appears to have been passed down through the family, for Edmund Bentley's father (Nicolas's grandfather) was the same (27); the mother too (Nicolas's grandmother), "uncommunicative" (24), "never seemed entirely sober," her state of continual inebriation gauged by the angle of her wig (25). This may help to explain E. C. Bentley's turning to drink in later life. However, journalism and writing as reflected among Detection Club membership had a strong heavy drinking culture and some of Bentley's contemporaries such as John Dickson Carr and, later, Edmund Crispin, drank heavily and as a consequence suffered poor health in their later years.

Against the reserved somewhat cold British temperament there is a strain of humor and geniality "inherited." Eccentricity lay in the family of Nicolas's mother, the rarely mentioned and scarcely ever named Violet Boileau. Her father John Theophilus Boilieu (b. 1805) was a general attached to the Bengal Staff Corps (30) in the Indian Army. In a wry passage Nicolas describes such officers:

> In a group photograph, showing him, seated with his brother officers, they look as unregenerate a crew of Anglo-Indian military martinets as ever commanded the mysterious loyalty of a sepoy army. That's Sir Haley O'Grady sitting in the middle in his frogged frock-coat with his pudgy fists clenched on his ivory-handled sabre, looking like a fat, infuriated spaniel. And that one beside him, the

frail, upright, faintly priggish-looking type with a heavy black beard and gold-rimmed glasses of the kind that Schubert wore — that's my grandfather (28).

This grandfather was in fact "a good man" who in retirement at Brighton "scandalized" the neighborhood by becoming a cobbler, furniture repairer and odd-job man and refusing to attend church. He was a free thinker, but "unlike most cranks and political radicals, he apparently had an excellent sense of humor, beautiful manners, and a good deal of personal charm" (28). Nicolas's barrister grandfather (father's father) is described as "a genial old person with a large white beard and a library, which he and I seemed to be the only people to use" (26).

Violet Boileau was eccentric in a different manner. She is described as "extremely volatile ... obsessional, domesticated and intensely house-proud" by contrast with her four "phlegmatic" sisters (37). But Nicolas on viewing her "suffused and distorted face" at the point of death describes her as having been:

> The pretty and vivacious girl who had inspired my father at their first meeting [a fancy dress party] to record the occasion ... in his journal in these words: "she was clever, and unaffected, and distinguished, and nice-looking, and a study [something worth observing closely (COD)].... Shall I ever see her again?" (42–42).

Earlier Nicolas writes:

> If I had not seen with my own eyes the love that existed between my mother and my father, I should have found it difficult to believe. Two people less alike in their temperaments or habits or interests could hardly be imagined. My father, as I remember him early on, was shy, reserved, studious, athletic.... My mother was gregarious, excitable and indifferently educated (37–38).

Nicolas Bentley's reminiscences depict his father Edmund Bentley as a complicated human being: deeply reserved in the Victorian fashion who could at the same time love greatly and was possessed of considerable good humor; who somehow lacked the motivation to write the detective fiction at which he was so gifted, yet produced good work in that genre when he did write, as well as a notable failure; who was athletic during his Oxford years yet succumbed to alcoholism towards the close of his life.

Short Stories

Aside from newspaper writing, Bentley produced a small output of fiction as well as humorous verse. His oeuvre is largely detective fiction using the character of Philip Trent from the landmark novel *Trent's Last Case* (1913). Twenty-three years later, in 1936, another Trent novel was published, *Trent's Own Case* written in collaboration with H. Warner Allen. Soon after, in 1938 a collection of short stories featuring Trent was brought together under the title *Trent Intervenes* (OUP synopsis 1995; Baldick xxii). The book includes three short stories written during the First World War but Bentley's most productive period is the late 1930s with eight tales (two undated). Evidently the 1930s marked Bentley's return to more sustained detective fiction. He contributed chapters to two crime stories, "The Scoop" (1930) and "Behind the Screen" (1931), for the radio broadcasts of the Detection Club, and from 1936 to 1949 he was president of that club ("Edmund Clerihew Bentley"). An uncollected Philip Trent story was published in 1938, "The Ministering Angel" (Grost). It is listed as "Trent and the Ministering Angel" (1938) by Hacklehorn who also includes "Greedy Night" (1936) and "The Feeble Folk" (1953). On the whole the short stories are entertaining, clever though not especially memorable aside from one or two. This is a common weakness of the form. Short stories are good for a single idea, of which the surprise ending is an example, but if they allow for the development of character it may be at risk of weakening the plot.

Bentley's three short stories published during the years of the First World War are "The Clever Cockatoo" (1914), "The Inoffensive Captain" (1914), and "The Ordinary Hairpins" (1916). "The Clever Cockatoo" is not a murder mystery but instead concerns a bad marriage. Trent reveals to the husband Sir Peregrine how he drugs his vivacious young wife in revenge for her philandering so that on social occasions she falls into a stupor. Trent covers his removal of the drug from the lady's boudoir by allowing a pet cockatoo to trash the dressing table. It is one of several tales that end with a confrontation between Trent and a perpetrator that goes no further. Letting off the malefactor is one of the more unusual elements in Golden Age crime fiction; disguise or subterfuge is another.

In "The Inoffensive Captain" (78–99) the hiding place of diamonds stolen by an escaped convict is uncovered by solving a word puzzle. They had been hidden within the lintel of a door behind its upper hinge. Convict and diamonds escape. "The Ordinary Hairpins" (209–230) is a missing-person story that uses the ploy of disguise. After the death of her husband and child in a Sicilian earthquake, an opera singer (of *Carmen*) assumes a new identity by making it appear that she has thrown herself overboard from a liner, whereas she travels to Norway to live in obscurity. Trent tracks her down. The clues are the hairpins of the title: black to match the dark wig worn by the lady to hide her pale-gold hair. Trent does not betray her confidence. All three World War I tales are gentle in the sense that no one is murdered and that principal characters are never arrested or exposed. Bentley may have felt that enough killing was going on in the arenas of war.

Aside from these three short stories, most of Bentley's tales are produced in the 1930s. They are a mixed lot. Some actually have murders to solve while others stick to the gentler tone of the earlier efforts. For example, "The Genuine

Tabard" (1–20) is a fairly ordinary tale about Trent's uncovering of a confidence swindle. It appears to have no date but conceivably belongs to Bentley's First World War period, if we take the clue of the fraudster's mistake over the graduates of All Souls at Oxford (19–20) as a point more immediately in Bentley's mind than it may have been in the mid–1930s. "The Vanishing Lawyer" (1937) is another missing person story in which a clever disguise is used. "The Old-Fashioned Apache" (1937) is a further example of puzzle solving from a note written in the argot or secret language of underworld French. There is no murder although someone is badly beaten up. "The Public Benefactor" (1928) is a tale of revenge taken on a magistrate for wrongful imprisonment that involves a series of tricks to make the man think he is losing his memory. There is an allusion to the Alexandre Dumas revenge novel *The Count of Monte Cristo* (1844). "The Little Mystery" (1938) is how a woman friend of Trent describes subtle changes in her flat. Subsequently Trent discovers a secret loft in which hides a forger who had attempted murder.

In four short stories a murder is solved. "The Sweet Shot" (1937) — its title refers to a successful stroke in golf — is a clever tale about exploding golf clubs. The victim (of course) is "a foul-tempered, bullying brute" (36), the woman is the victim's widow, and the killer the brother of the widow. This is enough to justify Trent in letting the matter rest after discussing it obliquely with the brother. "The Fool-Proof Lift" (ND) is a variation on the locked-room tale in which the "locked room" is a lift well. In a touch of irony, the murderer while drunk is run over by a bus. "The Bad Dog" (1937) is a variation on the Sherlock Holmes tale of the dog in the night, today something of a cliché. It involves death by knife-thrower. Interestingly, the name of the Italian murderer Capazza is the same as a Corsican Bentley met on his travels (*Those Days* 303). (The Spanish word *capaz* means being competent or able). The last tale of homicide is "The Unknown Peer" (1938) in which the murderer impersonates his victim Lord Southrop. But the disguise is given away when Trent at the scene of the crime discovers a small shard broken from a monocle dropped by the murderer. This might be a veiled allusion to Dorothy L. Sayers' character Lord Peter Wimsey. Wodehouse characters also wore monocles. The single eyeglass represents a certain type of English upper class.

These short stories are slight but they contain elements that emerge frequently at the hands of other writers. Characters from earlier work, in this instance *Trent's Last Case*, make cameo appearances: general reference to "the Manderson affair" in "The Inoffensive Captain" (78) and to Murch in the same story; also to Murch in "The Vanishing Lawyer." Sir James Molloy, editor of the *Record*, is mentioned in "The Old-Fashioned Apache." Favorite place names reappear: Mewstone ("The Vanishing Lawyer"), Maidstone in "The Bad Dog." Several tales hinge on Trent's arcane knowledge of Oxford, the Anglican Church, heraldry and the French language.

There are a couple of nice touches of melodrama we might safely categorize under Bentley's humor, although it may have been unintentional: "Watkin staggered to a table and collapsed on to a chair beside it. For a moment he dropped his head on his arms; then looked up with a ghastly face at the inspector" ("The Old-Fashioned Apache" 135); or, "A sobbing sound came from Lambert Coxe. He sprang to his feet, pressing his hands to his temples, then crashed unconscious to the floor" ("The Unknown Peer" 207). Much of Bentley's humor depends upon one-liners but is not always fully evident otherwise. In what has been a cliché ever since Shakespeare gave it colloquial utterance in *Hamlet*: "it was his grave, in a manner of speaking. It was vicar's great-grand-father's grave, that was" (3). From "The Genuine Tabard," "it's a tabard. I have seen a few before, and I have painted one, with a man inside it" (8). "People like a great doctor to look more or less unhealthy" ("The Clever Cockatoo" 38). "This was a tall house, 'converted' from the errors of its pre–Victorian youth" ("The Fool-Proof Lift" 100). This fits in with Bentley's wit that finds more expression in *Trent's Last Case*.

This was a decade in which Bentley is settled in his journalistic career and evidently can devote more time to his participation in the Detection Club and the writing of more short stories, not, however, the writing of a novel. His experience of the pressure of work on *Trent's Last Case* appears to have stayed fresh in his mind. In *Those Days* he wrote: "The labour of writing the story, in my leisure from a regular newspaper job, had been so crushing that I want never to attempt a detective novel again" (257–258). So when it came to writing a new novel, *Trent's Own Case* (1936), the labor was shared with H. Warner Allen. The two men had known each other for many years. Bentley notes that in 1910 he spent time with Warner Allen when Allen was Paris correspondent for the *Morning Post* (*Those Days* 301). Indeed, aside from the groundbreaking first novel, Bentley seems to have preferred the short story form. His last attempt to write a novel failed him.

Writing *Trent's Last Case*

At the close of the first decade of the twentieth century E. C. Bentley decided to write a detective novel. The project was conceived and begun in 1910. With thirty years' hindsight, Bentley states that he devised the plot when walking to his office at the *Daily News* from his home near the Hampstead Cricket Club: "quick walking stimulated the faculty of invention" (252). He did not begin writing in earnest for "six or eight weeks" though he made notes. During this gestation period Bentley set down guidelines from the detective stories of the past that were to affect the genre in the future:

> One day I drew up a list of the things absolutely necessary to an up-to-date detective story: a millionaire — murdered, of course; a police detective who fails where the gifted amateur succeeds; an apparently perfect alibi; some fussing about in a motor car or cars ... the detective-hero ... a driver ... idiotically reckless ... a crew of regulation suspects, to include the victim's widow, his secretary, his wife's maid, his butler, and a person who had quarrelled openly with him ... there had better be a love-interest, because there was supposed to be a demand for this in a full-length novel. I made this decision with reluctance, because to me love-interest in novels of plot was very tiresome [253].

We have to remember that Bentley is writing in hindsight when, no doubt with some complacency, he could see these factors at play in other crime novels such as those of Agatha Christie, Dorothy L. Sayers, Margery Allingham and John Dickson Carr. One of Edmund Crispin's trademarks, for instance, is the hilarious chase scene by vehicle as well as on foot, as in *The Moving Toyshop* (1946) and *Love Lies Bleeding* (1948).

The opening chapter of *Trent's Last Case* is uncannily appropriate for the world economic crisis of 2008. Had there been a similar market downturn or industrial strife around the time Bentley began writing the novel? There were indeed two notable events in the United States: the Panic of 1907 and the New York shirtwaist strike of 1909. The former came about as a result of a fifty percent downturn in the New York Stock Exchange, made especially worrying because this was already a time of economic recession, and there were runs on the banks and other financial institutions followed by bankruptcies and the collapse of the Knickerbocker Trust Company ("Panic of 1907"). In the novel the "bombshell" is attributed to the market having been "'boosted' beyond its real strength" (8). In the real world there was even a financier who helped save the day, J. P. Morgan, who pledged a great deal of his own funds to prop up the banking system. It is possible that Bentley had Morgan in mind when he created the fictional Sigsbee Manderson, but he might just as easily have modeled the character upon some other tycoon of the day.

The other crisis was a strike in November 1909 among Jewish women employed in the shirtwaist factories, resolved in February 1910 between employers and the National Women's Trade Union League of America for "improved wages, working conditions, and hours," although another event, the Triangle Shirtwaist Factory Fire in 1911, demonstrated the physical dangers for women employed in that industry ("New York shirtwaist strike of 1909").

E. C. Bentley's work marks a watershed between what begins in the nineteenth century with Edgar Allan Poe and continues through the Golden Age of crime fiction. Bentley writes with a light touch in two senses of this metaphor: his literary style favors simple, cogent expression and not multisyllabic wordiness, and there is an element of urbane wit in the characterization of the detective Philip Trent. The first springs directly from Bentley's journalistic background. He went for a prose style that was simpler than the "old-fashioned journalese" of nineteenth-century reportage, remarking in *Those Days*: "As far as I am concerned, I cannot charge myself with ever having used a long word where a short one would do as well" (312). The second of the light touches is influenced by Bentley's conscious decision to write a detective novel that moves away from the tradition of the infallible crime investigator exemplified in Conan Doyle's Sherlock Holmes character: "who has been made ostentatiously unlike life, eccentric and 'peculiar,' with the idea of making him interesting" (251). In order to carry out what was not so much a parody of Holmes as an alternative to that detective, Bentley depicts his amateur sleuth Philip Trent as easygoing, affable, prone to verbal humor, and fallible. What Bentley preferred was "the originality, and the power of good, plain storytelling" (249). Ironically, Trent is included years later among the eccentrics of the Golden Age when works by Hammett and Chandler introduced noir literature to the United States in reaction to the English era of cozy crime.

Bentley also appears to be making a plea for a realist approach, but he is not listed in what critics care to call the Realist School where the later work of Chandler and Hammett enters in. Realistically, Chandler finds unconvincing Sigsbee Manderson's motives to "plot his own death so as to hang his secretary" (9), suggesting that Bentley does not know many international financiers. The point is, however, that Manderson had set out to plot an attempt on his life, only that circumstances took a different turn. In later developments among writers of the Golden Age occasionally an apparent murder victim's suicide is an attempt on the "victim's" part to harm some other.

Bentley's project followed what is purportedly a common pattern. He began at the end of the novel and worked backwards, as he says in *Those Days*: "The first part of the story to be put on paper was a draft of the last chapter" (256). The writing itself after the preparation period took "at least six months of my leisure time" (255). Like Hemingway he wrote standing at a special desk: "The thinking out was done while walking to Fleet Street; the writing was done [from his home] at a standing-up desk ... because I disliked the idea of a sedentary occupation" (256).

As writing continued, new ideas emerged from the unconscious. "It was not until I had gone a long way with the plot that the most pleasing notion of all came to me: the notion of making the hero's hard-won and obviously correct solution of the mystery turn out to be completely wrong" (254). This was an innovation that in time and in the hands of other writers helped form the character of the bemused detective-hero who often gets it wrong before getting it right, for example, Margery Allingham's Arthur Campion or Edmund Crispin's Dr. Gervase Fen. There was still plenty of scope for the other sort of character, more erudite and virtually infallible: John Dickson Carr's Dr. Gideon Fell, Sayers' Lord Peter Wimsey, Christie's Hercule Poirot. It was that character type, modeled upon Conan Doyle's Sherlock Holmes, against which Bentley was rebelling: "It does not seem to have been generally noticed that *Trent's Last Case* is not so much a detective story as an exposure of detective stories" (254).

Having completed the manuscript and deleted "some thousands of redundant words" (256), Bentley cast around for a publisher. He submitted it first to Duckworths who had advertised a fifty-pound prize for a "best first novel" (257), giving it the droll title of *Philip Gasket's Last Case*. However, at a dinner in his club in January 1912 he found himself sitting next to a young American bearing the catchy name of Douglas Z. Doty who was with the Century Company, a New York publishing house. Doty wanted to see the manuscript and suggested that Bentley withdraw it from the Duckworths competition. Bentley acted upon Doty's suggestion the next day by writing to the Duckworths reader Edward Garnett, who was also a personal friend. Garnett replied, also in writing, that the book was not in the running. Bentley immediately retrieved the manuscript and sent it to Doty, catching him at his hotel shortly before he was to leave for the United States.

A few weeks later the Century Company accepted the manuscript and purchased the book rights. They made a number of changes to which Bentley readily agreed. The hero was renamed Trent and the book retitled *The Woman in Black*. The American publisher may have chosen the title from chapter seven, "The Lady in Black," but they might also have had in mind Wilkie Collins's masterpiece *The Woman in White* (1859–1860) and perceived Bentley's much shorter novel as belonging to a similar genre. Bentley did not like this title (259) and was gratified eighteen years later when Alfred Knopf acquired the American publishing rights and reverted to the earlier title of *Trent's Last Case*. Soon after the deal with the American publishers, Bentley found a British outlet, this time through John Buchan who was a partner in the Nelsons publishing house. Buchan read the manuscript, liked it, and sent it to his Edinburgh partner who accepted it. Bentley was well satisfied, regarding himself a tyro in the field against Buchan's record at the age of thirty-seven of "over a dozen successful books."

In the end, the book was published in March 1913 concurrently in the United States and in Great Britain. It sold well. In the same year Italian, Swedish and Danish translation rights were sold and in 1914 Nelsons published a French translation. German and Polish translation rights were sold soon after. There was purportedly a pirated Yugoslavian edition. In 1922 a Russian translation was published clandestinely in Berlin and, ten years later in 1931, Bentley gave permission for an Irish translation (260–261). *See also* Baldick's summary (ix–xi) of these events from the same source. Bentley notes as well that two films of *Trent's Last Case* were made, one British and one American: "bad beyond description" (261).

In fact, three films have been made of the story. The first was a silent movie released in 1920 about which very little is known (britmovie.co). Another American version described in *Britmovie* as a "part-talkie" directed by Howard Hawks was released on 31 March 1929 with a running time of sixty-six minutes. Although the industry by then was well advanced in the transition from silent to sound, it was a silent movie. The story goes that the Fox Film Corporation were unable to obtain the sound rights but went ahead with *Trent's Last Case* as a silent picture. Hawks claimed that the decision was made in expectation that the film would be a failure (IMDb). The review by F. Gwynplaine MacIntyre (2002), though riddled with minor inaccuracies, states that Hawks aimed at making the film a comedy. MacIntyre's impression is that the film "went into pre-production as a talking picture but was filmed silent at the last minute." The choice of Raymond Griffith in the lead role as Trent was unusual inasmuch as Griffith was a silent film comedian with a boyhood track record in vaudeville and French pantomime (IMDb).

MacIntyre's interpretation begins by stating that Philip Trent is a "know-all amateur sleuth" modeled on past characterizations of fictional detectives. On the contrary, in the novel Trent is portrayed as fallible and with a love-struck indecisiveness when it comes to Mabel Manderson. This is communicated in the film as well. MacIntyre states that Trent has no recognizable job, whereas in the novel he is clearly described as an artist who in his spare time engages in journalistic reportage for a major newspaper. In the novel, says MacIntyre, Manderson's widow is referred to only as "Mrs. Manderson"; not so, for her first name, Mabel (Evelyn in the film), is used often enough. But MacIntyre is most careless in his claim that "the original novel was clearly not meant to be funny," yet Trent is relatively light-hearted, we could say laid back, and delivers droll observations and wisecracks throughout the novel, not surprising when we consider that Bentley wrote it with the intention of parodying the Holmes tradition. Many of the jokes are apposite. It is that feature in the novel which allows Hawks to cast a popular and successful comedian in the role of Trent. Disgruntled by the shoestring budget he was allowed, Hawks is reported as saying he would "have a little fun" with the production (IMDb). In some areas the film diverges from the novel. Evelyn Manderson is portrayed as indeed having an affair with the secretary Jack Marlowe, while an important point in the novel is that Marlowe as a younger man is infatuated with Mabel but does not have an affair with her, although Trent suspects it and thereby commits one of his two major errors. It is sometimes difficult to tell whether MacIntyre is referring to the film or to the novel but clearly the film was simplified.

The British version of *Trent's Last Case* (*L'Affaire Manderson* in its French release) came out in 1952 with a running time of ninety minutes (pedantically, eighty-six minutes in DVD format). It is a more ambitious production directed by Herbert Wilcox with a cast that includes Michael Wilding as Philip Trent, Margaret Lockwood as "Margaret" Manderson, and Orson Welles as Sigsbee

Manderson. There appears a tendency to alter the names of women actors from those in the original novel, perhaps to bring them up-to-date with present-day nomenclature for women, "Mabel" and even "Evelyn" perhaps considered old-fashioned. The costuming is early 1950s drab although Margaret Lockwood is chic enough in black and white. One thinks that a present-day version made in the UK would place the story in its correct time frame, the 1910s before World War I when the fashion in women's Edwardian dress had become less impeding to movement than in Victorian times though retaining its voluptuousness.

The film is relatively faithful to the novel. However, it is a disappointment. Slow paced and with wooden acting despite the presence of three stars, it is not redeemed by Orson Welles' powerful presence at the climax. The *Britmovie* entry describes the film as a "humdrum contemporary whodunit that is almost devoid of suspense" with a "remarkably insipid" Michael Wilding in the role of Trent. The lack of suspense is also noted by "brice-18" in the IMDb review. On the other hand, what two reviewers see as lack of suspense (slow pacing) is perceived by another reviewer as a virtue: "The real pleasure comes from the unforced pace and stalwart cast" and the fact that it is "a little dated ... is all part of its charm" (*MovieMail*). I share the disappointment of the first critics. While the novel is nicely paced there seems no reason why a faithful film version should not be treated similarly.

The Meeting That Comes Once

Sigsbee Manderson, a wealthy industrialist, is found dead under circumstances that suggest he has been murdered. Philip Trent, an artist who doubles as a part-time journalist for a major newspaper, is asked by his boss to cover the case. The suspects include two secretaries, a close family friend, and the dead man's wife. Trent pursues his investigations, interviewing the suspects and carrying out forensic studies on footprints and fingerprinting. He suspects one of the secretaries of committing the crime and that the widow Mabel Manderson is an accomplice. This becomes complicated when Trent falls in love with Mabel from the moment he first sights her from a cliff top. He writes his report implicating one secretary but instead of handing it to his bureau chief he gives it to Mabel. The novel ends with dénouements that prove Trent to have been wrong on several counts. The secretary under suspicion is innocent and the "murder" is a case of misadventure — Manderson shot during a struggle with the family friend — and the secretary, although he admired Mabel Manderson, was not in love with her. Trent and Mabel fall in love and effect a conciliation. In a later novel and some of the short stories Philip Trent and Mabel are husband and wife. As one might expect from Bentley's repeated polishing, the novel is lean and well structured at approximately 70,000 words, balanced between seriousness of purpose and different comedic elements influenced to a degree by current events.

The brutish character of Sigsbee Manderson stands in contrast to that of Nathaniel Burton Cupples who at one point is described as priestly: "a man of unusually conscientious, industrious, and orderly mind, with little imagination" (18), living in "the quiet, half-world of professors and curators and devotees of research" (19). In turn, Cupples is both a contrast and a foil to Trent, for as Trent sees life through his artist's eyes so too does Cupples see life through an intense awareness and "a connoisseur's eye" (18). Philip Trent is "a long, loosely built man, much younger," with "a high-boned, quixotic face," clad in tweed, his hair and short moustache a little untidy (19).

Over breakfast Trent and Cupples discuss the case in an approach that might be called amateur detective procedural, a forerunner to the police procedural decades later. It is also a setting down of clues, as much for the reader as for the fictional investigators. This was already a well-established tradition in crime writing since before Conan Doyle's Sherlock Holmes, though refined by Conan Doyle. Trent had viewed the body of Manderson at the surgery of Dr. Stock in the village: wrists scratched and bruised, noted by both Cupples and Trent. But Trent observed something Cupples had not noticed: "that there were no cuffs visible, and that they had, indeed, been dragged up inside the coat-sleeves, as yours would be if you hurried into a coat without pulling your cuffs down" (21). Moreover, Manderson's shoelaces had been tied hurriedly and he had not put in his false teeth, which were back in his room. Says Trent: "there are signs of great agitation and haste, and there are signs of exactly the opposite" (21). This establishes the central mystery of the crime.

The other theme alongside the explanation of these inconsistencies and ultimate solving of the crime is that of the relationship between Trent and Manderson's widow. For the first time Mrs. Manderson is referred to by her given name of Mabel as she expresses interest in Trent's past successes. At this early stage there is a mutual interest between Trent and Mabel although they have not met. Trent is surprised to learn from Cupples that Mabel is his niece: "Her father, John Peter Domecq, was my wife's brother" (22). The wife is unnamed. Cupples, then, is Sigsbee Manderson's father-in-law. Cupples describes Mabel Manderson as an intelligent woman, strong and "full of pride" (25): "unlike the simpering misses that used to surround me as a child ... with ideals of refinement and reservation and womanly mystery" (27–28). Concerning Manderson, Cupples knows more than he is willing to divulge.

Trent meets Marlowe, one of Manderson's secretaries and is immediately impressed by "the man's breadth of shoulder and lithe, strong figure ... his handsome, regular features ... his short, smooth, yellow hair" (33), a reflection I suppose of Bentley's interest in university athletics. Marlowe is tired: "I was driving the car all Sunday night and most of yesterday" (34), a detail that becomes significant much later. Marlowe becomes Trent's major suspect.

Trent meets with Inspector Murch of Scotland Yard, with whom he has a friendly rivalry. Such a relationship is another element that already has a long tradition in crime writing. Murch in a sense is to Trent what Inspector Lestrade is to Sherlock Holmes, except that Murch is not characterized as a buffoon. The name and very likely some of the character traits are taken from a person of Bentley's acquaintance. When Bentley joined the editorial department of the *Daily News* its head was a man named Murch (*Those Days* 225). As for the fictional Murch: "Trent's nonsense never made any sort of impression on his mind, but he took it as a mark of esteem, which indeed it was: so it never failed to please him" (47).

However, Trent is not as slapdash as it might appear. He uses a notebook in which he sketches the layout of rooms, and his forensic work on fingerprints and footprints is as rigorous a method as that implied for Murch. The use of layouts for rooms and grounds is another strong feature of the tradition. Conan Doyle used it on occasion ("The Priory School," 673; "The Golden Pince-Nez," 788), and many writers of the Golden Age such as Edmund Crispin (*The Moving Toyshop* 134), John Dickson Carr (*To Wake the Dead* 206), or Margery Allingham (*Mystery Mile* 199). More inconsistencies are noted in the case: "no weapon is to be found" (37), a whisky decanter is more than half empty (45), and the way in which Manderson was clothed contrasted against the misplaced false teeth: "I call that over-dressing the part. The only decorative detail he seems to have forgotten is his teeth" (49).

Trent inspects the adjoining bedrooms of Sigsbee Manderson and Mabel (they slept apart). At this point he encounters the French maid Célestine, a scene that allows Bentley to practice his schoolboy French (Bentley was a Francophile and has Trent remember his student days in Paris) and this leads to another clue. As the maid demonstrates, Mabel could not have seen into the room of her husband from her bed (55). This means that Manderson or some other might easily have entered and left the adjoining room without Mabel's knowledge. It is not exactly a locked-room touch of the sort that became popular in the heyday of the Golden Age but, with reference later to a window, it is very nearly so. Further background and/or clues include a photograph of Marlowe and Sigsbee Manderson together and a small revolver with twenty or more loose cartridges in a leather case (58). It is said in a later chapter that the carrying of firearms is a peculiarly American practice.

Trent next interviews Calvin C. Bunner, Manderson's private secretary: "Mr. Bunner was a thin, rather short young man with a shaven, pale, bony, almost girlish face, and large, dark, intelligent eyes" (62). Bunner had noticed a strong change in Manderson's mood from that of being someone who kept himself "well in hand" (64) to becoming: "gloomy and sullen, just as if he was everlastingly brooding over something bad, something that he couldn't fix" (65). Bunner puts it down to business dealings in America and possibilities for violence against Manderson from someone whose life had been ruined by the tycoon, rather than to strained relations between Manderson and his wife who had not borne him a child.

A pivotal chapter, "The Lady in Black," fixes the love interest. Its physical setting matches the psychological conflicts between violence and the pastoral, refined tastes and crude. Bentley, who was a strong swimmer in his student days, makes use of the sea, the cliff and the weather to elicit mood. Philip Trent is a man of action, a strong swimmer, physically fit who scales a cliff: "Between vast grey boulders he swam out to the tossing open, forced himself some little way against a cross-wise current, and then returned to his refuge battered and refreshed" (69).

Both beauty and danger are contained in images of cliff and sea. In popular dream imagery: "If you are scaling the cliff, this augurs a difficult climb either socially or careerwise. If you reach the top, you'll succeed.... Standing on the edge of a cliff indicates obstacles ahead that can only be averted by taking risks" (Global Oneness 2010). Carl Jung refers to the sea as the collective unconscious: "unfathomed depths lie concealed beneath its reflecting surface" (Campbell 330). The imagery is apt for the novel. Trent's investigations seek concealed depths that hinder the solution of a purported murder: "This morning as he scaled the cliff he told himself that he had never taken up a case he liked so little, or which absorbed him so much" (69).

When walking along the cliff top Trent comes upon Mabel Manderson sunning herself on a grassy ledge some feet below, unaware of his presence. Trent it is love at first sight, the way having been prepared by his growing interest in his potential suspect:

> This woman seemed to Trent, whose training had taught him to live in his eyes, to make the most beautiful picture he had ever seen. Her face of southern pallor, touched by the kiss of the wind with color on the cheek, presented to him a profile of delicate regularity in which there was nothing hard; nevertheless the black brows bending down toward the point where they almost met gave her in repose a look of something like severity, strangely redeemed by the open curves of the mouth. Trent said to himself that the absurdity or otherwise of a lover writing sonnets to his mistress' eyebrow depended after all on the quality of the eyebrow [70].

The reference is to a well-known passage in Shakespeare's *As You Like It* II. Vii. 139: "a woeful ballad/ Made to his mistress' eyebrow" (Cohen 311).

Trent's first sighting of Mabel is described in an eloquent — one might almost say elegant — use of language: "She ... stretched her limbs and body with feline grace, then slowly raised her head and extended her arms with open, curving fingers.... [Trent] knew suddenly who the woman must be, and it was as if a curtain of gloom were drawn between him and the splendour of the day" (71). Compare this with Edmund Bentley's reactions on first meeting his future wife Violet Boileau (8). There is a similar depth of feeling, though Bentley's reminiscences are a great deal more restrained. Writing fiction allowed Bentley more freedom to bare his soul. The sudden movement of the woman early in the paragraph is counterpointed against the equally sudden onset of gloom in the shorter paragraph following. Short paragraphs, sometimes of one or two sentences, are a means of emphasis.

The sight of Mabel Manderson is troubling to Trent for he knows that Mabel might be implicated in Manderson's death. Moreover, in keeping with his Edwardian chivalry he wishes to protect her from the worst of the inquest. Mabel evokes in Trent feelings associated with his art and his childhood, and to her is attached an angelic metaphor. Seeing her reminds him of his mother. Once again, the physical setting strikes a mood in Trent who feels "heavy, sinister, and troubled" (73).

Sigsbee Manderson had withdrawn a great sum of money from his London bank, yet Mabel tells Trent that her husband came to her that Sunday night and asked whether he might borrow ready cash, "notes or gold," of her own (74). This, it will be found, is part of Manderson's ploy to frame Marlowe for theft. Here Manderson is associated with the American frontier, a trope that appears several times in the novel. His character is likened to that of an American Indian, from which ethnicity he is descended, evoking images of savagery current at that time. The Rider Haggard tradition of adventure tales in frontier worlds was already well established. See *King Solomon's Mines* (1885), R. M. Ballantyne's *The Coral Island* (1857), Twain's *The Adventures of Tom Sawyer* (1876) and, specific to *Trent's Last Case*, *The Adventures of Huckleberry Finn* (1884). "I think the most American thing in that great American epic is Tom Sawyer's elaboration of an extremely difficult and romantic scheme" (75), says Marlowe to Trent as he speculates upon Manderson's business dealings, adding that Manderson: "is rather fond of his well-earned reputation for unexpected strokes and for going for his object with ruthless directness through every opposing consideration" (76).

This chapter contains the main ingredients of the novel: Sigsbee Manderson's ugly character, the puzzle of the crime, the main suspects, the wife and Trent's growing attraction for her, atmospheric language that relates physical setting to plot, and social issues including certain moral statements and cultural differences between Americans and the English. It is worth remembering that Bentley was reacting against the melodramatic situations of the penny dreadful of his day. As Ann Thwaite, A. A. Milne's biographer, says:

> The classic Golden Age detective story (which had been more or less invented by E. C. Bentley, whose *Trent's Last Case* had been written just before the war) was reacting against the thrillers of Rider Haggard, Edgar Wallace, John Buchan — the

imperial romancers — the tradition that returned with Ian Fleming, if it had ever really gone away. Thrillers rely on the hunt and the chase. The detective novel is an intellectual game. There seemed to be a great need for new games to play in that period between the wars. (It was the era that invented the crossword puzzle, the scavenger hunt and Monopoly, to name but a few). The body in the library was not yet a cliché [210–211].

Mabel's testimony, it will be seen later, reveals Manderson's plot against Marlowe. She is roused from a light sleep and is told by Manderson from the adjoining bedroom that the time is 11:30 p.m. and that he had decided against going for a "moonlight run" in his car. The husband did not ordinarily talk to Mabel about his business dealings, but he made a point of doing so on this occasion. Says Mabel: "I was rather surprised when he told me that he had sent Marlowe to Southampton to bring back some important information from a man who was leaving for Paris by the next day's boat" (80). This it turns out was to entrap Marlowe, to give the impression that the secretary was absconding with Manderson's funds.

Later Cupples visits Trent in order to thank him for looking after Mabel. Trent, "pale and nervous" (85), is preparing photographic negatives. At the end of the process he discovers large fingerprints on the bowl containing Manderson's false teeth, and upon the window of Mabel's room, which he has photographed. They are those of the same man (88). We find in subsequent chapters that Trent suspects the prints are Marlowe's and in his love for Mabel Trent decides to withhold his evidence and allow Marlowe to go free. Trent interviews Mabel ("The Wife of Dives") about her relationship with Marlowe. Mabel's unhappiness becomes more explicit. At the mid-point, this chapter is in itself pivotal for the love interest between them. Once again, the weather foresees the melodrama to follow: "the sky was an unbroken grey deadness shedding pin-point moisture that was now and then blown against the panes with a crepitation [crackling, rattling (COD)] of despair" (90). The passage is a metaphor of Trent's mood: "He had the jaded look of the sleepless, and a new and reserved expression [that] ... took the place of his half smile of fixed good-humour.... 'You look wretchedly tired,' she said kindly" (90).

Mabel tells of the unhappy marriage in which she entered at the age of twenty (she is twenty-six in the novelistic present) that is the strongest indictment against Manderson and all he stands for. This leads to an insight into Trent's feelings towards Mabel: "he had seen the real woman in a temper of activity, as he had already seen the real woman by chance in a temper of reverie and unguarded emotion.... With that amazement of his went something like terror of her dark beauty" (95). Trent is under a spell that he shakes off momentarily to ask: "Will you assure me that your husband's change toward you had nothing to do with John Marlowe?" (96). Mabel's reaction, however, renews the spell: "he saw nothing but her heavy crown of black hair, and her body moving with sobs that stabbed his heart, and a foot turned inward gracelessly in an abandonment of misery" (96). Trent departs, leaving the envelope containing his report for Mabel to read. In fine melodrama his soul is shaken, he has an impulse that clamors to throw himself at Mabel's feet to beg pardon, he rues the "crazy purpose that had almost possessed him," he might babble "with the tongue of infatuation ... to a woman who loved another man" (96).

This suggests the world-weariness that overtook Bentley in later life that was only incipient at this time. He was thirty-five when he began writing *Trent's Last Case* and had been married to Violet Boileau nine years, time enough for the honeymoon to end. The tropes of melodrama include a Victorian reference to the lady's hair that brings to mind the metonym "her beautiful head" in *The Hound of the Baskervilles* (438). The ungracefully twisted foot is a similar trope.

Trent's report is pivotal for the mystery just as the previous chapter is pivotal for the love interest. This appears to be on firm ground because, whatever is said earlier about Trent's intuitive approach in contrast to that of Inspector Murch, Trent nevertheless applies approved criminal investigation methods. Trent concludes that John Marlowe impersonated Manderson after shooting him, established an alibi by letting the butler Martin overhear a phone call while disguised as Manderson that he, Marlowe, was at a Southampton hotel at the time of the shooting. He then waits in Manderson's room until the house is asleep, once again impersonating Manderson by voice when Mabel calls to him, slips from the house with Manderson's clothes in which he dresses the corpse hurriedly — hence the cuffs dragged up into the sleeves of the coat and the shoes carelessly tied (100) — allowing time to drive to Southampton and return. The fingerprints found in Mabel's room are those of Marlowe. Some of this is correct — Marlowe had been in the room — but Trent's conclusions are flawed: Marlowe had not killed Manderson, Mabel is not privy to Manderson's death, nor is Mabel in love with Marlowe. She secretly fancies Trent.

"Evil Days" marks a pause in the investigative development of the plot and returns to the underlying love interest. Believing that Mabel and Marlowe are lovers and that Marlowe killed Manderson, Trent distances himself from the affair by living six months in Paris as an artist among other bohemians. If *Trent's Last Case* were a stage play, this chapter and the one preceding might belong to a complication point in the dramatic structure where fresh factors are introduced that "delay the solution" (Bayliss 11). If the novel were a film, this might be "Plot Point II" (or some other later plot point) in which a discovery is made that moves the action towards a resolution (Field 37). In the 1952 film version there is no Paris interlude. On Trent in the novel:

> The two things that had taken him utterly by surprise in the matter of his feeling towards Mabel Manderson were the insane suddenness of its uprising in full strength and its extravagant hopelessness.... Before the eye of his fancy the woman always came just as she was when he had first had sight of her, with the

gesture which he had surprised as he walked past unseen on the edge of the cliff; that great gesture of passionate joy in her new liberty [110–111].

An "uprising in full strength," the "great gesture of passionate joy," is the closest Bentley comes to specific sexual references.

Trent's emotional wounds begin to heal "under the spell of creative work" (114) and he thinks less often of Mabel. However, the artistic circles in which he moves are similar to those of Mabel and a meeting between them becomes inevitable, facilitated through a chance encounter with Bunner. During their conversation Trent becomes perplexed: "It became more and more plain that something was very wrong in his theory of the situation; there was no mention of its central figure" (115). Bunner tells him that Marlowe is in his father's flourishing business and soon to be married while Mabel lives in seclusion in Mayfair, owns another house in Hampstead, but mixes little in society although she has "all the good hard dollars just waiting for some one to spraddle them around ... money to feed to the birds" (115), one of Bunner's "verbal surprises" (114) that endears him to Trent.

Trent returns to London with the intention of seeking Mabel out, but he delays, partly because Cupples, with whom he wishes to consult, is away and because he would be mortified if Mabel were to see him "lurking" in her neighborhood (116). Instead, Trent, who knows Mabel's interests in music, attends the opera in the hope of seeing her. Their meeting is heralded by a light touch on his arm, reprising the moment at the inquest when Trent assisted her to White Gables. This time the assistance is on Mabel's part. With "a light of daring in her eyes and cheeks" she tells Trent: "I wouldn't miss a note of *Tristan*.... Come and see me in the interval" (117).

Bentley devotes two chapters to the resolution of the love interest. Trent and Mabel move in the same circles. For two months Mabel maintains a coolly friendly attitude towards the man: "a nicely calculated mean between mere acquaintance and the first stage of intimacy, [that] baffled and maddened him" (118). At their meetings, some of which are held at Cupples' "large and tomblike house in Bloomsbury" (119), Trent avoids discussing the case with Mabel, convinced he has misinterpreted it and done Mabel an injury. Mabel, however, invites Trent to visit and he takes up the challenge. Their conversation begins falteringly, body language slow, speech soft to create dramatic tension. Trent sits rigid, his head bowed. Mabel blushes but also smiles mischievously as she begins to tell her part of the story.

Sigsbee Manderson was jealous of John Marlowe, irrationally because to Mabel as an older woman Marlowe was almost a boy, clever, well mannered, but with "a sort of amiable lack of ambition" (123), but equally "incapable of a crime of bloodshed" (129). Mabel returns Trent's report, placing it in his hand with "a touch of gentleness" (123), and goes on to describe how Manderson became increasingly cold towards her. She began to suspect that her husband was planning "some sort of revenge" (123) against Marlowe while remaining on friendly terms with him. They travel to England and move into White Gables. (This is the physical setting where the investigation starts). What is said about Marlowe's lack of ambition might fairly be attributed to Bentley from what we know of his biography. Mabel's "quaint expression," mentioned twice (126), and laughter might easily be founded upon the vivacious personality of Bentley's wife Violet. In these senses, Trent's stiffness reflects Bentley's reserve and Mabel's liveliness that of Violet Boileau. I wonder whether Bentley was conscious of these parallels when he was writing the novel? We have again the leitmotif of the woman at the cliff:

> As I passed by you it seemed as if all the life in the place were crying out a song about you in the wind and the sunshine.... It was when I led you from the hotel there to your house, with your hand on my arm, that — what was it that happened? I only knew that your stronger magic had struck home [132].

Mabel's response is at first to reproach Trent for a loss of reserve. Trent admits his sentimentality and loss of self-restraint but adds on a further melodramatic note: "please believe that it was serious to me if it was comedy to you. I have said that I love you, and honour you, and would hold you dearest of all in the world. Now give me leave to go" but Mabel reciprocates: "she held out her hands to him" (133). After the long speeches it takes a few words to hint at their reconciliation, and it takes a much shorter chapter to bring about a resolution of their relationship as, in consultation with Mabel, Trent drafts an apology to Marlowe.

In representing the new affection between Trent and Mabel, and in contrast to Trent's verbiage, the lines are subtle, economical and evocative. This may have reflected Bentley's natural reticence but it works well stylistically. His fine touch comes to the fore:

> She led him to his abandoned chair before the escritoire and pushed him gently into it.... Mrs. Manderson looked down at his bent head with a gentle light in her eyes, and made as if to place a smoothing hand upon his rather untidy crop of hair. But she did not touch it. Going in silence to the piano, she began to play very softly.... She ran across the twilight room, and turned on a reading lamp beside the escritoire. Then, leaning on his shoulder, she read [136].

Words such as "gently" and "softly" repeated, "silence," "smoothing," even "twilight" and "piano" (softly performed music) evoke feelings of domesticity and peace that are reprised in the closing paragraphs: "When Mrs. Manderson returned, he was hunting through the music cabinet. She sank on the carpet beside him in a wave of dark brown skirts.... She lifted her eyes again to his, and for a time there was silence between them" (138). We infer that they embrace and kiss.

The remaining two chapters deal with the solution of the crime. At twenty-five pages the penultimate chapter "Double Cunning" is the longest in the book, and no doubt one of the first to have been written. It is a version of the drawing-room dénouement that became a stock device with later writers and for that reason is parodied innumerable times. Trent's next mistake becomes apparent. Marlowe tells his side of the story to Trent and Cupples: Manderson's scheme to frame Marlowe, Marlowe backtracking and his finding of Manderson's body, and the steps he takes to divert suspicion from himself as an innocent man.

Cupples' Dénouement

A year and a half has passed. Marlowe, Cupples and Trent meet in a tasteful bachelor flat above St. James's Park. Marlowe returns Trent's manuscript with the compliment that it is very close to the truth. Marlowe states that "Manderson was not a man of normal mind," then extends this to other American tycoons: "Most of the very rich men I met with in America had become so by virtue of abnormal greed, or abnormal industry, or abnormal personal force, or abnormal luck. None of them had remarkable intellects" (140). The backwoods theme of savagery recurs with references to Colonel [Davy/David] Crockett's coonskin hat, also Manderson's descent from "the Iroquois chief Montour and his French wife," and his ancestors' involvement in the fur trade.

Manderson sends Marlowe to Southampton. As Marlowe stands outside the drawing room window he overhears Mabel loaning her husband the pocket money he needs, and is surprised to hear Manderson say that he has been persuaded by him, Marlowe, to go for a midnight run in the car. The lie tells Marlowe that something is wrong. As he drives off, he catches a glimpse of Manderson's face in the rear view mirror: "It was that of a madman, distorted, hideous in the imbecility of hate, the teeth bared in a simian grimace of ferocity and triumph" (151). Marlowe stops the car beyond a bend in the road and discovers that the key to the lock of the letter-case had been placed in a pocket of his own overcoat. But Manderson had outsmarted himself, for his notecase had been locked in the larger case containing diamonds.

Marlowe turns back in order to have it out with Manderson. He hears a shot and comes upon Manderson's body on the eighth green of the golf course near the flag, a pistol at his feet. He assumes that Manderson has taken his own life, a plot device used by later writers as for example in Margery Allingham's Campion story *Police at the Funeral*. Marlowe places Manderson's body in the car and drives to the house. He leaves the body at the gardener's tool shed and enters the house disguised as Manderson, wearing the dead man's hat and coat. There he pretends to make a phone call in order to deceive Martin, keeping his back turned towards the butler and mimicking Manderson's voice:

"a strong, metallic voice, of great carrying power" (158). Back at the corpse and after other preparations at the house that explain the clues found by Trent, Marlowe strips the body and dresses it, removing the teeth in order that people believe Manderson had been moving about the house. He then drives very fast to Southampton where he acts out the movements that would have entrapped him.

The reactions of Marlowe's two listeners are in character. Trent shifts alternately from excitability and tangential comments to the stillness of marble, as he does during his meetings with Mabel. Cupples, who knows a great deal more about Manderson's death, becomes "more and more interested as Marlowe went on, and was now playing feverishly with his thin beard" (154). At the conclusion of Marlowe's account, Trent compliments him as a man of courage. Trent is mortified that he got things wrong, a feeling communicated through both physical immobility and the sudden flaring of emotion: "the red flag that flew in Trent's eyes" (162). It is the truth as Marlowe sees it. Cupples, on the other hand, surprises both men: "'For my part,' he said, 'I never supposed you guilty for a moment'" (164).

In the final chapter Cupples' reason for saying this is unfolded in another surprise ending. This chapter has a lighthearted beginning that is contrasted at its midpoint with the shock ending. In high spirits, Trent invites Cupples to dine with him, announcing that: "I am going to be married to the most wonderful woman in the world" (166). This brings the love interest to its conclusion. In words that sound almost like working notes for the plot, Cupples says: "A madman conceives a crazy suspicion: he hatches a cunning plot against his fancied injurer; it involves his own destruction.... Turn now to Marlowe's proceedings. He finds himself in a perilous position from which, though he is innocent, telling the truth will not save him.... He escapes by means of a bold and ingenious piece of deception" (169). Having said this, however, Cupples suggests to Trent that although Marlowe's acts were ingenious, it was "really not strange that it should occur to a clever man" (170). Cupples means himself. They debate capital punishment. A man named Abel Atherton had been hung at Durham in December 1909, a year before Bentley began writing *Trent's Last Case* (Clark 1995) so the question is topical.

Cupples drops his bombshell when he tells Trent how he witnessed Manderson's baleful farewelling of Marlowe:

> I saw his face raised in the moonlight, the teeth bared, and the eyes glittering, and all at once I knew that the man was not sane. Almost as quickly as that flashed across my mind, something else flashed in the moonlight. He held the pistol before him, pointing at his breast.... But I think it quite likely he only meant to wound himself, and to charge Marlowe with attempted murder and robbery [175].

Cupples attempts to take the pistol from Manderson. They struggle. Cupples achieves the pistol but Manderson "sprang at my throat like a wild cat, and I fired blindly in his face" (176). Hence Manderson dies by misadventure or manslaughter, shot by Cupples in self-defense. Cupples remains hidden and slips away when Marlowe busies himself with Manderson's body.

Trent, who has turned to marble (again the marmoreal metaphor), is finally crushed and sits head in hand. But he has the last ironic word in which there is a return to his former geniality: "I could have borne everything but that last revelation of the impotence of human reason. Cupples, I have absolutely nothing left to say, except this: you have beaten me. I drink your health in a spirit of self-abasement" (177).

As in many other chapters, there are shifts back and forth from humor and affability to the serious and troubling. Earlir in the novel, Trent makes a good joke about hotel furniture on Cupples' arrival before he introduces the paraphernalia of his fingerprinting, makes a short quip likening himself to the comic character of Hawkshaw the detective followed by a description of the fingerprints. The conversation between Trent and Mabel is a form of humor not often found in crime fiction. It fits well, however, with Bentley's depiction of Trent as a fallible detective. As we shall see, there is plenty of amusement in the depiction of such characters. After Trent makes an impassioned speech about Mabel in his eyes incapable of wickedness and apologizing for his "injurious blunder": "'I love to see you worked up,' she said. 'The bump with which you always come down as soon as you realize that you are up in the air at all is quite delightful'" (127). There is humor in their collaboration over the letter to Marlowe where for the first time (134) we learn Mrs. Manderson's given name: "Mabel and I are betrothed, and all is gas and gaiters."

Elephant's Work (1950)

Six years before his death Bentley remembered that during a chance meeting at Blackwell's bookshop his friend John Buchan suggested he write a parody of a crime thriller. They called them "shockers" in those days. Buchan's *The Thirty-Nine Steps* had just been published in 1915. Bentley's shocker came out in 1950 as *Elephant's Work: An Enigma*. In the novel's dedication to Buchan written in August 1949, Bentley said:

> We had not seen each other since the publication of his romance *The Thirty-Nine Steps*, about a year before. When I told him how much I enjoyed it, he said: "Why don't you write a shocker yourself? It is twenty times easier than writing a detective story, like *Trent's Last Case.*" His argument was that in writing a shocker one need not bother about probabilities, hardly even about possibilities — all that mattered was the shock.

Bentley bought the latest reprint of Buchan's novel and reread it, evidently with the intention of using it as a model. The result was a twenty-seven chapter,

277-page volume. Buchan's novel is, however, tightly structured and economical at approximately 36,000 words filling 103 pages in the Penguin 1992 omnibus. *Elephant's Work* is twice as long at about 83,000 words in the 1950 Knopf edition.

The weaknesses in *Elephant's Work* are doubly regrettable because the novel begins with an interesting premise. Its chief protagonist Severn (his first name is not given) suffers amnesia in a railway accident caused by a fractious elephant (hence the title) and unknowingly changes identity with a fellow passenger who is Nick the Chill, a hit man from the American underworld. He is taken under the wings of two shady characters, General de la Costa and his doctor friend Barlow, and becomes de la Costa's bodyguard, unintentionally replacing the American. The group experiences vicissitudes until Severn regains his memory and all is resolved. What makes the work potentially interesting is that we might see the operations of a criminal group from the inside.

Elephant's Work, however, is a failure. The narrative style becomes prolix and in its ramblings suffers from a lack of the pacing one would expect of the genre for which it is a parody. Most of it is in discursive dialogue between the main protagonists who are at pains to explain over again to one another how pleased they are to be friends on the same side, with disquisitions on political affairs and long accounts of technical matters such as de la Costa's manufacture of ersatz diamonds. There are digressions into the history of the Mayan Indians and the elicitation of comfortable domestic scenes, including a motherly woman, all of which detract from the atmosphere the novel should have had. After its promising start, *Elephant's Work* is rarely lightened by action and there is no "shock" to speak of. The revelation that Severn is Bishop of Glasminster can hardly be described as a shock, though a little droll perhaps to see a churchman mistaken as a gangster.

The novel is passed over by several critics, perhaps because it is an embarrassment. Hoch lists *Elephant's Work* as Bentley's last thriller, stating charitably that it is "more in the style of John Buchan and is less successful." In responding to Hoch's review, Grost says that he never got round to reading *Elephant's Work* because so many people had panned it. (We are influenced by the reviews we read). David Vineyard (2009) is more forthright, for after writing a short, and interesting, synopsis of the plot he calls it: "light as a soufflé."

Bentley is seventy-five years old when he writes *Elephant's Work*—six years before his death—and, unlike the time when at thirty-eight he does *Trent's Last Case* and is arguably at the height of his powers, *Elephant's Work* is loose, tiresome, and unpolished. John Buchan his editor appears to have been overindulgent, perhaps because Bentley was an elderly man as well as a personal friend. Buchan must have recognized its difficulties. It is sad to see such an able writer lose his powers. There are clues to this state of affairs in the report that Bentley's house was bombed during the Second World War, an event that made him so depressed he turned to drink. There are frequent references to an alcohol-strong beverage called "telque" in *Elephant's Work*, perhaps Bentley's rendering of "tokay" or a fictionalizing of that drink.

I think what we are seeing is the progress of a minor writer who produced several good works in his younger days only to slip towards mediocrity in later life. His triumph remains *Trent's Last Case*. But it is not unusual to find an author who writes one or two masterpieces while the rest of their oeuvre is indifferent. Published in 1913, *Trent's Last Case* is now a hundred years old. Reviewers describe the novel as containing wit and humor. I see in it three principal elements that we find in many later crime novels that belong to the Golden Age: good plotting, humor/wit and a love interest with subtle Edwardian/Victorian eroticism: "a wave of dark brown skirts" (138). Bentley wrote two other Trent books twenty years later in the mid–1930s that reviewers say are of the same quality as his first: *Trent's Own Case* with H. Warner Allen, and a collection of short stories with Trent as protagonist: *Trent Intervenes and Other Stories*. It is a pity Bentley did not write more.

CHAPTER 3

The Plush Toy Mystery:
A. A. Milne (1882–1956)

Alan Alexander Milne (variant spelling Miln) was born on the 18 July 1882 in the London suburb of Kilburn and died 31 January 1956 in Hartfield, Sussex, at the age of 74. His parents were John Vine Milne and Sarah Maria (*née* Heginbotham). During his education at Henley House School his teacher at one time was H. G. Wells, who was there from 1889 to 1890. Milne attended Westminster School and Trinity College in Cambridge on a mathematics scholarship ("A. A. Milne"). In 1903 he graduated from Cambridge with Honours in Mathematics (Mendelsohn). In common with many other authors from the Oxbridge academic factories, he took up a career that had little to do with his university qualifications. From this time he began contributing verse and essays to *Punch* magazine and in 1906 joined the staff of *Punch* as an assistant editor, in which role he wrote weekly essays (Mendelsohn). Seven years later, in 1913 on the eve of the First World War, Milne married Dorothy "Daphne" de Sélincourt ("A. A. Milne") who became his secretary (or "scribe" as Mendelsohn calls her). His livelihood had become a means of finding a spouse, for Dorothy was the goddaughter of Owen Seaman, editor of *Punch* (Mander).

In 1914 Milne joined the Royal Warwickshire Regiment and later, in the spring of 1916 (Mander), was posted to the Isle of Wight and then to France as a signal corps officer (Mendelsohn). During 1916 to 1917 Milne wrote plays as a way of filling in time (Mendelsohn), his first, *Wurzel-Flummery*, produced in 1917. James M. Barrie, author of *Peter Pan* (1911), assisted in its production and Dion Boucicault, producer-actor, produced it (Mendelsohn). Milne was discharged from the army in February 1919 (Mander) and in that year his next play, *Mr. Pim Passes By*, was produced. It is regarded as Milne's greatest stage triumph (Mendelsohn). The actress wife of Dion Boucicault, Irene Vanbrugh, created the stage heroine Olivia Marden for the drama (Mendelsohn). Milne's return to family life after his demobilization led to the birth of his son Christopher Robin in August 1920 ("A. A. Milne").

In the following year (1921) he completed *The Red House Mystery*, which through August to December was serialized in *Everybody's* as *The Red House Murder* (Thwaite 209–211). It was published as a novel in April 1922 ("The Red House Mystery") by Methuen and in July that year in America as *The Red House Mystery*. Thwaite (211) tells us that Christopher Isherwood at the age of eighteen dramatized the novel for his end-of-term school play, yet surprisingly Milne never did this himself, though I note that Milne occasionally adapted works by other authors, notably *Toad of Toad Hall* from Kenneth Grahame's *The Wind in the Willows* (1908). "*Toad*" went into rehearsal in 1930 (Thwaite 361).

Milne also concentrated on children's stories in verse and prose and in 1924 the collection of poems titled *When We Were Very Young* came out, its pages illustrated by the *Punch* staff cartoonist E. H. Shepard ("A. A. Milne"). The following year (1925) the family moved to a cottage in Sussex named Cotchford Farm and a Christmas bedtime story appeared in the *Evening News* introducing the plush character of Winnie the Pooh (Mander). A collection of short stories, *Gallery of Children*, was also published in this year ("A. A. Milne"). *Winnie-the-Pooh* was published in 1926 (Mander). A second collection of poems, *Now We Are Six*, came out in 1927, and in 1928 *The House at Pooh Corner* was published (Mander). The 1930s appear to have been years of consolidation. In 1929 *Mr. Pim Passes By* was published as a novel and in autumn 1931 the family traveled in the United States (Mendelsohn). Milne became a member of the Detection Club which was founded in 1930 by Anthony Berkeley Cox and a group of mystery writers, including Agatha Christie, Dorothy L. Sayers and G. K. Chesterton ("Detection Club").

By the time the Second World War broke out Milne was fifty-seven years old and his output appears to have slowed during the war years. In September 1939 his autobiography was published with the title *It's Too Late Now* (Thwaite 423), and in November that year he contributed a play, "The General Takes Off His Helmet," for *The Queen's Book of the Red Cross* as a means of assisting the war effort ("A. A. Milne"). He continued writing light verse for *Punch* from 1939 to 1940. In the main, Milne appears to have contented himself with penning letters to *The Times* and making public statements about the war through pamphlets. One of his biographers, Ann Thwaite (430) tells us that: "After the war, Milne told the *Evening News* that, while it had been going on, 'apart from political articles he had had little appetite for writing.' C. W. Chamberlain at Methuen would, from time to time, inquire about the progress of a novel he was supposed to be writing."

The last mystery novel he wrote was *Chloe Marr*, published in 1946 when Milne was sixty-four. It was well received and, says Thwaite, in the first six months sold 16,412 copies, having engendered "a general feeling that Milne had produced something rather original, certainly something quite different from anything he had written before" (465). Some reviewers call it among his best work. The theme that "nobody knows the truth about anyone else," says Thwaite (466) casts a mystery about the eponymous character and may be the last glimmer of Milne's skill at writing mystery tales, although *Chloe Marr* is a psychological mystery and not a crime story.

Milne's last book, *Year In, Year Out*, published in 1952, was also well received. But in October that year he suffered a stroke and lived on as an invalid for little more than three more years before he passed away. It was the same year, 1956, in which E. C. Bentley died.

The Red House Mystery

Milne was at work on *The Red House Mystery* as early as 1920. Thwaite cites him as observing in 1950 that "the result would have passed unnoticed in these days when so many good writers are writing so many good detective stories, but in those days there was not so much competition" (209). Thwaite notes against Milne's modesty that *The Red House Mystery* was written shortly before Agatha Christie's debut with *The Mysterious Affair at Styles* (1920) that Milne regarded as "the model detective story" (209). But *The Red House Mystery* was *published* two years after the publication of *Mysterious Affair*. John Curran, cited in Wikipedia, says: "It [*The Mysterious Affair at Styles*] was written in 1916 and was first published by John Lane in the US in October 1920 and in the UK by the Bodley Head (John Lane's UK company) on January 21, 1921" ("The Mysterious Affair at Styles"). Dorothy L. Sayers' first novel *Whose Body?* came out in 1923 ("Dorothy L. Sayers"). Milne is in good company but, arguably, is not influenced either by Christie or Sayers. Instead, he is strongly influenced by another "model detective story," that of E. C. Bentley's *Trent's Last Case* (1913). *The Red House Mystery* owes a lot to Bentley's masterpiece in both its structure and tropes.

Milne was already typecast as a humorist, as he would be shortly as a writer of children's verse and prose, and his agent and publishers were frequently unenthusiastic whenever he experimented in different genres. Thwaite says that:

> Milne was always eager to move on to something different.... A detective story has other criteria [compared with children's books, popular novels, or serious literature] and Milne's works brilliantly, within his own rules. He had a passion for the form and so did his father, to whom he dedicated *The Red House Mystery* [210].

But it was more than that. Milne had an eye for the saleable market and chose what he wrote accordingly. In a letter to E. V. Lucas in 1933, cited in

Thwaite (210), he said: "It has been my good fortune as a writer that what I have wanted to write has for the most part proved to be saleable. It has been my misfortune as a businessman that, when it has proved to be extremely sale-able, then I have not wanted to write it any more." Seven years earlier in April 1926, Milne wrote for the Introduction to *The Red House Mystery*:

> What the country wanted from "a well-known 'Punch' humorist" was a "humor-ous story." However, I was resolved upon a life of crime.... Another two years have gone by; the public appetite has changed once more; and it is obvious now that a new detective story, written in the face of this steady terrestrial demand for children's books, would be in the worst of taste [ix].

But there would have been a growing demand for mystery stories, for the mid–1920s marked the emergence of several Golden Age writers: Agatha Christie's *The Man in the Brown Suit* in 1924 and *The Secret of Chimneys* in 1925 (Christie 2006); Dorothy L. Sayers' Lord Peter Wimsey novels and short stories begin-ning with *Whose Body?* (1923), continuing with *Clouds of Witness* (1926), *Unnat-ural Death* (1927), and *The Unpleasantness at the Bellona Club* (1928) into the 1930s. It is true that other key writers did not emerge until the 1930s, such as Margery Allingham and John Dickson Carr, and Edmund Crispin did not reach his height until the 1940s, but the movement was well under way when *Winnie-the-Pooh* was published in 1926 and *The House at Pooh Corner* in 1928. Milne did very well from the children's books and poetry, but I think he misread his market where crime fiction is concerned and we are the poorer for it.

As we shall see, the aspect of Milne as a humorist reappears in *Red House*. He is included by Symons in a list of farceurs: "those writers for whom the business of fictional murder was endlessly amusing" (104). In this tradition, continues Symons: "More than twenty years after the book's publication in 1922 Raymond Chandler made an attack on it which successfully convicted Milne of characteristic farceur-like carelessness in plotting, and of condoning some outstanding improbabilities" (105). Reader response is often a good anti-dote to criticism. Symons "was able to re-read the story without much loss of pleasure, and even with admiration of Milne's skill in skating over thin ice" (106), and cites Rex Stout's comment that Milne's *The Red House Mystery* is "charming," for its "light, easy way with murder, its dexterous shifts of suspi-cion and emphasis," while ignoring the improbabilities. Thwaite (332) cites Dorothy Parker (1927) who "read '*The Red House Mystery*' threadbare" (332), although she found Milne's children's stories and poetry whimsical and exces-sively cute. Further, Thwaite reports on Swinnerton (1938), who "saw that Milne had made three reputations in a quarter of a century — as humorist, playwright and children's writer — 'unless we call them four on account of *The Red House Mystery*; and as many reputations, of course, to be assailed by all who find the combination of lightness of heart with love of virtue to be an anachronism in the modern sceptic world'" (450). All the same, as Thwaite notes: "*The Red House Mystery* had 22 printings between 1922 and 1975. It has rarely been out of print" (517). Such responses place Milne firmly among those crime writers whose work is characterized by geniality, wit, humor in general and farce in particular.

An elementary start to close reading is to count the approximate number of chapters and words in a novel and so evaluate its limits. *The Red House Mystery* is made up of twenty-two relatively short and equally balanced chapters and, at a fraction over 210 pages, has a length of about 73,000 words. This allows for an economy appropriate to a short novel but sufficient depth in which to develop character and plot. A little shorter and we have a novella, but that also has some of the advantages of a novel for plot and character. Shorter still and we shift to the restrictions of the short story mode because, as Jeremy Hawthorn (338–45) says, the short story is more concentrated and because of its restrictions in length makes use of impressions and suggestions on the reader, often with an abrupt surprise ending. The short story form is good for presenting a single idea but not as efficient for detailed or repetitive argument or for character development. *The Red House Mystery* compares favorably with the approximate 62,000 words of *Trent's Last Case*.

In *The Red House Mystery*, a young man of thirty, Antony Gillingham, arrives at the eponymous residence where his friend Bill Beverley is staying as the guest of Mark Ablett. Like Philip Trent, Gillingham leads a somewhat bohemian life, moving in and out of various occupations such as shop assistant, valet, waiter and seaman. Between jobs he visits friends. Milne introduces Gillingham self-consciously: "He is an important person to this story, so that it is well we should know something about him before letting him loose in it" (16). Breaking the boundary between audience and stage actor by speaking directly to the audience in an aside, more generally, "the imaginary boundary between any fictional work and its audience" is done by some authors "for dramatic or comedic effect" ("Fourth Wall"). Broaching the fourth wall is one of Milne's characteristics. He wrote a detective play with that title. Several of the authors in my list do it as well.

The character of Antony Gillingham is comparable to that of Bentley's Philip Trent in a number of ways. Both men are physically active:

> Above a clean-cut, clean-shaven face, of the type usually associated with the Navy, he carries a pair of grey eyes which seem to be absorbing every detail of our person. To strangers this look is almost alarming at first, until they discover that his mind is very often elsewhere; that he has, so to speak, left his eyes on guard, while he himself follows a train of thought in another direction.... His idea of seeing the world was to see, not countries, but people; and to see them from as many angles as possible [16–17].

I suspect that it is a quality Milne sought to cultivate in himself.

While Gillingham might not possess Trent's artist's eyes, he possesses another distinctive skill, that of a photographic memory by which he can visualize and reconstruct any scene. Using the word "develop" as a punning metaphor, Milne's omniscient narrator says: "Everything which he saw or heard seemed to make its corresponding impression somewhere in his brain: often without his being conscious of it; and these photographic impressions were always there for him when he wished to develop them" (26–27).

The occasion for melodrama is the sudden death from a pistol shot of Robert Ablett that takes place moments before Gillingham's arrival. The fourth person in what is a geometrical figure of principal characters is Matthew Cayley, pounding on the office door demanding that Mark Ablett let him in. (The geometrical figure comprises Gillingham, Beverley, Cayley and Mark Ablett — five if we count the corpse of Robert Ablett.) As in *Trent's Last Case*, minor characters are introduced in the first chapter: "the pretty parlourmaid" (1) Audrey Stevens, Mrs. Stevens her aunt (housekeeper), Elsie (one of the housemaids), and Matthew Cayley, who is Mark Ablett's cousin. The conversation between aunt and niece introduces an unseen character, that of Robert Ablett, Mark Ablett's ne're-do-well Australian brother. It is this returned brother who is killed. Mark Ablett appears to have absconded so that suspicion falls naturally upon him. Gillingham in a whimsical act chooses to play the part of amateur detective, his friend Bill Beverley becoming the Watson to his Holmes. The relationship is not quite comparable with that of Philip Trent and Cupples in *Trent's Last Case* because there is no Holmes-Watson pairing in the latter. Trent essentially works alone although Cupples is an interested sounding board revealed as crucially important at the end.

House guests include an actress, Ruth Norris, Betty Calladine, the eighteen-year-old daughter of the woman acting as hostess for Mark Ablett, and Major Rumbold. Such characters are to become stock figures in the later history of the country house crime story. The image of the major, for example, appears a forerunner of the suspect Colonel Mustard in the board game Cluedo. The name of the Middleston police Inspector is Birch. Compare Inspector Murch and the town of Marlstone in *Trent's Last Case*. They are relatively minor but they contribute to the plot in two ways. The actress stages an appearance as a ghost that she could only have done if a secret passage from the house to the bowling green shelter was known to her. The love interest, Cayley for Miss Angela Norbury, provides the decisive motive (among others) for Cayley's murder of Mark Ablett. A minor love interest is Bill Beverley's infatuation for Betty Calladine.

From the beginning Gillingham and Beverley suspect Cayley of being implicated in the shooting of Robert Ablett. Most of the novel is taken up with their investigations of Cayley's movements, including whimsical scenes such as Bill Beverley's diving into a pond to retrieve an object sunk there by

Cayley, preceded by the schoolboy trick of leaving dummies of blankets and pillows in their beds so that Cayley will think they are asleep in their rooms. This falls a little short of slapstick. Witticisms, drollery and parodic paraphrases of Biblical verses mediated through the eccentric amateur detective are other comedic elements. For example, Gillingham uses humor to cover up Bill Beverley's indiscreet questions because he knows that Cayley is eavesdropping outside the breakfast room window:

> One should modulate the voice, my dear William, while breathing gently from the hips. Thus one avoids those chest-notes which have betrayed many a secret.... Fain would I gyrate round the mulberry-bush and hop upon the little hills. But the waters of Jordan encompass me [89].

From Psalms 114:4 in the King James Bible: "Jordan was driven back. The mountains skipped like rams, and the little hills like lambs." The pastoral setting is parodied earlier in the novel: "As he came down the drive and approached the old red-brick front of the house, there was a lazy murmur of bees in the flower-borders, a gentle cooing of pigeons in the tops of the elms, and from distant lawns the whir of mowing-machines, that most restful of all country sounds" (19).

Milne's chief means of comedy is a light parody of methods employed by Conan Doyle's archetypal Sherlock Holmes. Says Gillingham to Bill Beverley:

> Now, it always seemed to me that in that matter Holmes was the ass, and Watson was the sensible person. What on earth is the point of keeping in your head an unnecessary fact like that? If you really want to know at any time the number of steps to your lodging, you can ring up your landlady and ask her [70].

Gillingham weakens his point by demonstrating that he can indeed calculate the number of steps taken, visualizing them in his photographic memory.

Milne takes issue on important factors, just as Bentley does for *Trent's Last Case*. In his Introduction, Milne writes:

> This is what we really come to: that the detective must have no more special knowledge than the average reader. The reader must be made to feel ... that he too would have fixed the guilt.... Death to the author who keeps his unravelling for the last chapter, making all the other chapters but prologue to a five-minute drama. This is no way to write a story. Let us know from chapter to chapter what the detective is thinking. For this he must watsonize or soliloquize; the one is merely a dialogue form of the other, and, by that, more readable [xi].

These considerations form part of the code of practice among crime authors generally and members of the Detection Club in particular.

The Red House Mystery makes use of the locked room puzzle that became another staple plot ingredient in later crime fiction. Some explanations are ingenious. What is probably one of the simplest is the existence of a secret passage that enables the murderer to make her or his entrance and/or escape. This is what Gillingham decides after he and Bill find the way to a tunnel behind library shelving: "The four walls of the library were plastered with [books] from floor to ceiling, save only where the door and the two windows insisted on living their own life, even though an illiterate one" (98). (Another of Milne's stylistic quirks is to anthropomorphize inanimate objects, his use of the pathetic fallacy). The precise spot where the lever or panel is located that opens the shelf is behind a book of sermons titled jokingly *The Narrow Way*. Through the tunnel the two men reach a shed set beside the bowling green. They surmise that this is how Mark Ablett escaped after shooting his brother Robert Ablett and that Cayley was somehow involved, perhaps assisting Mark Ablett in his escape.

Hence elements of plot and characterization in *The Red House Mystery* echo those in E. C. Bentley's *Trent's Last Case* so frequently that it seems scarcely a question of chance. Both novels introduce the crime through minor characters. In their overall structure they contain an inquest, although in *Trent's Last Case* this appears at the midpoint, whereas in *Red House* the proceedings occur towards the end of the twenty-two chapters. Both volumes are of similar length, almost novellas. The device of letter writing furthers the plot. Surprise endings exemplify the detective's fallibility. The characters of the amateur detectives as hero are very similar. Both Philip Trent and Antony Gillingham are men of action. Their ages are similar. They lead bohemian lifestyles in which they move from one occupation to another. Trent's career is more stable as a newspaper investigator when he is not immersed in his painting. Each man has a unique gift that assists his investigations. Trent has his "artist's eye" while Gillingham can visualize a scene from photographic memory.

The murder victim in both novels is a character unsympathetic to the reader. Disliked by those around him, we have motive for the crime and a number of suspects. The theme of insanity reappears in many of the Golden Age novels. Sigsbee Manderson in *Trent's Last Case* is a greedy tycoon insane with jealousy over a fancied affair between one of his secretaries and his wife. Mark Ablett in *The Red House Mystery* is a man of great vanity, a control freak and drunkard who influences the mother of the young woman he wishes to marry. This provides the chief motive for his death. He is not drawn immediately as a wholly unworthy person. It unfolds through the novel. Manderson dies in a struggle with Cupples, his wife's uncle, who shoots him in self-defense. Ablett is shot in cold blood by his secretary Cayley who is in love with the same woman. There is a major suspect in both tales: Manderson's secretary Marlowe who in the end is found innocent, and Ablett's secretary Cayley who is indeed the guilty party.

A love interest, however, is the chief motive behind the shooting of Manderson and Ablett in each case. It is prominent in *Trent's Last Case* (as a key motif too), when Trent falls in love with Mabel Manderson, who reciprocates.

In *Red House* the love interest is muted but nevertheless stands as the chief motive for murder. Milne had strong feelings about it: "for myself I will have none of it. A reader, all agog to know whether the white substance on the muffins was arsenic or face powder, cannot be held up while Roland clasps Angela's hand" (x). Notwithstanding these protestations, there is a place for holding hands in *The Red House Mystery*. Indeed, the restriction is not among the "Ten Commandments" of Ronald Knox although rule 3 of Van Dine's "Twenty Rules" states: "There must be no love interest. The business in hand is to bring a criminal to the bar of justice, not to bring a lovelorn couple to the hymeneal altar" (*gadetection*). Such rules were observed more in the breach than in the practice.

Good humor and wit in both novels rests a great deal upon jokes and wordplay that include intertextual references. The most obvious are the references to Conan Doyle's Sherlock Holmes and Doctor Watson. There are also classical allusions, as one comes to expect from persons taught Greek and Latin in their schooldays, more prevalent in *Last Case* than in *Red House*. There is situational humor, too, but in *Last Case* this is muted, if at all present, while it is more overt in *Red House*, for example in Bill Beverley's dive into the pond. We have to wait for writers such as John Dickson Carr and Edmund Crispin for pure slapstick.

The geographical settings bear similarities. In *Red House*, the town of Middleston is not far away. In *Last Case* it is Marlstone. Both stories are set in mansions or large houses in the English countryside. The deaths take place in one instance near a golf course, and in the other case near a bowling green (a croquet ground). Water is an important motif: the sea in *Last Case* and a pond in *Red House*. So too, some characters have cognate names: Inspector Birch of the Middleston police and Inspector Murch of Scotland Yard.

Motifs attached to the amateur detectives' forensic investigations are particularly striking. There is a pistol shot and presumed struggle over the gun, a window and footprint to be investigated, emphasis on the layout of rooms — an office, library and adjoining room in *Red House* and adjoining bedrooms in *Last Case*— ill-fitting shoes into which a larger man attempts to squeeze his feet, the teeth of the dead man — false teeth in Manderson's case and dental records in *Red House*. In both novels there is mimicry of the murder victims' characteristic voices.

Inspired by Bentley's character of Trent, Milne applied to good effect several principles now well-known in detective fiction: the fallible amateur detective who does not always get it right, the more fallible Watson figure (although Trent did not really have a Watson, Cupples being the closest analogue), and the "smoking gun" that leads the reader to expect a development unexpected by the fictional investigators. In fact, there can be several smoking guns a reader might spot. These are the various clues a writer might insert into the narrative. In his 1926 introduction to *The Red House Mystery*, Milne states that "it is the amateur detective who alone can expose the guilty man by the light of cool inductive reasoning and the logic of stern remorseless facts" (x). A counterpoint to this principle is that of the fallibility of the amateur. As Antony Gillingham says to Bill Beverley a number of times: "My dear Bill, I'm such an obvious ass that I should be delighted to think you are too" (163). Chris Baldick says of the Trent character in *Trent's Last Case*: "Bentley's radical innovation was the creation of a detective whose brilliant deductions could be flawed by oversights and misplaced assumptions.... Trent is susceptible to error.... His clear vision has a small "blind spot" which endangers his success both as a detective and as a lover" (xii). Concurrent with this is a rule of thumb that the sidekick or Watson character in these tales should be a little less perceptive than the average reader. This is number nine in Ronald Knox's "Ten Commandments" about mystery writing: "The stupid friend of the detective, the Watson, must not conceal from the reader any thoughts which pass through his mind: his intelligence must be slightly, but very slightly, below that of the average reader" ("Golden Age of Detective Fiction").

Another plot element is noted by Milne: "A scar on the nose of one of the guests might suggest nothing to a detective, but the explicit mention of it by the author gives it at once an importance out of all proportion to its face-value" (xi). This is sometimes called the "smoking gun" that ideally has to be made use of later in the plot after its first casual introduction. For example, if attention is drawn to a stiletto on the mantelpiece it is fair enough for the observant reader to suppose that it will reappear later as a clue, the murder weapon, or suchlike. When something like this is not followed up it is called a MacGuffin, an ambiguous plot element that, while important initially in driving the plot can fade into unimportance or be completely forgotten by the end of the story ("MacGuffin").

Considering the success of *The Red House Mystery*, a puzzle is why A. A. Milne did not write more crime novels. This is explained in part by Milne's taste to "move on" whenever a story in a particular genre proved successful, although the truth seems to be that he concentrated most of his energies on the plays and his plush toy books because he preferred them. He did not move on from stage drama, in which he remained active most of his life. In this sense *The Red House Mystery* in full is a sort of grand MacGuffin. In any event, Milne did write another mystery tale published ten years later. *Four Days' Wonder* stands in Milne's biography as a muddled affair just as *Elephant's Work* is for E. C. Bentley. But before that he also wrote *The Fourth Wall* that, among all the others, was his only country-house murder mystery for the stage.

The Fourth Wall (1928)

The Fourth Wall: A Detective Story in Three Acts was produced at the Haymarket Theatre in London on 29 February 1928. It opened at the Charles

Hopkins Theater, New York, on 27 November 1928 and ran for thirty-six and a half weeks for 255 performances under the title *The Perfect Alibi* (Thwaite 532). It does not contain much humor aside from the depiction in brief of certain characters — Mrs. Fulverton-Fane, "Sergeant" Mallet, and Major Fothergill — and some light-hearted banter between the two lovers Susan Cunningham and Jimmy Ludgrove. Milne's biographer Ann Thwaite considers it an "ingenious" play for a number of reasons: "In the first act it shows us a murder ... and who has done it. In the second and third acts we watch the other characters trying to unravel the mystery. Such a scheme is, of course, the very opposite of what happens" [in murder mysteries] (327).

An indifferent film version directed by Basil Dean with the American title, at some point re-titled *Birds of Prey*, was released two years later on 18 November 1930. An IMDb reviewer, "Malcolmgsw," says:

> This film is more of a battle of wits rather than a murder mystery. Nothing happens for the first half hour. Then the sole murder is committed. We see who commits the murder so no drama or suspense there. It is seeing how the leads manage to deduce the murderer and track him or her down that is the focus of the last part of the film.

By this token, the film version is faithful to the stage play, but that is also its weakness: "The initial production chief was Basil Dean ... basically a stage director ... responsible for many misjudgements [so that he was] fired from his job a few years later." It is interesting, however, to see that Milne's original purpose comes through in what by this account is a poorly produced film. Incidentally, this illustrates how the pleasure of the reader or viewer can be had from following the steps in the puzzle while the identity of the murderer is already known. It underpins my policy of including spoilers in these essays.

Edward Carter shoots Arthur Ludgrove with Ludgrove's own gun in order to make it look like suicide. Edward Laverick is Carter's accomplice. Together they take steps to establish their alibis. The investigating police are P.C. Mallet and his son Sergeant Mallet. They interview in turn Adams the butler, then Jimmy, Carter, the Major, Laverrick, Mrs. Fane, Susan and Jimmy once more. The technique is effective in establishing suspense when we know already who committed the murder.

Susan is one of two heroines in the play. She asks Jimmy to meet her after everyone has gone to bed and together they speculate about the crime using "A M S" as guidelines for enquiry: was it Accident, Murder or Suicide? Jimmy is described in the scene notes as "one of those charming and apparently not very intelligent young men whom the Universities empty into the world so hopefully and regularly" (6). He plays second fiddle to Susan who is by far the more intuitive of the pair, a quality that leads her to suspect foul play and which is frequently contrasted against deductive detection in crime stories of the Golden Age: "That's what intuition means. That spiritual things are more important than material things, I *know* Uncle Arthur didn't shoot himself, because morally he couldn't shoot himself.... He wasn't that sort of fool" (51).

The other heroine is Jane West. Her part in the final scene in conjunction with Susan uncovers Carter's alibi through bluff and courage. Jane is a sophisticated and self-assured woman of the world, described in the scene notes as "tall, long-legged, long cigarette-holder in mouth [who speaks] ... in a slow deep voice" (12). Jane West is a character type similar to that of Nancy Spain's Miriam Birdseye. Jane has an arch, dry wit that contrasts against the mild figure of fun represented by Mrs. Fane and her vanity-box:

"Susan darling, you look divine. Exactly like a what's-its-name."

Susan: "Thanks Jane. I don't know what on earth you're talking about" [13].

Between them Susan and Jane lay a trap for Carter. In order that Jane can enter the room, Susan slips a key under the door as she retrieves a dropped brooch. As Susan faces Carter, who is holding her at gunpoint, Jane glides in and hides behind a curtain up-stage. She is not seen because Carter is distracted by Susan's hint that the Sergeant has entered the room whereupon, calling Susan's bluff, he *does not look around* (71). As a second witness Jane overhears Carter's smug confession to Susan, whereupon the two women confront the man:

Carter: Life's easy for your sort. You just sit there looking beautiful and insolent, while somebody else works for you, somebody else dresses you. You've never had to fight for your life.... You think you've got me, don't you?

Jane: (*blowing out a cloud of smoke*). Stiff.

Carter: Well, I can take you with me. (*Pointing his gun at Jane*).

Jane: (*languidly*). Shall we tell him?

Susan: (*wearily*). There's so much to tell him.

Jane: (*turning to Carter, looks down barrel of gun and puffs smoke at him*). The morning bath. It must have been so difficult for you. So silly taking a loaded revolver *and* a sponge into the bathroom, and so awkward if the sponge went off accidentally; but if you leave your revolver behind you under the pillow — well, I mean, where else can you leave it?

(*Carter breaks open his revolver and finds it empty*).

Revolver surprised while bathing [74].

This is melodrama laced with wit and parody. As the narrator says when introducing Anthony Shaffer's *Whodunnit*, which arguably is more memorable:

What you have stumbled into tonight is nothing more or less than an old-fashioned closed circle, telephone wires have been cut, flood-waters have washed away the bridge, "My god you mean it has to be one of us" English country house whodunit. But it has a difference. In order to save you from the miserable banality of the last scene where the murderous clergyman, or whoever it turns out to be, backs weapon in hand towards the French windows, snarling "I warn you, stay where you are, all of you, you'll never put me behind bars," I have decided to tell you who the murderer is at the outset [6].

In Shaffer's play the murderer is the narrator himself, but his identity as the butler Archibald Perkins is not revealed until the last page.

 Whodunnit played on 30 December 1982 at the Biltmore Theatre in New York, fifty-four years after *The Fourth Wall* made its début, and ran for 157 performances ("Whodunnit" [play]). But its fictional setting is the 1930s and the two dramas have parallels. *Whodunnit* purports to reveal the identity of the murderer at the beginning without revealing who it is, whereas *The Fourth Wall* actually does so when the audience witness the shooting. The murderer's melodramatic snarling retreat appears in both plays, a stock situation in the dénouement of *The Fourth Wall* but part of the satire in *Whodunnit*. The principle of the murderer's one mistake is also in play. In *The Fourth Wall* Carter is at pains to make his alibi watertight and so removes an incriminating blotting-paper from the room where the murder takes place and substitutes a fresh sheet. The blotting-paper presumably has the stamp in reverse image of Ludgrove's letter. Susan, this time following observation (68) and not instinct (which equals intuition, hence showing that the two qualities can work together) with the aid of Adams takes the original blotting-paper from Carter's jacket. The final scene between Susan, Jane and Carter is one of bluff and double bluff until Carter gives himself away by more or less confessing in front of hidden witnesses, another favorite element in these stories.

 The idea of the fourth wall, the aside or stage whisper that makes the members of the audience confidants with an actor, in the stage play of that name may refer to reference clichés of the genre — "I didn't hear the handcuffs click," says Susan, "They always click in the stories" (75) — but more likely to be letting the audience in on key aspects that are usually revealed at the end, the identity of the murderer, and at a lesser level, observing Jane concealed behind a curtain.

Four Days' Wonder (1933)

 The only other novel of Milne's that falls strictly into the category of a murder mystery is *Four Days' Wonder* published by Methuen, says Thwaite (389), in October 1933. It is a strange work, teetering between a children's story in language suitable for a young adult and as a more serious whodunit. It is by no means Milne's best work and might be compared against Bentley's disastrous novel *Elephant's Work* or Nancy Spain's careless pastiche *The Kat Strikes*.

 Reviews of *Four Days' Wonder* when it first came out were complimentary. A critic for *The Times Literary Supplement* cited in Thwaite hailed it as: "An entirely delightful and brilliant novel.... Elegant and gay [light-hearted] — all capital fun" (391), and it sold 8,000 copies by the end of its year of publication and was translated into French, Hungarian and German. But its children's/adolescent style was not to all tastes and its extensive silliness was reviewed by Sylvia Norman in the *Spectator* as "a nursery satire on detective fiction" (cited in Thwaite 391, 536n). Thwaite observes too that "the heroine, Jenny, is far too silly for the reader to feel sympathetic or even entertained as she rushes off to avoid being accused of her aunt's death" (391).

Jenny Windell does more than that. Before fleeing the scene, she replaces a brass doorstop from the floor where her aunt lies "to its usual place upon the grand piano" (8-9), first wiping (blood?) stains from it with her handkerchief and so destroying evidence. Jenny speculates about international spy syndicates, and so on. Throughout the book there is a droll humor that would not have been out of place in *Winnie-the-Pooh* and *The House at Pooh Corner*. While it is one of Milne's trademarks in style, it grows tedious in a novel of approximately 95,000 words. Sylvia Norman's reading that *Four Days' Wonder* is a satire on the detective genre is compelling, whether it was seen that way at the time. Milne himself took it seriously and complained to his publishers Methuen for not making a sufficient fuss of it (Thwaite 389). Perhaps the publishers saw that it was not an especially good novel. Today, rightly or wrongly, it is sometimes included with *The Red House Mystery* as the second and only other detective novel by Milne.

Perhaps surprisingly, a film version was made that had its first showing on 24 December 1936, directed by Sidney Salkow for Universal Pictures (Thwaite 534n). Its plot and characterization is described by Hal Erikson (allmovie 2010):

> When a real murder occurs in the vicinity, Judy insists upon playing sleuth, dragging teenaged astronomer Tom Fenton (Kenent Howell) into her Sherlock shenanigans. It's no trick for Judy or Tom to out-guess dimwitted police detective Duffy (Walter Catlett), but the murderer isn't so easy to flummox, and for a while it looks as though our heroine will never reach adulthood.

Whether Milne intended it or not, those who adapted and reviewed *Four Days' Wonder* for the screen received it as an adolescent detective comedy. A review in the Internet Movie Database titled "Silly murder mystery," by someone called "jaybee-3 from New Jersey" describes the film version in the same terms as the book but categorizes it as: "A comedy mystery from the Charles R. Rogers–Universal period: "Film plays well enough for young children but adults will become a bit restless with some of the nonsense. Dante is a charming lead but her career never really took off."

CHAPTER 4

Best of the Farceurs I: Margery Allingham (1904–1966), from Thriller to Detective Novel

Margery Louise Allingham was born on 20 May 1904 in Ealing, a suburb of London (Jones 1; "Margery Allingham"). Her father was Herbert John Allingham and her mother Emily Jane Hughes, an ex-milliner, both of whom were journalists (Blain, Clements and Grundy 19). Allingham's biographer Julia Jones (25) says that these parents "put social and professional obligations first" and left a lot of the parenting to the children's grandmother (mother's mother) Emily Jane Hughes: "Granny bathed them, prayed with them, taught them to read and loved them. She also told them stories" (7). (Both Margery's mother "Em" and her grandmother were named Emily Jane). The grandmother also passed on to Margery's mother and the aunts a measure of insecurity and poverty brought about by her decision to leave her heavy-drinking husband William Walter. This made the aunts and Margery's mother "individual, assertive and alarmingly self-reliant," such that in compensation, thinks Jones (6), they flouted "the conventional contemporary roles of women." More to the point, Em was known to her children as "a loud, domineering personality with no cosiness and a wounding tongue" (3). The family became even more centered upon a domineering mother and aunts after the death of Margery's father in the 1919 influenza epidemic (238).

Margery Allingham, then, acquired a family environment that was an uneasy mix of individuality and independence, insecurity and emotional instability.

Such traits — evident in her mother — can be traced through Margery's life as well. As Jones says: "Autobiography tends to be a filial genre — whether for or against the parental influence" (64). Children who are subject to a degree of parental neglect, or who carry a relatively subtle physical disability such as partial deafness or a more serious disorder, often compensate by developing a skill in childhood that carries over into adulthood. For Margery Allingham it is writing. Says Jones (30): "Most children growing up in such a household would at some time or other have played at writing." Writing in this family, however, was more than just play. Blain, Clements and Grundy (19) note that when she was eight years old, Margery wrote a story for a magazine published by her aunt Maud Hughes for which she was paid. As noted earlier, journalism is the breadwinning career of a good number of authors in our list after their studies in something completely different and their graduation (or not, as it may be) from the major universities, usually Oxford or Cambridge.

Margery grew up at Layer Breton near Colchester ("Margery Allingham") and went to school at Colchester (Blain, Clements and Grundy 19). Later she attended Perse School for Girls at Cambridge ("Margery Allingham"). In 1920 she entered Regent Street Polytechnic, now part of the University of Westminster, where she studied drama and speech training to cure a childhood stammer (Jones 63). There she met Philip Youngman Carter who became her husband some years later ("Margery Allingham"). Jones reports (103) that Margery left the Polytechnic in 1923 aged nineteen and was well enough known by then to be invited to a dinner of the P. E. N. club in November that year, where she rubbed shoulders with such literary figures as H. G. Wells and May Sinclair. Sinclair (1863–1946) was a novelist and member of the Woman Writer's Suffrage League who wrote about the moral progress and sufferings of women trapped in Victorian marriage to develop artistically against obstacles set by family and husband. She is credited with having coined the expression "stream of consciousness" (Blain, Clements and Grundy 987) but another authority, Abrams (180), attributes the phrase to the philosopher/psychologist William James. Practitioners of stream of consciousness as a literary technique include James Joyce, Virginia Woolf, William Faulkner and (of course) Gertrude Stein.

Margery felt ill at ease in the P. E. N. group (perhaps a little like one of Sinclair's heroines). Her self-consciousness when in such gatherings remained through her life, the unease repeated years later in the 1930s when attending meetings of the Detection Club (Jones 102). Persons with bipolar disorder, as Margery Allingham arguably had, can experience degrees of agoraphobia. Her crime novels can be read, however, with little or no inkling that anything is amiss in her life. As Jones notes: "In her diaries Margery reveals aspects of herself that passed unnoticed in her lifetime — her depression and insecurity above all" (xxi). Yet there were moments in her professional work that might point to those conditions. For example, in a lapse of concentration she attributed the authorship of *Trent's Last Case* to the crime writer H. C. Bailey instead of to its creator E. C. Bentley (James xxix). Perhaps such lapses are more common in persons with discordant mental states and who mix writing with a very active social life, as Margery did through innumerable garden parties. Nancy Spain is another writer with similar flaws but she appears more scatterbrained than Allingham.

A crucial development in Margery's life was her engagement and subsequent marriage to Philip Youngman Carter in 1927 (Jones 116) when she was twenty-three. Carter was an able artist-journalist who collaborated with Margery by illustrating dust jackets for her books and proofreading much of her work ("Margery Allingham"). Books of other writers illustrated by Carter include his father's clerihews and cover illustrations for several of the Sir Henry Merrivale novels by John Dickson Carr such as *The Bowstring Murders* (1934), *The Judas Window* (1938), and *Death in Five Boxes* (1938) (personal communication David Young, Moderator of the John Dickson Carr Collector, http://jdcarr .com). After their marriage "Pip" and Margery moved into a house at Tolleshunt D'Arcy close to Maldon ("Margery Allingham").

Margery's disquietening mental state was present throughout her life. She suffered from manic-depression, what we today call bipolar disorder. As Julia Jones notes in her "Introduction to the First Edition": "Laughter was crucial if she was to keep a steady view of life. Depression was one aspect but gaiety was another and both aspects came together in her novels. By writing her bitter comedies she kept tragedy at bay" (xxii). This is an almost unique motive for writing among the authors in our list. Others such as John Dickson Carr and A. A. Milne seem to have written farce for the fun of it, and Edmund Crispin likewise as well as to emulate Carr. Nancy Spain is the other writer who appears to have been impelled into farce by her bipolarity.

Margery's new marriage helped, as Jones observes:

> Joyce, Margery's sister ... believes that part of the answer [why Margery married Pip] lies in Margery's lack of social and personal confidence. She possessed an enduring confidence in herself as an artist and an ambition which survived even fallow years such as 1925–26. Pip's quality of savoir-faire took care of life's surface for them both, enabling Margery to mine her own depths more safely than she could alone [115].

But Margery never quite succeeded in this. Like her contemporary Nancy Spain, with whom Margery was to have an unusual relationship, her feelings of imperfection made her awkward in social gatherings. As Jones notes, "She attended one or two of the Detection Club's functions in the 1930s and scuttled home to Essex feeling inadequate" (102). Later, Jones says that in the years 1930–1931 when Margery was now twenty-six and still a relatively young woman: "Instead of stabilizing in adulthood, this trait developed towards potentially more extreme bipolarity of mood" (148).

Philip Youngman Carter had his own demons, if this can be said of his increasing conservatism over political and social questions as he grew older together with a predilection for extra-marital affairs. Jones (115) wonders how Margery at all chose to marry such a man, and to live with him. In point of fact, Margery Allingham and Philip Youngman Carter lived separately some years later, reuniting from time to time where their collaborative work or social commitments demanded.

The potted histories about Margery Allingham tend to stop around this point and trace the rest of her life through her books. In short, but no less potted is the following from Julia Jones' biography *The Adventures of Margery Allingham*. In twenty-one chapters Jones breaks down the course of Allingham's life into periods such as: "Mersea Island 1921," "Enter Albert Campion 1927–1929," "What Is the Reason for Me? 1937–1938," "The World Was Changing 1941–1945," "How to Become a Jolly Old Fruit 1959–1966."

In the 1930s Margery widened her professional horizons socially. Her exposure to the Detection Club has been mentioned. In this decade, too, says Jones:

> She became friendly with fellow Heinemann novelist Kate O'Brien. Of fellow-detective novelists she knew and liked John Dickson Carr ... and Philip (Pip) McDonald. From the evidence available she neither met nor mentions Agatha Christie, Dorothy Sayers and Ngaio Marsh, the writers with whom she is usually listed, until the middle of the decade — the last not at all [146].

But Margery did meet some of them. Jones says a lot earlier in her study (44) that Margery's "first impression" of Dorothy L. Sayers is that she was "school-mistressy" (44) not surprising as much of Sayers' early life when she was in her twenties involved teaching subjects such as French and German at different girls' schools. Later, during the war years, Allingham reassessed Sayers, stating that she was not so much "headmistressy" as "'really quite a nice old duck when you get to know her" (Jones 270). The photograph of a helmeted Dorothy L. Sayers reproduced in Barbara Reynolds' biography of the lady (297) attests to this image.

In general, however, Margery Allingham tended to go her own way in her writing and was selective, too, about what she read of others' work: "As well as the novels of her fellow crime-writers, which she read somewhat sparingly, her bookshelves contain memoirs of retired policemen, accounts of actual crimes and reports by forensic scientists" (Jones 321). Allingham received practical assistance in business from her publishers, principally Charles Evans, the editor of Heinemann since 1933 who had a great influence upon the writers he attracted into his stable. For example, says Jones (192), he gave financial support to Graham Greene, "Margery's exact contemporary." In the period 1930–1931 Margery switched from her earlier publisher to Heinemann (Jones 146).

In 1931 Margery and Philip Youngman Carter moved to Viaduct Farm at

Chappel (Jones 162). Difficulties with staff (a housemaid who brought in a "follower") and quarrels with Pip over domestic affairs, in more than one sense, made this a bad period for Margery. Alan Gregory's colorful cartoon (Pike) of people lounging in armchairs and presumably carousing illustrates the physical reality of such a party: "Margery, Philip and friends at Viaduct Farm, Chappel, c 1932." The body language ranges from reclining and sprawling to prim and proper. Margery sits before what looks like a large bowl of punch with a ladle in one hand and a wine glass in the other hand that she is about to fill. She is wearing a voluminous green spotted dress with exaggeratedly large puff sleeves. Her back is to the company. To the background a man in spectacles raises a tankard. Another with both arms raised and holding in one hand what looks like a long-handled spoon appears to be beating time in singsong or making a toast. A man in a blue suit taking central place with long legs stretched out in a characteristic pose appears to be Carter. Two dogs, a black Scottish Terrier and what looks like a Dachshund, sit upon the carpet. (A Terrier figures in Margery's own sketches). A young woman in a blue top sits near them with her back to the viewer. She appears to be reading something or perhaps listening. Two glasses stand on the carpet near the dogs. Eleven people are present (not counting dogs). A slender woman with short dark hair and long dress sits upright to the far right of the picture, her arms folded demurely across her chest perhaps holding something or possibly in disapproval. A twelfth person sketched in bare outline is to her left, hands folded in her lap, and is perhaps the artist's false start on the fully drawn figure. It is a tableau that speaks of various levels of engagement and disengagement among the partying crowd. This is a period marked by the wild parties of Margery's "gang."

The "family trouble," says Jones, "financial insecurity and private self-exploration make no mark on [her novel *Sweet Danger*] — except insofar as it exemplified her much later view that escapist literature represented 'an escape from insecurity into sanity'" (159). In other books, however, Margery was to reflect more directly the stresses of life in a household crowded with mismatched persons. Either way, writing appears to have helped Margery distance herself from the real-life frictions. Writing for 1934, Jones discusses Magery Allingham's personality illness related to that of her mother, citing her psychiatrist Russell Barton who believed that both women "are sometimes prey to unfounded suspicion of those closest to them. A vivid imagination or the facility for spinning plots can be an additional curse in this respect. But Pip's reputation among his friends and his later open infidelity suggest that Margery's jealousy in 1934 was likely to have been justified" (163).

Towards the close of the decade Margery found a new professional interest. Around 1938 she was invited to become a book reviewer for *Time and Tide*, a weekly magazine: "the small sums earned and the steady chore of considering other people's writing was of great benefit in helping her through this period of reassessment in her own life and work," says Jones (199). It is a different development from that of her former selective reading of others' work. In this period she met Margery Sharp and A. A. Milne on her trips to London (Jones 198). Milne is mentioned once only in Jones' biography of Margery beyond their apparently casual acquaintance and so, affable and helpful to other writers as he was, Milne appears not to have influenced Margery's career as he had with that of John Dickson Carr or Nancy Spain.

Unlike John Dickson Carr, who avoided using the Second World War in his novels beyond passing references to "Hitler's war" (Joshi 93–95), Margery Allingham found major themes in the hostilities, in the Campion novel *Traitor's Purse* (1941), published in the United States as *The Sabotage Murder Mystery* (Blain, Clements and Grundy 19), and in non-fiction, a record of personal experiences of people's reactions to the war in *The Oaken Heart* published the same year. Jones notes that "few of her 1930s peers were thought to have adapted their style so well to the post-war world" (287). There came a hiatus of two years before she published again with *Dance of the Years* (1943), followed by a longer break until *More Work for the Undertaker* came out in 1949. Its humor must have helped compensate for the bad times she was experiencing, for Jones remarks that: "*More Work for the Undertaker* shows Margery's comic sense as its most expansive and most generous even at a time when her own life was not especially gay" (272).

Nineteen fifty-one was a bad year marked by poor health: the onset of thyroid trouble and the putting on of weight associated with that condition, together with an exacerbation of her manic-depressive periods, and the confirmation that her husband was indulging in extra-marital affairs. That year Margery discovered Philip Youngman Carter *in flagrante* with an unnamed woman in his London flat (Jones 276). While the woman may not have been Nancy Spain, Carter and Spain had a brief affair around that time, perhaps no more than a one-night stand. At the same time Allingham continued writing. Says Jones: "Between March and October of that traumatic year, 1951, Margery wrote the most part of the novel [*Tiger in the Smoke*] which is generally accepted as her finest achievement" (282).

By 1955: "She was now an established figure in the world of crime-writers, voted one of the world's top ten living practitioners by the Mystery Writers of America and thus a target for younger writers and critics wishing to mark out their own stylistic territories" (Jones 310). Not only that, as Jones (282) says, Margery Allingham's last post-war "Bayswater" novels were so different from the usual detective/thrillers of the past that they place Allingham among the better of the mainstream writers. These included *More Work for the Undertaker* (1948), *Tiger in the Smoke* and *Hide My Eyes* (1958). In 1956 a film version of *Tiger in the Smoke* came out, and it pleased Margery when *Tiger* and *Hide My Eyes* (1958) were both added to the school examination syllabus (Jones 340).

Panek finds patterns from ancient mythology in Allingham's works (129) and Margery herself recognized elements from the medieval mystery/morality play (see above). I am reminded too of Karal Čapek's motifs (109) of the fairy tale and the cave hunt: "pursuit, escape, defence, the rounding-up of the victim, [and] close fighting" cited in chapter one.

Now in her late fifties, Margery enjoyed the 1960s and liked the young people of that generation with their exuberant "manners, habits and hairdos" reminding her of her old Gang from the twenties (Jones 341) that had been her audience for the initial Campion tales (Jones 124). By now her contemporaries were aging and dying, for example Nancy Spain in 1964 and Edmund Crispin in 1968, and her own health was poor with the onset of breast cancer. Jones refers early in her biography to "the attitudes of the ageing Margery — more tired, more disillusioned, less disposed to self-celebration" (30). Dr. Barton saw her through to the end, diagnosing not only the cancer but also her long-standing manic-depressive state (Jones 350). She died in 1966 on 30 June at Severalls Hospital, Colchester, aged sixty-two.

Theory & Practice in Margery Allingham's Writing

Margery Allingham's fiction was her livelihood. Her predilection for large dinner parties and frequent disputes with the tax office were two of the circumstances behind the production line, but she also enjoyed writing in the different genres between which she moved, sometimes not always with clarity. In *Police at the Funeral,* Jones (141) notes a greater attention in Allingham's style to detection than to adventure novels. To the extent that this was a conscious choice there is Jones's (142) observation that Allingham lifted the faked murder idea in *Police* directly from Conan Doyle's *The Problem of Thor Bridge* (1922). This is not strictly plagiarism. Many writers such as John Dickson Carr take ideas from works other than their own and give them a new twist or a different modus operandi, as well as expanding a short story to novel length or reworking an older story of their own. It is difficult for writers to remain uninfluenced by the work of others they admire or against whom they react. Elements of the thriller as well as the supernatural remain in all Margery Allingham's writing (as in Conan Doyle's work). She also used her craft as a vehicle for working out relationships between herself and others. This is why many of her stories have psychological elements, for example, Layer Breton memories and father-daughter estrangement in *Dancers in Mourning* (Jones 31).

Allingham's *métier* is the adventure thriller as with her first novel *Blackerchief Dick* published in 1923 (Jones 85), to which form she adds elements of the supernatural tale, the crime thriller and detective story as her skills evolve. As Blain, Clements and Grundy say (19), she wrote magazine melodramas that often contained occult themes. In the foreword to Jones's biography of Margery Allingham, Nicci Gerrard says:

> Margery Allingham's novels ... are not just dense with multiple murders, locked rooms, cunning plots, sudden reversals, devilish twists, but also with *goofy comic turns and sudden anti-climaxes that are reminiscent of PG Wodehouse* [my emphasis] rather than Agatha Christie, and with unearthly portents, supernatural events, shadows and moonlight and troubling dreams, whose wildness takes us into the world that Wilkie Collins evoked in novels like *The Woman in White* and *The Moonstone* [vii].

Literary critics often compare Allingham's work favorably with such forerunners as Collins, Poe and, contemporary with Allingham, Conan Doyle, Christie or Wodehouse.

The influence of Wodehouse is attributed also to the work of other writers in crime fiction — for example, John Dickson Carr who, according to Douglas Greene, "had been reading P. G. Wodehouse" (139) when he wrote *Hag's Nook* (1933); or Edmund Crispin, whose work is sometimes compared to Wodehouse, although Crispin saw nothing especially funny about that writer (Whittle 244; also 132, 140). Dorothy L. Sayers' biographer Barbara Reynolds (175) notes similarities in mannerisms between Sayers' character Lord Peter Wimsey and Wodehouse's Bertie Wooster. Albert Campion's horse and hound enthusiast Guffy Randall, while not ubiquitous, appears in several of Margery Allingham's novels. This upper-class English drone might have leapt from the pages of Wodehouse.

In point of fact, P. G. Wodehouse to my knowledge wrote only one crime mystery, *Leave It to Psmith* (1923). Its dénouement (256–257) involves the turning of tables upon a gun-wielding criminal when the ceiling falls in upon him. The cover illustration to my 1988 Penguin edition, "by Ionicus," depicts the traditional standoff at gunpoint between Cootes and Miss Peavey (malefactors) against Eve (heroine) and Psmith (hero). The verbal narrative (252) is a pure parody of the thriller:

> "Hands up!" said Mr. Cootes with the uncouth curtness of one who had not the advantages of a refined home and a nice upbringing. He advanced warily, preceded by the revolver. It was a dainty, miniature weapon, such as might have been the property of some gentle lady. Mr. Cootes had, in fact, borrowed it from Miss Peavey, who at this juncture entered the room in a black and silver dinnerdress surmounted by a Rose du Barri wrap, her spiritual face glowing softly in the subdued light.

Cootes' sinister but clichéd appearance with the firearm is undermined the next moment by the revelation that it is a "dainty" lady's weapon (another cliché from the genre of the thriller) followed by the appearance of Miss Peavey as femme fatale (cliché number three). The situation descends to slapstick as Freddie Threepwood puts his leg through the ceiling above, and ends in another cliché with Psmith hitting Cootes with a chair and taking possession of his gun. The front cover illustrator Ionicus depicts the characters almost like adolescents with chubby, clean-cut faces, appearances appropriate for a boys' adventure story. It is a disappointment that Wodehouse evidently confines his extensive writing to satiric comedy of manners and not to crime fiction although, ironically, his work influenced many crime fiction writers of his day such as Margery Allingham.

Margery Allingham's output is impressive. Her works include *Crime at Black Dudley* (1928; 1929 in the U.S.), *The White Cottage Mystery* (1928), *Mystery Mile* (1930), *Police at the Funeral* (1931), *Look to the Lady* (1931) — in the U.S., *The Gyrth Chalice Mystery* — *Sweet Danger* (1933), *Death of a Ghost* (1934), *Flowers for the Judge* (1936), *Dancers in Mourning* (1937), *The Fashion in Shrouds* (1938), *Traitor's Place/Purse* (1941) — published in the U.S. as *The Sabotage Murder Mystery* — *The Oaken Heart* (1941, an autobiography), *Dance of the Years* (1943), *More Work for the Undertaker* (1949), *The Tiger in the Smoke* (1952), *The Beckoning Lady* (1955), *The China Governess* (1963), *The Mind Readers* (1965). In all, she wrote more than forty books, mostly novels but also several collections of short stories, a radio play, and serializations. S. T. Joshi observes (75) that although the number of her novels fall well below the output of John Dickson Carr, she wrote almost as many short stories as Carr and, Carr being in Joshi's view not a good writer of short stories, Allingham's strength in that medium is that she can "draw character with a few bold strokes."

In 1956 a film version was made of *Tiger in the Smoke* (Blain, Clements and Grundy 19; "Margery Allingham"), and from 1989 to 1990 a BBC television series of her Campion stories came out. From 1928 with *The White Cottage Mystery* to *Tiger in the Smoke* in 1952, she produced a book a year (with the exceptions of 1942, 1944 and 1951). Thereafter the writing slowed with gaps of two or three years between books until her death in 1966. *Tiger in the Smoke* was her last crime novel and arguably one of her best. Several more publications came posthumously. An unfinished novel *Cargo of Eagles* (1968) was edited and expanded by Philip Youngman Carter so well that Pike remarks: "the join is probably not apparent to most readers (though Edmund Crispin claimed to be able to see it)." Carter was also the author in his own right of two Albert Campion novels, *Mr. Campion's Farthing* (1969) and *Mr. Campion's Falcon* (1970) — in the U.S.: *Mr. Campion's Quarry* ("Margery Allingham").

Faced with so much, but keeping in mind the manageable and lighter theme of humor in Allingham's work, I take the three novels in the *Margery Allingham Omnibus* (1982) — *The Crime at Black Dudley, Mystery Mile* and *Look to the Lady* — and one other, *Sweet Danger*, as representative. I also consider the BBC Campion First and Second Series: *Look to the Lady, Police at the Funeral, The Case of the Late Pig* and *Death of a Ghost* (First Series 1996/2008) and *Mystery Mile, Dancers in Mourning, Sweet Danger* and *Flowers for the Judge* (Second Series 1990).

Like several of her contemporaries, Allingham found success with one protagonist, whereas other writers created more than one, such as John Dickson Carr's Dr. Fell, Sir Henry Merrivale and Bencolin. In Allingham's case it is the amateur detective Alfred Campion. The first novel that introduces this character is *Crime at Black Dudley*, in the U.S. published as *The Black Dudley Murder*. Campion appears in seventeen additional novels and in excess of twenty short stories through to the 1960s. He is the creation chiefly for which Allingham is known ("Margery Allingham"). A lot of her other work is forgotten.

The "adventure" theme promised in the subtitle to Julia Jones' biography of Margery Allingham has two general connotations. Firstly, it is one way by which Margery perceives her place in the world. Jones cites from Allingham's memoirs *The Oaken Heart* (1941): "I have had many mental and moral adventures" (xix). Secondly, adventure tales as exemplified in the thriller became Allingham's chief means of expressing her "mental and moral adventures" from the word go. They often reflect the condition of manic-depression. Jones (xxxii) states that Allingham's admirers see her novels as unique, but she hedges this observation by inserting the phrase "to some extent." In fact, Margery Allingham's "cast of characters and descriptive style"— though unique in the sense that such elements are one of a kind for each individual writer — nonetheless conform to the overall framework of the thriller.

Allingham's novels lie on a continuum that starts with the sensation fiction of the late nineteenth century through the picaresque adventure tale (the swashbuckler *Blackerchief Dick*) to the mystery story, the thriller, and the detective story. Her writing covers all that ground but with a distinct bias towards the form of the thriller, beginning with *The Crime at Black Dudley* to *Tiger in the Smoke* some twenty-four years later. *Black Dudley* is a "debut" novel, loosely structured and with an emphasis upon the comic. It is one of her weakest offerings; whereas *Tiger* is a tightly framed deep study of a psychopath. There is no humor to speak of. In both novels Albert Campion plays a lesser role than in the adventures published for the years between.

Panek notes that Allingham's earlier novels violated ("ignored") the "rules" of detective story writing. Some of the more prominent, and amusing, that relate to Allingham's work as well as to others include the following. She used elements often found in abundance in the thriller, such as secret societies, sinister not to say inscrutable foreigners, assorted henchpersons, and unexpected coincidences and accidents, and in particular the motif of the master criminal. Says Jones (32–33), Margery took an "organic, intuitive approach," in contrast to that of her father Herbert, who saw "plot as a cerebral, detachable thing" and on that basis produced lurid Victorian melodramas through to the 1930s for the women's magazines, grounded in Herbert's former writing of serials for boys' adventure stories, a medium (serialization) that relies heavily on plotting and suspense (Jones 55). Margery's intuitive approach shows through when writing about dramatic productions in 1921.

The next hint at Margery Allingham's preference for intuitive writing is to show that she was in good company. Jones (79) observes that one of Margery's models, Robert Lewis Stevenson, "learned to rely upon the workings of his subconscious in dreams to push his adventure stories on," but she adds that Margery did not have the self-confidence to use her imagination so systematically. This was in 1921 when Margery was only seventeen years old. In the 1924–1927 chapter Jones (105) pursues this point, saying that Margery: "was never a writer who liked to write in an orderly fashion to a plan," as did her father and mother. Stevenson appears to have melded the intuitive with the orderly, a different approach from either that of Margery or her parents.

This is during the 1927–1929 period where Pip took over the role of mentor from Herbert Allingham, and early in their marriage before complications set in. The book on which they were working, *The Crime at Black Dudley*, was not entirely successful, a difficult mélange, perhaps, of intuition with orderliness. It is an early example, however, of Margery's shift towards humor, something that Jones (127) notices. When *Black Dudley* was published by Jarrolds in 1929, Margery was twenty-five. The writing of her next two books was hampered similarly by her inability to write to a formula.

It seems that Margery Allingham's writing relied heavily upon her interaction with others and their approbation. Her method of dictating a story to a second party appears unusual, a practice that is more in keeping with the recording of oral tradition. She used this means of writing much of her life. Eight years later, during the 1937–1938 period, says Jones (121), her assistant was Alan Joseph Gregory, nicknamed "Grog," who was an old school friend of Pip's. Grog and Allingham worked together on *Dancers in Mourning* and Margery took greater pains in polishing and revisions.

By 1965 and at the age of sixty-one Margery Allingham appears to have come to some terms with intuition versus systematization. Jones reports her as saying: "I am by nature an intuitive writer whose intellect trots along behind, tidying, censuring ... it has taken me a very long time to comprehend this and to allow for it" (323). Margery liked concepts such as symbolism. They appeal to one's intuitive nature. This said, Margery's work does not contain much intellection. Her books are successful not because they "give the reader pause for thought," in Jones's words (136), but because they have a "brisk pace and agreeably frivolous tone." There is a somewhat jarring mix of "sophistication" with woolly-headedness. Perhaps Margery Allingham never managed to have completely ordered thoughts. Her bipolar condition might well have militated against it.

Julia Jones appears herself a trifle muddle-headed (323), committing the same error as her subject by confusing H. C. Bailey with E. C. Bentley. Aside from that, Jones, when attempting to explain that by 1958 a good degree of sophistication had emerged in Margery's outlook on her craft, cites Allingham who in a talk about "Crime for Our Delight" states:

> The killing we harp on is not just an ordinary killing [it is] the new and main literary idea of the century. We seem to be catching up with the Greeks at last. Enormous amount of our stories have this second meaning or main meaning: the way one keeps on murdering one aspect of a person to give birth to another [324].

Sophisticated this may be, but it is also muddled.

Margery Allingham seems to be foretelling the growing importance of psychological crime stories, accurately as it turns out, with her notable *Tiger in the Smoke*, one of the first contributions to that subgenre. She says that psychological crime tales with their symbolism are replacing the puzzle tale. But it is more difficult to understand what she is getting at when she refers to "the killing we harp on," or "murdering one aspect of a person to give birth to another." The harped-upon killing appears to be the central idea that at least one murder (and often preferably three) should take place in such fiction. The murdering of one aspect of a person to make way for another sounds a little like the idea that a writer figuratively "murders" part of herself/himself as they create their works, whether in travel, adventure and so on. The phrase "second meaning or main meaning" is simply muddle-headed. It is either one or the other, not both. Allingham's reference to the Greeks is probably to the psychological themes of Classical drama as in the tragedy of King Oedipus. It might also be a sidelong reference to Aristotle's concept of catharsis.

In Margery Allingham's case, the Edwardian habit of writing about international conspiracies remains a staple of her work, including *Tiger in the Smoke*, published four years before her death and the sixth-last book she wrote, aside from one other published posthumously in 1968 (*Cargo of Eagles*, which Philip Youngman Carter completed). Margery was aware of changes in writers' habits, but she continued to work in the thriller mode. The thriller already had a long history and was still a popular genre despite what Jones says.

The writer James Laver, with whom Margery Allingham exchanged a brief correspondence, assessed the era "Between the Wars" (the Golden Age) as "hectic, frivolous, frustrated, puzzled, frantic" (Jones 198). That era, says Jones (198), "was visibly coming to a close," but its spirit remained compatible with both the thriller and the crime/detective story and the two streams within them of puzzle solving and farce. In such an environment there was plenty of room for both approaches: thriller and detective story, puzzle and farce. Allingham, who always wrote a mix of the detective puzzle-tale and the thriller, is not out of date. *Tiger in the Smoke* is well written and successful. Margery was a realist inasmuch as when war broke out in 1939 she wrote "never go pretending that things were going well before the war" (Jones 198), a view of life counter to that of John Dickson Carr who was unable to cope with the new circumstances and set most of his postwar novels in the 1930s. So although she writes thrillers, Margery Allingham uses elements and plotting from the detective story.

I doubt that her novels might be sources for our knowledge of changes in social attitudes, as Jones (xxxii) suggests: "possibly a tendency to use Margery as a quarry to mine nuggets of information about changing social attitudes." However, they do reflect the more closely knit social world around Allingham, beginning with the influence of her father Herbert. E. S. Turner in *Boys Will Be Boys* (1948), a study of the penny-dreadful genre for schoolboys, mentions Herbert Allingham (116) as "a star performer" in the production of adventure serials. This paternal literary inheritance is not lost but continues in Margery's close collaboration with Philip Youngman Carter, who is acknowledged directly by Turner (6): "I am indebted to the late Philip Youngman Carter for the idea of this book, and for his help and encouragement." Youngman Carter died in 1969 (Pike). The acknowledgments belong to the Penguin edition of 1976. But even at this earlier point in her life Margery was influenced in another direction by George Hearn, a family friend whose advice ran somewhat counter to that received from her family and her husband. For example, there is "her father's commercial craftsmanship" as a writer of sensational fiction for schoolboys, as in *Boy's Own Paper* (a publication to which, however, he did not contribute). Hearn on the other hand encouraged Margery to make use of a different popular form, that of the murder mystery which could be "both vehicle and disguise for essentially personal statements" (Jones 40).

One social setting that appears frequently in Margery Allingham's work under different guises involves the frictions there can be among small, close-knit family groups living in part isolation from the outside world: "groups of dangerously cloistered 'intellectuals' attempting to live according to books or tradition, failing to see life as it is and incapable of adapting to change" (Jones 61). The novels reflect "the dangerous claustrophobia inherent in family life" (Jones 143). This was a conscious decision on Margery's part and is an important aspect of her philosophy of crime writing, but it is not new. It is the *sine qua non* of English crime/detective writing of the Golden Age and most of the writers of this period use these settings in their stories.

Associated with this is what Margery herself refers to as the "literature of escape" (Jones 217), about which says Jones (283): "Primarily her novels were to entertain, not to harrow or to shock." The motive to entertain, including that of inciting laughter while at the same time exposing the reader to serious thoughts is a key feature of the Golden Age. Margery saw that the fiction in which she worked had elements of the medieval morality play (Jones 285–286). To this we can add Strachey's idea of detective novels as "folk literature" (Jones xvii) with "the detective as the romantic adventurer, 'the rescuer, the dragon slayer, the wanderer in search of other people's troubles'" (Jones 322). Margery does not address much serious thought to her stories in the sense that they contain very little social comment aside from what is implicit about close-knit family and village groups. Instead, she often chooses to use elements of shock and awe that belong to the thriller and horror genres, and that we find today in the police procedurals and forensic investigations.

The Crime at Black Dudley (1929)

The Crime at Black Dudley introduces Alfred Campion. It is her third major novel after *Blackerchief Dick* (1923) and *The White Cottage Mystery* (1928). *Black Dudley* has approximately 78,000 words, which is a standard length for these novels. After the onset of World War I, as John Dickson Carr's biographer Douglas Greene says, "Novels of seventy-five thousand to ninety thousand words became the most common length for a detective story" (100). That benchmark is observed through the Golden Age. In Margery Allingham's work, *Mystery Mile* has about 72,000 words, *Look to the Lady* around 80,000, *Sweet Danger* approximately 75,300, and *Tiger in the Smoke* comes in at around 78,000 words.

The short chapters in *The Crime at Black Dudley*, like those in the other novels, betray the episodic structure of a thriller, influenced by Allingham's prior experience in serialization, suggested too by clichéd titles such as: "The Ritual of the Dagger," "Murder," "The Mask," "Abbershaw Sees Red," "The Round-Up," "The Darkest Hour," "Mr. Watt Explains," or "A Journey by Night." Defining elements include the physical setting within an isolated old house, a love interest introduced early in the first chapter (in fact, two love interests), a gang of international criminals, secret passages behind fireplaces and trapdoors in trunks, a damsel in distress, a corpse, fights, attempted escapes and other trappings of melodrama. Jones (129) observes that "Glevering Hall [is] the most likely original for *Black Dudley*, a forbidding stone-clad house from which a park slopes away." This was not far from the old Vicarage in Letheringham, Suffolk, where Margery wrote most of *Black Dudley*.

A group of young people is invited to the old mansion for a weekend of partying. Allingham's cast includes George Abbershaw as the chief protagonist, a "little red-haired doctor" (191) from whose point of view the events unfold. Abbershaw is a sort of anti-hero. References to his relatively small stature occur at least nine times on a rough count. He is "determined" (26), "a sturdy little fellow, a pugnacious little cove" (75), but he is also "the sober, deliberate man of science" who can, however, under the pressures of the adventure become an "impulsive, energetic enthusiast." There are moments of self-realization: "In a flash he saw himself as she [Meggie] must have seen him all along. A round, a self-important little man, old for his years, inclined to be pompous, perhaps — terrible thought — even fussy" (64). The development of Abbershaw's character suggests that Allingham intended him to be the main protagonist and principal crime-solver. The other principal player, Alfred Campion, is the only character to be accorded a similarly full description. It seems likely that as her writing progressed Margery changed her mind in favor of Campion.

Against his unpromising qualities, Abbershaw becomes hero material and in the end, to demonstrate that size does not always matter, he gets the girl. The love interest between George Abbershaw and Meggie Oliphant runs throughout the novel and, when Meggie is kidnapped by the gang that takes over the mansion, acts as a catalyst for one of the action episodes with which the book is studded, moving the plot along. Perhaps for reason of the love interest, however, Abbershaw is not quite the main character. After several failed attempts, Albert Campion with outside help effects the rescue of the group from the old house with touches of slapstick and so goes a step further as hero. Yet Campion exits the story with the closure of the mansion episodes and it is Abbershaw and other of the young men who follow up on the gang in London, and it is Abbershaw who solves the murder. The fact that Allingham mixes two separate plots and therefore potentially two separate novels, and creates two leading characters, helps to account for a disorderliness in *Black Dudley* that makes it one of the weakest of her novels. Perhaps for this reason it was not included in the BBC screen adaptations.

Albert Campion is a freelancer who sometimes works for Scotland Yard and the Foreign Office. A campion is a plant with "pink or white notched flowers" of the genus *Silene*, thought to come from Old French *campion* (= champion) used to form garlands for the brows of heroes (COD). The alias suggests that of another fictional character who behaves in the guise of a fool, Sir Percy Blakeney, Baroness Orczy's Scarlet Pimpernel. At several points Campion appears to play the part of coward: "There must have been something pretty big afoot, or he'd have had a minion in for it. Gosh! I wish I was well out of it" (70). On the other hand he takes control in dangerous situations and hints facetiously that his fearfulness and the foolish persona are intended to screen his true nature: "who would dream of the cunning criminal brain that lurks beneath my inoffensive exterior?" (143).

The use of aliases, masks or heroes with no names is a stock feature of the thriller. Alfred Campion makes light of his mystery. He has other aliases such as that of Mr. Mornington Dodd (70) or Mr. Twelvetrees in *Look to the Lady* (474). They hide the highest of aristocratic family connections and are never fully disclosed:

[Abbershaw] Campion — that is your name I suppose?

[Campion] Well — er — no … my own is rather aristocratic, and I never use it in business. Campion will do quite well [71].

We are no wiser at the end:

Mr. Campion leaned over the side of the car until his mouth was an inch or two from the other man's ear, and murmured a name, a name so illustrious that Abbershaw started back and stared at him in astonishment.

"Good God!" he said. "You don't mean that?"

"No," said Mr. Campion cheerfully, and went off striding jauntily down the street until to Abbershaw's amazement, he disappeared through the portals of one of the most famous and exclusive clubs in the world [166].

The true dénouement is left to Abbershaw in his pursuit of the gang member White Whitby (climax) and confrontation with Wyatt Petrie (anti-climax). Allingham hints again at Albert Campion's real identity in *Mystery Mile* where, in the climactic confrontation with Simister, he is told:

"I fancy it is time that you and I had a little discussion together, Mr. Rudolph K." He [Simister] mentioned a name which so startled the young man before him that he betrayed himself with an exclamation [366].

We are still no closer to Campion's real selfhood than in *Black Dudley*. The same happens in *Look to the Lady* (28) when Val Gyrth remarks to Campion: "When you took off your spectacles a moment ago ... you reminded me of..." at which point Campion quickly changes the subject. But later in the same novel (74) we return to the hints in *Mystery Mile*. Mr. Branch, himself an ex-con, tells his old associate Lugg: "Your Mr. Campion ... I shouldn't be at all surprised if 'is real name didn't begin with a K. And figuring it all out, 'is Christian name ought to be Rudolph." This might be a tangential reference to King Rudolph in Anthony Hope's *The Prisoner of Zenda* (1894).

Allingham uses the device of introducing most of the characters through dinner table conversation between Meggie and Abbershaw. This may be contrasted against Edmund Crispin's approach as omnipotent narrator where usually the character profiles are deliberately made the subject of the first chapters, or Gladys Mitchell's young curate as unreliable narrator in *The Saltmarsh Murders* (1392). In rough order of appearance, the cast in *The Crime at Black Dudley* comprise George Abbershaw (doctor), Meggie Oliphant (love interest, damsel in distress), Wyatt Petrie (owner of the mansion, murderer), Colonel Gordon Coombe (Petrie's aged uncle, victim), Michael Prenderby (doctor recently qualified), Anne Edgeware (socialite/actress), Martin Watt ("black-haired beaky youngster"), "little Jean Dacre" (Prenderby's fiancée), Chris Kennedy (Cambridge rugby blue), and Albert Campion. The stereotypes would not be out of place in a board game such as Cluedo.

Anne Edgeware and Jeanne Dacre — the latter described as a "little round shy girl" (13) — are reduced to tears and hysterics by the dangers. Meggie Oliphant is made of sterner stuff:

One of those modern young women who manage to be fashionable without being ordinary in any way. She was a tall, slender youngster with a clean-cut white face, which was more interesting than pretty, and dark-brown eyes, slightly almond-shaped, which turned into slits of brilliance when she laughed. He hair was her chief beauty, copper-coloured and very sleek; she wore it cut in a severe "John" bob, a straight thick fringe across her forehead [11].

The bob was fashionable at this time. See the chapter with Dorothy L. Sayers.

All told, the number of young people comes to nine, the same number as the underworld minions who staff the place for their boss. Most, however, are unnamed hired henchpersons aside from one or two who figure in the action to sufficient extent, such as Weston and Mrs. Browning the housekeeper and her dim-witted maid Lizzie Tiddy. The lineup of major villains includes a sinister German named Eberhard von Faber under the alias of Benjamin Dawlish and his accomplice Jesse Gideon. The Colonel's private attendant is Dr. White Whitby who is in league with the gang. Their physical descriptions mark them out as stock figures for any thriller and, often together with their names, are matters for subtle comedy as Margery gently satirizes the genre. Eberhard von Faber is described as "fat to the point of grossness, but tall with it, and powerfully built. The shock of long grey hair, brushed straight back from the forehead, hung almost to his shoulders, and the eyes ... were bright now and peculiarly arresting" (50). As well as being facially expressionless von Faber speaks in a "deep Teutonic voice" that is "singularly menacing." Jesse Gideon, on the other hand, is "small and insignificant," but he is also "languid and sinuous" (50), snake-like. Dr. Whitby is "grey-haired, sallow-faced" (18).

Physical disproportion, often to the point of the grotesque, is a very common depiction of villains in melodrama. The number of obese men must be legion in comics, pulp magazines, and books of adventure, espionage and horror, even romance. Women of large body size appear, too, but my impression is that they are not so well represented. The opposite of large body size for villains is a representation that goes back as far as Cassius' (368) "lean and hungry look" in Shakespeare's *The Tragedy of Julius Cæsar* (I: ii). Often the two physical types are found together as boss and lieutenant as in *Black Dudley*.

National stereotypes are seldom avoided in this form of novel and Allingham no doubt reflects English attitudes towards Europeans, Germanic people in particular, held at the close of the 1920s. Hitler and the Nazi Party were rising to power at the time *Black Dudley* was published, and there are still strong memories of the chaos of World War I a decade earlier. Interestingly, Allingham appears to conflate the stock figure of the Teuton or Hun with Semitic characters: the alias of "Benjamin" used by von Faber, the double-barreled Hebrew names of his accomplice "Jesse Gideon." Allingham's villainous characters appear to have been German Jews or pretending to those nationalities. One wonders whether Margery was purposely ironic. Although Hitler's full ascendancy and the implementation of the "final solution" were ten years off, the threat represented by him and the Nazi Party was palpable.

During a sort of treasure hunt, an ancient Italian stiletto is passed in the dark from hand to hand among the young people as they wander about the premises. The Black Dudley dagger is: "Under a foot long, it was very slender and exquisitely graceful, fashioned from steel that had in it a curious greenish tinge which lent the whole weapon an unmistakably sinister appearance" (17–18). Such a description would have pleased contemporaries such as John Dickson Carr, an aficionado of ancient weaponry. Allingham and Carr knew each other through the Detection Club and Carr would have read *Black Dudley*. Douglas Greene reports a remark of Carr's in a letter to a friend: "Well I remember a drunken weekend with Margery and Pip Carter at their home in Essex" (199).

Colonel Coombe is found dead, presumably stabbed by the dagger. But gang members carry away the corpse before the old man's doctor can examine it. They ask for a cremation certificate signed by Whitby and Abbershaw together. Abbershaw manages to see the corpse's face and judges from the signs that a massive loss of blood and not heart attack is responsible for the death. There is a fight between Albert Campion and a criminal manservant when a packet containing papers falls and is picked up by Abbershaw, who promptly conceals it. Subsequently Abbershaw destroys the papers while not understanding their significance, a strange act that stretches the reader's credulity. Compare Jenny Windell in Milne's *Four Days' Wonder*, published four years after *Black Dudley*. The destruction or concealing of evidence on the part of an innocent person is a comparatively rare element in crime fiction. This is one of several improbabilities in the novel. Tampering with evidence is usually the work of the criminal.

The German gang boss informs the group that they are under house imprisonment until one of them hands over the thing that was lost. There follow a series of escape attempts that fail one after another until by chance a local hunt club of horse and hounds arrives on the scene to thwart the German's plans and save the mansion from being burnt to the ground. In this conflict Abbershaw is teamed with Campion against von Faber and the gang. The German and his minions are working for a large international criminal syndicate, a hoary staple of the thriller. Leroy Panek in *Watteau's Shepherds* gives an excellent critical overview of the writing of a thriller in Margery Allingham's hands. He describes *The Crime at Black Dudley* as "part spoof, part detective story, and part thriller — a combination which Allingham kept returning to even after she was influenced by the regular detective story of the thirties" (127–128).

Chris Kennedy, the jock of the group, is a secondary comic character. He is a sportsman, described by Abbershaw as a "young prize-fighter" (13), a man of action in keeping with the spirit of the thriller. However, Kennedy comes off badly in several adventures in the novel and one cannot help thinking that Allingham is satirizing the type. In the first incident, Kennedy attempts to escape from the mansion grounds in one of their cars. The gang has drained all vehicles of petrol but Kennedy refuels from their stock of scotch and brandy. However, he is shot and injured by Dawlish. In the second incident in which the group of young men led by Campion turn the tables on the gang, Kennedy is knocked unconscious at the start of the mêlée and left on the staircase, so missing the action. (The group's attempt is unsuccessful and they are recaptured.)

The subplot is the death by stabbing of Colonel Coombe. If developed on its own this might have become a standard "detective story" puzzle. However, Allingham splices the two plots together. Like other writers, she often had a subplot running alongside the main line in her later work that is very often the progress of a love interest. The gang member Dr. Whitby tells Abbershaw: "Perhaps you don't know that for the greater part of his life Colonel Coombe had been under von Faber's influence to an enormous extent" (182). In other words, Coombe was a member of the Simister gang for which von Faber worked. Subsequently Abbershaw, in an interview with Wyatt Petrie, confirms his suspicions that Petrie is the murderer of Gordon Coombe, the motive being that Wyatt after long investigations into the gang finds a connection between it and his own extended family, "my aunt's husband" (191). This appalls him so greatly that, rather than notifying the police, Petrie resolves to take Coombe's life. As a cover, he selects the young members of the party for their spotless reputations hoping that by contrast suspicion will fall upon one of the gang members. Hence the group of young people is used as a cover twice over, both by the criminals as an established practice and by Wyatt Petrie to hide his part as the murderer. Von Faber's decision to conceal the death throws Wyatt's plans into disarray.

These circumstances led Margery Allingham to violate one of the basic rules of "fair play" by allowing the murderer to go free on the grounds that Coombs is virtually a member of the criminal organization and that Wyatt Petrie is single-handedly fighting a social evil, something that Abbershaw remarks "is always a mad thing to do" (192). Other writers such as John Dickson Carr did likewise but it was frowned upon by the writing fraternity of the day. It is one of those "rules" in crime and detective fiction that is broken from time to time and raises controversy but in general is adhered to by most writers.

Margery Allingham herself considered *The Crime at Black Dudley* "not a very good story" (Jones 154). Julia Jones agrees implicitly, saying that it lacks "structural humour" and her impression is "that the bright young things are laughing at their own jokes" (127). I wonder at what point parody ends and self-consciousness peters out before poor writing takes over? In fact, upon a second reading of *The Crime at Black Dudley*, it is not at all bad, and certainly not poor writing, and I do not perceive the young things laughing at their own jokes. Panek's view, with which I agree, is different from that of Jones.

According to Panek, Margery Allingham consciously employs a battery of comic devices to good effect:

> Puns (some good and some groaners), jokes, absurdities, travesties, burlesques, slapstick, and cross-talk acts. No one would call their villainous criminal mastermind "Simister" or Ali Fergusson Barber and expect readers simply to grunt and follow the direct line of the adventure. It is all meant for fun [132].

It is meant also for farce: the fight scenes in which the rugger blue Chris Kennedy is knocked out, and the overcoming of the gang by the horse and hound group are pure slapstick. Allingham's greatest weakness in *Black Dudley* is that, as Panek says (130) in *Watteau's Shepherds*, "she muddles the issue of the leader but realized this and remedied the situation in *Mystery Mile*."

Mystery Mile (1930)

Appropriately for a writer of serialized stories, Margery Allingham's next book, *Mystery Mile* is a sequel to *The Crime at Black Dudley*. When Marlowe visits Campion in his flat above the Bottle Street Police Station to request his aid he is ushered into a luxuriosly furnished room (213) in which is a souvenir, "the Black Dudley dagger" that lies upon a side table as a letter opener. In *Mystery Mile* the identity of Simister is revealed after a series of pursuits, narrow escapes and fighting, continuing the tradition of the thriller. By the end of the novel Simister comes to a sticky end and no less than two love interests are resolved.

This novel is more neatly constructed than the previous one. Once again a group of young people are brought together in an isolated mansion. They are fewer than the nine-strong cast of *Black Dudley*— consequently easier for the novelist to manage — and consist of two pairs of men and women who form attachments between one another, plus the main protagonist Alfred Campion, who in more than one sense is the odd man out. Marlowe Lobbett and Isopel Lobett are respectively son and daughter of the American Judge Crowdy Lobbett. Giles Paget together with his twin sister Biddy is the squire of the village attached to the mansion (or the other way round, the mansion attached to the village). The older cast members include the judge already named, the Reverend Swithin Cush, a family friend and rector of the village; the Rector's housekeeper Alice Broom; the housekeeper of the mansion, Mrs. Whybrow; Ali Fergusson Barber, who is Simister disguised; and Anthony Datchett, confidence man and blackmailer in the guise of palmist/fortune teller. There is also a sort of village headman, George and his son Henry ('Anry) "with their five sons" (239), and a dishonest postman named Kettle, new to the village, who liaises secretly with Datchett by intercepting people's mail in order to provide information with which they might be blackmailed. There are as well an assortment of colorful types and criminals outside the village such as Thos. T. Knapp who assists Campion, although the latter despises him, and Campion's sidekick, the ex-burglar Magersfontein Lugg, who, with his lugubrious nature and as foil to Campion's wit, provides comic relief. Other minor characters include Dr. Wheeler, Peck the police constable from the neighboring village, and McNab, a cipher expert in London. There is also the dog Addlepate who in the tradition of adventure tales is used to carry a note from one hero to others.

Albert Campion's manservant and sidekick in most of the Campion novels is Magersfontein Lugg, "named for a discreditable encounter in the Boer War," says Jones (133). Further, Jones tells us that the character was seen by Philip Youngman Carter as a reification of Margery Allingham's unconscious mind, representing "the stubborn, anarchic part of one's self that remains unsatisfied, uncheered and unconvinced by moments of success" (134). The remark from someone with whom Margery has such a close relationship, though "uncharitable" as Jones says, probably points to the depressive side of Margery's nature. In the fictional tale, the cause of Lugg's pessimism is in his survival of a military campaign that went wrong during a phase of the Boer War. The Battle of Magersfontein took place on 11 December 1899 in which, due to a failure in proper reconaissance, the British under Lord Methuen were defeated with heavy losses and had to withdraw ("Battle of Magarsfontein").

Lugg is not a Watson figure. Although he takes that role occasionally, it is more usually filled by one of the young men involved in the mystery such as Abbershaw in *The Crime at Black Dudley*, Val Gyrth in *Look to the Lady*, or Marlowe Lobbett in *Mystery Mile*. There is instead a joking relationship between Campion and Lugg that turns upon a mutual exchange of insults while at the same time assisting each other. Lugg warns Campion of dangers; Campion needs Lugg's expertise. Contacts from Lugg's criminal past (burglary) make him a unique ally. The incongruity is a source of comedy:

> "Think you're clever, don't you?" he remarked in a throaty rumble. "When you're goin' into really nasty business, 'oo do you get round you? Two ruddy amateurs and somethin' out of a carpet shop.... *Don't* lean against that wall," he added hastily. "It's *me* wot looks after yer clothes, don't forget" [*Mystery Mile* 318].

Campion berates Lugg similarly, which worries some critics. Jones points out that reviewers often do not like the character of Lugg: "His comments on Campion's behaviour are too apt, his treatment by Campion frequently too bad" (134). Jones does not go along with this interpretation and neither do I. When Lugg in *Look to the Lady* (491) is so terrified upon seeing a supernatural creature in the Pharisees' ("fairies") Clearing that he becomes bedridden (the creature is a local witch dressed in animal skins and masked), Campion exclaims: "I go and leave you in a respectable household, and you bellow the place down in the middle of the night" (491). But he is genuinely concerned when Penny Gyrth tells of Lugg's state a page earlier, to whom he says: "I only told him to improve the shining hour by finding out what it was down there. I'll go and see him at once" (490). Magersfontein Lugg is a principal character whose humorous episodes, "comic relief" (Baldick 41), allow for "relaxation after moments of high tension," which is a form of catharsis; but he is more than that because he and Albert Campion share what anthropologists call a reciprocal joking relationship based upon mutual respect hidden behind the masks of mutual disrespect (Gould & Kold 358).

Where does Allingham, and for that matter others such as Dorothy L. Sayers, find their names? Some we might guess. Marlowe, for example, is one of the two chief suspects in *Trent's Last Case* (but predates Raymond Chandler's Philip Marlowe by eight years), McNab is a slightly different spelling of the eponymous character in John Buchan's thriller *John Macnab* (1925). Guffy Randall, who has a small part in *Black Dudley*, while not appearing in *Mystery Mile*, is alluded to in one of Campion's (Allingham's) best jokes. As mentioned earlier, his name is evocative of Wodehouse characters. Some names reflect the occupation of the bearer. That of the housekeeper Alice Broom is self-evident.

The love interests together form an asymmetrical pentagon. Marlowe Lobbett falls in love with Biddy, who reciprocates; Giles Paget falls for Isopel, who also reciprocates. The odd one out of this otherwise neat arrangement is Alfred Campion who is in love with Biddy. These young people have strong qualities. Isopel is "dark, but whereas he [Marlowe] was tall and heavily built, with the shoulders of a prize-fighter, she was petite, finely and slenderly fashioned" (211), "a slim little figure wrapped in furs" (229). Giles too is a sturdy, heavily built man with a square-cut face that is not handsome, "but he had a charming smile" (219). Biddy is "tall as her brother, with a figure like a boy's" (219). She has "a practical nature" (270). The two women are lissome. Their men are hero material. There is a trace of the rugger jock Chris Kennedy from *Black Dudley* in their makeup. One of the women, Biddy, is heroine material. It is she who becomes the damsel in distress, kidnapped by Kettle and handed over to the London gang working for Datchett under Simister.

The physical setting of *Mystery Mile* is a small village of that name situated on an island connected to the mainland by a narrow isthmus cut off in times of storm and flood. It is modeled on a real place, Mersea Island: "connected to the mainland by a causeway, the Stroud, first built by the Romans, which is often covered at high tide" (Jones 73). When Margery was a girl her family used to go on holiday at this seaside village. The villagers of the fictional Mystery Mile are insular, close-knit, presumably somewhat inbred. They are believers in witchcraft and the supernatural. It enables a joke such as that on the new postmaster Kettle: "the village 'foreigner': that is to say, he was not a Suffolk man, but had been born, so it was believed, as far away as Yarmouth, a good forty miles off" (260). Henry, the village rustic, is described by Biddy (232) as a "bokel" that, she explains, "was father's word. It means half a barmy, half a yokel." Mystery Mile is a place that modern cosmopolitan England has passed by. Jones finds Allingham's sense of place "interesting and important" (130). Most of the action unfolds in this isolated spot with the exception of Biddy's rescue scene in London and the shipboard prelude in the first chapter.

That prelude introduces the major characters of Judge Crowdy Lobbett, his son Marlowe, Simister under the alias of Ali Fergusson Barber, and Albert Campion. It sets down immediately what Chris Baldick identifies as Aristotle's meaning of plot (Greek *mythos*) in his *Poetics*, that is, plot as the "governing principle of development and coherence to which other elements (including character) must be subordinated" (171). This governing principle or setup is that Judge Lobbett, who has pursued the Simister organization for years in the United States, is very close to uncovering the arch-criminal's identity and so his life is at risk. In order to protect his father, Marlowe persuades him to take the ship's cruise to England. There have been several attempts either to kill Crowdy Lobbett or to warn him off by murdering others such as his chauffeur, secretary, butler and personal physician (248). This is overkill and Allingham makes a joke of it when she has Campion's response (202) to Simister, identified at this early point by his physical appearance as a Turk with a "curious pear-shaped head": "Four murders in his house within a month? That ought to be stopped. He's been told about it, I suppose?"

The melodrama serves to demonstrate that Simister is a particularly nasty specimen. It is also the first instance of Campion's own ruse as "a mental case." This conversation takes place during the beginning of a disappearing act that is the occasion for another attempt on Lobbett's life. In a style worthy of a Fu Manchu script, the floor of the trick cabinet is electrically wired. Albert Campion prevents Lobbett's death by blundering forward and dropping his pet mouse Haig upon the steel grille. Consequently Haig has a very brief walk-on part. Barber/Simister is set back at the thwarting of his plan, registered (207) by his physiognomy in a nicely villainous touch: "His heavy jaws sagged, his greasy eyes grew blank with astonishment." (No mice were harmed in the 1990 BBC film version.)

Field Marshall Douglas Haig (1861–1928) is a controversial figure. In a an entry "disputed" on grounds of neutrality, a Wikipedia contributor states that in the 1960s "Butcher Haig" was roundly criticized: "for the two million British casualties under his command [during World War I], and ... as representing the very concept of class-based incompetent commanders" ("Douglas Haig, 1st Earl Haig"). From the 1980s, however, his leadership is praised for his new technologies and tactics by which (ironically): "the high casualties suffered were a function of the tactical and strategic realities of the time." This is special pleading. The military outlook appears very similar to that of twenty-first-century warfare, except that today the extensive casualties are among non-combatants as well as the troops. At the time Margery Allingham was writing, with memories of the First World War still relatively fresh in people's minds (the 1920s were a decade of post-war reconstruction) it is likely that negative images of Haig were already present by the time of his death two years before the publication of *Mystery Mile*. Perhaps Ailngham was ritually consigning the field marshal to the flames.

The chief action involves a cat and mouse game between the young people and the criminal groups along the lines of the best of thrillers. With Campion's assistance, the judge goes into hiding. The con man Datchet arrives to read fortunes. Reverend Cush commits suicide after hearing his fortune told. Ali Barber appears on the scene ostensibly as an art critic interested in buying one of the mansion's paintings. Just before Barber's appearance Judge Lobbett disappears when he and the young people are investigating a hedge maze. As in *Black Dudley* the game has sinister outcomes. Biddy is kidnapped by Kettle and taken to London. Campion with Marlowe and Giles and the assistance of Lugg and Thos rescue her, dragging Barber along unwillingly. The whole episode takes up a lot of the novel around its midpoint. They return to the island, having discovered in a newspaper report that Judge Lobbett's cover is blown. He is a participant on an archaeological dig.

The key to Simister's identity lies in a children's fairy-tale book, one among many packed into a suitcase. Upon returning to Mystery Mile they find the housekeeper and Barber chloroformed. Campion takes immediate steps to get the judge out of danger and at the same time to lay a trap for Simister. Returning to the tidal flats via the maze, Campion sends Giles and the judge off in a dinghy. He remains behind in a hut at the edge of the flats to await Simister's arrival. In the meantime he opens a fairy-tale book identified as the one containing the clue, *Sinbad the Sailor and Other Stories*. The title of one of the stories reveals the clue: "Ali Fergusson Barber and the Forty Thieves" Campion exclaims aloud (364). Barber and Simister are one and the same.

The long conversation that ensues between Campion and Simister satisfies one of the traditional dénouements for such thrillers. If it is not a drawing-room revelation before assembled suspects, as in a Christie tale, it is the sometimes gloating disclosure of the murderer to his intended victim. Compare this against the almost reverse scenario in which the investigator with the upper hand confronts the criminal, as in John Dickson Carr's *Night at the Mocking Widow*. In a neat reprise on *The Crime at Black Dudley* it is revealed (366) that it was Simister who commissioned Campion (through his contacts) to be involved in the affair and that when Campion failed he was from then on underestimated. In another touch intrinsic to the thriller, there is badinage between hero and villain about their identities. Simister boasts (368) that he knows Campion's record and implies that Campion risks his reputation by knocking him (Simister) on the head, to which Albert Campion ripostes: "My second name is Morgiana, Mr. Ali Baba." In the Arabian fairytale, Morgiana is Ali Baba's slave girl who thwarts the thieves' attempts on her master's life and so gains her freedom and marries Ali Baba (*Ali Baba*). Here Margery Allingham takes some authorial licence, for in the original medieval Arabic tale Morgiana is Ali Baba's ally and not his adversary.

Action now moves swiftly to conclusion. Campion smashes the lamp. Simister shoots him in the shoulder with an acid gun. Campion falls through a gap in the floorboards upon firm ground beneath the hut. Simister exits the hut and moves around its side in order to gain a clear view of Campion and finish the job. But he loses his footing and falls three feet into quicksand. His struggles are described in the best tradition of the thriller.

In the final chapter, the anti-climax, the last threads in the story are brought together. The Simister gang is no more (283): "Von Faber in Broadmoor; Simister dead," and the asymmetry of the love interests is resolved when Campion bows out. The love triangle between Campion, Biddy and Marlowe is handled subtly by Allingham. There is another good joke:

> "Shocking!" agreed Campion. "I don't know what my wife would say."
>
> Marlowe stared at him. "Good lord, you haven't a wife, have you?" he said.
>
> "No," said Mr. Campion. "That's why I don't know what she'd say" [347].

Its analogue is in Douglas Adams' *The Hitchhiker's Guide to the Galaxy* (65).

This is a case in which Campion employs humor for a more serious purpose, to hide his disillusionment at losing Biddy. The steps that reveal this mood appear at intervals throughout the novel. From the first Biddy sees Albert as a likeable friend more than as a potential lover. When Giles says of Campion "he's not a crook," Biddy replies: "He's not a detective either.... As a matter of fact, he's really a sort of Universal Aunt, isn't he? "Your adventures undertaken for a small fee." Oh, I like Albert" (220).

So when Biddy meets Marlowe it is love at first sight. The sexual cues are easily recognized: "Campion, looking down, saw that she had laid her hand upon Marlowe's arm" (289). In the BBC film version, Biddy complains to Albert Campion that he is a cold personality. As if that is not enough, Isopel with a woman's sensibility tells Campion: "Marlowe is in love with her, you know. I think they fell for each other when they first met" (314). A little later, when they are in the house where Biddy is being held, and as Campion is about to ascend to an upper floor in a dumb waiter to join in her rescue, Isopel asks him to watch over Giles: "you don't know how dreadfully worrying it is to be in love," to which Campion responds: "That's all you know, young woman" (317). By page 337 Campion, "All this time ... had studiously avoided Biddy." Later, Campion makes a joke of it as he prepares to become bait for Simister, but there is a touch of bitterness:

> Tell Biddy, "Smiling, the boy fell dead." ... Should I do so, of course. Tell her she can have Autolycus [Campion's pet jackdaw].... Lugg, too, if she likes. The

woman could hardly hope to forget me if she had those two about the house [354].

The rationalization is complete when he reads Biddy's letter of thanks written in an immature hand: it "might have been a schoolgirl's letter" (381). Campion burns it. The effect on Campion lingers. He broaches the subject of retirement to Lugg who says: "Find the Lady is a Mugg's game" (381). Alfred Campion brightens up, however, when a mysterious new job offer arrives by mail. This note, too, goes into the flames, but now it is the time-honored act of destroying sensitive evidence as a prelude to a new adventure.

The theme of unrequited love reappears in other Allingham novels. Says Lugg in *Look to the Lady*: "If it's anything about a woman, you can tell 'im. 'E's been disappointed 'imself" (35). On the other hand, Albert Campion is attractive to women — Penny (Penelope) Gyrth in *Look to the Lady* throws Campion "a glance of by no means unfriendly curiosity" (51) — and in *Sweet Danger* he meets his future wife.

Look to the Lady (1931) and *Sweet Danger* (1933)

Allingham's next novel *Look to the Lady* (1931) introduces the supernatural more strongly than in *The Crime at Black Dudley* with its sinister Italian dagger, or the background of village superstition and fortune telling in *Mystery Mile*. Popular interest in the occult and spiritualism had grown by the late 1920s. As Jones says: "The need for comfort felt by countless families after the deaths of loved ones, whether in the slaughter of the Great War or the flu epidemic which followed it, had precipitated a resurgence of interest in spiritualism" (72). The theme is taken up by other crime writers of the era. Conan Doyle (1929) wrote several short stories on spiritualism. Dorothy L. Sayers in *Strong Poison* (1930) has Lord Peter Wimsey's secretarial investigator Miss Katharine Climpson, while posing as a spiritualistic medium, use a trick (197) with wires and wrist-hooks inside her sleeves that allow her to move the table during a séance. John Dickson Carr includes plentiful elements of the supernatural in his novels through the 1930s and 1940s. Carr's interest is a special case, for he is an unusual writer with a fixation on the supernatural that, after 1940, had become less important in the English psyche.

Julia Jones states (138) that the tone of *Look to the Lady* is disrupted by Margery Allingham's "sensitivity to such occult survivals." I do not see it that way. The bogus witchcraft surrounding a death, Lugg's terrifying experience that serves also as comic relief, gypsies in the area, and the fall to her death of Mrs. Dick Shannon, head of the Cleaver gang, are key plot points, and the usual ingredients for an Allingham thriller where arch-villains meet a bad end in quicksand, in a mill race or falling from towers. The mystery of the horrifying presence surrounding the Gyrth chalice that resides within the tower is described simply and with enough of a hint to satisfy the frisson of the supernatural that Allingham liked: "As his eye travelled slowly down the great gyves to the wrists, he caught sight of the human hands, gnarled, yellow, and shapeless like knotted willow roots" (270). This image is reproduced faithfully and just as sparingly in the BBC film version. The ghost in the tower is a giant mummified corpse, evocative of Alfred Hitchcock's *Psycho* (1960), except that we do not see its face behind the visor. Like John Dickson Carr, who would have enjoyed this get-up with its tourney armor and giant sword, Margery Allingham provides rational explanations for what at first blush appears to be the supernatural.

Sweet Danger follows the broad pattern of its predecessors. A group of young men with names such as Dicky Farquharson, Jonathan Eager-Wright, and Augustus ("Guffy") Randall with Albert Campion are thrown together in the small village of Pontisbright. Guffy Randall, who has walk-on parts in *Black Dudley* and is the subject of anecdotal mention in *Mystery Mile*, is a major player in *Sweet Danger*. A lot of the story is told from his point of view. They meet a group of likely young women, including Amanda Fitton and her elder sister Mary, also an older woman Aunt Hatt (Miss Huntingforest), and a younger brother Hal. The supernatural is evoked with hyperbole to establish suspense and dramatic tension: "When I said a curse I meant a curse. The place is poisoned. The air you breathe, the soil you walk upon, the water you drink is impregnated, soaked, drenched with the poison" (92).

Alfred Campion at last finds his future marriage partner in a feisty little redhead, the Lady Amanda Fitton. Her physical description stands alongside those of John Dickson Carr's or Edmund Crispin's protagonists:

> Amanda Fitton, eighteen next month, was at a stage of physical perfection seldom attained at any age. She was not very tall, slender almost to skinniness, with big honey-brown eyes, and an extraordinary mop of hair so red that it was remarkable in itself. This was not auburn hair nor yet carroty, but a blazing, flaming, and yet subtle colour which is as rare as it is beautiful. Her costume consisted of a white print dress with little green flowers on it, a species of curtaining sold at many village shops. It was cut severely, and was rather long in the skirt [62].

Amanda is too young for marriage but by the last page she and Campion make a wager to become partners when she comes of age. There is a shadow of Campion's old love for Biddy Lobbett, now Biddy Paget, from *Mystery Mile* but Amanda appears to accept it. In later novels she is mentioned as Campion's wife but does not figure greatly in those stories.

These heroes and heroines are pitted against another criminal organization. There are robberies, kidnappings, a damsel in distress, chases, alarums, and clever ruses before the villains are rounded up. The damsel in distress is a stock figure of the thriller that Margery Allingham places in many of her novels. The criminals have the usual nicknames redolent of the underworld such as "Widow's Peak" and "Sniffy Edwards." The arch-villain Brett Savanake (the name suggesting "snake") comes to the expected bad end, in this instance suitably mangled by a millwheel. It seems even more evident in this story that Margery is parodying not only herself but thrillers in general. As Jones (159) observes, the American publisher retitled the novel *Kingdom of Death* or *The Fear Sign*: "This dark side of the rural coin, however, remains subordinate to the atmosphere of comedy, holiday and Margery's patent affection for the village she had known since she was a child." The criminals may be menacing, but they are thwarted as often as they cause trouble, and a lighthearted atmosphere comes through among the young men and women.

Margery Allingham's Comedy

Margery Allingham is among the best of the humorists. Indeed, she perceives herself as a writer of comedy rather than as a crafter of detection puzzles: "Murder as an intellectual puzzle, à la Dorothy Sayers and the Detection Club, was, Margery found, 'a chastening ride for any aspiring writer of Comedy'" (Jones 142). She never quite fit that mold and it is no wonder that she felt ill at ease among members of the Detection Club who put so much store on puzzle solving.

The primary figure of fun is Albert Campion, but there is an element of mystery as well, introduced very early in *The Crime at Black Dudley*, in his first appearance as an Allingham character. However, the circumstances in which he joins the group come with a trivial mystery, a magic trick: "He came down in Ann Edgeware's car," says Meggie (14), "and the first thing he did when he was introduced to me was to show me a conjuring trick with a two-headed penny — he's quite inoffensive, just a silly ass." Similarly, in *Look to the Lady*: "A tall thin young man with a pale inoffensive face, and vague eyes behind enormous horn-rimmed spectacles smiled out at him with engaging friendliness" (16). Albert Campion belongs to the type of disingenuous fool or eccentric whose odd behavior masks a detecting ability greater than those around him. It is a well-established character type that includes Christie's Poirot, Carr's Sir Henry Merrivale, and Crispin's Professor Gervase Fen.

But this is too broad because other forms of humor make the novels so enjoyable. For example, Albert Campion and others satirize the emotional responses of some players as well as their physical appearance. Abbershaw's reactions to Meggie's light-hearted declaration of her love for him because she finds him "adorable" (65) allows Allingham to satirize romantic love: "A slow, warm glow spread all over Abbershaw. His heart lollopped in his side, and his eyes danced." One pictures an ungainly dog (COD). Similarly:

> Wyatt Petrie looked what he was, a scholar of the new type. There was a little careful disarrangement in his dress, his brown hair was not quite so sleek as his guests, but he was obviously a cultured, fastidious man: every shadow on his face, every line and crease of his clothes indicated as much in a subtle and elusive way [11–12].

This would not be out of place in a satiric novel of manners.

Another form of joking is the wry or witty anecdote "real" or invented:

> "I knew a man once," [Campion] said, "who managed by stealth to attend a Weevil Sabbath at Mould. He went prepared to witness fearful rites, but when he got there he found it wasn't the genuine thing at all, but the yearly outing of the Latter Day Nebuchadnezzars, the famous grass-eating society. He didn't see a single weevil" [*Mystery Mile* 236].

This joke is both real *and* invented. There is a town called Mold in North Wales but Google Earth shows no place in England spelled Mould. At first this appears a trifle silly, but by chance I found a link to its likely origin in Barbara Reynolds' biography of Dorothy L. Sayers. In 1926 during the General Strike Sayers became involved in writing a humorous brochure for a stunt run by S. H. Benson, the advertising company for which she worked. This was the founding of the fictitious Mustard Club advertising Colman's Mustard. Reynolds cites from the Club's prospectus which "proclaimed that it was originally founded by Aesculapius, the god of medicine, in the days of Ham and Shem. *Nebuchadnezzar was one of the earliest members, finding mustard a welcome addition to his diet of grass*" [my emphasis] (165). Reynolds continues: "This is Dorothy of the Oxford days, frivolling among her witty friends, her happy and creative self again."

The Biblical allusion reflects Dorothy L. Sayers' well-read Christianity. The root source of Nebuchadnezzar's association with grass is in the Authorized Version of the *Bible* (Stirling 700) in the Book of Daniel 5:31–34. Sayers would also have seen the series of "Large Colour Prints" begun by William Blake in 1795 in *The Marriage of Heaven and Hell* now held in the Tate Britain art gallery on Millbank, London (*Nebuchadnezzar* [Blake]). Margery Allingham used it in *Mystery Mile* some four years later.

Campion is not the only character who tells humorous anecdotes. One of the best of Allingham's jokes is told by Giles Paget in *Mystery Mile*:

> He's an extraordinary chap. Apparently he turns up after dinner at country houses and shells out the past and present for five bob a time. Anyway, that sort of thing. Rather funny: he told Guffy Randall that a beautiful creature was going to throw him over and he was going to be pretty seriously hurt by it. Guffy was quite rattled. He didn't ride to hounds for a fortnight, and it wasn't until Rosemary Waterhouse broke off their engagement that he realized what the chap meant. He was awfully relieved [234].

Another element is the frequent use (and abuse) of puns and malapropisms.

"The time for maypolin's past," he went on, "and Pharisees [fairies] Day, that ain't come yet."

The young man [Campion] sighed. "None of these — er — feasts are movable?" he suggested hopefully [*Mystery Mile* 227].

"Monsieur Randall," he said with a gulp which he could not quite repress, "you are a veritable hero. The — how shall I say? — the pineapple of your race" [*Sweet Danger* 42].

He simply set himself up as a "fence," and let it be known in the right quarter he would pay a fabulous sum for the article indicated. I daresay it sounds rather like a "Pre-Raffleite" [*sic*] Brotherhood to you [*Look to the Lady* 26].

Mr. Barber appeared interested. "In the maze?" he said. "Ah, yes, I see now. He is in the bush, as the Australians say."

"Well, we're all a little up the garden this afternoon," said Mr. Campion [*Mystery Mile* 267].

The example from *Look to the Lady* is a visual pun for the reader on E. W. Hornung's eponymous gentleman burglar in *Raffles* (1899) perhaps not readily understood unless there is some sort of verbal inflexion to put the point across. The last pun, drawn on the expression to lead someone up the garden path — that is, to trick or to mislead — seems to be that the disappearance of Judge Crowdy Lobbett in the maze is glossed over for Barber's sake as an unwanted visitor. It gains more point later when it is revealed that (a) Lobbett's disappearance was engineered between him and Campion to hide him from the gang seeking to kill him, and (b) Barber's true identity is Simister the arch-criminal.

Albert Campion does not always have it his own way in repartee laced with humor. In an exchange between him and Amanda Fitton in *Sweet Danger*, Campion's absurd flight of fancy is neatly turned upon him:

"I knew a man once.... His name was Gosling, you see, so he always dressed in grey and yellow, and occasionally wore a great false beak. People remembered his name, of course. But his wife didn't like it. Of course, he had perfectly ordinary children — not eggs — and that was a blow to him. And finally he moved into a wooden house with just slats in front instead of windows, and you opened the front door with a pulley on the roof. It had a natty little letter box on the front gate with 'The Coop' painted on it. Soon after, his wife left him and the Borough Council stepped in. But I see you don't believe me."

"Oh, but I do," said Amanda. "I was his wife. Come and see the mill" [73–74].

We see that Campion and Amanda are soul mates.

To her cast of characters Allingham adds an assortment of village eccentrics. Another bird joke appears in *Sweet Danger*: "From the moment they approached the front door, an air of faintly hilarious unreality descended upon the whole proceedings," an atmosphere reinforced the next moment when they meet Scatty Williams:

The man really was amazingly like a duck. His head was very bald and very white, but his face was a yellowish tan. There was a ring just above his ears which showed quite clearly where his hatband finished, and his face and neck were exposed to the elements. Two little bright blue eyes almost hidden by shaggy grey eyebrows were set close together beside the narrow bridge of an enormous nose, which splayed out at the tip so very like a duck's bill that one almost expected him to quack. To add to the incongruousness of his appearance he was wearing a white dress waistcoat of ancient cut which had been fitted with white sleeves, so that it faintly resembled a cocktail jacket. For the rest, however, he was arrayed in corduroy trousers, enormous boots and a very bright blue shirt without a collar [59–60].

Animals figure in several of the Campion jokes, a motif that brings to mind Edmund Crispin's "totemic" beasts in such tales as *The Glimpses of the Moon* (dog, cat, tortoise), and in *Look to the Lady* (69–70). Albert Campion also brings together Allingham's theme of the supernatural as well as her predilection for animal witticisms. When Allingham writes several pages later that: "Mr. Campion, whose imagination ran always to the comic, was reminded of a conjuring trick" (87), she might as well have been writing about herself.

Some of the jokes are of the reference group sort, reflecting Margery's enjoyment of American film and pulp novels. Albert Campion, again in *Sweet Danger*: "I think like that. I spend so long at the movies that I've picked up their culture" (98), and Amanda Fitton's expression: "Speaking as a soul not yet mated, nerts" (198), an Americanism that could be straight out of Dashiell Hammett. When Campion enters Xenophon House to meet Savanake: "He had been prepared for a palatial office, but not for this. Here was a shot from one of the more fanciful German films" (119). Allingham may have had in mind Fritz Lang's Expressionist science fiction film *Metropolis* (1927).

Other puns more visual than verbal include the interior of Albert Campion's apartment above the Bottle Street police station as described in *Look to the Lady*:

There were several old trophies on the walls, and above the mantelpiece, between a Rosenberg drypoint and what looked like a page from an original "Dance of Death," was a particularly curious group composed of knuckle-duster surmounted by a Scotland Yard Rogues' Gallery portrait of a well-known character, neatly framed and affectionately autographed. A large key of a singular pattern completed the tableau [16].

Campion's entrance into the hands of the criminals while feigning toothache, his face partially hidden by a huge handkerchief, begins with satiric repartee when he is asked his business by the woman receptionist:

"Campion," said the young man again. "A hot, fiery plant under the jurisdiction of Mars. And I've come about the papers. Large, flat, white things. You must have heard of them. I'm sorry I can't speak more clearly, but I've got toothache" [115].

This is a key plot point, for Campion switches identity with an assistant under cover of the handkerchief so that Savanake thinks he has spirited his enemy out of the country on a ship bound for South America where his life would be short.

Julia Jones notes a shift in the presentation of Albert Campion over time that reflects a maturing in Margery Allingham's writing, saying that in the earlier novels Campion was a "type" and not a "personality" as he was to become in the later books: "In a generation still laughing off the effects of the Great War she was not the only writer who relished fatuousness" (128). For certain effects Allingham writes thumbnail descriptions of a character's physical traits including that of Albert Campion. The stock description of Campion's physical appearance begins of course in the first Campion novel, *The Crime at Black Dudley* as "the fresh-faced young man with the tow-coloured hair and the foolish, pale-blue eyes behind tortoiseshell-rimmed spectacles [with] slightly receding chin and mouth so unnecessarily full of teeth" (14). It is equally as unflattering as that of Abbershaw. When a principal character is set up in this way their description has to be repeated with each new novel. This calls for inventiveness in writing variations on the theme (see also Edmund Crispin's Professor Fen). In *Sweet Danger*, for example, Campion is described in the following terms: "As Guffy stared, a pale, somewhat vacant face came into view. Sleek yellow hair was brushed back from a high forehead and pale blue eyes were hidden behind enormous horn-rimmed spectacles. The expression upon the face was languid and a little bored" (20). This is an improvement on the receding chin and too many teeth.

Albert Campion's persona improved over time commensurate with a gradual reduction in the ruse to present himself as a fool, so that he becomes a lot more serious in Allingham's later novels. This shift is especially apparent in the short stories published in 1939 (*Mr. Campion and Others*) where the vacuous look is only fleeting, though with Campion this usually means that he is paying close attention to a problem. In "The Hat Trick," "Mr. Campion's lean face took on an even more vacant expression" (54); in "The White Elephant," "Mr. Campion's pale blue eyes grew momentarily more intelligent behind his horn-rimmed spectacles" (119). In the short stories Albert Campion shows emotions more readily, laughing, apologetic, apprehensive, protesting or long-suffering when bright young women make irrational statements or admit they are indiscreet. His role has become more like that of the universal aunt or uncle by which he is described originally or, more appropriately, that of an older man who is a confidant to young women. He is in his late thirties by this time. Chloe Pleyell in *The Question Mark*:

"Albert, my pet," she said, "I want your advice. I don't know if I've been frightfully clever or terribly childish."

Her host resisted the impulse to cover his eyes with his hand.

"Criminal?" he inquired casually [78].

This is a different sort of humor and a far cry from Margery Allingham's first Albert Campion stories. It achieves polish in the short stories. Badinage is still present but now there is maturity, as in "The Frenchman's Gloves" when Campion gently teases Felicity Carrington:

I deduce from certain phenomena, obviously invisible to you but stunningly clear to me, that you, young lady, have been buttering me up all the afternoon with intent to convert my power to possible use in the near future ... that you have a small private mystery that you'd like cleared up, and that that mystery is connected with the venerable old Balsamic [a hotel]. Am I right? [141].

The old trick of spinning a tall tale is present but now it has the imprint of an older man.

Virtually all the tales in *Mr. Campion and Others* open with a young woman in trouble, Allingham's damsel in distress in a slightly different guise, lovely but to be read not as stupid *per se* but as engagingly scatterbrained. When Albert Campion meets Susan Chad in "A Matter of Form," these thoughts pass through his mind: "Changing fashions produce changing women ... but there is one type of girl who never differs. In tiger skins, crinolones [*sic*], or A.T.S. uniform she remains herself, dear, desirable, and chuckle-headed as a coot" (247). Through Albert Campion, Margery Allingham reveals her accommodation to the end of the 1930s. This end as described in "The White Elephant" might refer equally well to Campion's age or to the close of the decade: "Mr. Campion smiled ruefully. It was a sign of the end of the thirties, he supposed, when one submitted cheerfully to the indignity of taking a young woman out only to hear about her hopes and fears concerning a younger man" (121).

World War II was touched upon in Allingham's description of Campion's lean body and face, suggesting not only aging but also the results of food shortages. From "A Matter of Form": "looking a trifle thinner and grimmer in these days" (241). While continuing to indulge in badinage as in "The Frenchman's Gloves" above, Albert has almost given up on it in "The Name on the Wrapper" because: "Idiotic conversation, although invaluable, was not a luxury which he often permitted himself now that the thirty-five-year-old landmark was passed" (42).

There is more of the puzzle element in the short stories, to which the form is well suited. Most have the framework of a dear and desirable young woman who comes to Albert Campion with a problem that is revealed often as a trick played upon her by a conman or blackmailer. There are complications, a trap is laid followed by conflict, sometimes physical, the trap sprung and Inspector Oates (Campion's good friend) takes away his catch.

Several major characters from the novels appear in the short stories; others do not. There is no love interest to speak of for Albert Campion, although the plots of the short stories usually involve the presence of a young lady and her swain, often with a hated rival who turns out more often than not to be the criminal. Campion's manservant, although mentioned frequently in passing, is never named. In the short stories Magersfontein Lugg, to all intents and purposes, is out of the picture. Campion's Scotland Yard friend Superintendent Stanislaus Oates (nicely played by Andrew Burt in the 1989–1990 BBC television series) appears in most of the tales where as often as not he is called in to wind up the case by arresting the suspect(s). The other ubiquitous character is that of the forbidding older woman. In one instance, "The White Elephant," there is a reference to "the Denver woman [who] lost her emeralds" (120), which must be a salute to Dorothy L. Sayers' character the Dowager Duchess of Denver, mother of Lord Peter Wimsey.

A growing seriousness in the characterization of Albert Campion continues in the later writing. By the time Margery Allingham writes *The Tiger in the Smoke* (1952), Julia Jones tells us: "Her Campion novels were becoming more profound but taking considerably longer to write" (286). We have our best samples of her comedy in the earlier novels, and some elements of it in the later short stories. Like many of the authors in our list, Margery Allingham becomes more serious in later life to the extent of world-weariness, and her shifts in outlook are reflected in these stories and the development in them of her long-standing characters, with her illnesses and personal troubles always watching over her shoulder.

Five Women of
the Golden Age

In addition to Margery Allingham, five women wrote what was in most cases detective/crime fiction, often with an admixture of the thriller. Like Allingham they were born at the turn of the century and lived through the Golden Age. Some are well known, others less familiar. Between them they represent the two ends of the continuum for humorous writing. Dorothy L. Sayers and Ngaio Marsh created dense mysteries characterized by wit and affable male detectives touched lightly with eccentricity. Sheila Pim wrote gentle satires on Irish village life and manners using horticultural settings and motifs. Gladys Mitchell with her creation of the crone-like Mrs. Bradley has a detective of considerable eccentricity. Caryl Brahms wrote satire with a strong flavor of slapstick based upon her intimate knowledge of classical ballet.

Dorothy L. Sayers (1893–1957)

The following comes largely from Barbara Reynolds' biography of the lady. Dorothy L. Sayers, pronounced "Sairs" according to Reynolds (361), was born in Oxford on 13 June 1893. She died on 17 December 1957 at the age of sixty-four ("Dorothy L. Sayers"). Dorothy came into a well-read middle-class family. Her mother Helen Mary Leigh was the daughter of a Hampshire solicitor ("Dorothy L. Sayers"). Her father Henry Sayers was an Anglican clergyman, headmaster of the Christ Church Choir School (Reynolds 1). He introduced her to Latin when Dorothy was six, read to her, and joined in her childhood theatrical games based on *The Three Musketeers* (Reynolds 206). In a somewhat unusual mental association, Dorothy, upon discovering Dante's *Inferno* in 1944 at the age of fifty-one, remembered having read *The Three Musketeers* when she was an adolescent. Both works gave her great pleasure: "I can remember nothing like it since I first read *The Three Musketeers* at the age of thirteen" (cited in Reynolds 354).

When she was sixteen Dorothy attended Godolphin School in Salisbury, starting in January 1909, and two years later won the Cambridge Higher Local Examination (top in all England) with distinctions in French and spoken German (Reynolds 42). In 1911 she gained the Gilchrist Scholarship to Somerville College in Oxford and became one of the few women allowed into the university sphere. She threw herself into university life, attended a lecture by G. K. Chesterton that she liked and one by G. B. Shaw that she disliked. In these years she took up smoking and remained a heavy smoker all her life. She graduated in 1920 with the degree of Master of Arts. Apparently in a state of political unawareness Dorothy with two friends left on holiday for France in 1914, returning to England within days of the outbreak of war, a circumstance similar to that experienced by John Dickson Carr and his wife and by Nancy Spain and her friend Winifred Sargeant in 1939. Dorothy took up her old life at Oxford where the First World War passed her by.

Wartime was not as personality-forming as other experiences. Sayers wrote poetry, was hospitalized for appendicitis, survived the influenza epidemic, and formed a close association with Captain Eric Whelpton. When Whelpton took up teaching at a boarding school in Normandy, Dorothy joined him as his secretary. She had fallen in love with the man but his affections lay elsewhere. This was the first of Dorothy's disappointments in love. She could have entered upon an academic career but this did not appeal to her, although her skills lay in that direction and she was a schoolteacher at different times in her life. In 1921 she returned to the rectory in Christchurch and completed a novel.

Sayers managed to lead an active social life in London despite living in "penury" as Reynolds puts it (106). Her London life was divided between writing her first two novels, teaching, and translating. She also fell in love a second time, with John Cournos, a writer of "pretentious" novels (116). Dorothy and Cournos lived together on and off. Cournos visited her in her London flat and made use of her. After her parting with Cournos and on the rebound Dorothy had a relationship with a man named Bill White, a motorcycle rider and car salesman with a rough, macho self-image. White left Dorothy when she fell pregnant to him: "On 3 January 1924, in Tuckton Lodge, Ilford Lane, Southborne, she gave birth to a son.... She named the baby John Anthony" (Reynolds 124). Like Nancy Spain more than twenty years later, Sayers did not fully own up as mother of the boy.

This practice of disowning the child while doing everything else to give the growing person economic and quasi-family support is notable. Social disapproval towards single mothers that clearly spanned thirty years (a generation) is a possible explanation. Individual shame at having been compromised may have been an additional psychological factor. In Nancy Spain's case she bore Thomas Bartholomew Laurie Seyler out of wedlock in 1952 after what was likely a one-night stand with Margery Allingham's husband Philip Youngman Carter (Collis 132). Spain and her partner Joan Werner Laurie included Tom in their family together with Joan's male child Nick Laurie, passing Tom off as Joan's child.

Dorothy L. Sayers did this a little differently. Sayers placed her child in the care of a cousin, Ivy Amy Shrimpton, who with Dorothy's aunt Amy fostered (boarded) children as a livelihood. Dorothy kept the child's parentage hidden from her aunt ("Dorothy L. Sayers") while she paid for the costs at the house and remained in touch with John Anthony throughout his life, posing as a sort of aunt: "Tony was told that 'Cousin Dorothy' and Fleming had adopted him when he was ten. As the legal parent, Dorothy had no need to adopt him.... Sayers continued to provide for his upbringing, although she never publicly acknowledged him as her biological son" ("Dorothy L. Sayers"). As Reynolds says:

> With Ivy's help she had given him everything possible, except the acknowledgment of him as her son among her friends. It has been said that he resented this in later life. If so, it was something she had also denied herself.... As her letters show, she continued to do so [doing the best she could] until her death, in 1957. Under her will, he was her sole beneficiary" [346].

This is special pleading, for Reynolds is Sayers' goddaughter ("Dorothy L. Sayers") and tends to be somewhat uncritical.

From this point Sayers may have begun suffering from an eating disorder brought on by emotional stress. Reynolds notes (129): that Sayers became "grossly overweight" due to her liking for wine and good food, the self-indulgences a reflection of her preference for "the decencies of life" (134) over the rewards of romantic love.

But in the second half of 1925, a fourth man enters Dorothy's life: Oswald Arthur Fleming, nicknamed "Mac": "a journalist, working for the *News of the World*, a member of that tough, masculine society she had come to know in Bill's company, the world of pubs, of car salesmen, racing motorists and journalists" (Reynolds 153), worlds in which many of the other writers in my list moved. Dorothy and Mac married on 13 April 1926 (Reynolds 154) and were together until Mac's death on 9 June 1950 ("Dorothy L. Sayers").

Dorothy continued to live well and to put on weight alarmingly. Fully conscious of her physical image in public, she made what Reynolds (204) describes as "one of the watershed decisions for women at that period: to bob or not to bob," and had her hair cut in the Eton style. She may also have taken to wearing mannish clothes, white blouse and jacket, perhaps indicated in a photograph some years later in 1937 (Reynolds 280). In general she favored loose fitting dresses that flattered her frame. She was strikingly handsome, but allowed herself in later life (during the 1950s) to become unkempt in private, neglecting her appearance at home as well as disregarding her health: "She smoked heavily and put on a great deal of weight" (Reynolds 361).

Against the background of the General Strike of 1926, Sayers settled into her life as copywriter for S. H. Benson's advertising agency in London, a position she held from 1922 to 1931, where one of her notable contributions was the founding of the fictitious Mustard Club ("Dorothy L. Sayers"). Although we associate the 1920s with the jazz era, flappers and gaiety, it was a time of immense social pressures. People looked for distractions from their troubles and writers tended to meet these needs with agreeable diversions, for themselves and for a livelihood as much as to entertain readers. Dorothy L. Sayers did this in the marketing campaigns and by consolidating her writing of detective fiction.

In her literary persona, Sayers met members of the Inklings group such as J. R. R. Tolkien and C. S. Lewis, although she did not join the group or attend its meetings ("Dorothy L. Sayers"). But she grew more active later as a founding member of the Detection Club when it was formed around 1929, becoming the club's president from 1949 to 1957. Ironically enough, her period of crime writing was over by then and she had turned to religious themes and non-fiction. In Douglas Greene's biography of John Dickson Carr, there is a diverting photographic plate (between pp. 266 and 267) of Dorothy L. Sayers posed fondly holding the Detection Club's mascot Eric the Skull. Sayers was nearly always an imposing figure with a strong scholastic temperament that placed her somewhat apart from her fellow writers of detective fiction, journalists and playwrights. She intimidated Margery Allingham who describes her as "school-mistressy" (Jones 44).

During the 1920s, Sayers studied criminology and gradually refined her creation of the two chief protagonists in her crime series, Harriet Vane and Lord Peter Wimsey. She wrote more than seventeen Lord Peter Wimsey novels and some short stories, most in the period from 1923 to 1939. In Dorothy's first novel *Whose Body?* published in 1923, Lord Peter Wimsey makes his début (101). Sayers' crime output in the Peter Wimsey stories includes: *Whose Body?*, *Clouds of Witness* (1926), *Unnatural Death* (1927), *The Unpleasantness at the Bellona Club* (1928), a short story collection *Lord Peter Views the Body* (1928), *Strong Poison* (1930), *Five Red Herrings* (1931), *Have His Carcase* (1932), more short stories in *Hangman's Holiday* (1933), *Murder Must Advertise* (1933), *The Nine Tailors* (1934), *Gaudy Night* (1935), and *Busman's Holiday* (1937). There were about nine other works of crime fiction, some published posthumously. Translations and commentaries on Dante (principally *The Divine Comedy*) came later, and many essays and various non-fiction, much of it with strong religious (Christian) themes. Her work, then, has two broad phases: crime writing through the 1920s and 1930s followed by Christian themes after the Second World War when she was in her late forties ("Dorothy L. Sayers").

Barbara Reynolds (307) suggests that Sayers' change of life may have had a lot to do with the sudden shift from writing crime fiction to religious novels, commentary and translation: "Not enough is made in biographies written about women of the dynamic effects of the menopause. It often happens that the change in hormonal balance and the realignment of psychic forces result in a clarification of purpose and a redirection of heightened energy," with, one might add, a complete change of direction. Sayers "got religion" and like other writers such as Nancy Spain and Edmund Crispin became more conservative in later years.

In Edmund Crispin's case, while he gave up crime writing more or less, it may not have been directly due to alcoholism because he continued working in other fields. He seems to have reached the point where he was burnt out on crime novels, with the exception of his tour de force *The Glimpses of the Moon*. In Dorothy Sayers' case, Reynolds adds that she reached the conclusion that "detective stories tended to have a bad effect on people, making them believe that there was one neat solution for all human ills and she would have no more part in encouraging such an attitude" (339). This is very like Nancy Spain's misgivings that her Miriam Birdseye and Natasha Nevkorina novels were unsuitable for the two boys she and Joan Werner Laurie were raising.

As well as Alexandre Dumas' picaresque adventure tales of *The Three Musketeers*, read when she was thirteen and dramatized in playlets performed at home, other literary influences on Dorothy L. Sayers in her early years are as diverse as Lewis Carroll and Joel Chandler Harris (the Uncle Remus Brer Rabbit stories) from the folklore and fairy tale genres that remained a passion all her life (Reynolds 190). When Dorothy was eighteen and preparing for the Cambridge Higher Local Examination, she read three texts: "Molière's *Le Misanthrope*, Corneille's *Le Cid* and Racine's *Britannicus*" (Reynolds 42). These are acknowledged as the three great playwrights of seventeenth-century France ("17th-century French literature"). Molière specialized in comedy, Racine and Corneille in tragedy. It is a big step for Dorothy L. Sayers from folk culture to high culture through childhood to late adolescence.

A few years on when she was with Eric Whelpton and twenty-six years old, Sayers slipped back into low culture by reading crime stories in her spare time (Reynolds 93). When in the same year (1919) Whelpton fell in love with a married woman and Dorothy by chance (or was it psychosomatic?) came down with mumps, she plunged deeper into low culture by asking her good friend Muriel Jaeger to send as many Sexton Blake thrillers as she could find: "The Sexton Blake romp was an anticipation of the contributions she was later to make to the higher criticism of the saga of Sherlock Holmes" (Reynolds 95). By 1921 Dorothy was studying books on criminology in the British Museum's Reading Room, and writing her own crime novel, *Whose Body?*

Sayers was herself to have considerable influence on the fields of literature in which she wrote. The one most relevant to us is introduced not only by her crime fiction but also through her literary criticism. Two essays stand out. The first is a statement so definitive of detective crime fiction that it remains highly readable today, her introduction to *Great Short Stories of Detective, Mystery and Horror* that she edited for Victor Gollancz in 1928. A second of note is the lecture she delivered at Oxford in 1935 on "Aristotle and the Art of Detective Fiction." On that occasion she met Roy Ridley, the chaplain of Balliol, whose "Height, voice, charm, smile, manner, outline of features" so impressed her that she used Ridley as the model for her character Lord Peter Wimsey, not recalling that she had met him many years earlier in 1913 (Sayers cited by Reynolds 56). The essay on Aristotle is collected in the 1946 volume *Unpopular Opinions* together with a variety of others on such topics as "Forgiveness," "Towards a Christian Æsthetic," "The English Language," "Are Women Human?," "Living to Work," and "Dr. Watson's Christian Name." Sayers wrote a number of essays about the Sherlock Holmes tales. Other writers who impressed her were G. K. Chesterton and P. G. Wodehouse.

It appears, however, that the detective story most influential in her writing was E. C. Bentley's *Trent's Last Case*, already a classic when Sayers was starting her Lord Peter Wimsey novels. Reynolds mentions Bentley's novel several times in her assessments of Sayers' work. For example, on Trent's levity, literary quotation, prattling, bursting into song or whistling a Bach piece, impetuosity, and mental agility, Reynolds notes that: "Some of Lord Peter's mannerisms are also deliberately evocative of P. G. Wodehouse's Bertie Wooster. She used them because they entertained her" (175).

Love interest is a special case. It would have been difficult for Dorothy to write upon this theme after experiencing one unrequited crush (Eric Whelpton), a lover who used her flat as a dormitory (John Cournos), and another lover who abandoned her when she became pregnant (Bill White), followed by a lukewarm marriage of convenience with Oswald Fleming. At the same time, Sayers felt that "there is a great deal in what Chesterton says about its usefulness as camouflage" (Reynolds 138). Sayers coped with love interest both real and novelistic by fictionalizing the undesirable qualities of her ex-lovers in what Reynolds (113) describes as "the novelist's way." Hence Bill White's coarseness is reflected in Lord Peter Wimsey himself when teasing another man in *Clouds of Witness* (Reynolds 120). John Cournos is mirrored in the character of Philip Boyes in *Strong Poison* (Reynolds 112). Appropriately, this character is Harriet Vane's former lover and murder victim. Like Cournos in real life, Boyes wishes Harriet to live with him out of wedlock, something that Harriet refuses to do. Later Harriet finds that Boyes is not against the idea of marriage and had been testing her, whereupon she breaks off their relationship. Through the strong poison of the title, Sayers fictionalized Cournos and presumably got him out of her system by indirectly revealing his hypocrisy and marking him out for murder (arsenic in the omelet).

Writing in order to entertain oneself is shared by most of the writers in our list. They do not write solely to entertain the reader and so to earn a livelihood but also take personal pleasure in the composition of their work. For Sayers, "pattern was always something she delighted in" (14). There must also be greater fun for those with a disposition for writing tongue in cheek. Dorothy L. Sayers, however, belongs to the more serious minded, as Reynolds says delighting: "in puzzles of all kinds — cryptograms, codes, and especially crossword puzzles, a new craze in the 1920s to which she at once became addicted" (195). This preference arguably prevented her from great flights of comedy. Her humor is light, subtle, ironic, and far removed from the flights of slapstick found in Allingham, Carr or Crispin, or the verbal burlesque of Nancy Spain. Sayers' writing is definable more as a comedy of manners with an underlying seriousness, a trait for which she is sometimes criticized.

One of Sayers' strongest critics is Julian Symons, who in general finds her work "long-winded and ludicrously snobbish" (99) and describes *Gaudy Night* as "essentially a 'woman's novel' full of the most tedious pseudo-serious chat between the characters that goes on for page after page" (118). Symons has a point. Sayers wrote in a dense and often discursive academic style that came straight out of her experiences at Somerville College, Oxford, in drama and prose literature, perhaps also her poetry. She was not alone in this respect. Michael Innes (John Innes Macintosh Stewart) wrote in a dense style, too, but I think with greater success. His detective output is impressive with forty-five novels over fifty years (Collins), at least thirty-two of which are Inspector Appleby stories ("J. I. M. Stewart"). But as for *Gaudy Night*, the long-windedness and pseudo-intellectual conversation is the whole point. Sayers was depicting through Harriet Vane a familiar aspect of academic life. Having spent most of my professional time lurking on the fringes of Australian universities, I assure readers that "pseudo-serious chat" does take place in those environments, though no doubt with an Australian rather than an Oxford flavor.

What Sayers was writing in *Gaudy Night* was an ironic comedy of manners fleshed out with elements of the gothic and the thriller. No person is actually murdered. It is a crime story with no corpse, but with plenty of gothic atmosphere supplied in the poison pen and destruction of property by a deranged staff member. Colin Watson, whose *Snobbery with Violence* I thoroughly recommend, cites a 1934 *Daily Express* review on Sayers which announces that she "eclipsed Edgar Wallace and Conan Doyle" (150). Wallace is well known as a writer of thrillers with a touch of the gothic, and Conan Doyle too produced adventure and supernatural tales as well as featuring his better-known detectives Holmes and Watson.

Gaudy Night was first published in 1936 when Sayers was at the peak of her powers with eight Lord Peter Wimsey novels behind her. As Binyon says, more charitably than Symons, *Gaudy Night* "treats, in subtle and interesting fashion, the problems of women's education and the role of women in society" (59). The following where Harriet Vane goes to the horse races and sees Lord Peter in the near distance is a fair instance of Sayers' mature writing:

> She went down to Ascot ... partly for fun and partly because she wanted to get local color for a short story, in which an unhappy victim was due to fall suddenly dead in the Royal Enclosure, just at the exciting moment when all eyes were glued upon the finish of a race. Scanning the sacred precincts, therefore, from without the pale, Harriet became aware that the local color included a pair of slim shoulders tailored to swooning-point and carrying a well-known parrot profile, thrown into prominence by the acute backward slant of a pale-grey topper. A froth of summer hats billowed about this apparition, so that it resembled a slightly grotesque but expressive orchid in a bouquet of roses. From the expressions of the parties, Harriet gathered that the summer hats were picking low-priced and impossible outsiders, and that the topper was receiving their instructions with an amusement amounting to hilarity. At any rate, his attention was well occupied [60–61].

Her artful satire is directed at several targets: detective-story plotting, women's colorful hats contrasted against the man's sober phallic top hat, Lord Peter Wimsey's tailored clothing, and frivolous racecourse betting. Harriet's sense of being an outside observer is communicated satirically through the religious reference to "sacred precincts" — the racecourse enclosure for the elite — contrasted against standing beyond the pale. Hats at race meetings are as traditionally absurd now as they were then. Metaphor of the sort called metonymy — "naming an attribute or adjunct of a thing" (Appignanesi and Garratt 61) — carries us through the rest of the paragraph. Lord Peter's slim shoulders "tailored to swooning-point" present the image of a dandy, contrasted immediately against the maleness of his "parrot profile." The topper and the flowery hats, attributes of the women and the man, are very subtle sexual images. A "froth of summer hats" billows against the topper in an old metaphor of water and phallic object (sea and cliffs, lake and island, tarn and tower). As if that was not enough we have the "orchid in a bouquet of roses," both flowers symbolic of womanhood and "slightly grotesque" because the center of attention is a man. The almost hidden sexual content is apposite because Harriet is trying to ignore her feelings towards Lord Peter. There is a lot more to Dorothy L. Sayers' writing than Symons appears to see.

When Dorothy L. Sayers passed away suddenly from a stroke on 17 December 1957, seven years after the death of her husband, she was well established in the two worlds of crime writing and Christian (High Church) commentary, drama (as in the 1941 cycle of plays titled *The Man Born to Be King*) and translation with Dante's *The Divine Comedy, Part 1: Hell* (1949) and *The Divine Comedy, Part 2: Purgatory* (1955). Today many of her Lord Peter Wimsey novels and short stories are available under the imprints of HarperCollins and

Hodder & Stoughton (New English Library), and three BBC 1987 dramatizations of *Strong Poison*, *Have His Carcase*, and *Gaudy Night*. As with many other writers in my list, television and film dramatizations of Dorothy L. Sayers' novels are available for the enjoyment of new generations.

Ngaio Marsh (1895–1982)

Ngaio (pronounced "Nye-o") Marsh was born in New Zealand on 23 April 1895 and died on the 18 February 1982 at the age of eighty-six. She received her education at Christchurch in New Zealand as a foundation member of St. Margaret's College, and at the Canterbury College School of Art where she studied painting before taking up live theater with the Allan Wilkie Company of touring players. She was also a theatrical producer and interior decorator (Collins). After 1928 when she was now thirty-three, she divided her time living in England and in New Zealand. Like many antipodeans of her time, Marsh was an anglophile, hence the frequent settings of her novels in English country houses *à la* Agatha Christie and the others. She never married, nor did she have children. For the Canterbury University College Drama Society she produced a modern-day dress version of *Hamlet* in 1942, and in 1949 with her students she toured Australia performing versions of *Othello* and Pirandello's *Six Characters in Search of an Author*. The University of Canterbury named their Ngaio Marsh Theatre in her honor and her home is preserved as a museum ("Ngaio Marsh").

Between 1934 and 1982 she wrote thirty-two crime novels that place her among other prolific writers of the Golden Age. Marsh's first novel, *A Man Lay Dead* (1934), introduces her favorite protagonist Chief-Inspector Roderick Alleyn, called by Collins: "a good solid and erudite character benefitting from one of Marsh's greatest strengths, her ability to give all of her characters depth and colour." *The Inspector Alleyn Mysteries* (2009) — originally aired in 1990 and 1994 — are adaptations from several novels for BBC television, with the omission of *Surfeit of Lampreys*.

Marsh has been classed with Sayers, Allingham and Christie among "the four original Queens of Crime" ("Ngaio Marsh"). The fashion for listing writers among "four originals" or one of a "big three," and so on has to be taken with a grain of salt. Gladys Mitchell, for instance, is named as one of the "Big Three women detective writers" (*see* below), although we are left to guess the identities of the other two. It is more accurate to say that there are in excess of three or four notable queens or kings of crime fiction in the Golden Age.

Surfeit of Lampreys (1941) is the tenth of Ngaio Marsh's detective novels and belongs with others that employ wry wit and understated, often elegant, humor. As Mike Grost finds on his web site *A Guide to Classic Mystery and Detection*: "The opening chapters seem like a sparkling novel of manners, with sophisticated characters and comedy, an interesting cultural background, often centering on either the theater or the arts, and a great deal of gracefully written prose." I find this too in *Surfeit of Lampreys* which as a comedy of manners has similarities with the writing of Dorothy L. Sayers.

Mike Grost writes a good critique of Marsh's compositional techniques. He notes that her novels:

> Follow a common pattern. There is an opening section, which introduces the characters and sets up the background of the crime. This section is quite elaborate, lasting roughly four chapters.... It climaxes with the actual murder. At this point, Police Inspector Roderick Alleyn enters, and spends the next 150 pages investigating the crime.

This is more or less the pattern in *Surfeit of Lampreys*. To Grost, Marsh's chapters introducing the murder and the rest of the novel devoted to solving the crime read "like two different books." One of the weaknesses of the framework, then, is that "the elaborate but boring murder investigations waste far too much time." It is a criticism similar to that of Julian Symons towards Dorothy L. Sayers' work. All the same, Grost sums up by saying: "The books fall proudly and clearly into the paradigm of the Golden Age detective story. Marsh was not at all ashamed of being a mystery writer. She just wasn't very good at it. At least much of the time." A likely explanation for this weakness in Marsh's work is that live theater was her passion and writing crime novels merely a pastime, as she herself said. Collins (who echoes Grost) thinks that:

> The theatre based novels are very successful, holding a fine balance between detail, authenticity and the danger of boring the reader with excess. When not based in the theatre, Marsh tended to set her novels in the "English Country Village" and these were not quite as polished.

Surfeit of Lampreys has a gruesome enough murder that we do not reach until page seventy-seven when Lord Wutherwood is found in the lift of the family's London flat, a long needle embedded in his left eye. The crime scene is disturbed and potential evidence compromised. Wutherwood is carried to another room where he takes time to die. The character from whose point of view the story largely is told, Roberta Grey, wipes blood from the wall of the lift. Contradictory and often obstructionist acts and statements among what Inspector Alleyn calls (144) a "collection of certifiable grotesques" move the plot along that it is Alleyn's task to unravel. The "inconsequent family manner" (13) or, put differently, "great industry [of the Lampreys] in underlining their eccentricity" (226) suggests the theme that things are not always what they seem. The family, like their namesake, are slippery as eels. The lamprey or lamprey eel is defined as a fish-like vertebrate. The play on words of the title that flags this characterization refers to King Henry I (c. 1068/1069–1135) who is said to have died of food poisoning after over-eating this favored meaty dish ("Henry I of England").

Her mind seemed to change gear and she found herself thinking of the Lampreys as strangers. "I don't know what they are like," thought Roberta in her cold panic. "I have no knowledge of their reality. I have fitted their words and actions into my own idea of them but my idea may be quite wrong." And she began to wonder confusedly if anybody had a complete secret reality or if each layer of thought merely represented the level of someone else's idea of the thinker [108].

Roberta's confused thoughts reflect the tenor of the novel, to which her conclusion might apply as well in the minds of some readers: "'This won't do ... Stop!' Her mind changed gear again."

In all of this there is not a deal of humor beyond the wry comedy of manners among irritating family members and gentle bantering exchanges between Chief Detective-Inspector Alleyn and his sidekick Detective-Inspector Fox. Alleyn, for example, often addresses his assistant fondly as "B'rer Fox." Instead, *Surfeit of Lampreys* tends more towards the serious puzzle-solving side of the dichotomy that in one instance is contrasted against fantasy. In a virtually obligatory reference to crime fiction Alleyn states to the gathered family members:

Detective fiction has made so much of homicide investigations that I'm afraid to most people they suggest official misunderstandings, dozens of innocent persons in jeopardy, red herrings by the barrow load, and surprise arrests. Actually, of course, the investigation in a case of homicide is a dull-enough business [114].

Caryl Brahms (1901–1982)

Born on 8 December 1901, Caryl Brahms did not commence writing farce in detective story mode until around the age of thirty-six when she collaborated for a productive period of twelve years with S. J Simon (Seca Jascha Skidelsky, nicknamed "Skid" by Brahms). Their first novel was published in 1937. Between them they wrote four comic crime tales: *A Bullet in the Ballet* (1937), *Casino for Sale* (1938), *Envoy on Excursion* (1940), and *Six Curtains for Stroganova* (1945) until Simon's death in 1949 aged forty-four (*Classic Crime Fiction*; "Caryl Brahms"). They also worked together on a number of comic unreliable histories about the Elizabethan, Queen Anne and Victorian periods and were involved in writing radio and screenplay adaptations, both together and separately. Simon was a championship player of bridge on which he wrote a book: *Why You Lose at Bridge* (1945).

Both are from Jewish families. Caryl Brahms (Doris Caroline Abrahams) comes from Sephardic Jews originally from the Iberian Peninsula (Spain and Portugal) that immigrated to Britain from Turkey. S.J. Simon, born in Manchuria in 1904, belongs to a Russian-Jewish family of Vladivostok ("Caryl Brahms"). Brahms was educated at the first Jewish boarding school in Britain,

Minerva College in Leicester, then became a student at the Royal College of Music before turning to journalism writing for the *London Evening Standard* and, later, as ballet critic for the *Daily Telegraph*. Brahms received the Ivor Novello award for composing and song writing in 1966. Simon went to the University of London and studied forestry in the 1920s before he met Brahms.

Both writers brought different skills to the collaboration, Brahms with her knowledge of ballet, "purposeful but disorganized" and Simon who was "anarchic," says Ned Sherrin (iv) although there must have been a level of organization with the assistance of a skilled bridge player. Sherrin too had a collaborative partnership with Brahms and wrote a memoir about her. The most striking thing in these collaborations is that they take place within a comic tradition. Sherrin, for example, worked for BBC television satirical shows like *That Was the Week That Was* and *Up Pompeii!* It is a feature common in the avocations of several others in my list that they write lighthearted crime stories while engaged in their day jobs with BBC radio and television (John Dickson Carr, Edmund Crispin, Nancy Spain). Sherrin (vii) remarks that Brahms' work with Simon "overshadowed" their other less frequent jobs, an indication of how well the partnership took off. Sherrin (iii) also cites a comment in Brahms' memoirs about the fun of collaborative writing and makes a distinction between two sorts of humor: "I carry as a true-penny [honest fellow] Skid's pejorative, 'That's not humour, it's wit'—OUT!— by which he divided humour that bubbles up from the diaphragm — from wit which is a mental exercise." In general, while wit also is a form of humor, that which bubbles up from inside is the chief characteristic of the humorists: satire, burlesque, quirky wordplay, and so on. These characterize the novels of Brahms and Simon. As Sherrin observes:

> Although the book can be read as a classic crime story, its great delight is comedy, and it is hardly surprising that there is some laughter at the expense of the Golden Age of the genre, not least through the offices of Detective-Inspector Adam Quill of the Flying Squad [v].

Collaborations are not always made in heaven and are unusual when they happen felicitously. Consider the mix of enjoyment and stress shared between Margery Allingham and Philip Youngman Carter in the production of Margery's Campion novels, or the awkwardness between a reluctant E.C. Bentley and H. Warner Allen over *Trent's Own Case*, or John Dickson Carr's diplomatic collaboration with the touchy Adrian Conan Doyle. But that between Brahms and Simon appears an exception. Brahms writes: "In *Bullet* the Brahms-Simon mix was all too apparent. Skid took over the detection and the love scenes and I did the ballet bits" (iv). Brahms is cited again: "Skid and I laughed our way through a World War and in doing so forged our reputation" (vii). On his collaboration with Brahms, Ned Sherrin says (vii) that it "began with a modern restatement of *The Beggar's Opera* for deprived children and an adaptation of the Brahms-Simon Shakespearean novel, *No Bed for Bacon*."

In the limited sources available — *Wikipedia* entries and *Classic Crime Fiction* — there is no hint that Brahms and Simon were sexual partners nor is there mention of Caryl Brahms having married. Simon married a woman four years younger named Carmel Withers. They were both relatively short-lived, Simon dying suddenly aged forty-four in 1948 and Carmel the following year at the age of forty ("Caryl Brahms"). Ned Sherrin was gay: "he was a patron of the London Gay Symphony Orchestra." He died of throat cancer in 2007 ("Ned Sherrin").

It may be argued that these farces are slight. *A Bullet in the Ballet*, which is generally regarded as the best, is the length of a novella at about 48,000 words. Brahms and Simon receive no mention from two major critics, Leroy Lad Panek in his two books and in Julian Symon's study. But they are acknowledged briefly by Howard Haycraft and T. J. Binyon. Haycraft uses the terms *farce* and *travesty*, the second reminding me of Bakhtin's definition of Carnival: "All out farce is the stock in trade of ... [Brahms and Simon], better known as serious writers on the ballet, who have outrageously travestied the world they know best in *A Bullet in the Ballet* (1938) and later scandalously funny works" (195–196). Binyon also calls it farce as well as identifying other elements of the genre such as allusions and parody:

> Among the comic extravaganzas written by Caryl Brahms ... and S. J. Simon ... are four which could be termed detective stories, although Inspector Adam Quill, who constantly consults his *Detective's Handbook*, seldom solves a case. It is the mixture of running gags, parody, allusions, exaggerated characters, and knockabout farce which makes them amusing and highly readable [124].

The focus on the major character Stroganoff, however, leaves the impression that *A Bullet in the Ballet* is a one-joke novella: "Go away. You must not interfere with the Inspector who has come to arrange an assassin for us" (13). There are points of comparison between *Bullet* and Nancy Spain's novels. As Ned Sherrin says: "Everyday Russian words masquerade as the names of characters" (v). Stroganoff, literally meat strips cooked in a sour-cream sauce, speaks in fractured Russo-English somewhat like Natasha Nevkorina: "Poof ... the money it interests me not. I am an artist. How much?" (49). Contemporary celebrities get a mention. Lord Beaverbrook, who Nancy Spain admired and for whom she worked, is alluded to in *Bullet* as Lord Buttonhooke (40). Spain's books were written more than a decade later and she might well have read *A Bullet in the Ballet*. The inversion of what is expected, verging upon travesty, is a nice example of the carnivalesque when the action of another ballet — Nevajno's *Gare du Nord* (this appears to be fictional) — is described in the following terms: "It did not help Quill much to be told that the station was the Universe, the train Fate, and the passengers the nobler emotions of the human soul, such as hatred, jealousy, vanity and greed" (132).

The puzzle that D. I. Adam Quill confronts is: "The murder of two dancers — in the same ballet, in the same role, at the same theatre, within four days of each other" (99), to which he attempts to apply: "the three cardinal clauses in the Detective's Handbook" (11): Means, Motive, and Opportunity. Quill is six foot three, of *matinée* idol material, a handsome appearance that contrasts against his fallibility as a detective who in his first case arrests the wrong person (10). Added to this fallible detective is a more general reference to the genre: "Almost, felt Quill, he would have preferred one of those cases where all the doors and windows were locked and nobody had been near the house; one of those cases where you had only to discover how it was done and the murderer fell into your handcuffs automatically" (103).

In the end, when the murderer proves to be the aging trouper Puthyk, it is Stroganoff who has the last word in a letter to Quill:

> First he kill Pilaff in Paris, but we all think it suicide. Then he stay up on the opposite balcony and shoot Anton, and still we do not suspect him. Even you, Mr. Quill, who are trained to catch assassins, did not suspect. And still the old one he do not get his role. So he say to himself— this Pavel — he is a dancer mediocre, good to support the ballerina, but he has not the fire for Patroushka. It is a crime against art that he dance it. Poof! I kill him before he can begin.... But when the time come Kasha has danced the role well. The old man is a connois- seur. He sees the role is safe in the ballet while Kasha he is with us. For himself he cares no more. And so he does not shoot [158].

While appearing unusual, the murders fit in with the typology that lists security among the motives. The shootings are committed in the name of art.

Sheila Pim (1909–1995)

There is no entry on Sheila Pim in the *Wikipedia*, perhaps because from a mass-market viewpoint she is a relatively minor writer with a small oeuvre, four of which are crime fiction. Three are "novels of Irish life" and three are non-fiction (Rue Morgue Press). The crime fiction she wrote in humorous vein comprises *Common or Garden Crime* (1945), *Creeping Venom* (1946), *A Brush with Death* (1950), and *A Hive of Suspects* (1952), all published by Hodder & Stoughton. They are country garden mysteries, Irish style. *Creeping Venom* at more than 56,000 words is a standard length. The brief profile on Pim in *Classic Crime Fiction* says that:

> Sheila Pim, born 1909 to 1995, only wrote six mystery books and had no series character. The books would appear not to have been issued contemporaneously in America. The books are not particularly common, especially so in their origi- nal dustwrappers, some of which benefit from attractive artwork.

This has since been set right by Rue Morgue Press.

Tom and Enid Schantz (3–4) tell us that Pim was born in Dublin on 21

September 1909. Her father is described as a Quaker, presumably Irish, and her mother as English. She had a twin brother who died soon after birth and a brother Tom two years older who was "developmentally disabled" and lived for fifty-seven years needing full-time care. Sheila became a Francophile, attending the French School in Wicklow County, going to a finishing school in Switzerland, and graduating from Cambridge's Girton College with a Tripos (Honours bachelor's degree) in French and Italian. Those student days were "one of the happiest periods of her life." Family responsibilities took over, however, and her mother's illness and the need to care for the disabled brother forced her to return to Dublin and discontinue most of her own projects. In 1940 her mother Margaret died and the household was left in Sheila's hands.

Sheila Pim herself fell ill and wrote about it in her first book, *Getting Better: A Handbook for Convalescents* (1943). The large garden attached to the Georgian house where the family now lived gave Sheila experience in horticulture (growing fruit and vegetables) that led to the writing of a gardening column for the *Irish Times* and a gardening magazine *(My Garden)*. Her manuscripts were neatly typed on good quality paper, a point that impressed the editor. Many of her contributions to that magazine were collected in *Bringing the Garden Indoors* (1949).

After her father's death in 1958 and another move to a house in Old Conna at Bray, Sheila again fell ill. During her illness and convalescence she brought out her next novel, *The Sheltered Garden* (1965), described by the Schantzes as "a witty novel of manners with a few mystery elements but a great deal of gardening" (4). At that time she was also researching her major non-fiction work *The Wood and the Trees* (1966, 1984) which was the biography of Augustine Henry, a famed collector of plants who co-wrote a definitive book about the trees of Great Britain and Ireland. When in 1964 brother Tom died in an accident and Sheila became free to follow her own path, she did not continue writing detective fiction but instead worked for the Friends Historical Society in their museum. She also espoused the cause of a maligned section of Irish society, the gypsy-like Travellers, sometimes derogatorily called Tinkers. Deafness in her final years forced Sheila to live in a "sheltered housing complex," and at the age of eighty-six she died on 16 December 1995.

Sheila Pim's literary heritage is the thriller. She read the nineteenth-century *Boy's Own* tales that probably included *Boy's Own Magazine* (*circa* 1855), the *Boy's Own Paper* (founded 1879) or *Boy's Standard* (c. 1883) and others (Turner 49, 73–74, 96–103). She was also alert to the argot, clichés, and street language of the American magazines, no doubt what we identify as the pulp trade. *Creeping Venom: An Irish Gardening Mystery* (1946/2001) is set in a small village. Pim's knowledge of horticulture makes the novel an opportunity for educating the reader in a variety of flowers and other plants that grow around the village both wild and cultivated.

An elderly martinet of a woman, Miss Hampton, dies suddenly after eating snails prepared in the French manner. The poison is aconite, found in the deadly nightshade that grows in out of the way places about the village. Several people fall under suspicion: Mrs. Shegog, a witch-figure who curses Hampton over the escape of her billy-goat, the male heir to the mansion Liam Hampton, and Priscilla Hoyle who was the old woman's general help. The subplot is a love interest built up slowly between Priscilla and Liam. A young man of twenty-one, Tim Linacre, a brash fellow wet behind the ears, plays at detective. He is a general nuisance to the others, including the police, but in the end it is he who solves the death as accidental.

The snails eaten by the old woman are in fact the vector for the poison, for they are fed on copious amounts of deadly nightshade. Apparently slugs and snails thrive on the plant, hence the title of the novel, a pun on the slow onset of the poison and the slow-moving snails. However, the title has a double meaning. "Creeping venom" refers as well to the insidious spreading of suspicion through unfounded village gossip. Ironic humor comes from the social interrelations between persons, conveyed through their private thoughts as well as through dialogue. There are also moments of near slapstick: the pursuit of the errant goat, the collapse of an upper story floor and discovery of horses' bones beneath the floorboards. Religious intolerance of the snobbery kind is expressed through the disapproval of "mixed" marriages between Protestants and Roman Catholics.

Pim's characters are treated with light satire and empathy. Miss Hampton, for example:

> Had been the richest woman in the district for eighty years, and had grown richer and richer through losing one kinsman after another. She had always had enough to eat, but had completely missed sex life, had found that most people sooner or later asked her for subscriptions, had learned to see through people and order them about. So they had come by different routes to the same level of lonely old age [22].

This by comparison with the other old lady, Mrs. Shegog:

> "I have never seen any the size of them [snails].... Wherever did they come from at all? [She is told from England].... Ah, the poor creatures!" Mrs. Shegog meant the English, not the snails. "I suppose they'd eat anything there, as things are at present [20].

Village gossip is nicely represented, as too are the names of characters and the apparent love triangle between Liam Hampton, Meriel Booley Browne, and Priscilla Hoyle. These elements come together in a conflict introduced in page twenty-six:

> Mrs. Booley Browne turned red.... She was not going to have it said that Meriel was flirting with Liam Hampton.... The other ladies thought that, if the friend-

ship was not likely to lead to anything, Miss Hampton would not be showing such anxiety to discourage it. Mrs. Linacre thought Liam was foolish to prejudice his prospects. Mrs. De Vigne feared he was being got hold of. Miss Tench thought it would be good for Miss Hampton not to get her own way. Biddy Gahan and Ursula Owler thought it was romantic. Miss Counsel thought Meriel was a minx. Mrs. Gahan, the bank manager's wife, thought of something her husband had let drop once about the old lady's financial position, something she still remembered because he had told her to forget it [26].

Intertextual allusions are scattered through the novel, but the examples are few, subtle, and not as labored as in Edmund Crispin's prolific treatments. For example: "Tea was to Mrs. Hoyle what a straight rye is to Mr. Lemmy Caution" (94). This character from detective noir fiction and film is "a witty, crafty womanizer.... When playing Lemmy Caution, Eddie Constantine often approached pretty ladies with a glass of whisky in one hand and a cigarette in the other" ("Lemmy Caution"). The situations appear appropriate to the intertextuality, with the contrast between a tea-drinking Mrs. Hoyle and a whisky-soaked fictional detective, or with characters from high literature (*Jane Eyre*, *Pride and Prejudice*) in the comparison of a romance between Liam, educated at a public school and Oxford, and Priscilla, a ladies' companion. Priscilla sees Liam through romantic eyes: "She had sized up the situation as regarded Liam by now, and could not help being interested because he was so handsome. He was like Rochester, or Mr. Darcy. She could not resist mentally fitting him out with the appropriate whiskers" (30).

There are serious overtones as well. Tim, the irritating boy detective, learns the ethical lessons of crime-solving: "Once you start suspecting people, there's no end to it" (102). And there is a touch of hysteria on the part of Mrs. Linacre: (129): "We know this dreadful wickedness is in the air, and that somebody capable of murder is still at large, and none of us is safe until the police find out what happened, and as far as I can see they never will" (129). But this is not a dark novel. No real murder is committed: "The solution of the mystery of Miss Hampton's death proved rather an anti-climax" (127).

Sheila Pim was thirty-seven when *Creeping Venom* was published and reflects a measure of wisdom I think gained from the family hardships she went through following the death of her mother six years earlier: "enchantment lies on the future when you are young; on the past when you are old" (145). To this is added a wry humor that rests upon gentle and often subtle irony. The seriousness of a suspected crime is counterbalanced by this humor that at times diverges entertainingly into slapstick as when Priscilla and her mother discover a chamois leather packet of diamonds hidden within the mattress of the deceased Miss Hampton's bed amid: "clouds of feathers [that] tickled the Hoyles' cheeks and hands, and caught in their hair" (89–90).

Gladys Mitchell (1901–1983)

Born on the 19 April 1901 at Cowley in Oxford at the start of the brief Edwardian era, Gladys Mitchell lived for eighty-two years until her death on the 27 July 1983 ("Gladys Mitchell"). After she began writing her Mrs. Bradley mystery stories, Mitchell produced a novel a year virtually throughout her life. She became a member of the Detection Club and in the 1930s was ranked among the "Big Three women detective writers," the other two doubtless Agatha Christie and Dorothy L. Sayers ("Gladys Mitchell"). Her first novel, *Speedy Death*, came out in 1929 and her last, *The Crozier Pharaohs*, was published in 1984. With sixty-seven Mrs. Bradley novels, she was almost as prolific as John Dickson Carr.

Despite this impressive oeuvre, Mitchell is another writer of the Late Golden Age whose work lay forgotten until comparatively recent years. She is omitted from Forshaw's "Rough Guide" and by Panek in his two critical studies, surprisingly, and receives only one or two lines in passing from several other critics. Julian Symons (109) gives her a paragraph in his overview of "Humdrums" in which he finds her virtually unreadable, her books "average" and spoilt by "travelogue details" and uninteresting dialogue. T. J. Binyon (26–27) is less harsh. He places the character of Mrs. Bradley in the sub-group of psychiatrist-detectives and flags the rising reputation of the author. His main criticism (27) is that too much is made of "witchcraft, the supernatural, folk superstitions" that rest upon intuition and so go beyond psychological (Freudian) deductions. Colin Watson (237) refers in passing to Mitchell's "end-of-chapter red herrings" when discussing "the pornographic core" of the Ian Fleming James Bond pulps. (In a quotation culled by Watson we find that Fleming actually used the old cliché of a Bond woman's "proud breasts"). Haycraft (195) calls Mrs. Bradley "an entertaining character ... if some of her psychological discussions are not quite fathomable." Since then, several of Mitchell's novels are in reprint from Vintage Books and the Rue Morgue Press:

Mrs. Bradley is one of the true eccentrics among unusual detective characters:

> She was smallish, thin and shrivelled, and she had a yellow face with sharp black eyes, like a witch, and yellow, claw-like hands. She cackled harshly when William was introduced and chucked him under the chin, and then squealed like a macaw that's having its tail pulled. She looked rather like a macaw, too, because her evening dress was of bright blue velvet and she was wearing over it a little coatee ... of sulphur and orange [*The Saltmarsh Murders* 1931, pp. 24–25].

There is a BBC DVD box set of the Mrs. Bradley stories (2007) with Diana Rigg at seventy-four in 2012. Still svelte and elegant, Rigg does not cackle, nor is she a crone.

The Saltmarsh Murders (1932) is the fourth in Mitchell's series of Mrs. Bradley stories. It is the first book in a list cited to illustrate Mitchell's "strengths and style" along with *When Last I Died* (1941) and a number of others ("Gladys Mitchell"). One of these strengths is the creation of suspense. There is intimation of murder done, or to come, in the second chapter "Maggots at the Moat House..." ("maggot" = a whimsical fancy, OED), but this does not take place until chapter six. In the meantime, the missing person, Mr. Gatty, is described (25) as "a horrid little man" in keeping with the tradition that murder victims in the Golden Age are generally not missed and provide more of a pretext for deduction and the fun of the chase and problem-solving than moral outrage. It is a feature of the genre at this time that readers are often met with lightheartedness during world crises such as the General Strike in 1926 or the rise of Nazism in Germany in the 1930s. It is a very old phenomenon of the human creative spirit.

In establishing suspense over Mr. Gatty's disappearance there is a touch of the thriller and the gothic: the unfortunate man is found (30) still alive in the crypt of an ancient church. Old quarry holes are traps for the unwary and have their share of the sinister. Stealthy movements are heard (35) on a cottage roof. Jason Hall sums it up in a capable review:

> Miss Mitchell seems to pay homage to her comic contemporary, the great P.G. Wodehouse. (The prolific author is referenced a couple times by Saltmarsh's curate Noel Wells, who under other circumstances would fit right in bunging breadrolls about at the Drones Club with Bertie Wooster and his ilk.) Yet the narration is not mere imitation of a comic novel; propelling the story is a very clever, very busy mystery plot, and one which succeeds nicely on the terms of the genre.

Hall's review finds the later novel *When Last I Died* equally praiseworthy though he is somewhat uncritical about Mitchell's "expert execution" and "the very quality of these qualities." He adds, however, that Mitchell in this later novel is more somber in tone than in the satires of her early writing. This is another feature common in work by Golden Age writers: they become more serious in their later years, often influenced by world crises such as the Second World War.

Irrespective of Hall's approbation ("quality of these qualities?"), I see why Symons finds Mitchell's novels unsatisfying. *The Saltmarsh Murders* and *When Last I Died* are clever, the plots interesting, the satire entertaining, and overall Mitchell's work deserves attention. But Carr and Crispin, whom she must have met through the Detection Club, were producing better stories. They too slipped into the literary shadows, forgotten in the disillusion of the Second World War, the Cold War that followed, and the shift in crime writing towards the noir end of the spectrum. It is perhaps a sign of our present times that they are rediscovered and their best work increasingly available to a new critical readership.

CHAPTER 6

Best of the Farceurs II: John Dickson Carr (1906–1977)

John Dickson Carr (III) was born an only child in 1906 on November 30; he died on 27 February 1977 aged 71. His father Wooda Nicholas Carr was a Pennsylvanian Congressman ("John Dickson Carr") whose career in journalism along with that of the grandfather John Dickson Carr I pointed his son in that direction. The grandmother Amanda M. Cook encouraged his interest in reading (Greene 2), as did some of his teachers when Carr was in his mid-teens: "His favourite classes were the literature classes taught by Reardon S. Cotton, who encouraged John to become a writer" (Greene 11). Three other influences, however, were not as auspicious: a domineering mother, a heavily drinking father, and relatively short physical stature. These influences dogged John Dickson Carr III throughout his life.

Carr's mother, Julia May Lenox Kisinger (*Books and Writers*), and his father appeared mismatched in the eyes of many of their neighbors. Carr's biographer Douglas Greene notes that: "While Wooda was mild ... Julia was emotional, temperamental, exuberant, and frequently sarcastic ... [with] a sharp tongue ... [and] absolutely no interest in books" (7). Whether this is indicative of a personality disorder such as bipolarity or schizophrenia is difficult to say. It certainly affected the son all his life. When family life became intolerable due to the mother's berating of both father and son, John would retreat to an attic room where he wrote or read. Carr in later life often preferred to work in an attic. Says Greene: "It seems safe to assume that every time a strong-minded or man-dominating woman appears as a character in one of his books, she is based at least in part on Julia Kisinger Carr" (9).

A feature of such appearances, notably in the Sir Henry Merrivale novels, is slapstick events in which such characters receive a pie in the face metaphorically if not in actuality. Carr's father Wooda reacted differently. Says Greene: "Later in life, he would have to be hospitalized for alcoholism before finally giving up the bottle" (8). Paradoxically, Wooda and Julia appeared to enjoy each other's company in later years — the woman appears to have settled down — and when Wooda was ill at the end of his life Julia nursed him without complaint (Greene 8). As for their son, the pattern applies of children taking up a parent's weakness: "Most of his life Carr was a serious drinker and smoker" (*Books and Writers*). Predictably, Carr died of lung cancer when he and his wife were living in Greenville, South Carolina ("John Dickson Carr").

John Dickson Carr was educated at Hill School and Haverford College (*Books and Writers*):

> As a student at the Hill School and Haverford College, he wrote stories in all these genres, but his most memorable was a series of creepy detective stories featuring Henri Bencolin of the Surete, the best of which featured murder in a locked compartment of a "Ghost Train" [*MysteryNet*].

Schoolday likes and dislikes find their way into a lot of his writing. For example, Greene (12) notes that his books often contain disparaging comments about mathematicians and mathematics: "the last refuge of the halfwit," while on the other hand his interest in journalism continues. When school ended for the day and during the summer vacations he frequented the offices of the *Uniontown Daily News Standard* (13) and by 1920 when he was fourteen he was already covering sports events and, more significantly, murder trials. Greene points out (15, 16) that Carr was influenced by his boyhood and adolescent reading of fantasy, detection and historical romance by such authors as G. K. Chesterton (Father Brown detection), Arthur Conan Doyle (detection), Gaston Leroux (horror, historical romance)—*Phantom of the Opera* (1910)— and the adventure tales of Dumas and Stevenson: "and a wide range of ghost stories from Washington Irving and Edgar Allan Poe to the macabre exuberance of H.P. Lovecraft" (*MysteryNet*).

In 1969 at the age of sixty-three, and eight years before his death, Carr wrote that like his father he was influenced for the surprise endings and the characters in the O. Henry tales (Greene 20). Too much can be made of influences in early life that set a writer upon their path. Tales such as those mentioned above were a staple for many young men of Carr's time (I read Conan Doyle, Dumas and Poe in my adolescence). What makes the difference is that John Dickson Carr was stimulated to write such stories himself.

The factors in Carr's early life are linked through a domineering mother, retreat to reading in isolation, engagement with the real world of crime journalism, and experiments in writing. On this evidence, John Dickson Carr's career alternated between seclusion and conviviality, fantasy and real life, brought together and somehow unified by his writing. Seclusion is generally expected of writing, which is in itself a difficult strategy. Compare the work habits of Margery Allingham who dictated many of her stories and whose output might be said to have been cooperative to some extent, and certainly sociable. Carr's work regime is similar to that of many writers in that it is done in isolation. As Liukkonen and Pesonen (2008) put it:

> It is reported that he often wrote for eighteen hours at a stretch, forgetting meals. For help with his plotting he relied on the substantial reference library of works on crime that filled the shelves of his New York home. His thorough research for details and visits to likely sets resulted in authentic settings, which especially gave his historical novels air of plausibility. However, Carr's tone was playful, and eerie atmosphere of the murder scenes was often created in tongue-in-cheek spirit and at the end all "supernatural" elements are explained by rational causes.

From 1922 John Dickson Carr lived in England, from where he went to Paris in 1928 ostensibly to further his education at the Sorbonne. There are conflicting versions of Carr's life in Paris. Liukkonen and Pesonen say that Carr "plunged into bohemian life and wrote his first novel, an historical adventure," and he may well have done so, but he was selective about the bohemians with whom he mixed. Greene (64) observes that Carr kept away from the coterie of Left Bank American expatriates who gathered around Gertrude Stein and would have included the likes of Ernest Hemingway and F. Scott Fitzgerald. Somewhere in his book, titled with conscious irony *Geniuses Together* (1987), Humphrey Carpenter observes that the time of this "lost generation" was "one long drunk" (drunken binge) rather than a period of great literary creativity. In his summing up, Carpenter writes: "The geniuses had mostly turned out not to be geniuses at all. Yet they had been geniuses at being together, drinking together, sleeping together, and quarrelling together" (220). At a later period in his life John Dickson Carr might well have thrown himself into that alcohol-sodden milieu but he was still a young man just beginning to establish himself in crime literature.

Carr was twenty-two in 1928 but he was precocious and already knew what he liked and disliked in literature. He "abhorred" in particular "the 1920s school of realistic fiction," says Greene (107), as represented by Hemingway and Fitzgerald, as well as the gritty noir crime stories of Hammett and Chandler. Hemingway's Paris novel *Fiesta* (*The Sun Also Rises*) was first published in 1927 by Jonathan Cape; F. Scott Fitzgerald's *The Great Gatsby* came out in 1926; several of Dashiell Hammett's short stories were extant in the 1920s such as "Nightmare Town" (1924) and "The Big Knockover" (1927). Raymond Chandler's work was not published until the 1930s, after Carr's Paris sojourn.

The literary tradition that Carr grew up with and which he adopted in his own work comes from the late Victorian and Edwardian novelists such as Dickens and Wilkie Collins and their offspring: Rider Haggard, H. G. Wells, Bram Stoker, Conan Doyle and Chesterton. By and large they are thrillers as well as detective tales that today critics label as genre writing (Greene 21–22). It is a narrow viewpoint, Green says, but it shows Carr's preference for narrative and plot above characterization and what nowadays we also call psychological crime writing.

After a hesitant beginning John Dickson Carr's time in Paris was productive:

> In 1928, he went to Paris to study — or so his parent thought — but actually to become a full-time writer. He tried to write a historical romance but tore it up. Either in Paris or when he returned to the States he produced a long Bencolin story that became the basis for his first published novel, *It Walks by Night* (1930) [*MysteryNet*].

Carr returned to England around 1930 but he did not stay. Instead he caught a liner to the United States and was living in Brooklyn Heights by the time *It Walks by Night* was published.

During the voyage he met Clarice Cleaves, a petite twenty-one-year-old English lady who lived close to Bristol and was taking a birthday holiday funded by her parents. When she reached America she found clerical work in a Scarsdale store to support herself and it was there that John Dickson Carr followed up their shipboard friendship. Greene describes Clarice as:

> An extremely pretty young woman, with blond hair, eyes of an unusual navy blue, and what one friend describes as "a kitten face and a typically English complexion of roses-and-milk." She was slim and petite, only about five feet, two inches tall.... In many of John's books the hero falls in love at first sight [and the heroine is often slim and petite, a mirror image of Clarice Cleaves] [82].

John Dickson Carr courted Clarice through 1931 to mid–1932 and they were married on 3 June 1932.

This decade, says Greene, was Carr's "most prolific period" (182). He joined the Detection Club in London in 1930 and attended its convivial dinners throughout the 1930s (Young). From 1936, Greene tells us, "at least thirty translations of his books were published in Dutch, French, German, Italian, Norwegian, and Swedish" (258). In this period he wrote the bulk of his oeuvre, including *Castle Skull* (1931) a Bencolin story; *The Lost Gallows* (1931) also with the Bencolin character: *Poison in Jest* (1932); *The Waxworks Murder* (1932) — U.S.: *The Corpse in the Waxworks—Hag's Nook* (1933) a Dr. Fell story; *The Mad Hatter Mystery* (1933), also with Dr. Fell; *The Blind Barber* (1934), *The Eight of Swords* (1933), *The Bowstring Murders* (1934); *The Plague Court Murders* (1934); *The White Priory Murders* (1934); in 1935 *Death Watch*, *The Hollow Man*, *The Red Widow Murders*, and *The Unicorn Murders*; in 1936 *The Arabian Nights Murder* and *The Punch and Judy Murders*; in 1937 *The Burning Court* and *The Ten Teacups* (in the U.S. *The Peacock Feather Murders*); in 1938, *The Four False Weapons*, *To Wake the Dead*, *The Crooked Hinge*, *The Judas Window*

(U.S., *The Crossbow Murder*), and *Death in Five Boxes*; in 1939 *The Black Spectacles* (U.S., *The Problem of the Green Capsule*), *The Problem of the Wire Cage*, *Drop to His Death* (U.S., *Fatal Descent*), and *The Reader Is Warned* ("John Dickson Carr").

S. T. Joshi says that: "the first Fell novel appeared in 1933, the last in 1967, whereas Merrivale makes his debut in 1934 and bows out in 1955 with the novelette *All in a Maze* (4). On a rough count he wrote twenty-nine novels in the 1930s, eighteen in the 1940s, twelve in the 1950s, eight in the 1960s, three in the 1970s, plus nine short story collections and a large number of radio plays that are virtually a separate *oeuvre* ("John Dickson Carr"). A feature of this impressive output is that Carr wrote two and often three novels a year with the policy of alternating between his two main characters Dr. Gideon Fell and Sir Henry Merrivale (or "HM"). Herzel (68) writes that Carr's novels fall into three groups before he turns to historical romances and that taken together they mark off fairly neatly three stages in his career. The first stage, which Herzel calls an apprenticeship, is the Inspector Bencolin stories begun when Carr was twenty-five. The second stage, through the 1930s and 1940s, has the detective mysteries with the protagonists Dr. Gideon Fell and Sir Henry Merrivale. Stage three is his historical-cum-detective novels. In fact to the end of his life Carr wrote novels belonging to stages two and three.

At different points in their fictional histories Fell and Merrivale present comic characters. As Douglas Greene says (142), the two Dr. Gideon Fell books, *The Eight of Swords* and *The Blind Barber* "are primarily comedies" and it was as a comic writer that Carr saw himself. In fact, Carr shifted the comic emphasis from the Fell character to the Merrivale character and back again and there is always a balance, often an uneasy one, between elements of comedy and those of the thriller and the supernatural/macabre. An entry in *MysteryNet* notes: "Carr's antiquarianism. He loved old armor, clocks, fortune-telling cards, castles, and legends, and he worked such lore into his books. At the same time, Carr balanced the creepy atmosphere of his novels with scenes of outrageous comedy."

John Dickson Carr's private life, however, was not as plain sailing or as successful as his publication record. Factors already mentioned stayed with him most of his life: a wanderlust that was rarely satisfied, the onset of heavy drinking, and (a wanderlust of another nature) an inclination for extra-marital affairs. Carr and his family moved frequently across the Atlantic and back depending upon his mood. He was a very conservative figure as were many of his contemporaries and when English politics did not agree with him he would leave the country. In 1932 or 1933 they moved from the United States to England (Young), and Greene says (213) he visited New York in 1934. Even on the eve of war in 1938 they were travelling.

In 1941 when the United States entered the Second World War after Pearl

Harbor, Carr volunteered for service but instead was advised to return to England. There he worked for the BBC on propaganda radio scripts and wrote the Appointment with Fear mystery series that became highly popular (*Books and Writers*). This continued from 1939 to 1945. At the same time his output of mystery stories was maintained. In the war years (1940–1943) Carr had nine novels published plus a collection of short stories, *The Department of Queer Complaints* (Greene 259). Kingsley Amis (*Times Literary Supplement*) remembers Carr in this period:

> By 1948 Carr, never progressive in his outlook, had ceased to like it here and he and his English wife took off for the States. They were back in 1951 after the Tory victory at the election, but things were never the same for him again. There may or may not be a link between the traditional detective story and the pre-war world, but there can be no doubt that, after the final departure of that world, Carr showed a loss of energy and imagination in the Dr. Fell and HM tales and others with contemporary settings ... between 1950 and 1972, the year of his last novel, he spent half his time wiring historical romances.... Like his colleagues, like the science-fiction writers of almost the same period, he was coming to the end of his material.

In fact, says Greene (370), Amis did not meet Carr until 1955 when they were introduced by Edmund Crispin (Bruce Montgomery) at the International Musician's Club where they became drinking partners. In his own words, Carr fell off the wagon. But his heavy drinking had begun many years earlier in Brooklyn Heights (Greene 77) from 1930 on. It was both part of his image but also one of the leisure vices of people in show business and associated arts. Kingsley Amis has a history of heavy drinking and is remembered by his brother in law Colin Howard ("Monkey") for "going upstairs at Gardnor House on all fours because he could not make it standing up" (Jacobs 325).

Carr rarely if ever drank while he was writing, but he would go on extended benders as a means of unwinding after finishing a project. By 1944 when Carr added radio plays to his repertoire — directing/"producing" them, too (Greene 233) — his drinking had reached a more serious phase. Greene writes:

> It is difficult to believe that Carr could write such brilliant radio plays at a time when his drinking was getting out of control, but that was the situation. In his early days in Brooklyn Heights and during his first years of marriage, he did not drink while at the typewriter, and his sprees resulted in nothing worse than hangovers. By the time the Carrs moved to Croton, however, he had persuaded himself that he could write while he was drinking, and as far as the quality of his writing indicates, he was correct.... Unlike many alcoholics Carr could control his drinking [253–254].

This is a moot point because by 1942 and 1943, Greene (255) tells us, Carr began taking the addictive sedative chloral hydrate as a measure against insomnia, a drug that does not go well with alcohol. Clarice's plans to rehabilitate Carr from this dangerous mix were interrupted by their return to England.

At this time there are two conflicting social attitudes towards heavy drinking and alcoholism: "people did not let such matters become public knowledge. They kept alcoholism hidden; they never admitted it to friends, and often never acknowledged it to the alcoholic himself [but] ... everyone who knew John knew about his drinking — and almost always liked him anyway" (Greene 254–255). Heavy drinking and partying was a way of life in this world of journalism, literature, film and theater. John Dickson Carr was deeply embedded within this milieu along with other writers who also succumbed to alcoholism such as Edmund Crispin and Kingsley Amis. Even E. C. Bentley was not unaffected. Parties, often riotous, that helped oil this machinery were thrown and/or attended by writers with disparate habits such as Margery Allingham and Nancy Spain.

Another factor in John Dickson Carr's life that was also kept under wraps is his involvement in extra-marital affairs. Carr's infidelities appear to have begun soon after his marriage with Clarice and continued on and off for years. Liukkonen and Pesonen record the period around 1932 when Carr settled in England with Clarice and their three children with the observation that "Carr was not a very faithful husband, and he had affairs with other women." Many years later, in 1943, Greene (275) tells us that Carr had a mistress in his flat at Haverstock Hill at the same time as Clarice was seeking permission to rejoin him in England. Evidently Clarice was in the U.S. Greene (275–277) discusses this at some length, saying that Clarice took Carr's behavior philosophically and that Carr on his part held Clarice uppermost in his affections. Greene speculates that Carr always needed a woman to watch over him when he began drinking, but that he also found attractive women irresistible and they in turn responded to his "courtly attentiveness" (275). Carr expected Clarice to overlook these affairs. On this score, S. T. Joshi remarks that "Carr reveals the most profound ignorance of female psychology" (57).

Greene (353) also reports Clarice Carr's thoughts in 1991 on her husband's deep-seated unhappiness with life that impelled him to move frequently from place to place, "somehow running away from himself," finding new venues where he could set up office and write. Toing and froing between England and the U.S. had to be an expensive proposition because Carr usually packed crates of books and his collection of exotic weaponry to take with him. Clarice hazarded that the problem lay with Carr's small stature. This seems a little farfetched but it is an insight from a wife who was with Carr over forty-five years.

The fourth factor that influenced Carr's life, then, is his physical size, of which he was painfully self-conscious. Carr was a relatively short man. Greene cites Frederic Prokosch on Carr's boyhood appearance at Haverford College as that of "a small, sickly boy who smoked incessantly, who wrote all night.... His physical smallness no doubt stimulated his bravado" (40). Carr's passport application describes him as "twenty years old ... five feet six inches in height, with brown hair and gray eyes" (Greene 61). He is described in the Swedish press as "a small man with a coquette moustache, who reminds you quite a bit of Agatha Christie's sleuth Hercule Poirot. But ... Mr. Carr is unbelievably English; a gentleman right out of London City ... with dark red braces," and is described less kindly by another Stockholm journalist as bearing "a thin moustache, a thin brown face and rather big ears" (cited in Greene 388). Being likened to Christie's pompous and fastidious creation of Poirot would conceivably make anyone self-conscious.

Indeed, by describing the characters in his fiction Carr may have been compensating for his comparatively short stature. Professor Gideon Fell is obese to the point of the grotesque and Sir Henry Merrivale is also a large man carrying a big "corporation." Other male characters are tall, or "lean" on the other hand, such as Brian Innes from *In Spite of Thunder* (10): "forty-six years old.... Long and lean." (Note the sidelong tribute to Carr's contemporary Michael Innes). On the other hand, while the male heroes are active fellows able to take care of themselves in a scrap — like Tom Lockwood in his struggle with a would-be killer in the maze of the 1963 novelette *All in a Maze* (151) — their physical appearance such as height and build is generally glossed over.

In John Dickson Carr's work we learn about his own character from those of his fictional personae by omission as well as commission. His heroines are nearly always described at greater length than their beaus. This is not an accident, for writers (usually) plan their characters' appearance carefully. Margery Allingham's heroes, although mostly described in thumbnail sketches, have greater detail, for example Giles Paget in *Mystery Mile* (32), Val Gyrth in *Look to the Lady* (3), or Dicky Farquharson in *Sweet Danger* (19), and many others. Carr's preference is for his ladies to be tall, not only in real life but also in fiction, as in *In Spite of Thunder*:

> Out of the lift stepped a gentle, modest, well-rounded girl, tall and slender, with black hair and a sympathetic manner. You thought "girl" rather than "woman," though she must have been in her middle or later thirties. Though she was not exactly pretty, a clear complexion and large eyes made her seem so. And, except for her fashionable clothes, she might have been the vicar's daughter on holiday [36].

— and to be petite as well, again in *In Spite of Thunder*:

> A small cool whirlwind, high heels rapping, marched out of the hotel and hurried towards him.... She was rather elaborately dressed for dinner, in a low-cut, white gown that set off the firm sleekness of her shoulders. Though her face remained in shadow, a dim light from the hotel-foyer touched her heavy, glossy dark-brown hair. As usual, breathing out emotion, she seemed all contradictory qualities: stolidness and yet fragility, poise and yet indecision.... Long blue eyes,

black-lashed and a little slanted up at the outer corners regarded him with an innocence which did not hide either anger or uneasiness [11–12].

Compare the second description against that of Clarice Cleaves cited earlier. Carr is projecting the image of his beloved wife onto his fictional characters. Not only that, he is also projecting qualities in his own character upon his fictional ones: fashionable clothes — his ladies are chic and in real life Carr is dapper; modesty — for this read courtesy in Carr's treatment of women; contradictions, for example self-discipline when writing but loss of control in his drinking.

In 1943 John Dickson Carr was writing half-hour radio plays titled collectively *Cabin B-13*. The individual story of that title proved to be one of his best and became a satisfactory film adaptation retitled *Dangerous Crossing* (1953). Carr's prolific radio scripts began from around 1940 and continued to 1957, at a quick count about ninety-two (Greene 486–490). "In addition to radio scripts and the Conan Doyle biography, Carr wrote eight detective novels about Sir Henry Merrivale and Dr. Gideon Fell between 1945 and 1950" (Greene 332). The comic potentialities were realized more fully than ever, where, for example, the Sir Henry Merrivale novels are introduced with "some kind of comic disaster or uproar" (Greene 303) as we shall see.

At the close of the war the Carrs moved to Mamaroneck in New York (*Books and Writers*). While not perhaps as productive as the previous decade, the 1950s saw good work and some major landmarks. These include a biography in 1949, *The Life of Sir Arthur Conan Doyle*, written with Conan Doyle's hypercritical son Adrian as adviser; a review in 1950 for *The New York Times* criticizing Raymond Chandler's *The Simple Art of Murder*:—"while, unexpectedly, finding some good things to say about Dashiell Hammett" (Greene 108); the script for the film *Dangerous Crossing* in 1953; the publication in 1954 of a collection of short stories, *The Exploits of Sherlock Holmes* written in collaboration with Adrian Conan Doyle.

The last-named was an uneasy alliance. Adrian Conan Doyle was intense, obsessive and protective of his father's (and his own) reputation, while Carr tended to write in a more lighthearted vein. Perhaps surprisingly, Carr's light parodies of Arthur Conan Doyle's Holmes and Watson characters passed Adrian's censorship, at least those passages we find in the tales.

> You do typewriting, I perceive. The double line in the plush costume a little above your wrist, where the typewrist presses against the table, proclaims as much ["The Wax Gamblers" 66].

> "It is possible," continued Holmes, snatching back the telegram to read it again, "that there may be in London two women with the singular and even striking name of Gloria Cabpleasure" ["The Highgate Miracle" 81].

Another cause for tension between the two men was Carr's drinking. After writing three pages for *The Adventure of the Sealed Room* on January 2, 1953,

Carr went on a drinking binge that lasted two months (Greene 360). Adrian Conan Doyle had to complete the project. The Conan Doyle biography won two awards, the Edgar Award and the Grand Master bestowed by the Mystery Writers of America ("John Dickson Carr"; Young).

Carr is seen by critics as a writer who has limitations, perhaps it is better to say weaknesses, that include those mentioned already and also the idea that he could not lift his mind from the Golden Years of pre-war writing that were to his mind, says Greene (260), happier times. Internal evidence in *Night at the Mocking Widow* shows that although it is published in 1950 its temporal setting is pre–World War II Britain. The character of the German philoso-pher-psychiatrist Dr. Johann Schiller Schmidt might be taken from Johann Christoph Friedrich von Schiller (1759–1805), German poet, playwright, philosopher and historian ("Friedrich Schiller"). In *Mocking Widow*, however, he is a sinister figure. Merrivale's Whitehall associates tell him that they suspect Schmidt of being a Nazi spy. There is another hint that the novel's setting is pre–World War II when Merrivale says to Schmidt: "Aren't your country and my country two friendly nations?" (222). Inspector Garlick's investigations find that: "Cordy bought the typewriter from old Joe Palmer, the Glastonbury dealer, in 1931" (252), and Merrivale comments on a postcard photograph of the Mocking Widow in Danvers shop that the typewriter was a light manufacture of "the kind used twenty-five years ago" (255). The provision of an actual date, 1931, gives us a further clue that the setting of the novel is prior to World War II. From a narrator's aside (291), we can claim definitively that the novel is set in pre–World War II: "With a fluttering loud sigh, not unlike those occasional fluttering V-1's we heard *in later years...*" [my emphasis].

To be fair, *In Spite of Thunder* is post–World War II and has as its setting a guest house near Hitler's infamous Bavarian retreat Eagle's Nest (*Kehlstein-haus*) where a murder is suspected as having taken place, investigated and recorded at the time by Nazi officials. Some years later, in the fictional present, another death occurs that has to be investigated. The tale is overblown with melodramatic dialogue that is sometimes unconvincing but, for that reason, has unintentional humor. It is a novel, but *In Spite of Thunder* rests heavily on dialogue and reads like one of the radio mystery scripts Carr was churning out in the 1940s and 1950s. Much of the action takes place in a drawing-room dis-cussion and dénouement between the persons involved, and as if the similarity between the novel and a radio or stage play was not enough, it is divided into three parts each titled Act One, Act Two and Act Three.

More than a decade later Carr himself records a slowing down in his capacity to work. In a letter to David Higham in 1959 he wrote: "Life grows grimmer.... I am in my middle fifties (cited in Greene 405). By the 1960s to the 1970s Carr was suffering poor health due to his heavy drinking and smoking and for a time he moved to the drier climate of Morocco (Liukkonen and

Pesonen). Carr travelled capriciously between London, Tangier, Mamaroneck, and New York, before plumping for Greenville, South Carolina in 1965 (Greene in *MysteryNet* 1988). In February 1961, Carr declared no more Carter Dickson novels (Greene 382).

In 1962 Carr's doctor William Barrett warned that if he could not control his drinking he was at risk of suffering a stroke (Greene 414–415). This came to pass early in spring the next year (1963) when he was living (again) at Mamaroneck in New York. The stroke paralyzed him in his left side ("John Dickson Carr"). Despite this handicap Carr continued to write reviews for "The Jury Box" section of the *Ellery Queen's Mystery Magazine* and he lived for a further fourteen years. During the 1960s Carr wrote predominantly historical romances full of mystery and supernatural atmospherics. John Dickson Carr died in Greenvale, South Carolina, on 27 February 1977 of lung cancer at the age of seventy-one (Greene in *MysteryNet*; "John Dickson Carr").

Critics

Book cover blurbs are chosen to make the new publication attractive so that it will sell and are often written by the authors themselves at the behest of their publishers. They are not necessarily reliable indicators of a book's literary or commercial worth. However, standard quotations in brief from reviewers may hit upon qualities important for our understanding of a particular writer, demonstrated readily from the work. For example, Nicholas Blake in the *Spectator* in (1937) notes Carr's "skill at blending the normal with the bizarre." Hacklehorn comments on a similar pairing of "high comedy cheek-by-jowl with passages of spine-chilling terror." Agatha Christie observes that "very few detective stories baffle me, but Mr. Carr's always do" (back cover blurb for the Zebra Books 1950 edition of *Night at the Mocking Widow*). Similarly, Dorothy L. Sayers in the single back cover blurb for the *Four Complete Dr. Fell Mysteries* (1988): "Mr. Carr can lead us away from the small, artificial, brightly lit stage of the ordinary detective plot into the menace of outer darkness." Julian Symons on *The Hollow Man* in the 2002 Orion edition states: "The best Carr is the most ingenious.... The conjuror's illusion here is marvellously clever," and T. J. Binyon for the same edition says: "Probably the most ingenious of all detective story writers in the creation of puzzles."

Kingsley Amis has more considered opinions. In his 1981 review of *The Door to Doom* (1980)—1981 being the same year in which Amis was awarded the CBE—he paraphrases Julian Symons' critique of Carr's puzzle writing whether unconsciously or intentionally, saying that it has "excessive reliance on formula and lack of human warmth amounting to an absence of characterization." Amis may have been referring to this paragraph in Symons:

> The trouble with exploiting a formula like that of the locked room is that everything else becomes subservient ... genuine feeling in many of Chesterton's short stories, but very little in any of Carr's writing after his first half-dozen books.... Since the whole story is built around the puzzle there is no room for characterization.... What one remembers about them is never the people, but only the puzzle [110].

Amis notes as well Carr's occasional lapses into "disastrous facetiousness" and the idea that "anything to do with drink is funny." This hinted moralizing is rich coming from Kingsley Amis who was himself a soak and bon vivant. Amis also criticizes Carr as "likely to plunge into the style of the novelette." A novelette (or novella) is longer than a short story but shorter than a novel — "short novel or extended short story," says Baldick (152) — and this limits the development of character. That is unless, I think, characterization is made the chief element as in Joseph Conrad's *Heart of Darkness* (1902) with Marlow's psychology and search for Kurtz: "The horror! The Horror!" (121). Other elements are underplayed that might be the more prominent, such as plot development with surprise endings (which is what a lot of short stories contain). John Dickson Carr is renowned for his plot twists and not so much for characterization.

Kingsley Amis is doubly ingenuous when he says a few sentences later that "of course there are no secret passages, hidden trapdoors or concealed apartments" in Carr's tales. Indeed Carr's tales abound with them because he was influenced, like most of his contemporaries in the business, by the movement in crime writing of the 1920s and what those writers owed to the thriller. Stories by Milne, Allingham and Sayers, for example, contain those elements (Amis calls them prescriptions). Amis is generous with the Golden Age in popular literature, dating it from 1890 to 1950. He calls the 1920s detective stories set in English country towns and mansions a subgenre and points out that when Carr emigrated from the U.S. to England he readily adopted that form, obviously liking it: "these novels supply some sympathetic insight into the social history of that vanished era." Amis does not find *The Door to Doom* a satisfactory compilation of Carr's shorter work, stories he says are poorly chosen by Greene, but he approves of an essay by Carr that "has dated little over these last thirty-five years," that is, by 1981.

Another critique that appears from time to time is that of the parodic and satirical review. Hacklehorn's "Scathing Attack on Celebrated Mystery Writer" (2009) comes from Dr. Caligula Marshmallow, an even sillier nom de plume, assuming that Hacklehorn is also a pen name. This parody covers ground already trod in relation to other writers: "his grasp of characterisation is weak"; there are interruptions and "hysterical outbursts"; Carr "does not interest himself in the possible themes of setting, situation, and solution. For him, the story always takes back place to the plot"; the "same characters" reappear, including "lovers with their "comical" misunderstandings"; his clues are not based on "dialogue or actions which, when interpreted the right way, mean something entirely different, but technical clues." In fact, dialogue is a mainstay of many of Carr's novels, as noted above.

In his review parody Marshmallow does not appear to know the difference between a theme and a plot. Situation, setting and solution are *not* themes, nor are they the story; they are plot elements, it seems to me, because they are part of the more complex *arrangement* of events from the storyline. That the story takes second place to the plot seems perfectly admissible and not a valid reason for criticism, considering that the formal definitions favor the plot because by implication they are a more useful writer's tool. Marshmallow weakens his argument when he says in his introductory paragraph that Carr "is one of the best devisers of plots," although he adds that Carr cannot be ranked among the top five.

Moreover, clues are indeed based upon dialogue and actions and not only "technical" hints to do with clocks or pathology, important though they may be to the solution. In *Night at the Mocking Widow* a technical artifact has a key place, the typewriter hidden in the eye socket of the Mocking Widow. But the principal clue comes from a form of written speech, the style of the official report. Maybe this can be argued as a technical point as well, but it is tied in closely to dialogue (by definition "spoken") because a similar style of phrasing in the spoken word alerts the writer West as well as Merrivale to the possible identity of the murderer.

One of the features of Marshmallow's satiric review is its inconsistency. There are books of Carr's, says that reviewer, "where the humour is kept under control," and he names *The Mad Hatter Mystery* (1933) and *The Arabian Nights Murder* (1936). He also likes *The Sleeping Sphinx* (1947) and several of Carr's short stories: "Terror's Dark Tower" and "The Wrong Problem." He says that "the humour does not come from people rolling around in the mud or stepping on bananas, but instead from false beards and horses in barrister's wigs." But I see very little difference between mud fights and false beards. They all threaten to elicit a chuckle from the reader and belong to slapstick. Perhaps this is another example of the divide between those who like to take their crime novels seriously and those who don't.

Another critique, that of Roger Herzel, is hailed by Douglas Greene (434) as among the best. Carr was living when the review was written. While referring to Sir Henry Merrivale as a "comic" character (73), Herzel does not discuss this theme beyond remarking that the two investigators Merrivale and Fell are depicted as "childlike," have "an eccentric amiability" (72), and that "their mystery-solving ability lies not so much in pure reason as in their habit of seeing all things, large and small, as of equal importance" (73). This appears a trifle self-contradictory because although the Fell and Merrivale characters are broad-focused in their investigations, they also reflect a "comfortable common sense" (72) that helps ameliorate crimes that are baffling, sinister and apparently supernatural.

By the time such novels as *Skeleton in the Clock* (1948) and *Night at the Mocking Widow* (1950) were published, Carr through restless travel was escaping from social changes brought about by the upheavals of the 1940s. David Lodge summarizes this period for one of John Dickson Carr's younger contemporaries, Kingsley Amis (1922–1995), whose début novel *Lucky Jim* came out in 1954:

> The received wisdom of the 1940s was that the Second Word War, the "People's War," the landslide victory of the Labour Party in the General Election of 1945, and the establishment of the Welfare State, with free secondary and tertiary education, had genuinely democratized British society, and got rid of its class divisions and inequalities for good. But to many young people who grew up in the post-war period, and benefited from the 1944 Education Act, it seemed that the old pre-war upper classes still maintained their privileged position because they commanded the social and cultural high ground [xi].

Carr belonged to that generation for whom the old privileged class distinctions and gentility gave greater comfort. By 1948 he and his wife had fled once more to the U.S. only to return in 1951 when the Tory government came back to power in England. That government's policy of "encouraging consumerism and free enterprise," as Lodge (x) puts it, no doubt appealed to Carr. Lodge adds that Amis's novel *Lucky Jim*, although published a few years later, is set in the former atmosphere "of socialist, 'austerity' Britain in the 1940s." It is interesting that Carr and Amis became drinking friends although their social opinions differed. But while Amis wrote arguably his best satire on the "provincial bourgeois world" (Lodge viii) of the privileged upper and middle classes, John Dickson Carr held on to that world and preferred scarcely to come to grips with the social changes taking place around him.

By dealing with the more serious elements of crime/detective fiction, Carr taps into the concept of reader response. For example, in Herzel, "the Fell-Merrivale novels are more appropriately designed as a test of the reader's wits, and it is traditional to assume that this is why one reads a detective story" (77). Here "design" can be considered a key concept because Herzel points out (68) that Carr establishes a pattern which is characteristic (that is, characteristic of him), and that he experimented as well with different compositional devices such as concocting "impossible situations." (This is thought a better term than "locked room" mystery with which Carr is often labeled). Setting a trap for the murderer is one of Carr's plot devices that not only misleads the police and other characters in the novel, including the murderer, but misdirects the reader as well. It violates the "fair play" rule that the reader should know no more and no less about the homicide and the clues than the investigating person. Yet Herzel says on the same page that Carr could bring together fair play and the impossible situation more efficaciously when he discards the policeman as chief investigator and substitutes the Fell and Merrivale characters. This Herzel sees as "an advance in technique" (76). The fictional investigator has more room to move because he is not a policeman. But here another rule of fair play is subverted because Merrivale (or Fell) often enough let the murderer go free, although in *Night at the Mocking Widow* this is to offer the wrongdoer the option of taking his own life instead of undergoing disgrace on the gallows.

Herzel is on the side of those who do not take the crime/detective story to be literature in the true sense, saying of Carr that "his flat characters, his implausible plots, and his deliberate misleading of the reader ... which would be serious deficiencies in a novel considered as 'literature,' are both justifiable and necessary in the particular kind of fiction Carr writes" (67). This is in keeping with the general theme of the collection in which Herzel's article appears, on *Minor* American novelists. Herzel may have been going along with his editor's wishes. Both the editor C. A. Hoyt and the writer of the book's preface, Harry T. Moore, are faintly disparaging about their minor authors and on this evidence belong to the school that does not recognize detective fiction as literature. Moore refuses to comment upon crime fiction beyond saying that it is "relaxing" (xii). Hoyt, in a self-conscious and somewhat pompous introduction, states that Carr "has applied himself almost exclusively, or most successfully, to a certain rather restricted genre, one which automatically confers minor status ... [and] seems often to be the result not of a writer's gifts, but of his conception and ambition" (xvii–xviii).

This suggests that other genres more readily identifiable as belonging to the mainstream and therefore to literature do not have deficiencies. But of course they do. There is, for example, a controversy over whether Tolstoy's *War and Peace* (1868–69) would have been improved by the omission of his epilogue on history and method (Briggs xix). To say dismissively that crime literature is relaxing is, however, to pinpoint one of the chief reasons why it is favored by both the puzzle-makers and the humorists. It is for fun and for the personal enjoyment of the writer as much as for the reader.

Night at the Mocking Widow (1950) and *Skeleton in the Clock* (1948)

Written under the pseudonym of Carter Dickson, *Night at the Mocking Widow* is the twenty-second novel by John Dickson Carr. It runs to approximately 95,000 words and is therefore a substantial work though of average length for the form. The protagonists in John Dickson Carr's two series of novels are, to say the least, rotund detectives: Doctor Gideon Fell in the John Dickson Carr series and Sir Henry Merrivale in the Carter Dickson offerings.

They are what we describe today as morbidly obese. Fell is modeled on one of Carr's admired crime writers G. K. Chesterton (1874–1936). He is analytical and laid back. Merrivale is modeled arguably on Winston Churchill. He is astute and irascible ("John Dickson Carr"). Carr alternated between them and in some years produced both a Fell and a Merrivale novel.

In the 1934 novel *The Blind Barber*, written under his real name, a group of bumbling young people are let loose on a cruise ship in which are madcap chases and wild fights with an eccentric captain. In roughness of conception it is similar to that of an equally chaotic group of young people alone in an eerie mansion in one of Margery Allingham's earliest novels, *The Crime at Black Dudley*. The farce in *Mocking Widow* has greater polish, though it includes more slapstick and eccentric characters than Allingham. Its madcap opening involves a suitcase with wheels that appears to have a mind of its own, and there are plenty of pratfalls as its pursuers and innocent bystanders alike come to grief when it runs away from them. Sir Henry Merrivale's suitcase reminds us of Terry Pratchett's character Luggage, the homicidal bodyguard to the wizard Rincewind in the Discworld novel *The Colour of Magic* (1983).

The first chapter of *Night at the Mocking Widow* sets the scene by introducing most of the principal characters in the village of Stoke Druid. Conventionally there is the Reverend J. Cadman Hunter whose uncle is the Bishop of Glastontor (cf. the Bishop of Glasminster in E. C. Bentley's *Elephant's Work*), his housekeeper Mrs. Honeywell, the squire Tom Wyatt, and Colonel Bailey (the murderer). Ellie Harris is the postmistress, and the chemist is Mr. Goldfish and his wife. Inspector Dave Garlick is the *de rigeur* official foil for Sir Henry Merrivale. Fred Cordy is an atheist shoemaker ("cordwainer" = cobbler) who becomes one of the Colonel's victims. Named appropriately, Miss Cordelia Martin commits suicide by drowning before the action of the novel. There is a tennis match and people in the village are upset by a spate of poison pen letters that have been sent to several hinting at their clandestine affairs.

Chapter two introduces Sir Henry Merrivale and the aforementioned suitcase as well as two new principals in the cast: Pamela Lacey, the adolescent daughter of Stella Lacey, and the bookseller Rafe Danvers. Pam is in the care of Dr. Schmidt, a charlatan psychiatrist. Merrivale sets this right by the end. It is a subplot. Danvers asks Merrivale whether he would investigate the poison pen letters in exchange for an obscure rare book. There are intertextual references, one to Victor Hugo, another to the works *Absolom and Achitophel* and another to *Barchester Towers*. There is an implied cross-textual reference to a method of suicide made to look like murder in the classic Dr. Fell novel *The Hollow Man* (1935) that was used by Margery Allingham in one of her novels. Says Dr. Gideon Fell:

> A man shoots himself with a gun fastened on the end of an elastic — the gun, as he releases it, being carried up out of sight into the chimney. Variations of the

trick (not locked-room affairs) have been the pistol with a string attached to a weight, which is whisked over the parapet of a bridge into the water after the shot [157].

Gordon West confronts the Reverend James and warns him not to read the letter in church. They are both men of action. West is a Judo expert and the Rev. James Hunter an ex-boxing champion. Physical activities are a strong feature of the novel: sport (tennis), runaway suitcase, chases, fights. In chapter three the clergyman Hunter makes a brisk athletic entrance into Danvers' shop, leaping over tables in a close approximation to slapstick though he does not fall, and later in the novel he and West engage in a public fistfight. The plot is progressed by Hunter's statement that he will read the contents of the poison pen letter, although it involves insinuations about a relationship between him and Joan Bailey.

Chapter five finds us at Gordon West's cottage where he and Joan sit together to discuss whether or not Joan is in danger. Gordon and Joan's *tête-a-tête* is overheard by different persons unseen at two separate moments. Two minor characters appear: West's housekeeper Mrs. Wych and the choirmaster Mr. Benson. This is one of Carr's means of inserting suspense into a tale to save the reader from being overly distracted by the mayhem. Eavesdropping at partly closed doors, for example, is used a lot more extensively in Carr's more serious, and melodramatic, novel *In Spite of Thunder*. The central mystery in *Mocking Widow* thus far is the possible association of the poison pen letters with an earlier death by suicide. The identities of a second pair of eavesdroppers are revealed in the next chapter. Stella Lacey and Marion Tyler unintentionally overhear part of a conversation between Merrivale and Colonel Bailey discussing Bailey's model of a battlefield. The battlefield model becomes an important motif-cum-clue.

Hunter gives his sermon. Another clue is introduced, speculations about the typewriter used to compose the letters. Like footprints and fingerprints, the identification of typeface is a relatively early forensic aspect in the detective novel so common as to be almost a cliché by then. Its discovery during the climactic chase scene neatly rounds off its importance as a clue, unlike the muddled way by which the poison-by-hypodermic-in-whiskey-bottle clue is handled in Nancy Spain's *Poison for Teacher*. Carr ties loose ends together, avoiding the smoking gun situation. Marion talks with the vicar whom she secretly loves. Merrivale sits in the shadows of the room's corner and is not immediately noticed by those entering, another case of eavesdropping.

After another confrontation with the Reverend James, Gordon West meets with Joan, who this time is wearing a green silk frock. Joan has another letter from "the Widow" to say that she will be visited in the night. Steps are taken to protect her, and the violent action that follows is a plot turning point. West and Cordy (armed with a revolver) are stationed outside Joan's bedroom window. Merrivale and the Colonel sit on guard outside her door. There are shots, Joan screams, the Colonel enters the room ahead of Merrivale. They find Joan terrified at the sight of "The Widow" but the room is empty. With an ironic touch Merrivale says: "everybody ... assumed I was the big detective with the big clue. Even your niece assumed it. When I met her in Rafe's bookshop, she said: 'You're the man who goes about solving locked-room problems and disappearances and miracles'" (155–156). Detective-Inspector David Garlick is called in.

After the terrifying of Joan, Carr's plot moves towards burlesque. Marion asks Merrivale to take part in the village bazaar to be held in the Gunpowder Room. Merrivale agrees because he wants to wear the costume of an Indian chief. But this is also the occasion on which he and the police lay a trap for the poison-pen writer/murderer. Merrivale and Garlick make their plans, including the trapping of the letter writer with marked stamps. Similar to the summary of motives for murder in novels by other authors, typology of different categories of poison-pen writer is suggested: "the Informer ... the Avenger ... the Crazy Busybody ... the neurotic woman with ... some kind of sex complex" (184–185). Making lists is a characteristic of Carr's detectives but more often done by Gideon Fell than by Merrivale. To fill in time, Merrivale reads his copy of *Edwin Drood*, Charles Dickens's uncompleted novel, perhaps symbolic of their unfinished investigations.

While the Colonel (Joan's "Uncle George") and Joan are out of the house, Merrivale and Danvers take the opportunity to inspect Joan's room with the connivance of the Colonel's maid Poppy. They are discovered by West and Joan. An important clue comes to light in a chance expression of the Vicar's (who joins them): "therefore I propose" (204). But its importance is not revealed by Merrivale until much later, although West has an inkling. Merrivale asks West what he has done with the revolver and West admits that it has disappeared. To the reader's mind this throws suspicion upon Gordon West.

Stella Lacey arrives and asks Merrivale to come to her house in his role as doctor. This leads to chapter fifteen and the resolution of the subplot. Merrivale confronts Schmidt over the psychological nonsense he's been telling Pamela and her mother. Merrivale comforts Pam in a tribute to the shockers and the classic detective and adventure tales:

> I want you to read some fellers named Dumas and Mark Twain and Stevenson and Chesterton and Conan Doyle.... They can still whack the britches off anybody at tellin' a story.... Don't you like swordfights, and bloodhounds, and robbers at lonely inns, and good old-fashioned blood and thunder?" [219–220].

John Dickson Carr liked those authors. Appealing to Twain (1835–1910), Stevenson (1850–1894) and by implication Charles Reade's *The Cloister and the Hearth* (1861) — "robbers at lonely inns" — introduces Pam to the nineteenth-century "school of romance" as their contemporary Algernon Charles Swinburne (1837–1909) calls (viii) the works of Alexandre Dumas *père* (1802–1870) and Sir Walter Scott (1771–1832). To include Chesterton (1874–1936) and Conan Doyle (1859–1930) in the same breath potentially opens the girl's mind to the early crime novels and suggests that Carr sees a continuity between the genres and the forming, I suggest, of the two branches: the crime novel and the adventure tale or shocker.

In this way an author can inject literary criticism into what is otherwise an entertaining crime story. Indeed, Carr's appeal to swashbucklers adds to the entertainment. Subplots such as the German psychiatrist's meddling with the mind of an impressionable young woman can add to the spirit of a novel, but it can also be an unnecessary distraction. It has to be done with care. The next chapter (sixteen) is a filler by which Merrivale continues to reassure Stella about Pam, and the disappearance of West's revolver is referred to once again.

The next chapter marks a climactic point. It is also the stage at which matters become serious. Cordy, who is found later to have been an accomplice of the murderer, is pursued by an unknown assailant. Shots are fired. He climbs the tower named the Mocking Widow but when he reaches its head the weathered stone shatters and he falls to his death beneath the rubble (killed also by bullet wounds). Cordy has hidden the typewriter inside one of the hollow eyes of the "Widow" and in his panic is attempting to retrieve it. The inquest reported in the following chapter ignores the question of the poison pen because the police with Merrivale's help are planning to trap the murderer/letter writer.

In the final showdown, Merrivale enters the drum tower to face Colonel Bailey, now entrapped, who awaits him sitting upon a ledge, a Webley .38 in his hand. There follows a long dénouement in which the "locked room" mystery is explained:

1. The figure seen by Joan was her own face painted by the Colonel with watercolours upon the wardrobe mirror to resemble that of a hag (the Mocking Widow). It is done during one of the moments of inspection when he and Merrivale sat guard. Other locked-room mysteries are solved when it is shown that the victim is shot or otherwise done away with from outside the room although it looks as though it was all done from within.

2. The clue that links the Colonel to the letters, Merrivale says, is in their style: "It's the ding-dong, back and forth, twelve-syllable, high-structure ponderousness of *official letterwriting*. Even you, who speak colloquially, fall into the habit of using it when you write. And you, Colonel, have been corresponding with the War Office for a long time" (306).

3. Having achieved his aim with no longer a need to continue, the Colonel overplays his hand. The idea that criminals do too much and so reveal themselves occurs in several novels of this type.

The Colonel's pre–1914 unregistered revolver taken from West's office is empty after their exchange of fire but Merrivale leaves his own Wesley .38 with the Colonel, thus allowing him the option of a dignified suicide, military style, to forestall the hangman's noose. Colonel Bailey avails himself of this opportunity. This is another convention, that the distasteful procedures of judicial hanging are glossed over or never mentioned, or when the murderer is allowed to exit the novel by suicide or happenstance (cliff fall, quicksand, drowning, and so on).

As in *Night at the Mocking Widow* the serious investigations in *The Skeleton in the Clock* are sandwiched between two scenes of pure slapstick. *Skeleton* came out in 1948 just before the Carrs moved to Mamaroneck (Greene 334). It is another Sir Henry Merrivale novel under the pseudonym of Carter Dickson. From the distraction of slapstick and love interest the novel moves seamlessly to its serious, not to say bizarre, theme flagged by the title. During the excitement, Sir Henry Merrivale inadvertently buys a grandfather clock containing a human skeleton. The information is conveyed by Jennifer West herself:

> "The clock," Jenny explained, "hasn't got any works inside it. There's only a skeleton, fastened upright to the back, with its skull looking out through the glass clock-dial."
>
> The effect of this remark was curious.
>
> Instead of showing surprise or even sarcasm, H.M.'s big face smoothed itself out to utter expressionlessness. His small, sharp eyes fastened on Jenny in a way that evidently disconcerted her. He did not even seem to breathe. The thin voice of the auctioneer sounded far away.
>
> "A skeleton in a clock, hey? That's a bit rummy. Do you happen to know any more about it, my wench?" [29].

Jenny explains that the clock once belonged to Dr. Laurier who lived in their neighborhood. Jenny's Aunt Cicely decides to buy it at the auction in order to present it to the doctor's son who is himself a doctor. Jenny's grandmother Lady Brayle was to bid for it on their behalf.

Merrivale's dénouement in the final chapter reveals Carr's ingenious use of the clock as both clue and motif. Dr. Laurier senior is an old family friend who at the death of Lord Fleet — "an overbearing man who would be little missed" (75) and who used to bully his son Ricky — realizes that it is the son who has killed his own father. The means of death is a fall from the old manor brought about by a blow from the edge of a cricket bat to the back of the legs just above the ankles, breaking the bones and precipitating the victim from the roof. In order to protect the family, Laurier at Aunt Cicely's insistence amputates the legs just above the two ankles soon after the autopsy that had missed the evidence of the broken anklebones.

Years later, filled with remorse and in an act of penance, the old and now somewhat senile doctor builds the clock and attaches the ankles and feet to the legs of a medical skeleton of a smaller man. He hides the joins and differing sizes of the bones of the larger man with a wooden platform. The son Ricky did not turn out well and as an adult kills another person. Hence Carr's tale begins with an old murder and proceeds to a more recent one in the fictional present of Sir Henry Merrivale's inquiries.

Carr's Young Ladies

The love interest in *Night at the Mocking Widow* is principally that of Joan Bailey who is described lovingly by Carr:

> [She] wore a plain white silk frock, with silk stockings and low-heeled shoes.... "Very nice-lookin' wench," he [Merrivale] has said, as one of his higher compliments. "One of those country gals who go about absolutely exudin' sex appeal, and never once knows it. Likes to be known as a good fellow. Polite and undemonstrative in public; demonstrative as blue blazes in private. Fall for some young feller — probably has already — and never think of anybody else. Loyal; pretty intelligent; loves gossip" [37].

Joan appears throughout the novel in plain but chic silk dresses and in one instance a silk slip. She reminds us of Edmund Crispin's "idealistic portraits of eligible young women" (Whittle 189) — often modeled on Carr's wife Clarice — and compares favorably with the heroine Sally Carstairs in Crispin's *The Moving Toyshop* (1946) published four years before *Mocking Widow* and which Carr must have read. They were both members of the Detection Club.

Mocking Widow has almost a surfeit of romantic attachments. The Colonel's ward Joan Bailey is the daughter of Colonel Bailey's brother and brought up by the Colonel's wife Eunice (deceased). Marion Tyler is secretly in love with the vicar. There is Stella Lacey (11) "whose real age was thirty-four ... a delicate and dainty woman with ash-blonde hair and large gray eyes," which is a fair description of Carr's real-life spouse. She is one of the beauties of the village along with Marion Tyler. Gordon West (15) is a writer who "wrote only popular stuff, roaring adventure romances which the British public loved ... he wrote a series of plays for the B.B.C.," much like John Dickson Carr himself. He is in love with Joan Bailey who returns his affections. Marion Tyler is another of Carr's handsome ladies:

> Marion, her fine teeth often flashing in a laugh, wore bobbed hair fashionably curved and without the slightest tinge of gray. She had a good sturdy figure, and excellent clothes. She had, too, a gentle hand with children and dogs and horses. As for men, she sometimes confessed, there wasn't much room for them in her life, though she got on admirably with them [79].

Love interest even extends to the main protagonist. Another character, Mrs. Virtue Conklin, is more than Merrivale's landlady. She and Merrivale, both large-bodied people, have an informal and somewhat raunchy relationship, although Merrivale is married to a woman who has her own career, as he says many pages later (231). In contrast to the well-endowed Virtue: "Clemmie's years and years younger than I am. But she's little and blonde and kept her figger." An interlude describing Virtue's ministrations to Merrivale teeters between love interest and burlesque with the latter dominant: "It was she who woke him, saw that he was shaved, whipped him into the adjoining bath with a splash like a hippopotamus, and finally saw to it that he dressed himself in neat dark clothes" (168).

In a lighter touch:

> "Listen," said West, in fierce and fiery earnest. "Let me warn you here and now. If you keep wanting to know what I'm thinking, after we're married, I am going to strangle you. I mean that! Like this."
> "You don't love me."
> "The hell I don't! I was merely pointing out..."
> "Go on," said Joan. "Go on and strangle me! See if I care."
> Since this seemed rather a drastic measure, he kissed her instead as she expected [131].

Joan Bailey entrances Gordon West in her costume as a Saxon maid who burnt King Alfred's cakes, taking liberties with history as West points out:

> Against the background of green leaves, and despite the galoshes she was compelled to wear, Joan was a trifle breathtaking. Her light brown hair, heavy and soft as fleece, was parted in the middle and rippled down her shoulders. Round her forehead she wore what might have been described as a gold fillet. Her dress, of smooth but heavy green material, fitted closely down as far as the waist, then spread in flowing lines to the ground. Round her waist was a golden rope, with tassels, loosely tied [275].

Carr describes his ladies with more sensual detail I think than does his friend and emulator Edmund Crispin. Crispin idealized his fictional women because in real life he tended to shy away from them while at the same time indulging in flirtations. He was attractive to women. There was something similar too in Carr's makeup. John Dickson Carr was attractive to women and had extra-marital affairs, although he idolized Clarice who stayed with him to the end. In a parody by Hacklehorn of what is called "trends found in the works of John Dickson Carr": "The audience, comprised of myself, my gorgeous wife, Dotty — a normal, cheery, healthy, girl — the sort of girl who likes to see other women in the nude, the sort of girl who will fight in her underwear in the mud at the drop of a hat, the sort of girl who looks at a man in such a way to make him puff out his chest." Readers might amuse themselves for hours identifying every woman in Carr's fiction who is a simulacrum of his real-time wife Clarice.

Carr's Humor

John Dickson Carr gently satirizes himself in *Night at the Mocking Widow* when Joan Bailey exclaims: "You're the man who goes about solving locked door rooms and disappearances and miracles" (38). One of the things we shall discover is that in contrast to the "rules" for writing a crime/detective story, evidently compiled in fun, there are conventions used over again in different ways through the Golden Age and well beyond. Self-parody is one of those conventions and might be the closest a humorist will approach to the more sober riddle- or problem-solving stream many readers prefer. Whether there is one sort of reader who prefers "serious" problems and another who likes better a humorous approach might not be clear-cut. There are no doubt many who enjoy reading both forms. The runaway suitcase and resultant chase takes place in chapter four with a mélange of village dogs, children, and Tommy Wyatt's gang, as well as Merrivale. Joan Bailey gives way to a fit of laughter. Stella admonishes her: "Humor, Joan ... is *never* vulgar knock-about farce" (55), when to the reader it is precisely that.

As loose ends begin to come together the comedy acts as a catharsis after the dramatic events of the previous chapters (fifteen to seventeen). The Reverend James absentmindedly proposes marriage to Marion as she, accepting, "raised her eyes with a look Virtue Conklin had taught her" (267). Several other resolutions over family bliss take place. Pamela and her mother are reconciled, Pamela becoming something of a tomboy hanging out with Tommy Wyatt's gang: "Pam's ash-blonde hair was disheveled and her frock begrimed, in a way that would have horrified her mother a week ago. Over one arm hung a pair of muddy roller skates, and clutched under her other arm was a book labeled *The Adventures of Sherlock Holmes*" (272).

In two farcical notes, attempts are made to dissuade Merrivale from going to extremes with his Indian chief outfit (he is not allowed to carry a real tomahawk), and the discovery that Dr. William Waterford, Bishop of Glastontor (Hunter's Uncle William) is better known to Merrivale from their schooldays as "Pinkey," who had once lost a wager that Merrivale would not descend Ludgate Hill on roller skates (278–279).

This leads to a slapstick ending at the town bazaar. As the penultimate chapter it can be regarded as part of the rise and fall of dramatic tension: chase and death — catharsis 1— catharsis 2 — dénouement and death. In a lower key this pattern marks the chapter progression throughout the novel. The mud fight from a purely slapstick tradition balances the runaway suitcase of chapter two. One of the more grotesque (and therefore hilarious) images in the novel is Virtue's expectation that: "Sir Henry Merrivale must appear, like Venus rising from the seen [sic], unseen until the appointed time" (288). This looks very like a misprint — Venus/Aphrodite rose from the *sea* in Greek and Roman tradition, and is depicted this way in the Botticelli canvas c. 1486 ("The Birth of Venus [Boticelli]")—but the alliteration and logic of the phrase "from the seen, unseen" is Carr's poetic licence. (One might compare a different edition of the novel.)

The mud fight commences. Merrivale and Waterford settle childhood grievances:

> Deliberately, Dr. William Waterford, Bishop of Glastontor, dived over and scooped up a handful of rich mud. There was no time, his quick brain told him, to harden it to a mudball; a rough pie must do. Partly by luck, partly by the accuracy of his good right arm, the mudpie landed squarely in the face of Sir Henry Merrivale [292].

Inspector Garlick sees "another one (Miss Bailey, a sweet girl, if one ever lived) with her hair down and wearing only one of those silk things, climbing over a counter with a pie in both hands" (296). Joan is in her silk slip, having removed the outer costume so as not to soil it.

Whereas the runaway suitcase in *Mocking Widow* serves to introduce some of the novel's main characters, the scenes in *Skeleton in the Clock*—hilarious or ridiculous depending upon the reader's mood—serve as well to reprise and close a running feud between Merrivale and Lady Sophie Brayle. Coming in the latter half of Carr's life and together with *Mocking Widow*, it is one of the last of the Merrivale stories. In it there is a continued working out of Carr's motif of the domineering older woman. At the close of the novel Merrivale and Brayle are reconciled. The feud between these two finds expression during the auctioning of the clock of the title when Merrivale and Lady Brayle make opposing bids for the item:

> Lady Brayle ... must have been a powerful woman. She caught up the shield with one hand on each side of the rim. Inspired, she took two sweeping steps backwards and swung up the shield with both arms—full and true into the face of Sir Henry Merrivale just as he entered the room.
>
> The resulting *bong*, as H.M.'s visage encountered the concave side of the shield, was not so mellifluous as a temple-gong. But it was loud enough to make several persons in the auction-room look round. The Dowager Countess, for a moment really taken aback, held the shield motionless before H.M.'s face as though about to unveil some priceless head of statuary.
>
> Then she lowered it.
>
> "Why, Henry!" she said.
>
> The great man's Panama hat had been knocked off, revealing a large bald head. Through his large shell-rimmed spectacles, undamaged because the concavity of the shield had caught him mainly forehead and chin, there peered out eyes of such horrible malignancy that Jenny shied back. His cigar, spreading and flattened, bloomed under his nose like a tobacco-plant [22].

The classic image of a squashed or exploded cigar is pure slapstick that must have its origins in the vaudeville clowns of the previous century. Carr's description of the mishap makes sure that Merrivale is not really injured by the Scottish shield, the object described satirically as an antiquity of a holy nature: a "monument of antiquity" (21). The humor in the statement comes from the incongruity of an item of weaponry being called holy. All that is injured is Sir Henry Merrivale's pride, as in his response to Martin Drake's concern: "I'm fine. Don't you worry about *my* feelin's" (23). The encounter is also a means of introducing a love interest by bringing together in the one room the two young persons Martin Drake and Jennifer West.

Sir Henry Merrivale attempts to take immediate revenge. He selects a halberd from a display in the adjoining room and nonchalantly returns to the auction-room in order to examine it more closely in the better light, but with Lady Brayle's "ample, flowered posterior" (23) in his sights. As he approaches, however, "on stealthy and evilly large feet" (24), Martin intercepts and seizes the halberd's shaft. However, fate, as they say, takes a hand:

> Lady Brayle threw up her arm like an opera star. She took two swinging steps backwards. And she landed full and true against the point of the shaft gripped by Martin and Sir Henry Merrivale.
> The sound which issued from the lips of Lady Brayle ... petrified the whole room [25].

Merrivale is informed by a "meek little man with a white moustache" (a little like Carr himself) that he is holding not a halberd but "a seventeenth-century guisarme." A guisarme as defined in *Wikipedia* is a variety of polearm fashioned by mounting a pruning hook with an added reverse spike onto a spear shaft, alternatively a crescent shaped axe blade (pole axe) mounted on the shaft. The point that met with Lady Brayle's posterior identifies Merrivale's weapon by the former definition. As mentioned above, John Dickson Carr was a weapons buff and used to transport his collection of swords and other accoutrements with him at considerable expense to and fro across the Atlantic.

CHAPTER 7

Best of the Farceurs III: Edmund Crispin (1921–1978)

Edmund Crispin is the pseudonym of Robert Bruce Montgomery, born in Buckinghamshire at Chesham Bois on 2 October 1921 of Scots-Irish parents (Literary Heritage; IMDb; "Edmund Crispin"; *Books and Writers*). He died at the age of forty-seven on 15 September 1978 from a heart attack after a history of alcoholism and financial troubles that began in the 1960s (*Books and Writers*). Like several authors in my list he ended his years in straitened circumstances: "Alcoholism combined with the onset of osteoporosis and a retreat into a semi-reclusive lifestyle resulted in him writing and composing virtually nothing during the last 15 years of his life" (The Book Depository). That last point is not correct. As David Whittle shows in a substantial and even-handed biography of the man, Bruce Montgomery produced good work to the end of his life.

From the age of fifteen (*c.* 1935), Montgomery studied the piano and before the onset of World War II traveled in Europe and especially Germany (*Books and Writers*), no doubt pursuing those studies. Deemed unfit for war service, he read French and German at St. John's College in Oxford, gaining his B.A. in modern languages in 1943. Two close friends made during his time at Oxford were the poet and novelist Philip Larkin (1922–1985) and novelist Kingsley Amis (1922–1995), an association that influenced those men in their own work. As Liukkonen and Pesonen say, Montgomery and Larkin "read each other's texts and Crispin also dedicated his third book, *The Moving Toyshop* (1946), to Larkin." Around the age of twenty-two and while he was still at Oxford, Montgomery wrote his first novel, *The Case of the Gilded Fly*, under his pseudonym of Edmund Crispin. It is said that he was inspired to try his hand at detective/crime writing in 1942 after reading *The Crooked Hinge* (1938) by John Dickson Carr (*Books and Writers*), a good example of how authors are influenced by the work of their contemporaries.

From 1943 until 1945 he was schoolmaster at Shrewsbury School where he was organist and choirmaster as well ("Edmund Crispin"). By these accounts Montgomery was something of a loner — although there is a paradox, see below — and soon after his two years at Shrewsbury "retired" to Devon where he built a bungalow and began a settled country life alone, writing, composing music, collecting classical records and becoming involved in church affairs (Literary Heritage; *Books and Writers*). Crispin's chief protagonist Dr. Gervase Fen similarly prefers country village sojourns in between his duties as university don, as in *The Glimpses of the Moon*. Montgomery married late in life, in 1976 at the age of 45, two years before his death at West Hampstead (Literary Heritage).

We should expect that a dispassionate and balanced biography will discuss its subjects' failures and personal flaws as well as their triumphs and contributions to their chosen field (or the field that chose them) and not necessarily be a hagiography like that of Barbara Reynolds on Dorothy L. Sayers, good though it is. One of the most striking themes in this reading of selected authors who make use of humor in crime fiction is how their personal worlds often became unraveled towards the close of their lives, as Shakespeare reminds us, through one or more defect (see *Hamlet* I, iv). To look a little more closely at them beyond their text(s) can be surprising and sometimes saddening.

David Whittle (190) describes Bruce Montgomery as a "dilettante socialite" who enjoyed good food, was popular among women as well as men, and met with success in his occupations early in life. "By the time he was 32 years old," says Whittle, "he had eight novels and 21 pieces of music in print" (191). Yet for these and other reasons, he was not fitted out to face adversity easily, so that when life grew tough he did not cope well. His domestic arrangements were sheltered. Until the age of forty he lived with his parents (Whittle 229), a circumstance not unusual in middle-class England at that time, and later in a string of expensive hotels (another structured environment) until entering semi-reclusiveness in his bungalow.

On the other hand, Montgomery was not always alone. He was attractive to women and there was often someone to look after him, notably his secretary Ann Clements whom he married in his last years. Montgomery was semi-reclusive because Ann was a continual protective presence. Whittle suggests that another woman who held a torch for him, Audrey Keir Cross, "felt sorry for this extremely clever man who was useless at coping with the realities of life" (231). Like E. C. Bentley, Bruce Montgomery's attitude towards women was ambivalent. Montgomery could never make the final moves in a seduction and, although he had many women friends, he shied away from close physical intimacy. "He was playing a game," says Whittle, which "could well account for the idealistic portraits of eligible young women he draws in his novels" (189). This contrasts with John Dickson Carr who is arguably Montgomery's mentor, who, though a womanizer had a long-standing marriage with the petite lady he adored.

Montgomery felt an underlying dissatisfaction with his work that is hard to pin down. Whittle suggests this was due to meeting with successes so early that when difficulties arose with publishers (in both the music world and that of books) he was pushed into depression as often as into activity. After 1957 he relied heavily on tranquillizers and sleeping pills (Whittle 191). Montgomery also found it hard to stay with a project over a long period, appearing to lose interest or become disheartened (Whittle 167). Whittle observes compassionately that Montgomery "rarely seemed to know where his greatest talents lay" (193).

By "the early 1970s, Crispin's drinking finally overwhelmed him and he started to have money problems" (*Books and Writers*). The heavy drinking that led to full-blown alcoholism meant that Montgomery failed to complete jobs on deadline. He could also be petulant, especially in money dealings or when annoyed by visitors interrupting his work, but at the same time had a deep-seated generosity of spirit. Publishers were loath to drop him because he was such a nice person, but eventually they did. He continued to live an extravagant lifestyle, including big parties and the purchase of wine and spirits (like Margery Allingham a decade or more earlier), and consequently he asked for loans from publishers and personal friends such as Larkin and Amis. His decline is associated with poor health, chain smoking and in particular the onset of osteoporosis from which Montgomery suffered a number of falls and broken limbs that also slowed him down.

By the age of forty Montgomery had made his mark in four fields. These were music, film (music scores), detective fiction, and science fiction appreciation. In more or less a decade, from around 1944 to 1953, Montgomery as Edmund Crispin wrote the Professor Gervase Fen novels. After that date he discontinued his output abruptly, a circumstance that puzzled some critics. According to Whittle (263), Montgomery was disenchanted with the encroachment of stylistic elements from the thriller into his preferred form of crime fiction (although this had been going on well before his time), plus the growing fashion in "naturalistic" crime writing that he deplored as well. But he had not given up writing. He was busy instead with other projects, hence his contribution to different genres. Under his real name of Bruce Montgomery he wrote musical scores for concerts as well as for around fifty feature films, the best known being the British comedies of the 1950s that include the *Carry On* theme music for their producer Peter Rogers ("Edmund Crispin"). According to IMDb, the six films are *Carry On, Sergeant* (1958), *Carry On, Teacher* and *Carry On, Nurse* (1959), *Carry On, Constable* (1960), *Carry On, Regardless*

(1961), and *Carry On, Cruising* (1962). He also wrote the original music for *Doctor in the House* (1954) and the original story and screenplay for *Raising the Wind* (1961).

Although *Wikipedia* and *Book Depository* record Montgomery's music and fiction writing as having virtually ceased due to alcoholism from 1960, he continued against these odds writing reviews of science fiction and crime novels for *The Sunday Times* ("Edmund Crispin"), in this capacity taking over from Julian Symons. Montgomery's judgment, critical in literary reviews but generous as well, assisted the careers of several new writers. He reviewed favorably P. D. James's *Shroud for a Nightingale* (1971), liking in particular "her ability to mix imaginative literature with detective fiction" — a trait Montgomery himself possessed to a large degree — and gave added confidence to Ruth Rendell who in 1970 thanked him for his "generous and enthusiastic" reviews of her work (Whittle 200). Whittle says that in this niche "he became one of the most influential critics of detective fiction" (182).

Montgomery was influential too in a revivification of science fiction that raised the standards of critical assessment for the genre (Whittle 179). As matters no doubt grew worse, Montgomery began to edit a number of anthologies in science fiction and horror through the 1960s, the seven volumes of *Best Science Fiction* ("Edmund Crispin"). These are, together with the horror anthologies, *Best Science Fiction* 1–7 (1955, 1956, 1958, 1961, 1963, 1966, 1970), *Outwards from Earth* (1974); *Best Tales of Terror* and *Best Tales of Terror Two* (1962 and 1965). Several seem to take up from the last years of his work for the *Carry On* projects. Interestingly, because his detective story writing is seen by Whittle (218) as belonging to an earlier era, Montgomery compared the state of science fiction in the 1950s with that of crime fiction in the 1920s (the Golden Age). He is paraphrased in Whittle: "It does not make the most of its material; its jargon appeals to a clique; there is a 'stuffy monasticism' in the sense that women rarely appear and normal relations between men and women are almost nonexistent; and the characters are of little interest in themselves" (177).

According to the entries in *Books and Writers* (Liukkonen and Pesonen), Montgomery's published music appears for the most part concurrent with his crime writing: *An Ode on the Resurrection of Christ* (1947), *Mary Ambree* (1948), *Four Shakespeare Songs* (1948), two suites for chorus and strings: *Christ's Birthday* (1948) and *Venus' Praise* (1952), *Concertino for String Orchestra* (1950), *An Oxford Requiem* (1950), *Concerto Waltz for Two Pianos* (1952), *John Barleycorn: An Opera for Children* (1962). Barry Forshaw observes that Crispin's "close attention to structure" in his plotting probably owes a lot to his skill as a composer (25).

Even if it were to stand alone, Montgomery's *oeuvre* as Edmund Crispin is impressive: *The Case of the Gilded Fly* (1944), *Holy Disorders* (1945), *The Moving Toyshop* (1946), *Swan Song* (1947), *Love Lies Bleeding* (1948), *Buried for*

Pleasure (1948), *Frequent Hearses* (1950), *The Long Divorce* (1952), a short story collection *Beware of the Trains* (1953), *The Glimpses of the Moon* (1977), and a posthumous short story collection *Fen Country* (1979).

Liukkonen and Pesonen write that Crispin is:

> Master of fast-paced, tongue-in-cheek mystery novels, a blend of John Dickson Carr, Michael Innes, M.R. James, and the Marx Brothers, as the critic Anthony Boucher once described. Crispin's nine humorous Gervase Fen novels are among the most individualistic works of the genre.... In his novels Crispin combined farcical situations with literary references, coincidences with nearly postmodern self-awareness, inappropriate behaviour and sharp observations of the language of various classes and professions [1].

Crispin is described by Symons (142) as the last of the farceurs of detective fiction — this strand of the crime-writing lineage is listed in his Index as the "Farceur school" (247) — and while Michael Innes (one of the pseudonyms for John Innes Mackintosh Stewart) was writing in the same decades as Crispin, Innes' work by comparison is subdued and "playfully highbrow" ("J. I. M. Stewart"), carrying on, I think, from the tradition of Dorothy L. Sayers, both writers setting their stories within the "cloistered world" of academe (Forshaw 24–25). Indeed, just as there is in mainstream English literature a subgenre of academic or "campus novels" (Wynne-Davies 678) such as those of Kingley Amis, David Lodge and Malcolm Bradbury, so too this subgenre is well represented in crime novel humor along with parodies of the country cottage mystery. Edmund Crispin's first novel set the format for the rest of his output in the cloistered worlds of his character Professor Gervase Fen.

There are other cloistered worlds aside from that of a university. In *The Case of the Gilded Fly*, Crispin has two cloistered worlds embedded within each other: a repertory company within a university. As Binyon observes:

> A repertory company provides the closed society dear to the heart of the classical detective novelist, and the building of the theatre itself, with its entrances and exits, passages, coulisses [wings, side scenery — OED], subterranean labyrinths, and galleries and gantries above the stage, offers as many opportunities for mysterious disappearances and appearances as a Gothic castle or a medieval manor [66].

So it is that one violent death takes place within a university residential building and another in the organ loft of a chapel, while the murderer himself comes to a sudden end on stage crushed beneath the heavy safety curtain. I think we can safely claim Edmund Crispin as a classical detective novelist.

The Case of the Gilded Fly (1944)

Crispin's first Gervase Fen novel, at about 73,000 words when he was twenty-three years old, establishes a pattern from which his later work rarely deviates. His novels almost invariably begin with a journey of some kind — a countryside walk, a taxi — but in several instances a train journey, reflecting Montgomery's knowledge of that mode of transport and a loving irritation with British Rail. In this first chapter the main characters are introduced, love triangles noted, and several motives for the shooting of Yseut Haskell established. There is a roundup of stock characters. In *The Case of the Gilded Fly* most of these are members of a repertory company en route from London to Oxford where they are to rehearse a play, *Metromania*. Thumbnail sketches establish their types.

Sheila McGaw (5) is "a tall young woman, with trousers, sharp-cut features, a prominent nose and straight flaxen hair cut to a bell" (the almost ubiquitous "bob" of the 1920s). The reading matter she possesses, and with which she attempts to entertain a farmer, is a set of illustrations by the scene designer, director and actor Gordon Craig (1872–1966), who laid out intricate sets for *Hamlet* and other plays. In desperation the farmer retaliates by becoming lyrical about animal husbandry and agricultural methods: "Sheila ... managed to persuade herself by a form of autohypnosis that it had all been very interesting" (6). The comedy of contrasts rests upon the lifestyles and interests of two very different persons.

Robert Warner is the playwright whose latest work, *Metromania*, is to be performed by the Oxford Repertory Theatre. He is accompanied by Rachel West, his Jewish mistress. Robert is "in his late thirties, with rather coarse black hair (a rustic forelock drooping over his brow), heavy horn-rimmed spectacles shielding alert, intelligent eyes, tall, rather lanky, and dressed inconspicuously in a dark lounge suit" (7). At the end of the novel he is uncovered as the murderer, a dénouement perhaps flagged in the character's name, "warning" readers in advance. Names, like titles, are often chosen consciously by writers to suggest themes, whether by allusion or more directly, as David Lodge points out: "Comic, satiric or didactic writers can afford to be exuberantly inventive, or obviously allegorical in their naming.... Realistic novelists favour mundane names with appropriate connotations.... The naming of characters is always an important part of creating them" (37).

Yseut Haskell, who is Warner's first victim shot in a "locked" room, "was still young — twenty-five or so — with full breasts and hips a little crudely emphasized by the clothes she wore and a head of magnificent and much cared-for hair" (8). Her father names her from his "intensive and entirely fruitless study of the French Tristan romances" (10). She is the prima donna/femme fatale of the repertory, vain and spiteful, a vamp almost universally disliked. This is in keeping with one of the more apparent "rules" in crime/detective fiction that the character of the victim is generally so unsympathetic that there is a certain degree of satisfaction taken at their untimely demise.

Helen Haskell is Yseut's half-sister, born to her father's second wife. She is the love interest: "short, blonde, slim, pretty (in a childish way which made her look much younger than she actually was), had big, candid blue eyes, and was entirely sincere" (10). She is the first of a long line of Crispin heroines. Yseut and Helen dislike each other intensely, yet Helen is to inherit handsomely from Yseut's will: "a deed leaving the whole of her [Yseut's] money in the event of death, to her half-sister." Nigel Blake is a journalist who, having won a first in English three years earlier, is on his way to Oxford to visit his friend Gervase Fen, to watch the new play, and to see Helen Haskell again. He is in love with Helen. In the novel he is Fen's sidekick, the Watson character. His courtship of Helen is the novel's love interest.

Yseut Haskell is not universally disliked, for Donald Fellowes is "very gravely in love" with her (13). But we find towards the end that he is also in love with Jean Whitelegge. Fellowes is "a quiet, dark little person, addicted to bow ties and gin and very inoffensive in manner ... organist at Fen's college ... St. Christopher's" (13). He becomes Warner's second victim (207) in the organ loft. Two traveling companions are Nicholas Barklay and Jean Whitelegge. Jean is in love with Donald Fellowes and Nicholas (13) admires Fellowes for his work as a musician and feels sorry for him because of his infatuation with Yseut. Jean is "tall, dark, bespectacled and rather plain" whose interests, aside from her crush on Fellowes, revolve around the Oxford University Theatre Club (14–15).

A traveler who fulfills the stock character of the police officer is Sir Richard Freeman, Chief Constable of Oxford. As for naming, we remember that "Dick" is a colloquialism for detective and "Freeman" possibly an ironic reference to someone whose work often ends with others no longer at liberty. The relationship between Freeman and his friendly rival Gervase Fen has the carnivalesque quality of overturning:

> Sir Richard's chief interest being English literature, and Fen's police work. They would sit for hours expounding fantastic theories about each other's work, and developing a fine scorn for each other's competence, and where detective stories, of which Fen was an avid reader, were concerned, they frequently nearly came to blows, since Fen would insist, maliciously but with some truth, that they were the only form of literature which carried on the true tradition of the English novel, while Sir Richard poured out his fury on the ridiculous problems which they presented, and the even more ridiculous methods used in solving them ... if they had ever changed places ... Fen would have found the routine police work as intolerable as Sir Richard, the niggling niceties of textual criticism [11–12].

In a loose sense, Freeman is the Inspector Lestrade type from the Sherlock Holmes stream, though he is more intelligent that Conan Doyle's character. One of the jokes in this description is Crispin's tongue-in-cheek theory of detective stories with its allusions to amateurs and methods, two themes often debated in literary criticism of the genre.

It is a social cliché that travelers take reading material with them, especially in trains. As noted above, this provides an opportunity for gentle parody at the expense of different genres in the passengers' choices, both actual and invented, as well as an outlet for Crispin's fondness for obscure literary references. Freeman reads *Minor Satirists of the XVIIIth Century* written by Gervase Fen. Helen reads *Cymbeline* "with a little frown of concentration ... not sure that she was enjoying it very much" (11). This is a play from Shakespeare's last period that, according to D. C. Browning, is more correctly described as a "romantic drama" (vi), although it is placed in the *Tragedies* in my 1956 Everyman's Library edition. Browning states that the character of Imogen is "one of the most appealing of Shakespeare's heroines" and rates *Cymbeline* as "one of his finest plays" (vi). Imogen's "moral purity" ("Imogen (Shakespeare)") is a nice trope for Helen Haskell.

A young artillery captain sharing the carriage with Yseut (9) reads the James Hadley Chase novel *No Orchids for Miss Blandish*. Notorious for its depiction of the rape and murder of the eponymous character, *No Orchids* was first published five years earlier than *Gilded Fly* and so is current in the novelistic present of Crispin's characters. George Orwell's critical review of *No Orchids* is even more current, appearing in 1944 in two publications for that year. It would be surprising if Crispin had not read both novel and the reviews. *No Orchids for Miss Blandish* is mentioned a second time (27) with the reappearance of the young captain in chapter two, now identified as Peter Graham, with some of the group at a local hotel, the Mace and Sceptre. He and Rachel flirt and he takes her to dinner in a scene where the members of the theater are forming and breaking up alliances for the evening. It is a walk-on–walk-off part inserted I suspect for the allusion to *No Orchids* but also to demonstrate the relationship between Rachel and Warner.

Three major literary allusions, one invented, are enough for the chapter. The novel is littered with them, which exasperates some critics. The references, such as to *Cymbeline*, by and large make a point in order to underline a person's character, or *No Orchids for Miss Blandish* to remind the reader ironically that the novel will shortly become a murder mystery. Another aspect of these literary asides is the satirizing of academic writing. On Nicholas Barklay:

> As an undergraduate reading English a brilliant academic career had been prophesied for him, and he had bought, and read, all those immense annotated editions of the classics in which the greater part of every page is occupied with commentary (with a slight gesture to the author in the form of a thin trickle of text up at the top, towards the page number), and the study of which is considered essential to all those so audacious as to aim at a Fellowship [14].

From experience I can assure readers that anthropological and sociological commentaries can be just as tedious.

The epitome of academic satire belongs to the main protagonist Professor Gervase Fen, described by Binyon as "one of the most successful academic detectives" (52). His physical appearance and eccentric behavior is described regularly in the opening chapters of Crispin's novels, as in the first, becoming a stock description in later tales:

> He coughed and groaned and yawned and shuffled his feet and agitated his long, lanky body about in the corner where he sat. His cheerful, ruddy, clean-shaven face grew even ruddier than usual; his dark hair, sedulously plastered down with water, broke out into disaffected fragments toward the crown ... his only distraction was one of his own books, on the minor satirists of the eighteenth century, which he was conscientiously rereading in order to recall what were his opinions of these persons ... and wondered if he would be allowed to investigate another murder, supposing one occurred [4].

Authors need remain faithful to descriptions of their characters when they reappear. Compare the passage in Crispin's second-last Fen novel *The Long Divorce* published in 1952: "He was a tall and wiry man of between forty and fifty, with a lean, ruddy, clean-shaven face. His brown hair, ineffectually plastered down with water, stood up in mutinous spikes at the crown of his head. His manner was eupeptic [having good digestion — OED] and affable ... he carolled lustily, to the distress of all animate nature, as he walked" (1–2).

While still on Chapter One, there are, in addition to the factors above, striking tropes hinting that deaths are to follow:

> The train stops just outside the station, the monolithic apparitions of a gas-works on one side, a cemetery on the other, by which the engine lingers with ghoulish insistence, emitting sporadic shrieks and groans of necrophilous delight. A sense of wild, itching frustration sets in: there is Oxford, there, a few yards away, is the station, and here is the train, and passengers are not allowed to walk along the line, even if any of them had the initiative to do so; it is the whole torture of Tantalus in hell. This interlude of *memento mori* during which the railway company reminds the golden lads and girls in its charge of their inevitable coming to dust [2].

The scene gains much of its entertainment value because it parodies gothic melodrama. The looming gas-works suggests a huge gravestone set opposite the cemetery, a faithful sketch of the back end of towns through which trains so often pass and provide the visitor's first impression of a place. Emotional frustration (itching) and the helplessness or disinterest of passengers is linked to a vision of the Ancient Greek underworld: "Tantalus became one of the inhabitants of Tartarus, the deepest portion of the Underworld, reserved for the punishment of evildoers ... welcomed to Zeus' table in Olympus.... He is said to have misbehaved and stolen ambrosia and nectar to bring it back to his people, and revealed the secrets of the gods" ("Tantalus"). In this pre–Christian vision of hell we are reminded that we all die: Latin, *memento mori* = "remember you must die" (COD). But embedded within these somber images is a quirky anthropomorphism by which the train shrieks — like the ghost train at sideshow alley — and takes pleasure in the scene. Words such as "ghoulish" are juxtaposed against "delight" and so their impact is blunted; the dispirited passengers without initiative (an amusing image in itself) are linked to an archaic image of hell; the warning that we are all mortal, originally voiced to Roman generals by an adviser during a triumphal procession, is attributed to British Rail. It is a good example of what Freud (10) calls comic contrast or, in David Lodge's terms (111), the combination of surprise with conformity to pattern.

Yseut's interrelationships between the group's principal members, and its conflicts, are played out in the hotel where they meet. A lot of it is told from Nigel's point of view. Once again, impending murder is hinted. An argument between Nicholas and Yseut is "an unpleasant little incident, one of several such, destined to culminate in murder" (25), and at the end Nicholas says: "Someone is going to kill or mutilate that girl one day" (30). In the next chapter the conflict moves to the first rehearsal of *Metromania*. With obvious irony Yseut sings: "Why was I born / Why am I livin' / What do I get, / What am I givin'?" (36). Here, and in later parts of the novel, Crispin's knowledge of stagecraft comes to the fore, gained no doubt from his time at Oxford but more particularly from his involvement in film. The chapter is a parody of a stage rehearsal with new characters in walk-on parts: a gloomy young man named Bruce in the orchestra pit (35); the director Robert's shouted cue line (35); latecomer Clive (37), oblivious of the delay he's caused; stage manager and understudy, Jane "a slim, attractive young woman of twenty or thereabouts" (39). The dominant theme is Yseut's sexuality. Again Nigel's point of view at the close of Yseut's song: "it's not very surprising ... that a woman should enjoy making an elementary form of sexual advance to a room full of men without the slightest chance, so to speak, of being taken at her word. It must be a most delightful feeling" (37). Before all this, Nigel overhears a brief exchange between Yseut and Donald Fellowes, who declares his love for her (34). The chapter ends in a stormy argument between Yseut and Jean Whitelegge. As a prelude, Nigel had been thinking:

> It's ordinary comedy ... a pure Restoration drama situation — but it refuses to be comic; it's bitter and dull and sordid and witless. Later he was to realise how bitter these quarrels were, and to reproach himself for not paying more attention to them [38].

The reader is reminded continually to expect the tragedy that is to unfold. Crispin puts suspense to good use.

By now we have reached the fourth chapter that completes the build-up of suspense. There is another gathering, this time at a party thrown by Peter Graham who is still hopelessly pursuing Rachel. It is the scene of an increasingly bitter argument between Yseut and others. Another minor character appears, Richard: "a tall, fair-haired young man in the late twenties" (49–50). Peter Graham clumsily shifts his attentions from Rachel to Jane. Fragmented, phatic conversation characteristic of such gatherings adds to the humor. Yseut becomes drunk and waves a revolver she has acquired somewhere. Peter takes it from her. Helen takes her home. We are reminded several times that the chronological setting is wartime England by the attention given to blackout restrictions at night, a sort of background suspense to the main action.

The movements of that revolver are very important. In another use of suspense, we are told by the omniscient narrator that the night porter dozing in his box fails to see someone "who flitted silently up the big staircase to Peter Graham's room, or what that person was carrying on its return" (55). Nigel, with a premonition, goes to Peter Graham's room and looks for the firearm: "The drawer was empty. Revolver and cartridges were gone" (55). Here, as in earlier classic crime mysteries such as *Trent's Last Case*, as well as in John Dickson Carr's/Carter Dickson's *Night at the Mocking Widow*, the disappearance of a revolver becomes a crucial plot element.

The build-up of suspense continues with a coincidental meeting between Nigel and principle characters on their way down to breakfast:

> He rose and breakfasted early, wondering as he did so what the more riotous members of the party must be feeling like. Then at half past nine he went back to his room to get a book. His way led him through the corridor where Robert's and Rachel's rooms were situated, and made him a party to a coincidence which afterwards proved to have been of some considerable importance. As he passed Rachel's room, she came out on her way down to breakfast.
>
> And it was at that precise moment that Yseut emerged from Robert's room opposite.
>
> All three of them stopped dead; and to Nigel at any rate the implications of Yseut's presence were obvious.... The expression on her [Rachel's] face was not pleasant to see [56].

Yseut carries "a thin red notebook; and in her eyes was an expression of mingled fear and satisfaction which was repellent to a degree" (57). The notebook is a true McGuffin, the significance of which becomes clear in the dénouement. They part without a word. In this description words are superfluous. Crispin establishes the drama of the encounter through movement, pause and facial expression accentuated by the short connecting sentence.

Yseut's death takes place at the bitter end of Chapter Five, "Cave Ne Exeat," that Crispin translates as "Do not let it get out" (70), referring to a university ghost. This chapter opens with an introduction to Gervase Fen's home life with a small group gathering in his room at the university. The drawing-room discussion had been a stock device since the nineteenth century. It can appear early in a novel, as in the opening chapter of Wells's *The Time Machine* (1895), or be the setting for a dénouement as in many of Agatha Christie's stories, and has been parodied many times. In this instance, Crispin places the meeting in the first third of *Gilded Fly*. The participants are Gervase Fen, Nigel

Blake, Fen's wife Dolly — "a plain, spectacled, sensible little woman" (64) — Sir Richard Freeman, and a ubiquitous comic presence, the ancient don Wilkes who appears in several Fen novels, somewhat deaf with a strong liking for whisky.

The first part of the chapter is occasion for further satire on the detective tale, a sort of intertextual relationship in which Fen in argument with Freeman says: "Detection and literary criticism really come to the same thing: intuition ... once the idea has occurred to you, you can work on substantiating it from the text — or from the remainder of the clues.... I'm the only literary critic turned detective in the whole of fiction" (65–66). Soon after the exchange between Fen and Freeman, Robert Warner joins the group. Wilkes proceeds to tell a ghost story about the university, to the dismay of his audience. The anecdote, from a different genre (that of the ghost or horror story), departs from lighthearted satire to re-establish the suspense that Crispin has been building upon since the beginning. At the close of Wilkes's tale, Fen does the blackout and switches on the lights in the room. Robert asks the whereabouts of the lavatory (toilet) and leaves. There is some disbelief about the story. When Dolly expresses it, Fen looks upon her "with something of the triumphant and sentimental pride of a dog-owner whose pet has succeeded in balancing a biscuit on its nose" (75). Wilkes insists that the story is true and adds prophetically: "It is the killing, after all, which is the essential thing, however it be contrived. Killing always engenders more killing" (77). At that moment they hear a shot.

In the next chapter, Crispin touches upon an element that is both a stylistic and a moral controversy within crime fiction: comedy and the lighthearted in uneasy alliance with the sordid impact of the crime of murder, which is another way of addressing the tradition of employing elements of comedy to explore serious purpose (*see* Lodge 164). Generally speaking, the act of murder is glossed over in comedic crime and in some instances is barely mentioned, while in others it is revealed that no crime is committed (for example, in Shelia Pim's *Creeping Venom*). But occasionally a writer will remind us how serious it all is:

> Like most people, Nigel had often tried to imagine how he would feel in the presence of violent death. Like most people, he had thought of himself as being calm, collected, almost indifferent. So the conscious part of him was totally unprepared for the sudden acute spasm of nausea which seized him at the sight of that motionless, lifeless form. He went quickly back to the sitting-room, and sat down with his face in his hands" [81].

A little later Nigel experiences an epiphany: "It was an honest admission that without life the most beautiful body is an object of no interest. We are not bodies, thought Nigel, we are lives. And oddly, there came to him at that moment a new and firm conviction of the nature of love" (86). To underscore the serious tone of this chapter there is a corresponding change of mood in

Gervase Fen: "His usual slightly fantastic naivety had completely disappeared, and its place was taken by a rather formidable, ice-cold concentration. Sir Richard, who knew the signs, looked up from his conference with the Inspector and sighed" (90).

In this relatively long chapter the build-up of suspense that began in chapter one reaches a conclusion with the discovery of Yseut's body. It does not end there, of course. This is a plot turning point from which the next layers of suspense are generated in the investigations to uncover the murderer. In a sort of catharsis, there is a return to relief in comedy, when in order to demonstrate how unwieldy the revolver would have been if held in the way Yseut appears to have done it, Fen requests Dolly to commit suicide (96).

In the following chapter the first round of police interviews begin. The gun that belonged to the military man Peter Graham is stolen from his flat on the night of the party. Nigel phones Helen to give her the news. Fen and the Inspector interview Robert Warner who uses Rachel as his alibi and, at the point of leaving, turns suspicion upon Jean Whitelegge by saying that he saw her coming from Peter Graham's room. There are allusions to other works in crime fiction. The epigraph heading the chapter is attributed to Thomas Campion (1567–1620), an Elizabethan songwriter, "comparable to Shakespeare and Jonson" (Bloom 136), but Campion is also the name of Margery Allingham's fictional detective. (Each chapter carries an epigraph from one of the English poets.) When Fen speculates that Fellowes could not leave the college after dark unless he went "through the President's garden," adding "irrelevantly" that "it all comes of having a system which is half monastic and half not" (104), he is alluding to the comparatively closed communities writers choose as their settings, and playing on the title of Malcolm Innes' novel *Death at the President's Lodging* (1936). Montgomery (aka Crispin) admired Innes' work and probably modeled his style upon that of Innes as well as Carr. Whittle (266) states that Montgomery made "relatively little use" of the enclosed world of the university college, but this is splitting hairs. Montgomery may have chosen to make *less use* of the enclosed world of the college setting, but he settled upon alternative closed worlds all the same.

Allusions to other works in the genre continue, including reference jokes. After complaining that "we have completely lost the point in a maze of routine investigation," Fen says: "If there's anything I profoundly dislike, it is the sort of detective story in which one of the characters propounds views on how detective stories should be written. It's bad enough having a detective who reads the things" (123). Another example: "I know: it can't come out till the last chapter" (124). Crispin is fond of stage whispers, "breaking the fourth wall," as are many other authors in crime fiction. It is a relatively common comedic device and a means by which an author may quietly poke fun at her/his contemporaries.

A lot of Crispin's literary allusions are faint suggestions or obscure and sometimes inaccurate quotations from literary classics difficult to recognize. This is a striking aspect of Crispin's humor that annoys some critics. Crispin not only has us running to our encyclopaedias for the obscure literary references, we have also to dive into our dictionaries for the meaning of multisyllabic words, such as (121) "constatation" = the process of verification or assertion; "gnomic" (131) = sententious, using aphorisms (OED); "aposiopesis" (132) = becoming silent, breaking off a sentence (Wik); "apolaustic" (133) = dedicated to enjoyment (Wik); "finical" (133) = finicky (COD); "cinereous" (138) = ash-grey (COD). This is what happens when a writer holds a first in English literature from the Oxbridge schools.

This chapter also contains one of the statements on death by violence that is *de rigueur* in most if not all of Crispin's crime novels. As usual it comes through an internal monologue on the part of a Watson character, in this case Nigel Blake:

> His earlier reaction to the murder [in page 81] he felt had been sentimental, and he was now inclined to believe that Yseut's death might from many points of view not have been at all a bad thing; if she had been run over by a bus, the effect would have been the same, so why be disturbed by moral considerations? ... This was in his conscious mind; in the unconscious there lived and grew still a superstitious terror of death by violence, impervious to the niceties of rational calculation, and which the consciousness was trying to suppress by refusing further speculation on the problem. The superstitious fear was there, no doubt, because the agency was mysterious — an atavistic throwback to a belief in the powers of the spirits of earth and air [130–131].

We remember that Crispin was influenced by the crime stories of John Dickson Carr, who went in for supernatural explanations ultimately debunked by Carr's Sir Henry Merrivale or Dr. Gideon Fell.

Compare this with a similar passage in *The Moving Toyshop*. Fen says: "A criminal has no rights in any sane society" (132). Cadogan's thoughts are very different:

> Euthanasia, Cadogan thought: they all regard it as that, and not as wilful slaughter, not as the violent cutting-off of an irreplaceable compact of passion and desire and affection and will; not as a thrust into unimagined and illimitable darkness. He tried to see Havering's face, but it was only a lean silhouette in the fading light. Something took root in him that in a week, a month, a year perhaps, would become poetry. He was suddenly excited and oddly content. The words of his predecessors in the great Art came to his mind. *"They are all gone into the world of light," "I that in heill was an in gladnesse." "Dust hath closed Helen's eye...."* The vast and terrifying significance of death closed round him for a moment like the petals of a dark flower [165].

This is one of the strongest passages on the topic that we might read in Crispin. One like it appears in most of his novels. Note the atmosphere elicited by repeated uses of images of the dark: "unimagined and illimitable darkness," "silhouette," "fading light," contrasted with "*the world of light*," immediately set against the closing of eyes, and the final simile immediately after repeating the verb to close: "the petals of a dark flower closed round him." At the same time there is Cadogan's excitement and odd contentment, in a sense perhaps for the reader too, because they are closer to uncovering the identity of the murderer and approaching closure. It is an interesting touch to raise the soliloquy to a poetic level by citing yet another literary source, the sixteenth-century poet Thomas Nashe (1567–1601), in Kermode and Hollander, *The Oxford Anthology of English Literature*: "Beauty is but a flower, / Which wrinkles will devour; / Brightness falls from the air; / Queens have died young and fair; / Dust hath closed Helen's eye. / I am sick, I must die." In *Gilded Fly*, Nigel's internal thoughts continue:

> This is the stage, he told himself, at which the stark, terrible realisation of the thing envelops you with a sudden rush; fortunately it is nothing of the sort; on the contrary, its supreme unimportance is most impressive and is resulting in a perceptible lightening of spirit [138].

This is the stage, too, at which the author smooths the emotion for the reader in order to continue with the main goal, that of resolving the mystery. As a stage in the plot, this chapter is concerned mostly with the thoughts of a number of persons: between Nicholas Barclay and Sheila McGaw, between Jean Whitelegge and Estelle Bryant and between Rachel West and Robert Warner. Nigel accompanies the inspector for the cross-examination of Helen. Helen is shown the ring taken from Yseut's hand that appears to have been placed there after her death. It means nothing to her. The inspector states that he believes the death was suicide. The ring is a key motif in the plot but receives little discussion and, as we shall see, its significance is an afterthought. It is a McGuffin of the forgotten kind.

Back to the rehearsal and Nigel and Helen, after some dalliance, receive Fen through the window. He is "muffled in an enormous raincoat and had on an extraordinary hat" (153), a parody of John Dickson Carr's Gideon Fell. Fen announces that he knows who committed the crime. Nigel remains in the dark as at Fen's bidding he summarizes the case to Helen. The rehearsal is a minor interlude in which "Fen prowled about getting in everyone's way, exhibiting an exaggerated interest in the proceedings, and asking idiotic questions" (157). The comedy continues when they retire to the "Aston Arms," where Nigel is bitten on the finger by a featherless parrot that quotes from *Die Lorelei*.

From the ridiculous to the serious, Fen questions Nicholas about movements into and out of the room he and Donald Fellowes were sitting in at the time the shot was heard. At Fen's request Nicholas delivers a short and scathing disquisition "on the ethics of murder" (161). Fen questions Sheila McGaw about where she was at the time of the murder. He argues with Fellowes who is upset because he believes he is under suspicion. Fen's forceful reply has purpose. He moves on to Robert and Rachel. Fen is playing the part of devil's advocate when he remarks about the rehearsal and hence the play:

> In this, as in a very few other works of literature, there are things which one can only put down to divine inspiration. Normally one can easily follow the rather laborious and mechanical processes of an author's thought. It's the unexpected, inconceivable things that don't fit into that process, and which yet are absolutely right, that I mean [166].

Robert, referring to this as "a bag of tricks," says he will shortly be writing another play that is even better. There follows a subtle sparring match between Fen and Robert:

> Robert: "Is it usual ... for the detective to discuss the crime with his suspects in this impartial and informative fashion? ..."
> Fen: "A *sine qua non*.... In the course of the discussion they are supposed to give away their innermost feelings. But do you regard yourself as a suspect?"
> Robert: "Well ... I suppose I could have rushed out of the lavatory, shot the girl, rushed back again, and reappeared at the appropriate moment." [Which is in fact what he did] [167].

They return to the rehearsal. Fen suggests that he can help Helen in her career by introducing her to a celebrated actor: "I have a hold over him. We were at school together, and he did awful things" (173). Compare a similar schooldays relationship between Sir Henry Merrivale and the bishop in "Mocking Widow." Fen questions Jean Whitelegge. Jean admits that she took the gun from Captain Graham's room because Robert needed it as a prop for the play. Later the gun disappeared. Back at the stage there is brief mention of the safety curtain: "a heavy contraption which was abruptly lowered, narrowly missing the head of the husbandly Clive, who leaped out of the way with a startled oath" (179). As in several other instances, this is a "smoking gun," a harbinger of what is to come in the climactic scene. It is a principle in detective writing that features strongly in John Dickson Carr's work that Crispin admired so much and emulated. In a short essay written at the age of fifteen the precocious Carr — who calls this "realistic" story writing — stated that "putting here and there a casual remark that, unknown to the reader, is the keynote of the plot; increasing the suspense bit by bit until the reader is being hurried along at a terrific speed; and in one astounding flash revealing the whole truth" (Greene 455).

Fen surprises Nigel by saying (181) that in this particular case sexual jealousy is the motive. The chapter's title is "The Questing Beast." This is another example of the casual remark turning out to be a keynote. Earlier, in a discussion with Sir Richard, Fen states categorically: "I don't believe in the *crime passionel*, particularly when the passion appears, as in this case, to be chiefly frustration. Money, vengeance, security: these are your plausible motives, and I shall look for one of them" (124).

The next chapter (twelve) is a similar interlude. It stretches out the suspense, marking a quiet point, a prelude before the onset of action. In the "story" it refers to the opening night of the play, but it is also an ironic touch in the plot: "It was an interlude of calm before the final effort, before the culmination of that effort on the Monday night, and before another culmination more serious and less pleasant" (185). It is also like the point in a film before the final action where the love interest is resolved. Thus, the "Vignettes" in this chapter are (1) Donald and Jean walking in one of the parks of the university, where Donald declares his love for her; (2) Nicholas and the blonde discuss the case as Nicholas buys her a drink; (3) Robert and Rachel, also strolling, discuss theater and the case, and when Robert asks Rachel to marry him she accepts; (4) also in a park, Fen and his wife discuss the case as their little son plays with the family cat; (5) Nigel and Helen cycle together and picnic at the riverside where Nigel asks Helen to marry him and she accepts. This is one of the few insights into Fen's domestic life. In the next chapter we learn that he is forty-two.

Fen tells Nigel that he has mailed a letter to the murderer to say he is discovered. He shows Nigel a timetable of the movements of various suspects but Nigel can make nothing of it. They attend the chapel. The organ player, Donald Fellowes, fails to come in on cue at the closing hymn. Fen and Nigel (207) investigate and discover Fellowes, "lying across the organ stool with his throat cut from ear to ear, and a blood-stained knife on the floor near him." The play is performed and ends: "on a note of sudden personal tragedy, delicately and movingly hinted at" (219), a case of the play within reflecting upon the plot line without. The actors, Fen and Sir Richard gather at the theater bar. Helen and Nigel wait hand in hand "for the curtain to go up on the last act of another play" (220). The facts fall into place in Nigel's mind. Jean Whitelegge has disappeared. Fen warns that the police have the theater surrounded. The murderer, Robert Warner, faces them with an automatic pistol in hand. He runs onto the stage pursued by Fen, Nigel and the inspector, who fires, wounding Warner in the leg. Warner falls. The safety curtain drops and crushes him. Nigel enters the electrician's gallery where the switch that raises the curtain is located and finds Jean Whitelegge there.

Back in Fen's rooms there follows the traditional drawing-room explanation. The shot heard by the witnesses was a blank cartridge and not the one that killed Yseut. She had been shot from the west courtyard through a number of open windows, the sound of the report drowned by the loud music played by Donald and Nicholas. The motive is that of security and not of sex, for it was Yseut's loss of her red notebook and subsequent search for it in Fellowes' room. The notebook contains something incriminating Warner with which Yseut was blackmailing him. Fellowes had taken the notebook accidentally when gathering up his music from the bar and was killed because he would have read the notebook. This is one of the MacGuffins.

"a plot element that catches the viewers' attention or drives the plot of a work of fiction" [*MacGuffin*, Princeton University, WordNet 3.0]. The defining aspect of a MacGuffin is that the major players in the story are (at least initially) willing to do and sacrifice almost anything to obtain it, regardless of what the MacGuffin actually is.... Common examples are money, victory, glory, survival, a source of power, a potential threat ... common in films, especially thrillers.... It may come back into play at the climax of the story, but sometimes the MacGuffin is actually forgotten ("MacGuffin").

Donald Fellowes, Fen speculates (231), assumed that Jean Whitelegge committed the murder and, because "he was infatuated with her" said nothing in order to protect her. Fen himself is reluctant to follow up (232) because the suspect (Warner) was "a great creative artist." After Fellowes' death, Jean privately tells Fen that she did indeed witness Robert Warner shoot Yseut. The chapter closes with a remark that Jean could not be prosecuted for releasing the stage curtain because she was helping stop an escaping killer. The reader sees that Jean took the only revenge she could over the murder of Fellowes, who loved her and with whom she was in love.

There remain a few pages of anti-climax in "Epilogue: The Gilded Fly." Six people travel back to London by train during the week in 19–24 October 1940, as they had come. It is unusual for an author to give such precise dating. The two train journeys at the beginning and the close are like bookends to the novel. It is a neat way of rounding it off. The blonde tells Nicholas she is going to marry him. Fen and Sir Richard discuss literature. Helen and Nigel are honeymooners, having married a few days before. Crispin has a more romantic end for young lovers than in some of his later novels such as *The Moving Toyshop* in which Cadogan, the Watson character equivalent to Nigel, does not win the lady.

The ring called the "gilded fly" is a true McGuffin. It is barely explained when Nigel asks Fen about it. Fen replies that Warner, prone to over-elaborating or "decorating," had placed the ring on Yseut's finger as an ironic symbol of "measure for measure," that she lived and died by sex, citing vaguely the Shakespearean tragedy *King Lear* they are attending, possibly Act IV, Scene 4 (241). It is a vague reference, intentionally I think, and I find in it nothing to suggest an ironic tit for tat, or, in the corresponding act and scene of *Measure for Measure* reference to sexual promiscuity, although there is mention of "A deflow'd maid" that hardly fits the case.

The Moving Toyshop (1946)

The Moving Toyshop is Edmund Crispin's third in the Professor Gervase Fen series and is considered by many to be among his best. Howard Haycraft includes it in *The Haycraft-Queen Definitive Library*. By his lights Crispin is a latecomer (xxiv): "among the new writers [with] ... the necessary staying-power" (xxiv). But the names of Crispin or Montgomery do not appear in the book's index. At approximately 61,500 words, *The Moving Toyshop* is almost but not quite a novella, a little shorter than the début novel *The Case of the Gilded Fly* at about 72,300 words. The advantage of a form of this length is that it encourages the writer to be economical in words, if one aims at a certain length in the first place, and sometimes this can mean tighter control of the plot. Contrast it with Nancy Spain's *Poison for Teacher* at around 110,000 words, longer but not necessarily as tightly or as neatly structured. However, one disadvantage of a shorter length novel is that while it need not preclude character development, in my opinion it tends to make this a little difficult. Compare Margery Allingham's psychological novel *The Tiger in the Smoke* (1952) at approximately 89,000 words, sufficient for her study of the psychopath Jack Havoc, or Graham Greene's character Pinkie in *Brighton Rock* (1938) at around 98,000 words.

In Crispin's novels, such as *The Moving Toyshop*, sufficient room is allowed to sketch in the characters of two or at the most three of the protagonists. The others tend to be one-dimensional stock figures. Crispin's poet Richard Cadogan, in a sense Professor Fen's Watson figure from whose point of view the story mostly is told, is vaguely Holmesian: "He was lean, with sharp features, supercilious eyebrows, and hard dark eyes. This characteristic appearance belied him, for he was [sic] a matter of fact a friendly, unexacting, romantic person" (9). Set this beside Conan Doyle's portrait of Sherlock Holmes from *A Study in Scarlet*: "excessively lean ... his eyes ... sharp and piercing ... his thin, hawk-like nose gave his whole expression an air of alertness and decision" (15). Richard Cadogan does not quite match up to the last part of Conan Doyle's description of Holmes. Sally Carstairs, when fleeing from Fen and Cadogan is frightened unnecessarily by "that man with the cold eyes," meaning Cadogan (89). The subtle humor, if he is indeed a physical parody of Holmes, is that Cadogan is a romantic rather than a decisive hero, and unexacting rather than alert.

Toyshop has an attention-grabbing opening that introduces mood variation from seriousness that will throughout descend or rise to satire and farce: "Richard Cadogan raised his revolver, took careful aim and pulled the trigger" (9), and misses the target. He negotiates with his publisher Mr. Spode (an important minor character by the end of the novel) for an advance that will allow him to take a holiday. (A character with the same name appears in the Wodehouse stories.) Spode prevaricates and Cadogan contents himself with a train journey to Oxford. As in *The Case of the Gilded Fly*, there is an almost loving tilt at British Rail. Cadogan misses his connecting train (none were running) and gets a lift from a passing lorry driver whose leisure reading is *Lady Chatterley's Lover*. The driver makes two further important appearances in the story. Cadogan is dropped off on the outskirts of the city and comes to a toyshop. He ventures inside and finds the body of an elderly woman who has apparently been strangled. Someone knocks him unconscious. He recovers to find himself in the storeroom from which he escapes through a window and reports to the police. But when the police investigate there is no toyshop but a grocery instead.

We are introduced in the next chapter to Gervase Fen, Cadogan's old teacher. Fen is an active creation — he "strode with great energy across the lawn" — and is described (27) in almost athletic terms as:

> A tall, lanky man, about forty years of age, with a cheerful, lean, ruddy, clean-shaven face. His dark hair, sedulously plastered down with water, stuck up in spikes at the crown. He had on an enormous raincoat and carried an extraordinary hat [27].

As in *The Case of the Gilded Fly* the last touch appears a faint parody of one of John Dickson Carr's principal characters, Dr. Gideon Fell in cape and hat, a Chestertonian or Falstaffian figure markedly inactive, unlike Fen. Carr's other large-bodied detective, Sir Henry Merrivale, is by contrast with Fell irascible and physically active, modeled upon Churchill it has been suggested. Crispin admired and emulated Carr without taking it to extremes. He introduces faint elements from these models into Fen's character but otherwise makes Fen his own creation. Gervase Fen is vain and often wrong on minor matters while good at solving crimes. This is one source of humor when he claims: "There's something romantic about me.... I'm an adventurer *manqué*: born out of my time," to which Cadogan's sobering reply is: "What nonsense" (126).

Fen believes Cadogan's story and they drive to the shop in his car Lily Christine III. They hide from the grocer in the upper floor and effect a slapstick escape out the back. They observe in passing (34) the spot where Cadogan had been sick during his night adventure. In the next chapter they phone the number found on a piece of paper Cadogan had pocketed when he discovered the corpse. It is the proprietor of a boarding house, Mrs. Wheatley. They visit her and Cadogan learns of a Miss Emilia Tardy, who travels a lot. Note the pun on the dead woman's name: tardy meaning late. Tardy's nearest of kin was another old lady, her aunt Miss Snaith: "very rich and eccentric ... lived on Boar's Hill, and had a liking for comic poems" (39).

Fen gets in touch with his friend the police inspector, Sir Richard Freeman (who also lives on Boar's Hill), and tells him that there was indeed a body. By now Cadogan is wanted by the police. Freeman has a larger part in *The Case of the Gilded Fly*. In *Toyshop* he makes cameo appearances, phoned by Fen from time to time to check on a point (including literary discussion). The trail leads to a solicitor, Mr. Aaron Rosseter, mentioned by Mrs. Wheatley. Rosseter had placed a cryptic notice (44) in the personal column of the *Oxford Mail*: "Ryde, Leeds, West, Mold, Berlin" (44). Fen and Cadogan interview Rosseter who tells them that Snaith's estate was to be left to her niece Emilia Tardy, but under such conditions that unless Tardy read of it in English newspapers within six months of Snaith's death, her inheritance was forfeit. Miss Snaith did not approve of her niece traveling about the Continent and sought revenge for that and for neglecting her. Fen does not trust Rosseter and believes he is lying to them, although it turns out that the main substance is correct, for it drives the plot. In this chapter we have the puzzle element in the cryptic words of the advertisement and the eccentric bequest.

Fen and Cadogan go to the Mace and Sceptre public house where they review the case. In an enjoyable parody of a university pub, we are introduced first to the character of Mr. Hoskins, an undergraduate: "more like a vast, lugubrious blood-hound than ever ... sitting at a table with a dark and beautiful girl called Miriam" (51). Hoskins' ploy for winning over beautiful young women is to listen to them sympathetically while feeding them chocolate. As in *Gilded Fly*, a minor character, "with horn-rimmed glasses and a long neck," sits nearby reading a book. In this instance it is *Nightmare Abbey* from which he moves on to other gothic tales at later points in the novel: *Crotchet Castle* and *Headlong Hall*. Another frequenter of the pub declaims Marxist arguments to his audience. Fen and Cadogan briefly follow the pastime of listing Detestable Characters in Fiction. They encounter a "rabbity man" (57) who identifies himself as George Sharman, an ex-schoolteacher, who drunkenly boasts that he has come into "a large sum of money." At the end of the novel it is revealed that Sharman is the murderer, but at this stage Fen suspects Rosseter of the crime. They find that *The Nonsense Poems of Edward Lear* might be a key to the obscure newspaper notice:

> The Old Man of the West ... wore a pale, plum-coloured vest ... a Young Lady of Ryde ... purchased some clogs and some small spotted dogs ... Berlin ... was an Old Man whose form was uncommonly thin [66].

Fen sees a "shaky train of correspondences; Miss Snaith — comic verse — Rosseter — advertisement — Sharman's inheritance ... it had occurred to me that Sharman and the 'others' he talked about might be the legatees in case Miss Tardy didn't put in her claim" (66–67). This is the central puzzle.

The next and fifth chapter contains the first of several slapstick chase sequences for which Crispin is justifiably notorious. Fen and Cadogan set out on a search of Oxford shops, an undertaking described tongue-in-cheek:

> It is true that his [Cadogan's] sense of the fitness of things was somewhat impaired by beer; but it is also true that the improbable has less weight in the City of Oxford than in any other habitable quarter of the globe. But still, even at the time, he felt that a poet and a professor who insisted on combing the shops of the town for a blue-eyed, beautiful girl with a small spotted dog, in the hope that her discovery might throw some light on the disappearance of the toyshop from the Iffley Road, were hardly likely to remain long at large in a sane and self-respecting society [68].

In the Cornmarket they see a girl matching the description. Cadogan shouts. The girl runs. They give chase, followed by "two men in dark suits" (72). Fen nicknames them Scylla and Charybdis, but their real names are Weaver and Faulkes (168). The pursuit leads them to the Sheldonian building where a choir of the Handel Society is rehearsing. The girl takes refuge among the altos and escapes as Cadogan and Fen create havoc and argue with the conductor. They follow the Dalmatian (fully grown) and almost catch up with the girl as she enters St. Christopher's. But she goes to the women's section of the church and leaves at the end of the Blessing. Fen and Cadogan follow as quickly as the order for exiting allows. They lose the girl this time and return to the chapel where they are ambushed by the two men in black and rendered unconscious. They regain consciousness to find themselves tied up in a cupboard. Wilkes rescues them and they leave the building in time to see the girl being hustled into a car.

A second slapstick chase ensues, with assistance from the lorry driver met earlier. The man is now reading Lawrence's *Sons and Lovers*. This is using English class consciousness for satirical effect in the reading habits of the unnamed lorry driver:

> "Industrial civilization," said the driver unexpectedly, "is the curse of our age." Cadogan stared at him. "We've lorst touch with Nachur. We're all pallid." He gazed with severity at Fen's ruddy countenance. "We've lorst touch" — he paused threateningly — "with the body." ... Enlightenment was upon Cadogan. "Still reading Lawrence?" he asked [87].

Although the chief point of view is that of Cadogan, the omniscient author who makes occasional appearances include those of others, Fen's from time to time and, in this chapter, the events from the girl's viewpoint. Her name is Sally Carstairs. At first she trusts Scylla and Charybdis, who take her to a country cottage to meet the man named as Berlin in the limerick. The dog is shot when Sally attempts to escape but it gets away in time to die in front of Fen, Cadogan and the lorry driver who has stopped upon hearing the shot. When Sally regains consciousness she is in the safe keeping of Fen, Cadogan, Wilkes and the lorry driver, but she distrusts them and refuses to tell her story. Fen asks Hoskins to come to the cottage. Hoskins feeds Sally chocolate and reassurance. Sally relents, but she admits that she has no idea what is going on.

This chapter with the car chase, firing of a shot, and kidnapping of the heroine is a light parody of the thriller. Sally perceives Fen and Cadogan in their appearance "like something out of a bad thriller" (90). Now at the novel's midpoint there is a kind of summing-up from Sally's point of view. We learn that Sally works at the lingerie shop. The old lady (Snaith) takes a liking for her and includes Sally in the group of legatees. Sally responds to the advertisement and meets Rosseter. She is in the house when Miss Tardy is murdered.

Rosseter warns her not to go to the police but to keep quiet so that she will get her share of the money.

Sally Carstairs is one of Crispin's notable young ladies almost to rival those of John Dickson Carr:

> She was about twenty-three, tall, with a finely-proportioned, loose-limbed body, naturally golden hair, big candid blue eyes, high cheek bones, and a firmly moulded chin. Her scarlet mouth broke into an impish smile as she called back to someone in the alley-way [70].

Like his mentor, Crispin tended to idolize his heroines. Sally is not the kind of girl who faints when in physical danger (91) although she is knocked out. Such heroines in these novels often have weak background admirers such as "Philip Page, who was safe if rather pathetic" (98).

In chapter eight, Sally, Cadogan, Fen, Hoskins, and Wilkes head off in Fen's car to confront Rosseter. On the way they discover the "real" toyshop in another road. The red-haired young man on duty tells them that the owner is Alice Winkworth. Continuing, they find Erwin Spode waiting in Fen's room. Leaving Spode, Fen and Cadogan go to Rosseter's office. Rosseter, however, gets the drop on them and at gunpoint tells (122) his side of the story, solving the chief mystery. Someone killed Tardy before Rosseter could do it, and Cadogan blundered into the shop. Rosseter intends to kill Fen and Cadogan but is shot instead by an unknown marksman from outside. The central mystery is now resolved and cleverly replaced with another mystery: who shot Rosseter?

Cadogan and Fen pursue the marksman unsuccessfully. Fen asks Hoskins (a) to attempt to discover the identity of the member of the group called Berlin and (b) to protect Sally in his (Fen's) room. Fen and Cadogan stop in a teashop to discuss the case and by coincidence meet Alice Winkworth who overhears them mention her name: "Her face was fat, yellow-complexioned, and moon-like, with a rudimentary black moustache, a pudgy nose, and small, suiline [piggy] eyes — the face of a woman accustomed to exercising egotistical authority" (129). At first she is belligerent, but Fen makes her reveal her part in the business. It was she who moved the toys from the Banbury Road shop to the one in Iffley Road. She describes how Rosseter had the members of the group wait in separate rooms while Tardy was dealt with. Fen is now able to identify almost all the group: "Mold (equals our Mr. Sharman), Berlin (the doctor, unidentified), Leeds (this creature here), Ryde (Sally), and West" (136). The last-named is not yet identified. In Winkworth's description and accompanying diagram (134) this is like a locked-room mystery.

Chapter ten opens with a satirical scene in the rooms of Adrian Barnaby (138) whose "Restoration tea-and-madeira" party is crashed by a number of university jocks, the rowing Blues. Hoskins asks Adrian to help identify an "abnormally thin" doctor for Fen: "'For Fen...? I know: someone has committed some *ghastly crime.*' Mr. Barnaby enunciated the words with relish" (139). They consult a hypochondriac Welshman named Gower, who suggests the heart specialist Dr. Havering. Hoskins proposes they recruit some of the brawny athletes in the party: "When about twelve more or less interested and intoxicated people had been got together, Mr. Hoskins addressed them collectively with dark allusions to murder and young women in distress, and they all cheered" (142). Meanwhile, in a parody of a university lecture, Fen recruits from his seminar class on *Hamlet.* In order to throw the police off the scent, two students disguised as Fen and Cadogan drive off in Fen's car. The police give chase. In the Mace and Sceptre, Fen with Sally, Cadogan and Wilkes confront Sharman, who confesses that he helped in the moving of the toys. Hoskins tells Fen by phone that his university gang attempted to corner Havering but that the doctor escaped on a bicycle.

In the next chapter we have a third slapstick chase. Havering is pursued down South Park's Road (there is a useful schematic map of Oxford provided) until he becomes trapped in Parson's Pleasure, a free (naked) male bathing area of the river. The two London tough guys Scylla and Charybdis make an appearance. They attempt to seize Sally and a fight ensues between them and Cadogan, aided by the Oxford Blues. Havering is bundled into a punt by Fen, Cadogan, Wilkes and Hoskins while Sally is asked to wait in Fen's room. Scylla and Charybdis take the next train to London. Havering is cross-examined and forced to confess his part. In the old woman's plan he is the member of the group with the alias of Berlin. He sees an opportunity to benefit from the situation and persuades Rosseter to become involved, blackmailing him with knowledge from a past association: "Like Rosseter, Havering conveyed obscurely an impression of seediness and professional ill-success" (157). He continues to claim his innocence of the murders by saying that the group were all together between the times of 11:35 and 11:45 when the murder is thought to have taken place, calculated by Havering upon examining the body (which is now in the river nearby).

There comes in the next chapter a gentling of pace and the dénouement, but two more chapters are to follow. Cadogan and Sally sit in a summer house smoking and discussing poetry and the case. Cadogan tells the girl about his ex-lover of years ago (174) and states that he is now middle-aged and will never marry (176). This is a nororiously bad move for any man trying to impress a new lady. They return to Fen's room where Fen proves enigmatically that Sharman (a) was not the murderer and (b) is the murderer. Spode is the missing link, the Old Man of the West. Fen sums up the group of which Spode is almost a part:

> Rosseter, yellow and Asiatic, with his prominent jaw and professional ease; Sharman, rabbity, muffled, drunk, and contemptible; Miss Winkworth, with her moustache and pig-like eyes; Havering, neurotic, thin, rigid, frightened. A

lawyer, a schoolmaster, a fake medium, and a doctor. It was into their hands that a foolish old woman had put her affairs, and with them, the life of her niece [179].

Fen does not immediately reveal how Sharman did the crime. First they prepare for a raid on Sharman's house assisted once again by the Oxford Blues.

The penultimate chapter has yet a fourth chase scene. This one has more serious consequences than the others and more closely parodies the thriller. Fen enters Sharman's house. A shot is fired and Sharman escapes. The chase leads first to a cinema where the film is a B-grade thriller reminiscent of a Raymond Chandler or a Dashiell Hammett novel. From there Sharman steals a bicycle and Fen appropriates a car in which to follow him. The chase leads to a fun fair and a fight on a runaway merry-go-round — "Like a scene from a Graham Greene novel" (194) — that ends with Sharman thrown off by the centrifugal force.

The final chapter is short and anticlimactic. In the best tradition the murderer gives himself away: "Rosseter could have testified, if he'd been alive. The only people, apart from the murderer, who knew he was dead were ourselves and the police. Argal, Sharman killed Rosseter; Argal, he also killed Miss Tardy" (204). This is a joking usage (argal = therefore, thus) but more specifically the timing is important. Miss Tardy was not strangled but died of suffocation while Sharman was with the others. Sharman then removed the evidence of suffocation and substituted the string around the dead woman's neck. It is a touch worthy of a more hard-boiled story than the mostly satirical and farcical goings-on of *The Moving Toyshop*.

The Short Stories (1953, 1979)

There are two collections of Edmund Crispin's short stories. The first is *Beware of the Trains* published in 1953 and compiled by Crispin. The title reflects one of the chief motifs in his work, his fondness for British Rail. As he says in the 1952 foreword to my 1987 edition, all the tales except for one are published in the London *Evening Standard*. The exception, "Deadlock," appears to have been written for the collection. There are sixteen short stories all told and no date of publication is given for individual tales. Crispin extensively revised and rewrote them for *Beware of the Trains*, so in that sense they are a new entity. Many of the tales are forgettable while nonetheless entertaining. Crispin himself notes at the start of the foreword that "a short story can aim either at atmosphere or at the anecdote; those which follow belong, with the exception of 'Deadlock,' to the second category." Atmosphere or mood and ambience, says Abrams, "it the tonality pervading a literary work, which fosters in the reader expectations as to the course of events, whether happy or (more commonly) terrifying or disastrous" (11). By anecdote I think Crispin is referring to the single incident that in crime writing is the presentation of a murder and the puzzle surrounding its execution, followed by the crucial clue(s) that lead to the unveiling of the criminal which is often a surprise ending. A longer, atmospheric short story can of course include elements found in the shorter form. This is one of the few tales that does not have Proessor Gervase Fen as protagonist.

"Deadlock" is about a murder told in flashback from a young man's point of view. Daniel Foss, fourteen, and his friend Margaret Porteous, thirteen, sneak out at night to eavesdrop on Margaret's sister Helen, who is visiting an unpopular boatman named Murchison. Daniel and Margaret split and rejoin each other some minutes later when their parents call them in. Subsequently, Murchison's body is found floating near the lock where a canal enters an estuary (Crispin provides a sketch map). A sequence of events is gradually uncovered by Inspector Watt who often talks about the case with Daniel as a witness. He concludes that Murchison is clubbed and left for dead by a group of itinerant Maoris, an unusual but welcome change from the sinister antipodean ne'er-do-well Australian roustabout. But someone comes upon the scene and pushes the unconscious man into the lock. Death is by drowning and not a result of blows from a carved Polynesian club. Different characters in the tight-knit family groups see a body lying at the door of a house and take it to be a drunken neighbor (body #1). Minutes later the body is not at the door and by the pools of blood appears to have been moved to the side of the canal by the drunken man (body #2). The only person without an alibi is Daniel's moralistic aunt, who is grown senile. She is convicted of the drowning and placed in an institution.

Daniel has a better inkling of what has taken place but this is not summed up until nine years later in novelistic time. It is wartime. Now eighteen and in the military, Daniel realizes that it was Margaret who pushed Murchison into the canal in order to protect her sister Helen from the man's attentions. But Margaret dies in an air raid and Captain Vandeloor, who also witnessed events and kept quiet to protect Margaret, goes down with his ship. Over the years, Margaret and Daniel (157) tacitly keep silent about the affair: "she must have been aware of what I knew, and yet trusted me implicitly ... I had always thanked God that the doctor had interrupted us before I was able to tell the Inspector about the blood on my shoes" (157). The blood at the lock's inner gates is a key clue.

The title is a play on words: The body found in the canal (dead lock) and confusion about the identity of a body lying outside a doorway (a deadlock or impasse). It is a surprise ending but one that is presented thoughtfully, with a touch of reverie and nostalgia and a sense of loss for the protagonist Daniel. The story is sober and, as Crispin says, atmospheric. It contains no humor to speak of. This might be explained partially by our knowledge that Bruce Montgomery is entering into a problematic stage of life with his heavy drinking, except that we have to reckon with his last novel *The Glimpses of the Moon* published twenty-four years later. The other tales use more traditional surprise endings and have smatterings of humor, but it seems fair to say that Crispin gave freer rein to humorous episodes in his novels than in the short stories.

Elements and motifs that have come to be associated with Crispin's novels appear just as much in the short stories. Crispin is an astute observer of human nature and we are rewarded from time to time with insightful character sketches:

> The second porter, who was very old indeed, and who appeared to be temperamentally subject to that vehement, unfocussed rage which one associates with men who are trying to give up smoking ["Beware of the Trains" 10–11].

> He had the precarious, *constricted* air you notice in people who are trying to think of two things at once ["Humbleby Agonistes" 22].

> It was a wholesale reversal of normal personality which you scented the instant you met the man ["The Golden Mean" 112].

> Consequently there were quantities of personal belongings — books, sewing, and whatnot — scattered about it, and they contributed to a much more friendly, informal atmosphere than is usual in such places ["Deadlock" 148].

With an especially striking figure of speech:

> It was more the sort of sensation you have when in crossing a road you hear a car coming at you and you can't for the moment either see it or judge, from the sound of it, what direction it's coming from ["Humbleby Agonistes" 23].

Stylistic elements include the pathetic fallacy: "Rain was falling indecisively" ("Beware of the Trains" 9); "the lightning winked" ("Express Delivery" 71); "the gathering darkness was accentuated by a fog which had appeared dispiritedly at about tea-time" ("Otherwhere" 119), a twist on Bulwer-Lytton's "it was a dark and stormy night"; also literary and classical allusions: "Lacrimae rerum" (45) meaning according to one interpretation "tears of things" for human suffering ("Lacrimae rerum"), a Classical pathetic fallacy from Virgil's *Aeneid* and which appears in Crispin's short story "Lacrimae Rerum" as a personal joke that becomes a clue in a murder. In his foreword, Crispin feels compelled to explain the title source for the story "Abhorrèd Shears" (56–63), that it comes from Milton's *Lysidas* (1637) and refers to the shears (blade) wielded by a Fury, the avenging deity, as a metaphor for poison in a murder case that Fen solves. In a more general serve to English literature: "Gervase Fen — for whom, thanks to the repetitious insistence of the English poets, such moralising had long since lost its first freshness" ("The Drowning of Edgar Foley" 27) and, from Fen once more: "More matter ... with less art" when Humbleby's debriefing of Fen becomes a parody of literary expression: "horrid little cottages, and in one of these, tended only by a sister of advancing years, lived the protagonist of my tale.... unconscious of his doom" ("Otherwhere" 121).

Then there are the self-referential allusions and in-jokes about detective fiction and well-known characters and plot situations. They reflect Crispin's close friendships, especially with John Dickson Carr. The locked-room cliché comes up a number of times:

> I'll tell you what it is, Humbleby: you've been reading too much fiction; you've got locked rooms on the brain.... Gideon Fell once gave a very brilliant lecture on The Locked-Room Problem, in connection with that business of the Hollow Man ["The Name on the Window" 109].

This is a common conceit in the subgenre, to treat in one's own fiction as real-life a fiction from another author, which is often an implicit tribute to that writer. The fictional characters Gervase Fen and Gideon Fell know each other, just as Bruce Montgomery knows John Dickson Carr.

Other allusions to the subgenre are more general: "There are three possibilities, and suspicion's divided between them in that horrid ounce-for-ounce fashion which one associates with detective fiction" ("Abhorrèd Shears" 56–57), and the somewhat startling claim that "detective stories *are* anti-social" ("The Quick Brown Fox" 84) on the grounds that criminals get ideas from reading them. This leads to a clever notion about pitfalls attendant upon criminals reading detective fiction. In the same chapter: "their training in imaginary crime — which as a rule is extremely complicated — tends to make them over-elaborate in the contriving of their own actual misdeeds; and that, of course, means that they're easy game" (84–85). It is another way of looking at the motif of the criminal making that one fatal mistake by either neglecting something or not leaving well enough alone; fatal because before the abolition of capital punishment from 1957 it ended off-scene at the hangman's rope. In this particular short story: "she [the murderess] was a reader of detective stories; and what she dreamed up — in the hope that everyone would make the deductions Wakefield has just been making, and probe no further — was in consequence a detective-story device" (95). In saying this, Fen — and Crispin over his shoulder — takes care to state that he is not mocking detective tales. But there is a touch of satire or, because the criminal uses the tales as a model, of parody.

This is not the only example of the criminal's mistake. In "Black for a Funeral," Constable Tyler "having killed Derringer ... found that his victim *wasn't* wearing a black tie [and was] obliged to do something about it, in order that your suspicions shouldn't be aroused by a discrepancy between his statement on the telephone and the clothing you saw when you reached the scene" (101). It is one of the few examples in Crispin's fiction that the situation of a murderer's good public image be resolved by allowing that person to take the way out through suicide rather than go through the disgrace of a trial and execution. Fen does this by allowing Tyler to overhear from the adjoining room

when he (Fen) speaks loudly to Sergeant Beeton. This crooked cop motif gives
rise to one of the few confronting outcomes in Crispin's stories. It is more characteristic of John Dickson Carr, from whom Crispin might well have got the
idea. Members of the Detection Club (as well as non-members in the game of
course) would have read one another's stories, hence such motifs as these were
common knowledge with a comcomitant temptation to use them in one's own
writing, to see how it might be done better, or to parody or to salute.

Concerning the obstruction of formal justice, "Otherwhere" has a nicely
ironic ending:

> "Justice?" Fen reached for his hat. "I shouldn't worry too much about that, if I
> were you. Here's a wife who knows her husband killed her brother. And here's a
> husband who knows his wife can by saying a word deprive him of his liberty and
> just possibly — if things didn't go well — of his life. And each knows that the other
> knows. And the wife is in love with the husband, but one day she won't be any
> more, and then he'll begin to be afraid. And the wife thinks her husband is in
> love with her, but one day she'll find out that he isn't, and then she'll begin to
> hate him and to wonder what she can do to harm him, and he will know this, and
> she will know that he knows it and will be afraid of what he may do" [127–128].

In another instance, "The Name on the Window" the murderer attempts
to destroy evidence in a clumsy struggle against another man, during which
they crash through a window and shatter the pane (107). The victim writes the
name of his murderer upon the glass as he dies. There is a touch of Holmesian
parody in reference to dust on the floor trampled by rescuers, but more of a
general broadside it seems to me against motifs in the thriller and John Dickson
Carr's writing in particular: "Nor was the weapon the sort of thing that could
possibly have been fired from a bow or an air-gun or a blowpipe, or any nonsense of that sort" (108).

Familiar images of Fen reappear in some of these tales: "His ruddy, clean-
shaven face was pensive; his long, lean body sprawled gracelessly, heels on the
fender; his brown hair, ineffectually plastered down with water, stood up, as
usual, in mutinous spikes at the crown of his head" ("Humbleby Agonistes"
24), as well as his predilection for staying in country pubs or cottages: "*The
Norton Arms*— whose only guest at the moment ... was an Oxford Professor
seeking peace and quiet in order to finish a book" ("Black for a Funeral" 95).

Justice overtakes a police sergeant in another crooked cop tale. Crispin
makes a particularly incisive social comment that must reflect what he was
observing in the London around him. It is one of the strongest statements I
have read in Crispin's fiction:

> Fen, as he gazed out across the river at the expanses of South London, was think-
> ing of old women in little shops who might one day go in intolerable fear because
> their protection against the thug and the delinquent had become a mockery and a
> sham; of pimps and bawds who might flourish at the cost of a few pounds

slipped weekly into the right hands; of night-watchmen burned alive without hope of reprisal in well-insured warehouses, and of little girls violated by degenerates whose services were valuable to their bosses and whose immunity was therefore worth paying for ["Within the Gates" 54–55].

The date of the foreword, 1952, shows that these *Evening Standard* tales predate the ones in the second collection and are at a guess written in the decade before, that is, during the 1940s, a period when Crispin is at the height of his powers and producing his best novels (for example, *The Case of the Gilded Fly, The Moving Toyshop, Love Lies Bleeding*).

Fen Country is posthumous (Crispin died in 1978) and is evidently compiled by "Barbara Montgomery" as copyright holder, listed as Montgomery's wife in the Copyright Renewal Database for *Beware of the Trains*: "Renewing Entity Barbara Montgomery (W)." To clarify, Ann is the preferred (second) name for Bruce Montgomery's secretary—Barbara Ann Montgomery (*née* Clements)—who is recorded in the Whittle biography (241) as marrying Bruce Montgomery on the 19 February 1976, and who died in 1986 shortly before Whittle began to research Bruce Montgomery's life, something Whittle has always regretted (personal communication David Whittle). The collection has twenty-six stories, most published in the *Evening Standard,* for all of which the year of first publication is recorded. The tales are shorter and lighter than those in *Beware of the Trains,* with the exception of two longer stories in *Winter's Crimes.* The shorter pieces in the *Evening Standard* have a touch of the *feuilleton* about them. Nineteen fifty-three to 1955 are the most productive years:

1950	1	"Who Killed Baker?" *Evening Standard* (Co-written with Geoffrey Bush)
1952	1	"Shot in the Dark," *Evening Standard*
1953	6	"Death and Aunt Fancy," "The Pencil," "The House by the River," "After Evensong," "Merry-Go-Round," "Wolf!" *Evening Standard,* "Outrage in Stepney," *Ellery Queen's Mystery Magazine*
1954	6	"The Hunchback Cat," "Blood Sport," "Windhover Cottage," "Dog in the Night-Time," "Man Overboard," "The Undraped Torso," *Evening Standard*
1955	7	"The Lion's Tooth," "Gladstone's Candlestick," "The Man Who Lost His Head," "The Two Sisters," "A Country to Sell," "A Case in Camera," "Occupational Risk," *Evening Standard*
1960	1	"Death Behind Bars," *Ellery Queen's Mystery Magazine*
1969	1	"We Know You're Busy...," *Winter's Crimes*
1972	1	"The Mischief Done" *Winter's Crimes*
1979	1	"Cash on Delivery," *Fen Country*

These short stories come after Crispin's second-last novel, *The Long Divorce*, published 1952 in the period of his life when he was turning his hand to different projects, such as composing musical scores for the *Carry On* series and compiling science fiction and horror anthologies. The latter clearly suggested ideas for *The Glimpses of the Moon* where, as well as the motif of dismemberment, musical composition and bug-eyed monsters come together in the character of the musician Broderick Thouless. In his blog on writing *The Glimpses of the Moon*, "The Passing Tramp" suggests too that Crispin is influenced by Gladys Mitchell's tale of dismemberment in her second novel, *The Mystery of a Butcher's Shop* published by Gollancz in 1929.

Crispin rarely used a co-author for his crime fiction but music and film often invite if not necessitate collaboration with others. His co-authorship of "Who Killed Baker?" with fellow composer Geoffrey Bush (1920–1998) is an exception. Lewis Foreman felt it important enough to include it in his 1998 obituary on Geoffrey Bush: "A lifelong fan of detective fiction, he collaborated with his friend the composer Bruce Montgomery (more familiarly known as 'Edmund Crispin')" (*The Independent*).

Pretty much the same motifs and themes jump from the pages of this book as in the earlier collection, not to mention the novels: the unlikeable victim, slapstick, animal references, sidelong references to motifs and themes from the thriller, striking single-sentence character sketches, occasional references to real-life events, in one instance realpolitik when the Petrov affair is mentioned ("Outrage in Stepney" 61), solving a crime by knowledge of a foreign language, also the astute reading of a character's traits, and so on. Among the better examples:

[Slapstick]. "Haldane ... contrived adroitly to upset his port into Wakefield's lap" ["Who Killed Baker?" 10].

[Non-English expressions]. "Dandelion. English corruption of the French *dent-de-lion*—which of course means a lion's tooth" [37].

[Criminal's mistake]. "I realized she was shamming deafness.... A genuinely deaf person would have felt the vibration of that heavy fall, conducted through the floor and walls" ["The Two Sisters" 59].

[Character]. "A flabby, fluttering young man, the superintendent had thought, like the furry, overblown kind of moth," a line that would have been worthy of Nancy Spain ["The House By the River" 102].

[Melodrama]. "Humbleby struck his brow with his clenched fist, in a transpontine manner which was nevertheless perfectly sincere" ["The Mischief Done" 177].

[Thriller]. "there was an automatic pistol in his hand." ["The Lion's Tooth" 36]; "at midnight a certain private plane would be taking off for the Continent from a lonely field in Norfolk." ["Cash on Delivery" 146]; "the muzzle of Elliston's pistol halted him" ["Cash on Delivery" 148].

[Justice]. "Writers of fiction get very heated and indignant about blackmail. Yet, by and large, it's always seemed to me personally to be one of the least odious and most socially useful of crimes. To be a blackmailer's victim you do almost invariably have to the *guilty* of something or other ... blackmail has a — a punitive function" ["Man Overboard" 202].

The Glimpses of the Moon (1977)

The Glimpses of the Moon is Edmund Crispin's last novel. He died in 1978, a year after it was published. *Glimpses* is also the final appearance of Professor Gervase Fen. It is a long work that proceeds at a leisurely pace for approximately 118,000 words and stands as a creditable swan song after a gap of twenty-four years since the publication in 1953 of the short story collection *Beware of the Trains* and Crispin's second-last novel *The Long Divorce* in 1952. *The Glimpses of the Moon* is leisurely in another sense. It took "the best part of twenty years" to write, observes Whittle (166) who adds that the description of Thouless the comedy-film composer (33–36) may have been penned around 1967, if the Thouless character aged forty-six is modeled upon Montgomery himself at the same age. Ten years after, by 1977, Bruce Montgomery was a hopeless alcoholic often shielded in public places by embarrassed friends (*see* Whittle 240), yet he was capable of good work to the end, whereas some of his contemporaries, such as E. C. Bentley, John Dickson Carr and Nancy Spain, lost their edge in their final years and produced mediocre work.

It can be argued that Ellis the tortoise is a metaphor for the novel itself, in its slow pacing and apparent circularity that never quite reaches a dead-end. Extending the metaphor, *The Glimpses of the Moon* has a spiral structure in which characters and events are revisited over again so as to stretch out the plot in a leisurely way. Even the faster chase scenes have an unhurried aspect about them because they are drawn out and introduce one by one elements that help tie the plot together (the police pursuit of Luckraft, the man from Sweb, the Pisser, Fen and the Major as interested observers from the branches of a tree, even Ellis the tortoise). Ellis may have found freedom on the open road where the protestor's van blocks the progress of a motorcycle club (among others) and the chemist Dodd trips over a tortoise (220).

One of Crispin's touches is the introduction in almost every novel of a totemic animal, often more than one. In *The Glimpses of the Moon*, this is Ellis the tortoise whose slow progress across Broderick Thouless' garden is noted periodically. There is a cat named Stripey to whom Fen talks aloud (61). The major has a cocker spaniel called Sal (101). A pig farmer communes with a sow named Wilfreda (37). A horse figures prominently in the chase scene and the *mêlée* that follows (225), as does a cow, its digestive processes from stomach to stomach described.

I suspect Crispin enjoyed writing this novel, which reads as an unhurried ramble taken by the author among an assortment of eccentric characters in the village of Glazebridge. The tranquility and eccentricity does not end with the occurrence of mysterious deaths but continues as a sort of *mise en scène* to the investigations of the crime. The novel might just as easily have been written as a quirky comedy of manners with no murders and detection, and with the element of conflict no doubt embodied in a different way. The plot's improbabilities tend to flow over the reader if he/she who studies it pauses less to note quotable lines than with Crispin's other books. It merits a re-reading, and in May 2012 I observed that it is overdue for republication. Since then, *The Glimpses of the Moon* is republished in a June 2012 edition by Felony & Mayhem. Appropriately, the cover photograph by the digital artist Drew Medina is that of a tortoise.

The Glimpses of the Moon opens in the local pub with gossip about a murder. The group include the major, a writer Padmore and Professor Gervase Fen. A farmer named Routh has apparently been killed and dismembered by one of his employees, an Australian named Hagberd. Routh, described (5) as a "horrible man," fits the stereotype in these English garden village mysteries that murder victims are generally not likeable and do not overly excite the reader's sympathy. Hagberd, regarded in the village as "mad as a hatter" (9), is another fond stereotype of the coarse colonial with a shady past, Australians being well known to become bushrangers at the drop of a cork-brimmed hat. Crispin provides a short biography of the man, describing him in hyphenated terms:

> Hagberd not only was an Australian cattleman, he looked like one. He was sinewy, lanky, long-armed, easy-striding. He wore broad-brimmed hats. His weather-beaten face was a yard of muddy pump-water, his nose a beak. He had small, intensely blue eyes, set very close together. His ears stood out like jughandles [47].

For all his peculiarities Hagberd is not thought by the villagers to be murderer material. As the Major says: "All that hacking and hewing afterwards, don't you know — somehow *that* fitted in with Hagberd all right. What doesn't seem to fit in was the killing itself" (5).

At this point another of the more eccentric characters, Gobbo (Gorley, Gorman, Godwit), claims that Hagberd could not have done it because he had been talking to him at the time the crime is said to have been committed: "Gobbo gave the impression of having been left over unaltered from a very early novel by Eden Phillpotts" (6). The Phillpotts literary reference is one of many similar inter-genre allusions sprinkled freely throughout Crispin's novels together with other loves such as foreign language quotations and obscure words that have one leaping to the dictionary. *Wikipedia* tells us that Eden Phillpotts (1862–1969) was a writer of the Dartmoor series with titles such as *Widecombe Fair* (1913). His literary friends include Agatha Christie who admired his work, Jorge Luis Borges, Conan Doyle, Arnold Bennett and Jerome K. Jerome, who wrote *Three Men in a Boat* (1889). Phillpotts is perhaps better known for writing science fiction and fantasy such as *Saurus* published in 1938 (*see* Clute and Nicholls 928). That's one I missed in the Animal Fable study.

The most characteristic element in *The Glimpses of the Moon*, as in other novels by Crispin, is his satirical treatment of social institutions and life's

chances that are often founded upon self-reflection. The funniest of these is
the depiction of the music composer Broderick Thouless drawn from Montgomery's own experiences. The passage below satirizes not only the occupation
but also the genre of the shlock horror movie of the Hammer kind:

> By nature and inclination a gentle romantic composer whose idiom would have
> been judged moderately progressive by Saint-Saëns or Charminade, Thouless had
> launched himself at the task of manufacturing the *Bone Orchard* score like a
> berserker rabbit trying to topple a tiger…. Ever since then he had accordingly
> found himself occupied three or four times a year with stakes driven through
> hearts, foot-loose mummies, giant centipedes aswarm in the Palace of Westmin-
> ster and other such grim eventualities, a programme which had earned him quite
> a lot of money without, however, doing anything to enliven an already somewhat
> morose, complaining temperament. A bachelor of forty-six … his single state was
> accounted for locally by the theory that on his visits to film studios he seduced
> starlets, a breed which no one realised had long since become extinct [34].

Bruce Montgomery is working on similar projects in musical composition
and the science fiction anthologies during the decade in which *The Glimpses
of the Moon* is put together. Similarly, his character Thouless is composing the
score for *The Mincer People* when visited by Professor Fen:

> "Terrible stuff, you've never *heard* such a noise. There was one bit of kiss music,
> for a marvel, but by the time I got to it I'd done so many murders that it
> sounded exactly like another one. *Derngh!*" he exclaimed in his nose, imitating
> sforzato [suddenly accented] stopped horns. "And then *erk*, *skerk*," he added…. I
> can't remember anything nastier I've done except for those sickening wailing vio-
> lin harmonics in *Thing of Things*" [36].

Crispin does not forget to describe Professor Gervase Fen as he has always
done, but this time his character is aging:

> In the fifteen years since his last appearance, he seemed to have changed very lit-
> tle. Peering at his image now, he saw the same lean body, the same ruddy,
> scrubbed-looking, clean-shaven face, the same blue eyes, the same brown hair
> ineffectually plastered down with water, so that it stood up in a spike at the
> crown of his head. Somewhere or other he still had his extraordinary hat. Good.
> At this rate, he felt, he might even live to see the day when novelists described
> their characters by some other device that that of manoeuvring them into exam-
> ining themselves in mirrors [43].

Self-reflection (literally in the example), says Chris Baldick, applies to
works of literature "that openly reflect upon their own processes of artful composition." Lately the term "metafiction" is used to label this device as though
it were new. In fact, the deceit goes back a long way. Baldick cites *Tristram
Shandy* (1759–67) as the type example. In the English country village and campus crime stories of the Golden Age (and other closed community settings
such as live theater) this sort of self-consciousness is more prevalent as different

writers get to know one another and to read one another's works. Often enough this reflects the approbation of one writer for another in which there is a degree of modeling. Another element in this movement is the use of multiple points of view (140), well illustrated in *The Glimpses of the Moon* where the observations and theories of different characters such as Fen, the major, the rector and Thouless bounce of one another.

Self-parody continues throughout. Trade secrets are revealed: "When I finally run out of inspiration, which I'm bound to do sooner or later, I can crib bits from them [Thouless' music scores] for other films" (78). Literary criticism is an obvious target, at one point "intoned" in the mode of a university lecture:

> "Spark, Muriel," he said. An idea began to fizz feebly at the bottom of his mind, like stale effervescing aspirin dropped into a glass of water. "The use of ellipsis in Mrs. Spark's earlier work," he intoned, "imposes patterns on her narrative which in addition to their intrinsic shapeliness sometimes make the reader — sometimes make the reader — sometimes make the reader wonder if his wits are failing" [105].

So too is detective fiction singled out: "'Facts first, theories after. *In*duction, not *de*duction.' He [Detective-Superintendent Ling] had read of this distinction years before in a Pelican Book, and never tired of repeating it" (107). Pelican Books were the scholarly editions of Penguin Books founded in 1935 by Sir Allen Lane and added in 1937 to the Penguin list. Pelican was discontinued in 1984 ("Penguin Books").

Crispin slips in fond references to his own and to others' work: "There had been some business about an Oxford toyshop, Widger [Chief Constable] remembered" (182). On page 271: "Crispin writes those up," said Fen, "in his own grotesque way. And there's not much money in it, John. In writing about any murders, I mean." To this Crispin adds a footnote that treats the fictional character of Professor Gervase Fen as a real person: "I include this fragment of dialogue only at Fen's personal insistence.— E.C." As for other writers: "You could read aloud to me over lunch, then. John Dickson Carr, *The Crooked Hinge*. Good stuff" (256). *The Crooked Hinge* was published in 1938.

Earlier in the novel, Crispin introduces us to a family best described as Dickensian, the tedious Mr. and Mrs. Bust and their children: "The Bust children were pitied ... because of their parent's joint sense of humour, which was almost unbelievably imbecile in character. In the Michael Innes phrase, the Busts were not people with whom a joke readily loses its first freshness" (50). Also in the tradition of Dickens, Crispin attaches names to some of his characters that are not so much ridiculous, although many are, as indicative of their temperament or habits: Gobbo, Mrs. Clotworthy, Mr. and Mrs. Bust, Mrs. Leeper-Foxe, the two sisters Titania and Tatiana (129), Constable Luckraft, Chief Constable Widger, and the man from Sweb.

Michael Innes (1906–1994) was another of Montgomery's/Crispin's contemporaries. According to David Whittle (74) J. J. M. Stewart met the younger man for lunch late in 1945 ("Michael Innes" was Stewart's pseudonym). Clearly Innes, like John Dickson Carr, became a model for Crispin. Whittle compares their work favorably, although they are also very different. Innes writes more calculatedly and with greater complexity than Crispin, who often becomes sidetracked by his "memorable cast of characters" and sticks to "smaller struc-tures" and "the carelessness of plotting that marks out the *farceurs*" (268). Be that as it may, readers often confused Crispin and Innes because their styles were similar.

Serious crime solving and horrific events in *The Glimpses of the Moon* would not be out of place in a novel by John Dickson Carr and Crispin pays tribute to another of his literary models, G. K. Chesterton, whom Carr too admired:

> There are two Chesterton effects, actually, which are used in the Father Brown stories.... The first ... consists in asking the wrong question.... The second and more important Chesterton effect: even when you've picked the right question, the answer to it is a paradox. So: "Why was the dead man's arm cut off?" Answer: "Because he hadn't got an arm" [292].

Carr likewise mixes horror and the supernatural with humor but Crispin has a lighter touch that is never far removed from farce. At first this appears not the case. Routh's corpse is dismembered, its wrapped head passed from person to person in a series of both intentional and accidental swapping to be replaced at times by that of a pig and the bust of a statue. But the gruesomeness of all this quickly shifts to very like that of bedroom farce where different characters come and go in hiding from one another, except in this case it is the heads of unfortunate victims.

Most of our attention is taken up with the farcical situations that Crispin devises. The chase scene includes the man from Sweb carrying a mysterious box that some pursuers think might contain the missing head. Slapstick ensues, over-indulged, some might think, in the climactic chapter as though Crispin were trying to outdo himself. Not only is there an attenuated chase scene (instead of two or three as in Crispin's earlier novels) in which motor cars, horses, cows, motor cyclists and an assortment of villagers participate to come together in gridlock within a narrow road, the discovery of the box's contents is the com-pletion of the rector's practical joke on the man from Sweb, for immediately after the Pisser explodes: "it soon became evident what this third element in the booby-trap had been. It had been hydrogen sulphide. The man from Sweb smelled like a cargo of broken addled eggs" (250). The Pisser is a MacGuffin brought to a powerful conclusion that neatly resolves one of the subplots, the activities of the man from Sweb. This almost literal "smoking gun" and the naming of the electricity pylon introduce an element of mischievous scatology into Crispin's writing.

Bruce Montgomery was fond of mayhem all his life, see the orchestral melt-down in the 1961 film *Raising the Wind* made sixteen years earlier, for which Montgomery wrote the score and in which he played a cameo part as conductor. Interestingly, there is a rare allusion to racism in the simile of a berserk and protesting make-up artist. An earlier sketch of the ambitions of Dermot McCartney (70) might be considered politically incorrect by some readers when in my opinion it is described best as ironic. The exploding mix of powder and hydrogen is a well-known clown's device, in both senses of that word, as well as suggesting a schoolboy prank.

This climactic *mêlée* takes place in the penultimate chapter. In the succeeding and final chapter, the dénouement is in traditional fashion over dinner in the kitchen of Fen's rented cottage. Fen delivers his summation (272–293). Police Constable Andrew Aloysius Luckraft discovers that Ortrud killed Routh. He blackmails Ortrud in order to pay George: "That was really the only link between the two cases. Its unique, though, as far as I'm aware — A blackmailing B for the cash to silence C, who in a sort of circlet is blackmailing A" (274). Hagberd finds the body and dismembers it because he dislikes the man for mistreating animals. Luckraft kills George in the Botticelli tent at the local fête and cuts off his head. George was blackmailing him with a letter from Mavis with whom he had been having an affair. But Luckraft does not confess to the murder of Mavis Trent that took place before the action of the novel. Mavis dies at Hole Bridge either by misadventure or killed by Luckraft. Fen states that it was very likely the latter because fingerprints had been cleaned from Mavis's handbag: "the sort of detail that would be likely to be known to a policeman rather than to anyone in any other profession, except perhaps detective-story writing" (287). Fen deduces that George is an amputee, which explains the missing arm (the Chesterton effect).

The last words of *The Glimpses of the Moon* return to both literary parody and a repeated pun: "I shall write my own novel.... It will be called *A Manx Ca*.... I shall really be able to get down to it — in, as you might say, detail" (296). Cats of the Isle of Man bear a naturally occurring mutation producing tails that are either shortened or non-existent. Crispin makes a double pun on Fen's proposed novel that might well remain unfinished unless he can get down to its subject matter, the detail in the tale.

In his essay on "The Poetics of Excess," Umberto Eco suggests (121) that Victor Hugo wrote his tales with two sorts of reader in mind, contemporaries for whom the history of events described by Hugo is still relatively fresh in their minds, within living memory that is, and people reading the novel hundreds of years later. Similarly, but within a much shorter time frame, the novels of the Golden Age writers are received differently by those reading soon after the year of first publication and readers two or more generations later.

Edmund Crispin's *The Glimpses of the Moon* is a striking example of this change over time for its literary allusions. It should be remembered that Crispin and many other authors of his era are graduates from the big universities, mostly in literary studies, and that their readership would have included a great many fellow graduates as well, the English intellectual middle class, so that literary and classical allusions read by many of us thirty years later (that is, a generation) are more familiar to those earlier readers than to us. For us, a great deal of Crispin's vocabulary is perceived as dated or arcane, at the worst pretentious (one acquaintance said "showing off") because in general we do not have the benefits of a Classical British education. Other writers as well as Crispin indulge in erudite, often obscure allusions — Dorothy L Sayers and Michael Innes come to mind — but Crispin is virtually in a class of his own. A lot of Crispin's allusions are faint suggestions and sometimes inaccurate quotations from literary classics and so difficult to recognize. His self-satire is often to do with books and publishers. But this is by no means the most prominent aspect of his humor. He is more important for witty dialogue and quirky situations.

There is a passage in *The Moving Toyshop* that reads very like a manifesto on fiction writing. For "poetry" read "prose" or, more exactly, crime fiction:

> Poetry [crime fiction] isn't the outcome of personality. I mean by that that it exists independently of your mind, your habits, your feelings, and everything that goes to make up your personality. The poetic [crime fiction] emotion's impersonal: the Greeks were quite right when they called it inspiration. Therefore, what you're like personally doesn't matter a twopenny damn: all that matters is whether you've a good receiving-set for the poetic [crime fiction] waves. Poetry's [crime fiction's] a visitation, coming and going at its own sweet will [173].

CHAPTER 8

Best of the Farceurs IV:
Nancy Spain
(1917–1964)

In her autobiography *Why I'm Not a Millionaire* (7), Nancy Spain says she was born at a maternity home named Rose Villa close to Jesmond Street in the maritime city of Newcastle-upon-Tyne. Her home life was "supremely happy." (Spain makes heavy use of adjectives.) She had a sister, Elizabeth. Her father, Lieutenant-Colonel George Spain, took part in several radio plays and broadcast on Newcastle United events ("Nancy Spain"): "George Spain, our father ... used to write very funny articles for *Punch*, very scholarly articles for the *Cornhill* about witchcraft and Roman Britain" (9–10) and "Father says that the Spains are descended from terribly grand Hugenots [sic] called Despaigne" (15). Nancy's mother Norah was Irish and, it was said, experienced a harsh life with ten brothers and sisters (13). Nancy describes her as "one of the great English eccentrics who has ... for some years been getting away with every sort of electrifying outspokenness on account of her alleged Irishness" (12). Norah's father was an Englishman, William Holmes Smiles, and her mother Lucy (Nancy's maternal grandmother) was sister to Mrs. Beeton, author of the famous cookbook. Nancy wrote a biography of Mrs. Beeton as she did too of a mentor in her early life. Both Nancy's parents were eccentric and indulged in practical jokes.

It is easy to see that from both sides Nancy Spain finds her own brand of underlying eccentricity, which is a profound unsettlement in her personality. The outspokenness "inherited" — that is, learned — from the parents in her eyes and in the eyes of others made her something of a social misfit. If it does not all lie in her family background it is possible nonetheless to explain in part her rebellion from the class structure and regulatory life of Roedean School for girls that Nancy attended in her mother's footsteps. In later life Nancy drew upon memories of her schooldays for her crime novels. Frequent references to childhood infections such as scarlet fever, as in *Poison for Teacher* (280), resonate from that earlier period. As Nancy said: "Mum was an old Roedeanian ... she even knew when people were not catching infectious diseases fast enough" (16).

There was enough in that school environment for Nancy to rebel against, but her critical comments about the place veil a good degree of affection for it:

> Girls and staff at Roedean were without exception high-minded, pure-souled conformists. Most of the time they couldn't make out what I was laughing at ... [and] there was a lot of fuss made by Old Roedeanians, who will do anything to hold back time. They said there could be no Public Spirit without djibbahs. And no one smiled.... The Old Roedeanians are a very rich, tremendously reactionary body [19, 22].

A common means of rebellion is reflected in one's choice of clothing. Nancy describes this sack-like garment the girls were required to wear, modeled upon the Middle Eastern djibbah (djellaba). The "fuss" made by Old Roedeanians was on account of the discontinuance of the djibbah at the school in 1935. Nancy appears to have liked that garment under some circumstances: "I refused to wear any but home-made djibbahs. A really swanky djibbah, and some girls had about six of them, made by Debenham and Freebody or Forma or Liberty's, could run you into ten guineas a djibbah, even in 1931" (21–22).

One critic states that Nancy wore "mannish" clothes at school ("Nancy Spain"). This choice is not mentioned by Nancy when writing about her school-days and I do not think a djibbah qualifies. Both Middle Eastern men and women wore them with differences in style. It was later in life when she was writing her biography of Mrs. Beeton (109) that Nancy "threw off forever the last rags of conventional dress and behaviour," adding that: "I had always worn great heavy hairy tweeds and thick brogues," no doubt the mannish clothes with which she was identified earlier. Some characters in *Poison for Teacher* dress like that. Now "with Barbara [Cole] I wore dungarees [bibbed overalls of Indian calico] and never went to the hair-dresser." Not all her friends approved this choice. Noël Coward told her that she looked like "a *degringolée* [sic, *dégringolé*, lit. "tumbled down"] farm hand" (110). Barbara Cole, described by Nancy as an architect, was a Russian émigré who allowed Nancy to live in her flat gratis as a "chum" on the understanding that she paid the phone, gas and electricity bills. The wearing of overalls is a fashion cliché for lesbians and much is made of Spain's dressing mode by commentators. The major, and seemingly only, biography about her of any weight is titled *A Trouser-Wearing Character*.

Spain says (18) that in 1931 at the age of fourteen she sat for her scholarship examination. Eight years later she traveled to the south of France with an old school friend nicknamed "Bin" (Winifred Sargeant) and: "When we got back in September war was declared" (33). John Dickson Carr's biographer Douglas Greene (120) describes a similar experience had by Carr and his wife Clarice. During World War II Nancy served in the WRENS on Tyneside ("Nancy Spain") where she met Joan Laurie for the first time (Contrasola). She also began writing about "becoming a lorry driver at North Shields at the mouth of the River Tyne on 1 November, 1939" (38). Some of the writing was done on her knee, she says (57), while sitting in first-class train compartments.

This is the first of two autobiographies, *Thank You, Nelson,* for which she received £50 from the publisher Hutchinson. A further £50 came as an advance on her first crime novel, *Poison in Play,* to which good fortune was added a part-war service pension: "I became a Naval Pensioner" (74). *Thank You, Nelson* received a favorable review in the *Sunday Times* by A. A. Milne. Citing that reviewer, Nancy (77) writes: "'A Wren's-eye view of the Proper Navy,' it said, by A. A. Milne. I promptly burst into tears." After that, Spain requested a meeting between them and subsequently she and Milne had a long-standing friendship. This was in 1945, the same year her second novel, *Death Before Wicket,* was published by Hutchinson. The first novel is unlike her later works such as *Poison for Teacher, Cinderella Goes to the Morgue* or *Not Wanted on Voyage* in that it is darker and reads a little like a noir script while containing the elements that characterize her later work, such as rapid facetious dialogue and farcical, often slapstick scenes.

Nancy Spain wrote ten crime novels over a period of ten years on an average of a book a year, all published by Hutchinson: *Poison in Play* (1945), *Death Before Wicket* (1945), *Murder Bless It* (1948), *Poison for Teacher* (1949), *Death Goes on Skis* (1949), *Cinderella Goes to the Morgue* (1950), *R in the Month* (1950), *Not Wanted on Voyage* (1951), *Out Damned Tot* (1952), and *The Kat Strikes* (1955). To these she added two biographies: *Mrs. Beeton and Her Husband* (1948), *Teach Tennant: The Story of Eleanor Tennant, the Greatest Tennis Coach in the World* (1953), and three autobiographical works: *Thank You, Nelson* (1945), *Why I'm Not a Millionaire* (1956), and (posthumously) *A Funny Thing Happened on the Way* (1964) ("Nancy Spain").

In common with many authors in crime/detective fiction, Nancy's background was journalism. Over the 1950s and 1960s Nancy was a columnist with the *Daily Express*—"I became Book Critic of the *Daily Express* in the spring of 1952" (175)—and for the magazine *She* (founded in 1955 by Joan Werner Laurie) and *News of the World* as well as taking an active part in radio broadcasts, such as *Women's Hour* and *My Word!* and becoming a panelist on *Juke Box Jury,* a program on BBC television ("Nancy Spain").

She died at the age of forty-seven on the 21 March 1964 in a light aircraft accident along with her partner Joan Werner Laurie (1920–1964) and others ("Nancy Spain"; Contrasola; Collis 1997). Laurie was a rally driver/navigator and was learning to fly at the time. In the words of a Golden Age of Detection

Wiki (*gadetection*) reviewer, Spain's career was "flamboyant and high-profile." No less flamboyant a writer, Noël Coward said in characteristic manner: "It is cruel that all that gaiety, intelligence and vitality should be snuffed out when so many bores and horrors are left living" ("Nancy Spain").

Sexual Preferences

There is a sort of intertextuality between Nancy Spain and her contemporaries, for several commentators say that Spain lived in an open lesbian relationship with Laurie, and they together raised two sons. One, Tommy, was the product of Laurie's six-year marriage with Paul Seyler. Nancy records in her memoirs (130–134) that some time after Paul Seyler's death she joined Joan Werner Laurie's struggling magazine *Books of Today* and was then invited to move in with Joan at a house in Carlyle Square around 1950–52 (187). The other son, Nicholas ("Nicky"), was evidently the child begotten between Nancy Spain and Philip Youngman Carter, Margery Allingham's straying husband. One source states that Spain disowned her offspring: "publicly unacknowledged during her lifetime" ("Nancy Spain"). While she talks about Nicky, her affair with Carter appears to have been a well-kept secret, for Margery Allingham did not identify Spain as one of Carter's paramours, as far as her biographer Julia Jones says, and Spain in her autobiography does not allude to this while she records meeting Margery and Philip on several occasions. Philip Youngman Carter was "a gregarious and convivial man, who disliked solitude and greatly enjoyed entertaining his friends and associates" (Pike) and more than one woman was involved in his extramarital activities. He was attractive to women. Margery with her manic-depression (bipolar condition) was often difficult to live with. On more than one occasion they had blazing rows that ended in physical violence. Margery Allingham had her suspicions from the early 1930s (Jones 163) and by 1951 discovered her husband *in flagrante* in his London flat with an unnamed woman (276). Up until then Allingham, like many wives of that time, had turned a blind eye. But by now she gave up on Carter and felt some relief that her doubts had been justified: "She need no longer be responsible for him" (277). Instead, Allingham worked out her emotions in her fiction.

Jones (270) tells us that Nancy Spain visited Allingham's D'Arcy House: "Margery couldn't help wondering whether what Nancy really wanted was a book review for her magazine or the promise of a story for Joan Werner Laurie's *She*." Nancy records (122) those visits to Margery Allingham as well:

> I am also very fond of Margery Allingham, whom I met about this time. I wanted to write a piece about all the lady detective story writers, so I rang them all up and went along to see them. Marge was the only one who invited me to stay. She is a perfect darling, who lives in a big Georgian house in the middle of

Essex and is married to Philip Youngman Carter, the editor of the *Tattler*. Marge has never been to one of *my* parties, more's the pity, but I have been to several of hers and gigantic things they are too.

It seems unlikely, though not impossible, that Nancy Spain was the woman Margery Allingham found with Philip Youngman Carter in his flat. If so, Margery evidently did not hold a grudge, for some fifteen years later, Jones tells us (342), she was "shocked" to learn of the deaths of Spain and Laurie and grieved for them.

The magazine *She* broke new ground that encouraged other experiments in women's publishing. The Contrasola profile on Werner and Spain draws upon the biography by Rose Collis:

> In 1955, a quiet revolution occured [sic] in the hitherto cosy world of women's magazines: *SHE* was launched onto an unsuspecting world.... The magazine's editor was Joan Werner Laurie and its main contributor was Britain's best-known female ... media personality, Nancy Spain. What most *SHE* reades [sic] were unaware of was that Joan and Nancy had been a couple since 1950 and were rais-ing two sons in what was, for the time, a remarkably publicly avowed "pretend family." Nancy's flamboyant, show-off articles, coupled with Joan's steady, astute editing, made *SHE* the women's magazine that broke the mould and paved the way for the likes of *Cosmopolitan* and *Marie Claire*.

Cosmopolitan appeared in the late 1960s as a woman's magazine (it was founded in 1886 in the U.S.). *Marie Claire* was founded in 1937 in France, banned during the German occupation in the Second World War and relaunched in 1954 ("Marie Claire"). *She* magazine itself went through several periods of decline and rebirth, its risqué beginnings perhaps too heady for later publishers. Nancy Spain was living in Baker Street at the time, around 1948, when her book on Mrs. Beeton came out. One of the magazines alluded to by Margery Allingham would have been the *Tribune* "by courtesy of Michael Foot" (Hennegan ix).

Movements can go out of fashion within a generation or two and reappear just as whimsically. The 1993 introduction by Alison Hennegan for the Virago Press edition of *Poison for Teacher* appears dated only eighteen years later. It is a hagiography with faintly smug allusions to hidden sexual (gay) cues in the narrative. The word "gay" as a colloquial reference for homosexual/lesbian preferences had not achieved its present-day connotations when Nancy Spain was writing in the late 1940s. By the mid–1990s a generation later (forty-four years after *Poison for Teacher*) the so-called "gay revolution" was taking place.

Nancy Spain was writing in a decade where the additional usage of the word "gay" to refer to homosexual or lesbian preferences was gaining ground, and she no doubt enjoyed subverting the more neutral use of the word. There is a carnivalesque tone as well as satire, parody and slapstick in *Poison for Teacher*. It seems a little unfair, however, or perhaps lacking in foresight, for

Virago Press to appropriate Nancy Spain to its cause. If we take Nancy's word for it, she had sexual preferences for both men and women. In her autobiography (26) she mentions several times men with whom she was in love, including "a dear boy called Arthur ... I love him yet. He was killed in a night raid over Germany in 1942" (40), and she jokes ruefully a number of times that most of her boyfriends left to marry wealthy heiresses. The reader must not expect the autobiography or Nancy's crime novels to be a lesbian polemic, although there are plenty of lighthearted allusions to gay characters in both senses of the word among women and men. Spain's writing can be enjoyed by any reader, not only those who get the in-jokes.

What most stands out in *Why I'm Not a Millionaire* is that Nancy Spain is a deeply troubled person. This comes through many times despite her claim early in the book — written on her thirty-eighth birthday in 1955 — that her intention is to "catch the happy hours" and that writing about death cannot be done happily, especially by "a frivolous person like myself" (34). But there is sadness in her memoirs. She needed badly, and revelled in, the stable home life and relationship she had with Joan Werner Laurie and the two children, and several women and men were unforgettable mentors to her at different points in her life.

Photographs of Nancy seem to have been taken at high points in her life when she was either most sparkling or at rest and content. The cover illustration attributed to the gay celebrity photographer Angus McBean (1904–1990) that appears on the Virago Press 1994 edition of *Poison for Teacher* shows a relatively young woman with a mop of thick dark hair standing and likely through trick photography superimposed against the backdrop of a book manuscript. The page of typescript is decorated with objects appropriate to a crime novel: a knife embedded in the page, revolver, hammer (traditional blunt instrument), handcuffs. Their shadows, including that of Nancy, are thrown upon the backdrop. The two pages of the typescript are identifiable. They are from *Cinderella Goes to the Morgue,* published in 1950 when Nancy was thirty-three years of age. The last line of Chapter Six, Book Two reads: "was quite dead" and the first page of Book Three: "Poor banjo's dressing-room" in pages 106 and 107 respectively of my World Distributors Consul edition (1963). Nancy is wearing a thick cardigan with the collars of a white shirt folded over the neckline. Her left hand rests upon her waist. Her eyes are open but hooded. Her face is in repose but alert.

The study of Nancy taken on the balcony of the Montego Beach Hotel by the Caribbean, according to the caption on the frontispiece of *Why I'm Not a Millionaire*, shows the same hairstyle. Her face is partly in shadow and she is squinting a little into the sun. She wears a whitish short-sleeved shirt with two pockets and what appear to be jeans. Later photographs show an older woman whose face is narrower but still with the mop of dark hair. The flattering profile of Nancy on the front cover of Rose Collis's study *A Trouser-Wearing Character* (1997) is that of a self-assured woman, pen in hand, wearing shirt and waistcoat. A silk scarf against the neck gives mixed messages. It adds a feminine touch but at first glance it looks like a necktie.

A photograph taken in 1958 during the BBC Home Service and BBC Radio 4 panel game *My Word!* with Denis Nordern is the only study from this group that is not posed and is therefore less self-conscious. She is wearing a light-colored pullover from which a white shirt collar protrudes. In another photograph of the panel of experts she wears a white shirt, dark jacket and what appear to be matching dark trousers. Her head is down as she writes or reads. Denis Nordern adjusts his spectacles. The one member of the panel aware of the camera and smiling towards it is Valerie Hodgetts, secretary to Tony Shryane, the co-deviser of *My Word!*

Nancy Spain's quirky and punning narrative reminds us that she had a way with words. She took part in the panel game as Denis Nordern's first partner from 1956 until 1964, the year of her death ("My Word!"). Writing in 1958 for the BBC staff newsletter *Ariel*, Tony Shryane, who devised the program with Edward J. Mason, says: "The four permanent team members are E. Arnot Robertson, film critic and writer; Nancy Spain, journalist; and Frank Muir and Denis Norden, scriptwriters of sound radio's *Take It from Here* and television's *Whacko*."

In her professional life Nancy Spain had a "scatty style of column-writing" that led to the *Daily Express* being sued twice, successfully, by Evelyn Waugh ("Nancy Spain"). The issue must have involved more than being scatterbrained and disorganized, qualities that although slightly alarming appear harmless in themselves. Nancy drops Waugh's name several times in her memoirs (it appears six times in the index). She was outspoken and by her own account crossed swords with more than one celebrity, including the crime writer Christianna Brand (1907–1988) — ten years Nancy's elder — who in her lifetime produced around twenty-four novels, most of them detective stories ("Christianna Brand"). Brand was on the Committee of the Detection Club and likely enough behind a move to have Nancy blackballed. Nancy in a wry mood tells it this way: "I failed to write a single word of the detective story that Mrs. Webb was wanting. Worse still, I failed to pay the rent.... Looking back, I am sure all my misfortunes at that time arose from having been black-balled from the Detection Club" (123). Mrs. Webb was one of the principal editors at Hutchinson who was, in Nancy's words, her "*almer mater* [sic], guide, philosopher, and friend for eleven years" (63).

The Detection Club is described delightfully by Nancy:

> This splendid body of men and women meet once a year to praise each other in a vault near Westminster. They carry skulls about on cushions, they light candles and they intone a terrible oath which conjures the members on pain of diminishing

sales and returns to stick to the rules of clues and foot-prints. Christianna Brand, a witty doctor's wife, author of *Heads You Lose* [1941] and other noble works, who is a member of the actual Committee of the Detection Club, delights in teasing me about this, calling me "Little Spoil Sport" and "Little Nothing Sacred" simply because in those days I was so bad at working out plots. I am sure that terrible oath of the Detection Club was the reason for all my financial insecurity [123].

It is a satirical description but I think some hurt underlies it. Nancy cared a lot about what people thought of her. She moved in circles of the literati — in the autobiography she is a great name-dropper — among whom certain persons are very important to her: Noël Coward, Joyce Grenfell, Mrs. Webb, A. A. Milne, Orson Welles, Barbara Cole, Nancy Mitford, Colette, Joyce Cary.

Noël Coward (1899–1973), to whom *Why I'm Not a Millionaire* is dedicated, was a lifelong friend. "Coward was homosexual but, following the convention of his times, this was never publicly mentioned" ("Noël Coward"). Nancy describes an amiable interview she had with him in New York (161–162) that may have been their first meeting. In 1955 she sang a wartime song for him, "Tommy, Tommy Atkins" (22), that moved him to tears. He had a pet nickname for her (23) "Old Wimbledonia," from Wimbledon House at Roedean School. They had lunch together (59) probably on more than one occasion and attended a hilarious séance with two friends, possibly Nancy's "last sublime experience of 1954" (230). Another influential friend was A. A. Milne. Nancy owed Milne a lifelong debt of gratitude after his gracious review of her first book of war experiences. She recalls (78–79) visiting the Milnes at their Sussex home, Cotchford Farm, where she had lunch and sat with A. A. Milne in the garden discussing writing and poetry (80). Around 1955 Nancy met Orson Welles who summed her up insightfully: "He also said (which was very surprising to me constantly told by one and all that I was a divided personality) that he thought I was very, very nice. This set me up for days" (240).

It is uncertain which mental condition she was coping with: bipolarity/manic depression (from which Margery Allingham suffered as well), schizophrenia or some other condition such as autism or depression. Eccentrics and non-conformists in the literary and theatrical worlds tended to accept Nancy, who was obviously drawn to them. Her earliest acquaintance with one such (70) was at the Vincent Square Hospital for Women during the war where she was sent with an asthmatic condition, seeing "a very rebellious rating from Limehouse and Stepney called Joan Werner Laurie who had appendicitis. But I didn't meet Joan until later." When they became involved with each other through their journalism around 1950, Nancy saw herself in negative terms as a "lame duck" (133). Elements from her fiction mingle with her account of this time:

Until I met Jonnie [Nancy's pet name for Joan Laurie] I was a miserable sort of creature, a failure, hating everybody, living in a sort of ivory tower of work, refusing to allow Real Life in the shape of Family Life to intrude on me at all. I had become a terrible cynic, chiefly because all my boy-friends had darted off and married someone else.... Jonnie and Nicky awakened my fondness for humanity, which had lain hidden for so long; hidden away under a sort of barrage of smart attempts at wit and brisk repartee and clever little detective books [135].

Whether sharing the same residence and bringing up their two children between them means that Nancy Spain and Joan Werner Laurie had a lesbian relationship is beyond the point. Same sex couples can live together without necessarily wearing the gay label. But Nancy did, or at least many others thought so. What is more important is the way their friendship changed Nancy's life. It is interesting that she thought the writing of her detective novels was one of the ways by which she escaped from the real world. Yet the wit and repartee with which she chides herself is a defining mark of her crime writing that makes those novels so enjoyable to read, and it comes from her character and involvement in a world of print and radio often infused with sparkling dialogue. Hiding behind one's writing can be said of many authors. The irony is that if a work goes into publication, it enters the public domain, and so the writer engages with the world whether they like it or not.

This is something of which Nancy says she became aware nine pages later when she met Joyce Cary, an Oxford writer whose "incendiary mind" (184) rekindled Nancy's drive to review books: "Reading and writing is not a simple business. It is a complex relationship between reader and writer, as difficult and exasperating as a love-affair." Cary (1888–1957) was one of the "remarkable people" (182) Nancy met in 1952, her "vintage year." He struggled as a writer in his early years, a fact that may lie behind the encouragement he gave to Nancy. Some pages on, Spain makes an informative statement about her work schedule that might well have been influenced by her meeting with Cary:

I have got into the habit of getting up at five a.m. to work. This is surprisingly enjoyable, particularly in the summer.... I work until seven, when I am always so ragingly hungry that I go and get myself breakfast. This regime, carried out faithfully, morning after morning, produces the necessary tight string of continuity to finish a long piece of work like a book. So after breakfast I have a whole ordinary day left for broadcasting, journalism, answering the bloody telephone and meeting people. This is the way that I managed to finish two detective novels, two books for children (and I illustrated them myself, too, which I deeply enjoyed) a short novel, various magazine stories and this book. In the daytime I was writing my stuff for the *Daily Express*, *SHE* and working on various programmes for the B.B.C. [232].

Over the years Spain honed her professional skills to a fair standard. When she was working on radio plays she used to sketch small pictures in the margins of the scripts as self-reminders to polish them (37). She wrote "silly clerihews" (71) when convalescing from asthma in the WRENS hospital. But she felt insecure in her work and had strong reservations about her ability as a writer of detective stories, saying around the time *Mrs. Beeton* was published (1948) that she was no good at it (116). By then she had written three crime novels: *Poison in Play, Death Before Wicket,* and *Murder Bless It.* What is arguably her best, *Poison for Teacher,* came out in the following year. She agonized over reviews, observing once — and revealing a "secret" of the craft — that it was a pity a writer could not write one's own reviews the same way they wrote their own blurbs (126).

Because she "had suffered for years from not being reviewed" (139), Nancy began a column in *Books of Today* about "Looking In on Crime" under the iconic "Chad" inscription from the Second World War, also known as "Foo" in Australia and related to the American "Kilroy was here" ("Kilroy was here"). Her column was blessed by Joan Werner Laurie, the editor, a detective story addict herself. Among the insights Nancy had from A. A. Milne were the ideas that "all writers write to please themselves.... No sensible author wants anything but praise" (79). It is a mark of Spain's sensitivity to the craft that on the whole she tried to write favorable reviews of the work of others, perhaps with Evelyn Waugh as an exception.

At some date in the early 1950s, after they moved in together, Nancy Spain and "Jonnie" visited Nancy Mitford and Colette in Paris a number of times: "we met Nancy Mitford and Colette and Christian Dior. In between whiles we lay exhausted in our beds at our hotel, reading French and American women's magazines. I can see now how the inspiration for *SHE* stemmed from that staggering forty-eight hours so long ago" (143). That magazine came out in March 1955 (247–248).

Nancy Mitford (1904–1973) was a comic writer, known affectionately to many through her wonderful parody *Love in a Cold Climate* (1949). After the Second World War she lived in Paris for much of her life. She appears to have had two marriages and several affairs with men. Her first romance was with a gay Scotsman, and her marriage to the Hon. Peter Rodd failed (Rodd was unfaithful and could not hold a job), and she had an affair with Charles De Gaulle's Chief of Staff, Colonel Gaston Palewski, that brought her to Paris but was otherwise a failure. ("Nancy Mitford"). She certainly had enough experience of upper-class life for her novels.

Colette (1873–1954), on the other hand, had numerous lesbian affairs as well as heterosexual relationships (one of her male partners was bisexual). ("Colette"). When Nancy Spain met her, Colette must have been in her late seventies. Of Nancy Mitford and Colette (150): "There are people whom one loves immediately and forever. Even to know they are alive in the world with one is quite enough. And Colette was like that."

The fulfilling love of Nancy Spain's life was Joan Werner Laurie. Writing, it must have been around 1955 to 1957, and starting in what at first glance appears hero-worship but which gained some degree of balance, Nancy says: "she likes really good music and really feeds upon it, loving Beethoven and Bach and Sibelius and César Franck in the way that I love Sousa and Novello. And she can read books on comparative religion for pleasure ... in the same way that I might read a modern novel" (134). Of particular interest, because it is one of the more striking elements in Nancy Spain's crime fiction, is the improving effect on her of living with Jonnie and her son (and with Nancy's own son), a greater tolerance towards children: "Why, she has even taught me, by precept, how to love little children and animals. Quite *beastly* little children with dirty faces" (136). The juxtaposition of children with animals reveals her mixed feelings. It took time.

Ralph Wood, cited in *gadetection* reviewing Spain's third-last detective novel *Not Wanted on Voyage* (1951), finds a "darker side" that has an element evocative of King Solomon:

> Nancy Spain's biographical notes say she had a son by Philip Youngman Carter, Margery Allingham's husband. The boy was brought up as the youngest son of Joan Werner Laurie, Spain's partner. A character in *Not Wanted on Voyage*, an author, has a neurotic lover who cannot have her own children. So his wife has allowed their daughter to be brought up as the lover's child. The wife dies by being literally cut in half, and nobody will tell the baffled child what has happened to her "Auntie." You wonder what was in Nancy Spain's head when she wrote it [*gadetection*].

This is Spain's eighth novel, dedicated to her good friend Hermione Gingold. It is more polished than her earlier works. There is greater attention to characterization but there are variants on much the same elements as in her earlier novels. She was thirty-four at the time of its publication and arguably at the height of her powers. More care is taken in its overall structure but there are also hints of the ennui that led to Spain deliberately abandoning writing in this form.

Nancy Spain's insights into her own character came about both through her work and her personal relationships, especially that with Joan Laurie. The main theme of her somewhat rambling, confessional autobiography appears summed up in the penultimate chapter where she brings the two areas of her life together when discussing the BBC radio programme in which she participated:

> "Who Said That?" ... showed me up, to myself, once and for all as the same indiscreet, talkative, enthusiastic, apprehensive, Conservative, insular miss who left Roedean in 1935 labelled "Speaks before she thinks." Life, they have promised me, will begin at forty. So perhaps on my fortieth birthday ... I shall become, by some miracle, discreet, quiet, disillusioned, brave, Liberal, and cosmopolitan. But I doubt it [243–244].

Those words can be read as an unintended epitaph, for Nancy Spain died at the age of forty-seven in that aviation accident seven years after the publication of *Why I'm Not a Millionaire*.

The autobiography *A Funny Thing Happened on the Way* (1964) reflects Nancy Spain's slapdash writing. She jumps back and forth from one period in her life to another so that discovering a clear chronology is not easy. Some of the later chapters appear to be taken from earlier work, perhaps reviews or other columns, for there are changes in style. There is a glaring error in her consistent mispelling of the name Morihei Ueshiba, founder of the martial art of Aikido, with whom she met during a trip to Japan (137–139) as "Veshiba," no doubt misreading the "U" in the name as a "V." The same approach can be recognized in her crime novels except that a tale such as *Poison for Teacher* appears on the whole tighter and more ordered in its structure. Spain was not a stylist like some of the other authors in my list but she wrote delightful satire.

Poison for Teacher (1949)

Nancy Spain writes in a racy, tongue-in-cheek style that, in *Poison for Teacher*, satirizes two enclosed settings, one within the other: a girl's school and, part of the curriculum, a group of amateur actors rehearsing the J. M. Barrie play *Quality Street* (1902). It is a setting broadly similar to that chosen by Edmund Crispin for his first novel *The Case of the Gilded Fly* (1944), published only five years earlier and which Spain had probably read. *Poison for Teacher*— Spain's fourth crime novel — is written from a similar standpoint to that of Crispin, that is, using memories of Spain's own time at Roedean School, East Sussex, founded in 1885. Crispin's model was Oxford University.

Poison for Teacher is an irreverent romp satirizing several different institutions, genres and character types. The critic Curt Evans (*MysteryFile*) observes that Spain is satirizing girl's schools, and certainly Nancy's sentiments towards her schooldays appear ambivalent. She is quoted as learning to ride horses on the Roedean Town Moor "with other little bourgeois tots" and at the school she adopted mannish clothes ("Nancy Spain"), perhaps a rebellion against school life as well as affirming her sexual preference (*see* above). Roedean school is described as "an independent girls' school in Roedean village on the outskirts of Brighton, East Sussex.... The school overlooks the sea and is situated close to the marina" ("Roedean School").

The setting of *Poison for Teacher* is Radcliff Hall, a girl's school very like Roedean. The satire largely involves frequent references to physical and personality flaws. Schoolgirls are often described as horrid, and are teary, frequently clumsy, and mean-minded. Evidently Nancy did not entirely enjoy her school years, and perhaps her dislike for children stems from this period. A quick content analysis finds words and expressions a little old-fashioned for today's readers, "horrid" (a key word), or "somewhat shaming" as frequently used in the Evelyn Waugh novel *Vile Bodies* (1930) and in its film version *Bright Young Things* directed by Stephen Fry (IMDb).

This places Nancy Spain among the post–World War II humorists in crime fiction along with Edmund Crispin, Ngaio Marsh, the later Margery Allingham, the later John Dickson Carr, Colin Watson and Sheila Pim. If we were to represent this subgenre by points along a continuum from dry humor to satire, farce and slapstick (ribald humor), Dorothy L. Sayers' restrained wit as in *Gaudy Night* lies at one end of the continuum, Nancy Spain's *Poison for Teacher* at the further end. Margery Allingham's oeuvre lies somewhere in the middle, and the shenanigans of John Dickson Carr and Edmund Crispin rub shoulders with the novels of Nancy Spain. One big difference between Spain and Carr or Crispin is that Spain does not construct her novels as neatly as those two humorists.

Stylistically, the most striking impression is the rapid pacing of *Poison for Teacher*, assisted by short, often one- or two-page chapters, and facetious dialogue. Despite the apparent brevity of the chapters and their sections, the novel is substantial at approximately 110,000 words in the Virago Press edition. There are touches of slapstick as well as satire. Sharp though two-dimensional character types are differentiated by droll names: Peter Bracewood-Smith (detective novelist and murderer); Theresa Devaloys, the first murder victim (French mistress at Radcliff Hall School for Girls); Miss Zwart (English mistress); Gwylan Fork-Thomas, the second murder victim (chemistry mistress); Roger Partick-Thistle (camp organist); Dr. Philip Lariat (principal suspect); Mrs. Puke; Mrs. Buttick; Miss Helena bbirch; Major Bandarlog, who lives in Pondicherry Parade; Mrs. Grossbody, the Matron; her assistant, Miss Bound; Mr. Intrikit, and so on: "There was Major Banderlog, the old fool who was always complaining about noise and dogs' filth, who lived in the Indian quarter beside the pier.... There was Mr. Intrikit, the manager of the Brunton Hotel, who went in for spiritualism and witchcraft and black magic" (85–86).

This predilection continues in Nancy Spain's other works. *Not Wanted on Voyage*, for example, has a cast of equally colorful personages often with appropriate Dickensian names: a writer called Bunyip, the ship's Dutch captain Van der Vaterloo, passengers Commander and Mrs. Fryteful, the Italian couple Mr. and Mrs. Polyo, Kenneth and Beryl Tennis-Racket, two spivs Albert Earole (with his wife) and Stanley Chew, the chief steward Mr. Creep, and a drunk named Bert Canteen.

As well as satirical and punning names, the language often rises to melodramatic cliché. Natasha "threw back a lock of hair and watched the sergeant with the innocent, limpid gaze of a startled fawn" (275). This figure of speech appears to date back to Felix Salten's *Bambi* (1928) that Spain would almost certainly have read, although the expression was doubtless in popular use by the time *Poison for Teacher* was written, and Raymond Chandler (111) uses it, also with satirical intent, in *The Little Sister* (1949) that Spain might not have read, both *The Little Sister* and *Poison for Teacher* published in the same year. However, *Poison for Teacher* is not a one-joke novel based solely on funny names that allude to bodily and other functions. It is more complex than that.

Naming the fictional school Radcliff Hall, Curt Evans tells us, is a play on the personage Radclyffe Hall, a prominent lesbian of the 1920s who wrote *The Well of Loneliness* (1928), a groundbreaking novel that treats lesbian themes directly and with compassion. There is a double pun in Spain's choice in that an underground publication titled *The Girls of Radcliff Hall* appeared in 1932 privately circulated. It is described as a *roman à clef,* a "novel with a key" in which readers in the know recognize characters from real life (Abrams 165), including themselves. It created a storm at the time. The author Gerald Berners — a composer of classical music described in *Wikipedia* as eccentric, a humorist and homosexual — wrote of lesbian schoolgirls engaging in "indiscretions," the characters based upon himself and a number of close intimates, including photographer and costume designer Cecil Beaton and artist and stage designer Oliver Messel ("The Girls of Radcliff Hall"). A contributor to the web site Selvedge Yard, identified by the initials "JP," observes scathingly that while Cecil Beaton "will always be remembered for his huge influence on the world of photography and fashion ... his persona and image was [of] ... obsessive vanity, insecurity and posturing." These men were ripe targets for Berners' lampoon. While many in the group were amused by the novella, Beaton took exception to it and attempted with limited success to find and destroy all copies.

The two amateur investigators in *Poison for Teacher* are the stage actress Miriam Birdseye and her sidekick, the former ballerina Natasha Nevkorina/ DuVivien who speaks (249) in fractured Russo-English: "I am still doing of six things at once ... this is how I am been going on ever since I am come to this place." Vagueness is one of her attributes as well as beauty (2): "Her lovely shining ash-brown hair fell to her shoulders. Her enormous hazel cat's-eyes looked balefully at her husband." Nancy Spain uses a lot of cat imagery. The combination of tenses imparts a fluid speech that helps to reflect Natasha's character sympathetically and is not abrasive upon the reader, unlike the parody in Brahms and Simon, *A Bullet in the Ballet* (1937), where Stroganoff continually tells Stanley his secretary to go away. Miriam Birdseye, unlike Natasha, is "tall and thin and blonde and not very handsome" (6). There are frequent satirical asides about the live stage: "Miriam's hatred of blood transfusions dated more or less from the spectacular failure of her musical version of *Dracula*, in which she had played the Countess (The Undead) a year or two before. Her resemblance to a lady vampire was only superficial" (159).

Natasha is independent in her own right, a wish-fulfillment for Spain who always worried about her financial state. Of Natasha's possessions:

There was Amy the Pekinese, and a block of rather tiresome shares that were re-invested every ten years in Government gilt-edged. And there was the house on Hollybush Hill in Hampstead and a half-share in all Johnny's, her husband's, terrible night-clubs and road-houses [180].

Natasha joins up with Miriam in her new detective agency at 44P Baker Street (Sherlock Holmes's fictional residence in that street is 221B). Johnny's fruitless search for his spouse during which their paths cross several times unbeknown to each other is a subplot in later chapters (headed as Interludes). Many of Nancy Spain's male characters are depicted as weak and ineffectual, culminating in her last and flawed novella *The Kat Strikes* in which men burst into tears, but there are also male tears in the better novels.

Someone has been playing dangerous pranks at Radcliff Hall. The headmistress of the school asks for their assistance: "It was the Hon. Miss Janet Lipscomb, of Radcliff Hall School for Girls.... She strode into the showroom with an ashplant and a red draught-excluding jacket and brogues with big, fringed tongues" (8). Lipscomb might well be a self-parody. Later in the novel she wears "a grey silk shirt with a high semi-stiff collar and a dark-green tie" (97), suggesting the photographic portrait of Nancy described earlier, and jacket and brogues were often Nancy's preferred attire. Lipscomb is accompanied by Julia Bracewood-Smith whose father, Peter Bracewood-Smith, writes potboilers, each with diminishing printruns. Natasha had read and enjoyed one of his books. Miriam and Natasha travel to the fictional seaside village of Brunton-on-Sea to get to the bottom of the mystery. There they meet Bracewood-Smith: author of *Death and the Archbishop*, 68,000, and *Death and the French Governess*, 9,000, and *Love and Murder*, 5,000 (18).

They also meet Miss Theresa Devaloys the French mistress who is to become one of Bracewood-Smith's victims. Devaloys, described in subtle damsel in distress terms: "proved to be a miniature pink-and-white model of a woman with a neat cat's face and hair cut in a fringe as for the 1920s. Her clothes inclined to frills and she wore *crêpe* taffeta blouses with little pleated fronts" (22). Teresa conducts them through a garden of concrete birdbaths and gnomes where she leaves them at one of the school's Houses, departing with Bracewood-Smith. There they meet an old friend from an earlier adventure in the European country of Schizo-Frenia, Roger Partick-Thistle:

An exquisite young man with golden hair minced in. He was wearing a ginger tweed coat and a pair of whipcord trousers, and he had on a neat bow tie. He stood for a second aghast, staring from Miriam to Natasha and back again with a wild surmise. Then with a great cry he flung himself on Miriam [22].

These are stock comedic characters found within a stock English seaside setting, differentiated by the clothes they wear (as well as by their actions): Janet Lipscomb, the stereotype of a tweedy outdoors woman; Peter Bracewood-Smith, the eccentric writer of mediocre novels; Julia Bracewood-Smith, a lost and sardonic adolescent — compare her with the similar character of Pam Lacey in Carter Dickson's *Night at the Mocking Widow*— Theresa Devaloys in feminine frills and silks in marked contrast to Lipscomb; and Roger Partick-Thistle as the stereotype of a camp young man. This is not deep character development. The strength of *Poison for Teacher* lies in the madcap humor and sparkling repartee between the participants. It is a wonder that at least one critic (Hennegan) takes the novel seriously.

As their cover, Miriam is to teach English and Natasha dancing. They attend dinner at the school, an occasion for a satiric description of the girls as they enter the food hall. Another mysterious prank occurs: the lights go out and the cocoa urn is overturned, scalding one of the girls. In search for a better meal, Miriam and Natasha drive to Brunton-on-Sea in Roger's Austin Seven where at the Brunton hotel they again meet Bracewood-Smith. In the next chapter as Natasha and Miriam take their first classes, Theresa Devaloys visits Gwylan Fork-Thomas's room and discovers a letter in draft warning her to keep away from Philip Lariat, the doctor. At this point Nancy Spain follows one of the conventions of crime writing by hinting at the impending demise of a victim: "It *did* stay out nice all day, and this was just as well for Theresa Devaloys, for it was the last day she spent alive" (46).

After establishing rivalry between Devaloys and Fork-Thomas, Spain complicates the plot by adding motive for a suspect other than Fork-Thomas. Devaloys goes to the doctor's consulting rooms and accuses Lariat of making her pregnant. At the dress rehearsal Theresa Devaloys "as Miss Phoebe as Miss Livvy" (56) falls dead, poisoned by the whiskey she had been drinking as part of the stage props. Another convention often found in crime stories of this form is that of moving the body to hinder the investigation. This goes back to the founding tale for the Golden Age, *Trent's Last Case*, in which Marlowe, upon finding Manderson dead near the golf course, carries the corpse to the grounds of the house. At Radcliff Hall Devaloys' body is removed from the stage so as not to terrify the next class of schoolgirls about to use that venue.

Miriam and Natasha accompany Sergeant Tomkins on his cross-examination of witnesses. They visit Bracewood-Smith's bungalow and the chemist and meet in Epsom's teashop as Mrs. Puke, the town gossip, eavesdrops nearby. Subsequently Mrs. Puke gossips about it to Dr. Lariat. Miriam and Natasha go to Devaloys' room and find what they guess is a blackmailer's notebook. Tomkins reconstructs the scene and in Chapter Six, Bracewood-Smith gives a public talk about writing detective stories. This might well be satire on John Dickson Carr's "essays" on aspects of the detective story as voiced through his character Dr. Gideon Fell. In keeping with several decades of tradition, Nancy Spain lampoons the genre in which she herself is writing, Referring to Bracewood-Smith's book *Death and the French Governess*, "'I can't read detective stories myself,' said Miriam politely. 'It is an intellectual exercise, like poker'" (198).

Natasha and Miriam drink at the hotel and stroll to the sea front. On the way Natasha has a premonition of danger and indeed moments later they discover Gwylan Fork-Thomas dead in a wind shelter. She is the third victim if we count the death of Bracewood-Smith's former wife who is thought to have killed herself. This is the convention of having a mysterious death take place before the action of the story. In *Not Wanted on Voyage* a similar murder takes place before two more deaths occur during the voyage. In that novel an unusual touch is frequent reference to one of the passengers as the murderer without revealing his or her name. Confronting images of murder and eerie surroundings, although they are present, are downplayed in keeping with the conventions. *Poison for Teacher* is a parody of English country garden mysteries that are indeed often self-parodies. The discovery of Gwylan Fork-Thomas' body, "The whole of the back of her head ... blown away" (124), is not dwelt upon. The death of Theresa Devaloys on the stage is melodramatic rather than eerie.

The matron, Mrs. Grossbody, lies ill in the sanatorium (130) where she tells her assistant Miss Bound that she saw Fork-Thomas leave for Dr. Lariat's house across a stretch of ground called Lovers' Loose that has a notorious reputation, but that she did not see Fork-Thomas return. In the next interlude, Bracewood-Smith wipes his face on a silk scarf that Natasha mislaid on their earlier visit. This is a crucial McGuffin appearing late in the plot. It is part of the irony that Johnny DuVivian meets and speaks with principal characters and misses the clue of the scarf as well as the sighting of Natasha herself. In the next interlude, Johnny talks to Henry, a fellow club owner, who tells him about the murders at Radcliff Hall. Meanwhile, Natasha, Miriam and Tomkins question Lariat, who breaks down and admits (149) that he had an affair with Theresa Devaloys. He needs a drink and offers them John Haig whiskey. It was a John Haig bottle that had been poisoned at the rehearsal. The evidence points increasingly to Lariat. The three investigators find a bicycle with a blood-soaked shopping basket attached (158). They search for bloodstains in Lovers' Loose and, caught in a rainstorm, enter Bracewood-Smith's cottage where they find Partick-Thistle asleep in a guest room (166). They are discovered by Bracewood-Smith. The Bally Netball match between students and staff (209–210) is a slapstick scene.

The clues are scattered through the novel and, as the above summary reflects, are not well organized. Natasha's suspicion that the poison was delivered by a syringe into the bottle of whiskey is undeveloped. Natasha phones Miriam and tells her she thinks she knows who committed the murder, and the motive. With a touch that is today associated with the so-called post-modern style, the omniscient author tells the astute crime reader that they will have already guessed the answer so the rest of the page remains blank "to indicate this information" (229). Fisher (see below) is critical of the novel because she sees it as "too post-modern." Miriam and Natasha tell Tomkins that he is making a mistake by arresting Philip Lariat (232). They believe, correctly as it turns out, that the murderer is Bracewood-Smith.

They prepare for another rehearsal. Brentwood-Smith now has a full-blown head cold. This is moving towards the end of the novel and the clues are beginning to come together, though still in haphazard fashion, the pace of the novel quickening. Natasha, crouched over the gas-fire "like a beautiful Siamese cat" (236), says:

> Roger is saying ... that Gwylan is telling him that whoever put the poison into that whiskey must have put it into the bottle *off* the premises. Like in an off-license. With a hypodermic. And Bracewood-Smith *must* have done it because he brought in the bottle himself [237].

They need to find the hypodermic, the revolver and the headscarf Gwylan Fork-Thomas was wearing when she was killed. Miriam arranges with Julia Bracewood-Smith for the girl to hand over a parcel her father gave her to mail (239). There follow a series of ironic events that help to establish suspense. Grossbody the matron keeps Julia at the sanatorium with suspected scarlet fever and sets out sadistically to destroy all her possessions including the parcel. Later Miriam and Natasha force the matron to admit where she put the parcel. In another slapstick scene (256), Miriam rescues the parcel from the boiler house where it was destined for fumigation while fending off the amorous advances of Cyril the Welsh boiler man.

Tomkins has new evidence and the inquest is adjourned (247). They visit Lariat in his cell and have an exchange with his solicitor, Charles Gracchus-Tiberius (248). Miss Juniper arrives on the scene. She is a gossip reporter for *The Daily Glass* working for Lord Cute (read Michael Foot or, more likely, Nancy's boss Lord Beaverbrook whom she admired), who appropriately enough likes her drink (250). Juniper invites herself into Miriam' room where in an apparently drunken state and ignored by them, she overhears their discussion of the case (257). Juniper then reveals that Bracewood-Smith is a drug addict whose "arms are *pitted* with punctures" (259), and in what must be the worst pun in the novel: "'From a hypodermic,' said Natasha slowly, getting the point."

The penultimate chapter begins with preparations for the play: "Natasha arrived backstage, looking very pretty. Her hair had been elaborately dressed in the conventional ringlets (a little too long for the usual *Quality Street* manner)" (269). Janet Dunbar writes:

> *Quality Street*, set in the period of the Napoleonic Wars, is about two spinster sisters, the younger of whom has a romance with a dashing army captain. He goes off, however, without "declaring himself," and the disappointed Miss Phoebe puts on spectacles, hides her ringlets in a muslin cap, and determinedly looks forward to being an old maid [156–157].

As he prepares to go to the play, Brentwood-Smith who is still fighting off a head cold, picks up a scarf lying on his kitchen chair to use as a handkerchief.

This is Natasha's silk scarf left accidentally when she was questioning Partick-Thistle. Juniper phones in to her office with the story (263). She then interviews Bracewood-Smith who is too drunk to realize what he is saying (though he can remember everything afterwards except to whom he was speaking). Tomkins confronts Bracewood-Smith backstage. Bracewood-Smith prepares to blow his nose. Tomkins takes the scarf from his hand and asks whether it belongs to Miss Fork-Thomas. In a brainstorm Bracewood-Smith gives himself away:

> It *wasn't* a handkerchief. It was a white silk scarf, worked all over with a pattern of edelweiss.... In the distance Bracewood-Smith heard his own voice, scarcely human, growling, barking, wailing. He could not stop it. It said: "A scarf? Gwylan Fork-Thomas' scarf? How *can* it be hers, you fool? I burnt Gwylan's. I tell you ... I burnt it" [273].

As a final interlude (274) and comic anti-climax, at Brandy's Club in Brunton-on-Sea Johnny DuVivian receives a phone call from Black Market Bob to say that someone fitting the description of his wife had just been spotted leaving on the train to London. So Miriam and Natasha in the company of Tomkins make their return, first having to endure the Radcliff Hall School song in farewell.

Critical Reviews

There appear to be no critical studies of *Poison for Teacher* let alone of Nancy Spain's oeuvre. The web site for *Classic Crime Fiction*, while listing ten novels by Spain, appeals for further information. The *gadetection* site owner, after entering a short history of Spain's career, includes a bibliography of her ten novels linked to mini-reviews. But only two of those novels have reviews: *Murder, Bless It* (1948) and *Not Wanted on Voyage* (1951). The other links no longer lead to their relevant page and need contributors. Nor is Spain mentioned in Symons, Watson, or in Panek's two books. Binyon, however, is aware of this oversight and observes: "Though the books are ignored by reference works on the detective story, they are worth seeking out" (124). I agree and find it unusual that Spain's work is not greatly acknowledged in crime fiction.

Curt Evans' review in *MysteryFile* provides less than four pages on the novel and might be the best we have. Evans writes:

> While Nancy Spain's mysteries maintain a formal commitment to the puzzle structure, nevertheless *she is typical of the time in which she wrote in placing greater emphasis on other elements, namely humor and character* [my emphasis]. Especially notable in her books is her sly subversion of sexual mores of the post–WW2 era.... There's humorous satire directed against girls' schools ... and sexual foibles, as well [as] some interesting asides on detective fiction. The mystery is rather a mess, however. While there is fitful investigation, intricate clueing is absent; and

the solution is handed to the investigators. You may be left with questions at the end, assuming you care about the mystery. Most of Spain's readers probably did not.

Cinderella Goes to the Morgue has a different touch from *Poison for Teacher* in one respect: more of the supernatural appears. Greater emphasis is placed on Natasha's clairvoyance: "Childishly clairvoyant herself, Natasha quite often refused to admit the gift in others" (92). This observation from the omniscient author takes place at a tealeaf reading by the wardrobe mistress Estelle Furbinger. The woman tells Natasha that there will be a second death and that Timothy Shelly — "if that is his name" — whom Natasha fancies is "in it up to the hilt" (93). Spain is no doubt drawing upon her experience of the séance she and Noël Coward once attended. This piling of suspense upon suspense is one of the elements that make these two novels enjoyable. Spain's writing does not follow the puzzle-solving stream in Golden Age crime fiction. It belongs indisputably to the tradition of farce and satire in the genre as Curt Evans recognizes.

There are moments in *Cinderella* when the omniscient author intrudes: "Liberty Hall, or Bayleyside, as *I* should prefer to call it" [my emphasis] (42). Then too, there are sometimes light parodies of romantic cliché: "Natasha ... already knew that one night, in the dark, very soon, she would wake, her eyes wide with fierce surmise, and realize all that had not, at the time, appeared to her significant" (68). This is another suspense-making device: short staccato phrases, and a contrast implied from dark to light, together with a melodramatic cliché: "Fierce surmise." "Wild surmise" occurs in *Poison for Teacher* (22) when Miriam and Natasha meet Roger Partick-Thistle. In *Cinderella*, too, Nancy Spain often describes colors and shapes evocatively:

> The grill-room upstairs also glittered with chromium. The chairs were scarlet leatherette. The tables were round. At the back of the room there was an unpleasant bar with a chromium rail for the feet, a looking-glass that multiplied all these horrors by fifty (it was cut up into fifty fragments, each a foot square), and a neat little round-about man in a white linen coat [168].

Such passages occur as breaks in the pacing, from the rapid exchange of dialogue with short descriptive sentences that characterize Spain's writing.

Some descriptions of room interiors or open countryside in *Cinderella Goes to the Morgue* have critical merit, although they are clearly parodies of literary writing. They are frequently acerbic:

> They left behind them the rows of terrace houses, and their unfortunate dirt-clogged fronts and greasy gardens. They began to pass City Building Schemes and rows of council cottages. Here and there among them swallowed up by strips of unhygienic brick, and equally unhygienic pavement, were fine Georgian or Queen Anne Mansions, left futile, in two acres of unproductive soil. Many of them had already been turned into Orphanages or Cripples' Homes and proclaimed the

fact, shamefaced, with hoardings and dark-green, gold-lettered notices. By and by the tram-tracks ceased and then the houses, and then they were stealing along Westward, through the purple countryside towards the last streaks of the fading day [42].

Such a description is worthy of George Orwell as in *The Road to Wigan Pier* (1937) or, closer to home, Edmund Crispin's agreeable descriptions of British Rail. Note use of the pathetic fallacy near the end of this citation.

Some of the comments made in the *gadetection* reviews of *Murder, Bless It* and *Not Wanted on Voyage* are equally pertinent to *Poison for Teacher*. Jon (the webmaster) observes tongue in cheek that:

Novelists in post–Waugh England had it easy. Take a few art students; add a handful of exotic foreigners, and a mysterious underworld figure or two, and stir in some theatrical personalities. Garnish with sparkling conversation, and top with decorous hints of homosexuality. Strain out the compassion. Plot is optional, but a thrilling title is a *must*.

Another reviewer, Ralph Wood, on *Not Wanted on Voyage*, says in more sober vein:

The device of the cruise makes the story something like a country house murder. For the duration of the voyage, none of the suspects can leave, and no help can arrive from outside.... The book is witty and camp, with comically class-conscious details of late forties tourism. Miriam Birdseye's friends Natasha Nevkorina and Roger Partick-Thistle are also on board. So far, very much in Nancy Spain's usual style.... But perhaps it also has a darker side.

There is a careless one-paragraph review on the Amazon.com site that focuses on trivia and misses the point of Spain's satire. Mrs. L. R. Fisher, who is a prolific producer of one-paragraph reviews for that site, gives *Poison for Teacher* one out of five stars. She ridicules the novel for Spain's description of her protagonists' clothes and because:

It's much too long and wordy. She's not as funny as she thinks she is. Alcohol is used for a cheap laugh every few pages (it's never funny). There are casually denigrating references to Jews, and to people being "queer as coots." There are no characters you can like or believe in — it's too post-modern (this is a "detective story"). It's no surprise that she's forgotten and unread.

Nancy's lively repartee, dialogue the chief form in *Poison for Teacher*, helps to explain what Fisher saw as wordiness. To have the best effect of the satire one must read the passage more fully:

She had walked over to prayers and breakfast in a splendid make-up that epitomized (Miriam thought) Enunciation and Controlled Breathing. She was rather sorry that Natasha was not there to see, for everyone else seemed to take it for granted. It consisted of a low-waisted mauve cardigan, trimmed with yellow worsted flowers, a dark-blue jersey with strings at the neck and a *splendid* shapeless mustard-coloured hairy tweed skirt that she had discovered in a cupboard outside her door. Miriam wondered who it belonged to and thought perhaps Miss Zwart. (She was perfectly right). Her shoes and stockings had already been used in a revue sketch.... They were size nine and they strapped over the instep and fastened with buttons.... At breakfast and prayers, Miriam was quite indistinguishable. She melted among them, in her appalling protective clothing, like an animal in the forest [43–44].

Animal imagery is strikingly satirical in the description of Miss Lipscomb's drawing-room:

There were a number of good mats and a great many small skins belonging to animals like snow leopards, martens, badgers and skunks. They had all been snared or shot by the late Baron Lipscomb, and his daughter would not have parted from them for the world. In front of the fire lay Miss Lipscomb's revolting dog Scharnhorst. He was an angry, self-assertive, barking, worrying rough-haired fox-terrier with bad points. He smelt of fish [36].

The Scharnhorst was a German battle cruiser launched in October 1936. It saw action in World War II and was sunk at the Battle of North Cape in late December 1943 ("German battleship *Scharnhorst*"). This would have been fresh in English (and German) minds when *Poison for Teacher* was published.

Spain's characters are likable on the whole whether they are brief sketches for the purpose of satire or more solid characterizations (though still two-dimensional) like Natasha and Miriam. The violent and drink-sodden Peter Bracewood-Smith is less likable, but he is a caricature of an English garden cottage murderer and is not altogether unsympathetic. His susceptibility to alcohol (whiskey and gin) proves his downfall. In fact, alcohol is not a running joke but an important plot element, for the poison was delivered by its means. Had Fisher wanted to draw a moral, she might have noticed this principle.

Fisher's criticism about "casually denigrating references to Jews" is to be seen in context. On a quick inspection, five pages contain passages Fisher might have found offensive. Two refer to one of the schoolgirls: "Maud Stuckenheimer ... a little sharp-faced intelligent Jewess like a Japanese painting" (54), and "this nasty little Jewess" (90). The first comment is complimentary and comes from the "omniscient narrator"; the second, uncomplimentary, is spoken by Natasha. This swing from like to dislike, approval to disapproval, occurs at many places in the novel and, I think, reflects Spain's characterization of individuals as much as it might reveal her own feelings. The broader context is Spain's general dislike for children and of schoolgirls in particular at the time of writing.

The other noteworthy references concern the characterization of Philip Lariat. This is probably the nub of the matter. When we meet Lariat for the first time he is described approvingly as: "a stoutish, handsome young Jew" (32). Several pages later his biography is stated in neutral terms: "His father, Mr. Emmanuel Lariat, a moneylender of Harrogate ... had originally been called Emmanuel Lazarus, and he had changed his name by deed poll before Philip's birth" (49). A third example is the one that might have aroused Fisher's ire: "He turned his hands in a helpless little gesture, palms face upward, and swung round in his chair towards Natasha.... 'I am weak, I suppose,' said Lariat as though talking in his sleep. 'And conscious of my social inferiority. Being a Jew, I mean'" (148).

This exchange between Lariat, Natasha and Miriam revolves around Lariat's disingenuousness. Lariat is a ladies' man and a liar as revealed (32) by his change from "thick, sobbing tones" in his attempt to seduce a woman in the Brunton hotel to normal speech when he greets Roger. Natasha and Miriam do not believe him for one moment: "Natasha's large hazel eyes grew wide and troubled as she looked at him"; "Miriam sniffed. This sort of humility always failed to move her" (148); "Natasha, who had never yet observed Doctor Lariat do anything but smile and smile and smile, like a dog, found this hard to believe" (149). Subsequently Lariat with "his nerves and his sentimental Jewish heart" breaks down and tells Miriam, Natasha and Tomkins about his affair with Theresa Devaloys. There is a complexity in these two pages of cross-examination of an unreliable witness that goes well beyond a facile judgment about ethnic prejudice.

Several ethnic groups are mentioned in the novel, sometimes with national traits lightly satirized. Natasha's husband, Johnny DuVivian, is an Australian wrestler and proprietor of a string of nightclubs (2). Natasha is Russian. Cockneys, the Welsh, the Portuguese, and an irascible Indian are represented. The novel is rich in small satirical moments. It is the sort of novel that polarizes the two traditions that flow uneasily side-by-side: the serious, puzzle-solving crime story and the crime novel written for laughs. They have parallel histories, different terms of reference, one may slide into the other, and they appeal separately to different readers.

Another critique that takes itself too seriously and appears to miss the author's intention is that of Alison Hennegan in her introduction to the 1994 Virago edition. The review is written with a polemic that serves the feminist spirit of the early 1990s. It praises Nancy Spain as a lesbian who broke the mold (xiii) by subverting familiar expectations to make them "unsettlingly alien and bizarre." Hennegan (xiv) describes the novel as inverting "conventional moral judgements" and so "remarkable" for that time (but she has it both ways by adding "any period"); disconcerting readers by conflating tragedy with comedy (xi); having an absence of moral judgment (xiv); her comedy reflecting "fascination and delight" with "human difference" rather than danger and fear (xvi). This reading is close to my theme of exploring social reality through satire and other forms of humor as David Lodge (164) tells us. Yet I can't help feeling that Hennegan takes Nancy Spain far too seriously for the entertaining romp that *Poison for Teacher* leads us through.

Hennegan notes with approval Nancy Spain's debt to the "mistresses of the Golden Age of detective fiction" (ix) such as Christie, Sayers, Gladys Mitchell and Josephine Bell and says it "makes supreme good sense" to combine a murder with one's old school. But this is commonplace — it is one of the traditions in crime writing — so too the "cogent one-liners" such as the cliché that Mrs. Puke likes "a good crime" (xiii). Gladys Mitchell (see Chapter Five) wrote the Mrs. Bradley series of detective stories, some of which are parodies of Agatha Christie while some of her other stories poke fun at the conventions of crime writing. Josephine Bell (Doris Bell Collier Ball, 1897–1987) wrote many detective stories with medical backgrounds (she was a doctor along with her husband) that could make her a forerunner of the "forensic" crime novels so popular in the first decade of the twenty-first century ("Josephine Bell"). She does not appear to have received much attention lately. Neither Bell nor Mitchell appears to have had a lesbian inclination and the note than Mitchell never married is insufficient evidence. Hennegan seems to be stopping short of claiming that Nancy Spain's work places her in the company of the Golden Age writers, but she comes close to saying it. Spain is a minor writer when her work is compared against that of her forerunners, although in my opinion the exuberant humor places her up there with the other humorists.

Cinderella Goes to the Morgue (1950)

Nancy Spain's sixth novel *Cinderella Goes to the Morgue* is so closely modeled on *Poison for Teacher* published in the previous year that I suspect Spain used the broad framework of the earlier novel when she planned *Cinderella*. The first three chapters of *Cinderella* contain much the same ingredients as *Poison*: a general distaste for children — "Tottenham Tots, who scattered, whispering and cooing like a lot of dirty little pigeons" (28); passing references to the Wrens (44); the absent or "vague" mental states of the two protagonists Miriam Birdseye and Natasha DuVivian (10, 11); Natasha's Australian ex-wrestler husband Johnny DuVivian, still estranged from Natasha, a direct carryover from the previous "Radcliff Hall" novel to which there is direct reference (48).

The male characters contain another beautiful and feckless young man, Tony Gresham: "It was not a girl. It was a good-looking young man with fair hair in flannel trousers and a lemon-coloured slip-over whose face was already glazed and shiny with weeping" (14). We have a grotesquely hirsute male with an equally unlikely name who is the star of the pantomime: "Hampton Court was square and hairy and in the distance he looked like an angry baboon.... He presented the appearance of an ape, dressed as a pin-striped financier" (16). Compare this with the ape image of the rector in Edmund Crispin's *The Glimpses of the Moon*.

There are as well in *Cinderella* unusual minor characters such as a "Jewess" (30) and Hampton Court's "fat, personal confidential maid with glittering eyes like boot buttons, called Sary O'Driscoll" (16). (There appears to be a tradition among writers to name some of their characters from prominent public places). A Jew, Ephraim Goldsack, makes a brief appearance much later (158). There are the two partners, Harry DeFreeze (third "victim," a suicide) and his brother Banjo DeFreeze (second victim) in *ménage a trois* with Vivienne Gresham (first victim) who marries Harry then cuckolds him for his younger brother Banjo (23).

Miriam and Natasha pause in their Christmas shopping at Newchester-on-the-Tame, a thinly veiled rendering of Newcastle-on-Tyne. Miriam and Natasha decide to visit one of three theaters in this fictional provincial town: the Theatre Royal, the Pallindrome (a double play on the word "palindrome" and the London Palladium), and the Universe. There they meet Tony Gresham, the press agent who is crying because Hampton Court has been bullying him. Tony's mother Vivienne Gresham is mentioned as "principal boy" (15) in the pantomime and Miriam remarks a little callously: "*That* old trout. She may *easily* drop dead." At which point Natasha has a premonition: "I am only feeling a shiver when Miriam says Vivienne Gresham may be dropping dead." They meet Hampton Court and learn that he has sacked two of the girls for being drunk on stage and is consequently two persons short for the chorus, so Natasha and Miriam are persuaded to join the troupe. They stay overnight in an uncomfortable local hotel until, after meeting the lord mayor Thomas Atkins (the murderer), they are invited to stay at his house Bayleyside, where they meet Atkins' wife Kidder.

Aside from Natasha's premonitions that supply dramatic suspense, there are other hints of foul play to come: "I hope to heaven *this* doesn't develop into one of darling Natasha's murder dramas" says Miriam (40), and "darling Natasha suddenly felt the oddest sensation. She felt that Mr. Atkins was not everything that he appeared to be" (38). As in *Poison for Teacher*, it is Natasha who does most of the detecting. Hampton Court introduces the subject of murder and its motives at the dinner table, discussed among them subsequently: madness, jealousy, passion, hatred ("the usual things"), lust and anger ("the Seven Deadly Sins"), and one character (Kidder) adds financial security (money). This leads two pages later (55) to the death, where Vivienne Gresham during the rehearsal falls through the stage-trap because the platform had not been raised back up following the exit of a Fairy Queen. In the resulting investigation, the character of Sergeant Robinson comes on the scene: "a neat, clean man with a neat, clean mind" (121).

The deaths when they occur have features similar to those in *Poison for Teacher*. Vivienne Gresham (55) dies from a fall and Banjo DeFreeze (106) is shot in the forehead by a revolver that had been mislaid by Timothy Shelly.

Once again there is a stark description of the murder: "Banjo was lying on the floor in a dreadful heap, like a bundle of old clothes. In the middle of his forehead there was a neat blue bole. He was quite dead." As usual, it is brief enough to mitigate the horror. The novel towards its end has a third death in the suicide of Harry DeFreeze (188), just as there is a purported suicide in *Poison for Teacher*.

The romantic interest this time is between Timothy Shelly and Natasha who has "an unfortunate love of wastrels" (50). There is a lot of sexual farce, from various advances by drunken actors towards women characters to the more subtle reaction of a drinks waiter who, after "watching Natasha's inconsequent beauty," departs "reverently, his little silver salver clenched against his black trouser leg" (40).

Mislaid revolvers are a frequent element, as in Carter Dickson's *Night at the Mocking Widow* or Milne's *The Fourth Wall*. Natasha, who fancies Timothy Shelly and wishes to shield him, demands that he hand over his revolver (118). At that point Timothy realizes he no longer has it. This is stretching the reader's belief but is consistent with Timothy's not-so-bright character. Later they have the following exchange:

> Timothy closed one eye.
> "But I *ought* to be all right," he said. "Oughtn't I? I mean, I never fired it. Innocence will out."
> "Do not be being such a fool!" cried Natasha, infuriated beyond endurance.
> "It is not *innocence* will out. It is murder" [131].

The missing revolver appears during the pantomime lying on a cushion carried by Marilyn Franklyn in her part as Dandini (148–149). Miriam quickly conceals it in her clothing. A ration book swindle is exposed (151). Natasha gets Timothy to admit that Vivienne was his wife who refused to divorce him (161). Timothy hated her (165). A child actor breaks a tooth on a bullet hidden in a packet of sweets (162). Robinson addresses a crowd of actors brought together as suspects/witnesses, a parody on drawing-room dénouements (166). Motives dot the novel here and there.

The pathetic fallacy has a good airing. The oily darkness of the city streets — "The city now glistened like a black oilskin" (197) — establishes a mood of foreboding as the novel moves towards its climax in the department store of Atkins and Marshall. Natasha produces a revolver bullet and says to Sergeant Robinson: "I am observing Mr. Tom Atkins, trying to light his cigarette with it last night.... And I am also realizing that he is *pretending* to be drunk all the evening" (217). Natasha says she searched Atkins's room while he was taking a bath and found the bullet. Subsequently Robinson shows Natasha a letter written by Banjo to Marylyn ("Maryella") fearing for his life at the hands of Tom Atkins because they were in the coupon scam together. Banjo believes that it was Atkins who pulled the lever that opened the stage trapdoor (220).

Of the motives discussed by characters earlier, madness and jealousy appear to be uppermost where Thomas Atkins is concerned. Here is Atkins's soliloquy as he slips towards insanity:

> Ever since he had picked up the revolver by the telephone switchboard at the Theatre Royal, and had realized, with a start of pleasure, that it belonged to Timothy Shelly, he had been perfectly aware that he was going to make the usual murderer's mistake.... *He* had seen how gone Kidder was on Shelly.... But where the hell was the mistake? *That* was what he couldn't think. He could hardly think at all [220–221].

A quick transition to slapstick a few pages later that would have been worthy of John Dickson Carr or Edmund Crispin blunts the seriousness and makes Atkins more a figure of fun than of evil: "Miriam Birdseye ... had peeped out of a roll of battered oilcloth, giggling helplessly.... He had run berserk down the store, dressed unbecomingly in his underwear, apparently in satyr-like pursuit of Sary O'Driscoll" (227). In the ensuing fracas several persons descend upon the department store where Atkins has taken refuge in his office: Marylyn Franklyn, Hampton Court, Miriam, Natasha and Timothy, and Robinson and assorted police. Atkins fires a shotgun, wounding Robinson. The characters take cover behind a number of store counter displays. Atkins mounts to the cash desk above his office and continues firing. He starts up the mechanism that operates the cash canisters that flow through the overhead trolley railway, while the police close in: "It was Bowes, the dependable, who first had the idea of advancing on Tom Atkins like Burnam Wood on Dunsinane concealed behind the wax models from the window" (226). It ends when Atkins attempts to escape by swinging from the overhead wires until he brings them down upon himself.

The final chapter is a true anti-climax. Atkins is likely to be declared insane. Kidder remains faithful to him. Tony Gresham and Miriam plan to go into partnership in a theater with Tony's insurance money. Timothy declares his love for Natasha, which pleases her. But she is less enthusiastic (that is, "vague") about marriage and having his children. There is a final ironic twist to the murder investigation when Natasha in the last page says: "I was not going into the bedroom. It was not finding the revolver shell. I was making it all up. But the Sergeant believed me" (234). They drive towards County Cork (Timothy's home) unaware they are being followed by Natasha's ex-husband Johnny DuVivian.

The Kat Strikes (1955)

The Kat Strikes, which is the last of Nancy Spain's crime novels, is generally regarded as her weakest. As her biographer says, by this time in her life Spain had grown tired of writing detective stories. *Kat* places Nancy Spain with

E. C. Bentley as an author who in later years produced a flawed and eccentric novel; or A. A. Milne's perhaps experimental *Four Days' Wonder*. At approximately 64,000 words, *The Kat Strikes* is more like a novella. It is certainly nothing like Spain's wordy forerunners.

The flyleaf blurb claims *The Kat Strikes* to be an "extremely exciting story in the true English tradition of Buchan and Edgar Wallace." The restrained style of the reviewer suggests that he/she may have held doubts. Certainly *Kat* has elements of a thriller. The protagonist rescues Jimmy, "a little man," when he attempts to suicide in the Thames, only to find him murdered in a warehouse soon after. There is a sinister housekeeper and houseboy, drug running is involved "under cover of a respectable publishing firm" (190), and a rhetoric flourish towards the end (168) sums up: "The whole business, Jimmy's death, Creyke's corpse, the burning warehouse, Cyril down by the river in that nightmare villa, our happy hour on the Serpentine" (168). The iconic river figures throughout the novella from the suicide attempt to the barge gifted to Kat and her swimming naked into the boatshed of the criminal gang.

The usual autobiographic allusions to persons and literature are few: "Lord Cute. Who owns me body and soul *and* the *Daily Glass* and *The Banner*" (165), and eccentric names: Terence O'Flaherty Fingal O'Kelly with "enormous shoulders" (22). Similarly Spain attempts noir imagery in a bar scene vaguely modeled on the 1942 film *Casablanca*:

> There was a bar, of course, with various characters draped along it; pathetic waifs in little black bursting dresses; sad lisping boys with volumes of Tennessee Williams gripped like a one-way railway ticket, a piano where an unconcentrated young coloured lady wandered about the keyboard. The pianist didn't seem to have the energy to play a complete tune, just as the characters sitting around didn't seem to be capable of living complete lives [60].

Like the pianist she depicts, Nancy Spain is not concentrated on the craft of writing. There are flashes of her old form such as those cited above, and this one: "The tide was coming in fast and the water was coiling along Millbank, clutching and gulping and chuckling like a live thing" (10). But the novella appears to have been thrown together haphazardly as though it is a first rough draft. It has glaring inconsistencies. Where is Cyril carrying his gun? Is it in his hip pocket?—"it was quite easy for me to feel the bulge in Cyril's hip-pocket" (74)—or in his trouser pocket?—"The other [hand], the left one, was in his trouser pocket, guarding his gun" (74)? The weapon finds its way to Cyril's right hand, a clever feat if in the left pocket, easier if in a hip pocket: "Cyril seized me with his left hand and shook his gun at me with his right" (76). In the climactic scene of the burning boathouse Spain seems not to make up her mind whether, as she swims, Kat is holding in her teeth a book that contains heroin in its hollowed pages or is clutching it to her chest (192–193). The latter would have made swimming difficult.

The key to this creative lapse I think is the date of publication. In 1955 it is fair to say that Nancy Spain was heavily preoccupied with a number of issues that had a profound impact in her life and self-image. In that year *She* magazine was founded and Nancy became involved in BBC radio and was a member of a panel on BBC television. She met with and was sustained by a number of mentors, principally Noël Coward, A. A. Milne and Orson Welles. But the most important factor is the establishment of a family life centered upon the circle of Nancy, her partner Joan Werner Laurie and the two boys. This brings about a crucial shift in Nancy's self-awareness, leading her to opt out of detective/crime writing from a new conviction that it was not quite proper to depict death and lightheartedness when she was increasingly responsible for two young children, one of which was her own. The priorities in her life had changed. Nine years later Nancy Spain and Joan Werner Laurie died in the aircraft accident.

Today Nancy Spain's work, by all accounts, is "forgotten and unread." *Wikipedia* has no entry for Spain and Laurie's *She* magazine, although other sites advertise later incarnations of *She*. Neither Nancy Spain nor Joan Laurie is profiled in *The Feminist Companion to Literature in English* (1990) much less the *Bloomsbury Guide to English Literature* (1989). Nor is Nancy Spain included in the list of "Notable Roedeanians" at Roedean School ("Roedean School"). It is uncertain whether this is due to snobbery towards the genre or towards gay authors, or some other oversight. Perhaps her life was so outrageous that even the feminist establishment disowned her, but I think that unlikely. It is similar to the unjustified fate of others who were active writers during the Golden Age. As Curt Evans says: "Nancy Spain had a gift for humor and character portrayal that makes her mystery novels worth reading even today, over half-a-century after the last of them was originally published. Just don't expect Crime Queen level plotting, and you should not be disappointed" (*MysteryFile.com*).

CHAPTER 9

Continuing the Tradition

It seems to me that a lot written in the present day does not compete with the best from the Golden Age, but this assumption may be unfair. The handful of post–Golden Age humorists whose work spans the last decades of the twentieth century and in some instances carries though into the twenty-first suggest a slow dilution of the "pure" forms that utilize wit, satire, burlesque or slapstick. In their place has come a gradual shift towards more serious crime fiction. That stream had always been present in the Golden Age puzzle-solving crime novels and remains strong today with an infusion of forensic and psychological themes. Today, although humor remains present in many crime stories, it is often presented as comic relief, sometimes tangential to the plot instead of taking pride of place or sharing equally in importance with the mystery to be solved. I am thinking of writers such as Andrea Camilleri and Kerry Greenwood, for whom humor is not paramount. On the other hand, Michael Innes, Colin Watson, Anthony Shaffer, Leslie Thomas and Simon Brett cheerfully carry on the tradition of humorist crime writing. Individually they stand at opposite ends of the spectrum from subtle wit and dense satire to the comic extravagances of burlesque and broader satire. Having said this, it might be useful to preface a discussion on these writers by considering one of the earlier humorists, Ronald Knox, whose life of sixty-nine years spans not only the Golden Age but some years before and after that era, importantly because Knox's rules for detective crime writing influenced his contemporaries and those who came after.

Monsignor Ronald Knox (1888–1957)

Ronald Arbuthnott Knox was ordained as a high-church Anglican priest in 1912 but found Roman Catholicism more to his taste and chose to be ordained into that church six years later in 1918. He came from a Leicestershire

Anglican family and before his ordination was a brilliant Classics scholar at Oxford where he continued as chaplain. Ironically, G. K. Chesterton interested Knox in the Catholic Church before he himself chose to enter Catholicism. It may have been the connection with Chesterton that led Knox into crime in his early career, in between broadcasting and writing about Christianity. Later in life when he appears to have given up crime, he translated the *Vulgate Bible* (1950) and the *Imitation of Christ* (begun in 1953) among other classic works of faith ("Ronald Knox").

Behind his spiritual vocation Knox was a satirist. This seems to have begun with a radio hoax in 1926 about the shelling of the Savoy Hotel that may have influenced Orson Welles in his *War of the Worlds* dramatization, also in radio, in 1938 ("Ronald Knox"). Both hoaxes were taken seriously by many listeners and with resulting panic. Knox's satirical tales of this period are brought together in *Essays in Satire* (1928). Some belong to "the genre of mock-serious critical writings" ("Ronald Knox") such as treating Holmes and Watson as though they were living figures ("Studies in the Literature of Sherlock Holmes"), or an essay attributing the authorship of Tennyson's poem *In Memoriam* to Queen Victoria, and in "Reunion All Round" lampooning the tolerance of the Anglican Church by absorbing Muslims, atheists, and Catholics who murder Irish children, the last-named a shift towards serious social comment which is a hallmark of satire.

As a founding member of the Detection Club, Knox is responsible for the codification of ten rules that he called a Decalogue in imitation of the Ten Commandments (Exodus 20:3–17). He wrote six crime novels, five of which feature the detective character of Miles Breadon, from 1925 (publication of the first) to 1937 (the last novel). The decade from the mid–1920s to the mid–1930s belongs to the first wave of Detection Club writers. Knox's crime oeuvre include *The Viaduct Murder* (1925), *The Three Taps* (1927), *The Footsteps at the Lock* (1928), *The Body in the Silo* (1933), *Still Dead* (1934), and *Double Cross Purposes* (1937). There are three collections of short stories: *Saved by Inspection* (1931), *The Motive* (1937), and *The Adventure of the First Class Carriage* (1947). He also contributed to three collaborative works from the Detection Club: *Behind the Screen* (1930), *The Floating Admiral* (1931), and *Six Against the Yard* (1936). These "round-robin" tales are a curious mix of plot, characterization and the uncovering of more than one villain, each chapter often becoming more unwieldy and complex than its predecessor at the hands of every new contributor; as in *The Floating Admiral* in which at least one writer, Clemence Dane (305), gives up on solving the mystery. The form is entertaining but is a showcase, perhaps unwittingly, of the individuality of some stylists, and to my mind does not really work.

The examples here are from Knox's first novel, *The Viaduct Murder*. Symons calls Monsignor Knox "the super-typical Farceur of the decade, one who never allowed into his half-dozen detective stories the faintest breath of seriousness to disturb the desperate facetiousness of his style. *The Viaduct Murder* (1925), with its amateur investigator who gets everything wrong, owes a good deal to Bentley" (105). In the best tradition of a murder tale, the discovery of the body near the foot of the viaduct confronts the reader with the unpleasantness of violent death:

> Together they approached the prostrate body; it lay face downwards, and there was no movement of life. The thrill of distaste with which healthy nature shrinks from the sight of dissolution seized both of them. Gordon had served three years in the army, and had seen death; yet it was always death tricked out in the sacrificial garb of khaki; there was something different about death in a towncoat and striped grey trousers — it was a discord in the clear weather. The sun seemed to lose a shade of its brightness. Together they bent; and turned the body over, only to relinquish it again by a common instinct. Not only did the lolling head tell them that here the architecture of the human frame had been unknit; the face had disappeared, battered unrecognizably by some terrible and prolonged friction [18].

The victim has apparently fallen from a passing train or from the top of the viaduct. The preliminary pages (reverse of title page both sides) provide a map of the area and a rail timetable. A little like Edmund Crispin many years later, Knox, with a touch of the pathetic fallacy, voices his liking for railways: "Let the Wordsworthian say what he will, railways ennoble our landscape; they give to our unassuming valleys a hint of motive and destination" (16).

Apart from having the stamp of Knox's personality, *The Viaduct Murder* touches upon several staple elements in the genre that hark back to Conan Doyle, E. C. Bentley and A. A. Milne. The Merion Press introduction (iii) to this approximately 70,000-word novel states, "There are no less than ten references to Holmes and/or Watson including the title of one of the chapters." This is Chapter XVIII, "The Holmes Method" (177). In the Merion Press synopsis (Shelley's Bookshelf):

> Marryatt (the clergyman), Carmichael (the retired don), Reeves (the former member of the military intelligence), and Gordon (the vacationing golfer) are playing golf in Paston Oatvile when Reeves slices his drive from the third tee. In searching for the ball they come upon the dead body of Mr. Brotherhood below the railroad viaduct. When they find his hat 15 yards away from the body they suspect "there's been dirty work." The foursome set out to solve his murder.

Knox's humor has two chief components. It is first of all characterized by a dry wit, as one might expect of the obverse nature of an otherwise very serious churchman, and devolves upon a number of singularly fallible investigators. In these two respects it might owe a little to Chesterton and a lot to the tradition of the fallible detective/investigator already established by E. C. Bentley and played closer to Knox's time by A. A. Milne. Reeves's thick-headedness is evident from the start, for along with his golfing companions Marryatt, Carmichael and two caddies, he moves the body (19) to a nearby tool-house. During the inquest "disturbing the clues" (77) is tacitly forgiven and Reeves instead is thanked for his action. This is satire directed at the conduct of an inquest and the moving the body. Other conventions in the genre reflect those of a rival form, the thriller. There are the three investigatory questions: "was it accident, suicide, or murder?" (27). The dead man is suspected of being in disguise: "Brotherhood is Davenant, Davenant is Brotherhood" (65). The golfing club-house has a secret passage (121).

A great deal of Knox's wit, it appears, raises questions about how best to establish knowledge and is often self-referential: "distrust the author whose second paragraph does not come to ground in the particular" (1) [after an intro-ductory paragraph giving the physical setting]; "People can never tell you a story without putting their own colour upon it — that is the difficulty of getting evidence in real life" (11); "What do we really know about one another down here?" (12); "Headlines are especially destructive.... Under this treatment, all the nuances of atmosphere and of motive disappear; we figure the truth by try-ing to make it fit into a formula" (11).

These concerns appear earlier in the novel but they are revisited in the penultimate chapter, "The Consolation of Philosophy" with Alexander Gor-don's advice to Reeves: "I don't mean the guess-work by which we live from day to day, and which is necessary to living: I mean the theories learned people propound to tell us about the past, about the meaning of human history" (238). On finding a vocation to which Reeves might be best suited, Gordon satirizes in turn anthropology (239), psycho-analysis (240), and literary crit-icism (241): "If the worst comes to the worst, you can always fall back upon literary criticism, and there you are on perfectly safe ground. A man with a documentary hypothesis can defy the rudest assaults of common sense."

Michael Innes (1906–1994)

Michael Innes is the pen name for John Innes Mackintosh Stewart. He was born in Edinburgh on 30 September 1906 and died at the age of eighty-eight on 12 November 1994 at Coulsdon, a town on the southern edge of Greater London. He graduated in English Literature at Oxford, studied psy-choanalysis at Vienna in 1929, and from 1930 to 1935 was Lecturer in English at the University of Leeds before becoming Jury Professor of English at the University of Adelaide, South Australia. He has, then, experience of comic university life from the inside. Stewart's time in Australia evidently lasted from 1936 to 1946 until, after the Second World War, he took up a position equiv-alent to that of a Fellow at the Queen's University of Belfast in 1949, called a Student in University of Belfast nomenclature. He retired in 1973 when he was by then a professor at that university.

Stewart was prolific. Under the pseudonym of Michael Innes he wrote more than forty crime/detective novels between 1936 and 1986. Under his real name of J. I. M. Stewart, he wrote also six critical works (on Joyce, Conrad, Shakespeare and Hardy, for example), twenty novels, six volumes of short stories, and an autobiography ("J. I. M. Stewart").

The two novels profiled here are forty-four years apart. *Death at the President's Lodging* (1936) is Michael Innes's first crime novel when he was thirty. It is also the first Inspector Appleby mystery, published in the U.S. as *Seven Suspects*. Michael Innes's age and the date of publication of *Lodging* place him within the time frame of the Golden Age writers. Indeed, he is described this way by Grobius Shortling as a "later" writer of Golden Age detective stories. The protagonist of the other novel written when Innes was seventy-four years old, *Going It Alone* (1980), is not a police inspector but a scholar in French literature. *Going It Alone* is in a more lighthearted vein than *Lodging*. It too is satirical with touches of the thriller in its premise and plot progression.

Innes made a conscious choice to use comedy as the dominant mode while at the same time he wrote what Shortling calls "complicated" plots. In a note to the story, Innes says:

> The senior members of Oxford and Cambridge colleges ... are, as Ben Johnson would have said, persons such as comedy would choose; it is much easier to give them a shove into the humorous than a twist into the melodramatic; they prove peculiarly resistive to the slightly rummy psychology that most detective stories require [v].

This says a number of things about Innes's approach. Firstly, he is fond of often tongue-in-cheek literary allusions. His books are sprinkled throughout with scholarly references but are a little less arcane than the extremes Edmund Crispin throws at us. Secondly, his settings are nearly always enclosed within old houses, rural villages or universities and so adhere closely to that Golden Age preference. Several of his works can also be described as campus novels. Thirdly, his training in psychology (Freudian analysis) helps to inform his tales while at the same time he is wary of the uses to which psychology is put in other detective stories. Innes writes melodramatic tales, too, as in *Going It Alone* which parodies the thriller, so his rules are flexible. Grobius Shortling in his survey of Innes' work lists another novel, *The Secret Vanguard* (1941), as a parody ("pastiche") on Buchan's *The 39 Steps*. Shortling describes *Death at the President's Lodging* as "murder at a pseudo-Oxbridge college; very complicated plot with the eccentric dons involved in different aspects of the case and covering up." Similarly, R. D. Collins writes that: "Innes has a colourful and urbane writing style which is, unusually in this field, weighted towards dialogue, verbal exchanges and well rounded characters rather than the usual plot-driven whodunit."

Julian Symons calls Michael Innes "the finest of the Farceurs, a writer who turns the detective story into an over-civilized joke with a frivolity which makes it a literary conversation piece with detection taking place on the side" (115). For Symons the Innes stories have a "flippant gaiety" (116). T. J. Binyon compares Innes's method with John Dickson Carr and Ellery Queen but, a little like Symons, describes the novels as using "intellectual conceits, in which a complex, logical plot is set against an elaborate, often highly artificial background peopled with eccentric characters, whose conversation is witty, amusing, and erudite ... he is always concerned to entertain" (94).

The plot of *Death at the President's Lodging* follows a traditional pattern. The president of a university College, Dr. Josiah Umpleby, is found dead in his study in bizarre circumstances: "Just beside the President's grotesquely muffled head lay a human skull. And over the surrounding area of the floor were scattered little piles of human bones" (15–16). There is a suggestion of the twenty-first-century preoccupation with forensics and body parts (one current television drama is titled *Bones*) but the imagery with its exaggerations of chalk-scrawled death's heads, human skull, and scattered bones to my mind appears more similar to the front cover illustration on the 1979 Methuen edition of Watson's *Snobbery with Violence*.

For that book of criticism, a Lord Peter Wimsey simulacrum in starched collar, tailored overcoat and wearing a monocle holds a magnifying glass in one hand while with the other hand he passes his hat to the butler. He stands at the entrance to the crime scene, the victim at his feet a woman in 1920s flapper costume, a knife between the shoulder blades. While death by knife is a serious matter, the many images (one hesitates to say overkill) present a more comic impression. In the case of the illustration its costuming with a hint of snobbery parodies the upper-class Golden Age detective, whereas in Innes's novel an element of the facetious peeps through the overabundance of death images. (The "common offices of death" attached to the academic gown suggests a shroud.)

There is another touch, that of the thriller, referred to explicitly:

> *Why* had Umpleby met his death in a story-book manner? For that his death had been set in an elaborately contrived frame seemed now clear.... He had died in a literary context; indeed, he had in a manner of speaking died amid a confusion of literary contexts. For in the network of physical circumscriptions ... there was contrivance in a literary tradition deriving from all the progeny of Sherlock Holmes, while in the fantasy of the bones there was something of the incongruous tradition of the "shocker" [23].

Innes goes on in this manner for more that 82,000 words. The novel is built up in a dense style somewhat in the tradition of Dorothy L. Sayers but with touches of the more active thriller.

Written many years later in the autumn of Innes's life, *Going It Alone* is a parody in the tradition of the thriller. It has an interesting premise. The protagonist Gilbert Averell temporarily switches identity with that of Georges,

Prince de Silistrie, a look-alike acquaintance who lives in France but likes to visit England regularly. (Silistra is a place in Bulgaria and may or may not have anything to do with Innes's choice of name). Georges has a wild temperament and enjoys partying, preferably in England where he is less likely to be recognized. Gilbert, an "elderly" man in his mid-fifties, prefers a quiet life but endeavors to live much of his time in France as a tax dodge. Georges persuades Gilbert to change identities more or less by forcing the arrangement upon him. Passports are exchanged. Averell is dogged by a man calling himself Flaubert after attaching himself to Averell during the flight from France to England. Gilbert passes through English Customs as the Prince. He visits his sister Ruth Barcroft, nephew Timothy, and the two nieces Kate and Gillian at a country house named Boxes.

The socio-political unrest of the time is frequently referred to in the novel (at about 57,000 words, it is really a novella). Tim, for example, now twenty-one when Gilbert sees him again, was at the age of twenty what we would call a student activist: "he had come to hold strong views on the evils of capitalist society, nuclear weapons, sub-human housing, racialism, the CIA, and numerous other conditions and institutions that ought simply not to be" (23). Satire is even more evident, but so too is the serious undertone. This is Margaret Thatcher's England. She was prime minister from 1979 to 1990 ("1970s"). What is more, many of the generalities might just as easily apply to the second decade of the twenty-first century.

Characteristic of Innes, intertextual literary allusions and parodic references to Golden Age crime novels are sprinkled through the text, starting on the first page (7) with a reference to the Hardy novel *Tess of the D'Urbervilles* (1891), and continuing with mention of Shakespeare (9) as well as leading French authors (29) such as Balzac, Proust, Malraux and Flaubert. Joseph Conrad and Robert Louis Stevenson are drawn in (110, 116), Samuel Becket (130) as well. There is a playful tribute to Agatha Christie's choice of titles when Gilbert catches "Monsieur Gustave Flaubert" prowling near the summerhouse, a very English setting for this sort of thing:

> From somewhere close at hand, in fact from just outside the summerhouse, had come a most alarming sound. It was the sharp *click!* surely to be associated (Averell thought) with the cocking of a pistol, if pistols are in fact things one does cock. He was uncertain about this — but in no doubt of the resurgence of what a writer of romance might entitle *Peril at Boxes* [96].

A pistol does not have a cocking mechanism like the revolver because its chamber is integral with the barrel ("Pistol"). The parodic reference is no doubt to Christie's Hercule Poirot novel *Peril at End House* (1932). Later in *Going It Alone* there is another allusion to the adventure and thriller genres: "a roughly sketched skull and crossbones had been appended by way of signature ... rather like the Black Spot in *Treasure Island*" (110).

By now Averell is in the company of his nephew Tim and his friends and there follow in succession more prowling, this time on the part of the heroes, chases, a fire to discomfit the criminal gang (bank robbers), and rescues. The person rescued from an attic was known to "Do It Yourself. Or Go It Alone" (149), hence the title of the novel. The ending verges on slapstick, though Crispin would have done better. There is a brief anti-climax in which Gilbert Averell and the prince meet over lunch in Paris. The mysterious Flaubert tailing Gilbert is a private investigator sent by the prince's jealous mistress Minette.

Colin Watson (1920–1983)

Born in the first year of the 1920s, Colin Watson is too young to be included in the assemblage of Golden Age writers. But he made up for it with his twelve Flaxborough novels, beginning with *Coffin, Scarcely Used* (1958) when he was thirty-eight years old and ending with *Whatever's Been Going on at Mumblesby?* (1982) aged sixty-two, a year before he died on 17 January 1983. When he was at the ripe age of fifty-one, Watson also wrote one of the best overviews of the genre for its wit and wry humor, *Snobbery with Violence* (1971). Its theme, the English class system in Golden Age tales, is a particular aspect of humor (satire) in crime fiction. Writing in 2004 for an internet issue of *Mystery Magazine* that he edits, Jeffery Ewener remarks that Watson has been out of print "for more than a decade." Ewener would be pleased to note that since then Rue Morgue Press republished *Coffin, Scarcely Used* in a 2008 edition.

The Wikipedia entry on Colin Watson is slight. We learn that Watson was a journalist in Lincolnshire and that he modeled the characters in his Flaxborough chronicles on real people known to him, a common circumstance. According to Tom and Enid Schantz who paraphrase Jeffery Ewener in their introduction to *Coffin, Scarcely Used*, Flaxborough is modeled upon Boston, the town in Lincolnshire where Watson worked. Jeffery Ewener writes that:

> There are no biographies, no critical examinations beyond a couple of character studies by the late Earl Bargainnier in the journal *Clues*, and not one doughboy or doughgirl in the army of Ph.D. students in EngLit, CrimeLit or PopCult has seen fit to grind the man up into thesis mulch. On the web there's only a single site devoted to Watson [6–7].

Ewener notes what appears the only useful web site on Colin Watson, run by William Nedblake, but the site appears to have been removed.

Watson kept a low profile, as Ewener says, but he was active enough, aside from his novels, to be elected to the Detection Club in 1970 (in the members list contained in Wikipedia) where H.R.F. Keating's wife noticed him at one of their dinners. H.R.F. Keating wrote the Inspector Ghote mysteries set in

Bombay (Symons 189). Watson is described as a "quiet grey-haired, grey-moustached man," perhaps "a schoolteacher — the quiet, scholarly, typically English kind."

Jeffery Ewener extrapolates from Colin Watson's career as a newspaperman to show a little more of the personality. Watson, says Ewener, worked for "the Canadian-born press baron Lord Thomson's chain of exuberant English publications" where his job was to write on daily events. There was no byline. The leading articles were published in various regional newspapers with a decidedly conservative leaning towards giving the readers what they liked. This needed, says Ewener, "an instinctive grasp of the unspoken attitudes, assumptions, beliefs, prejudices, aspirations and fears of the English middle-class." It was good experience for Watson's satirical crime fiction — not to mention his critical study *Snobbery with Violence*— and he quit his full-time job when the novels became popular, entering into a "process of observation, intuition and expression [that] became the basis of his satire over the next twenty years."

Symons includes Watson under "Entertainers" in the chapter "Crime Novel and Police Novel" instead of placing him among the farceurs (104–106), I think because he is following a chronological order and the earlier humorists had their heydays in the 1920s and 1930s. But he clearly ranks Watson among them, using phrases like "fireworks of comedy," "tactful dealings with comic characters," and "brilliant comedy" to describe the Flaxborough tales. Similarly, Binyon places Watson in his section on "Comedy"— in a chapter titled "Oddities"— where he sums up Watson's work as "extraordinarily funny, in both plot and narration, the books also turn a sharply satirical eye on modern British society" (125).

On the other hand, Panek in the only mention on the last page of *Watteau's Shepherds* ranks him among the later writers "like Colin Watson and Julian Symons" who "left the fun and unreality behind and wrote crime novels full of bitterness and unpleasantness" (199). Surely not, but Watson's first novel came out just after the Suez Canal débâcle and his last when Margaret Thatcher instigated the Falklands War in order to gloss over social and political ills she caused at home (Ewener). Satire often has a serious edge. The Suez Crisis was in late 1956 ("Suez Crisis"), twenty-three years before the publication of *Watteau's Shepherds*. But the single mention of Watson scarcely fits the point, and Panek unaccountably omits him from his later study. There are more snippets such as these among the critics than biographical material on the man himself, but they are few.

Colin Watson's twelve Flaxborough novels are *Coffin, Scarcely Used* (1958), *Bump in the Night* (1960), *Hopjoy Was Here* (1962), *Lonelyheart 4122* (1967), *Charity Ends at Home* (1968), *The Flaxborough Crab* (1969)— in the U.S. as *Just What the Doctor Ordered, Broomsticks Over Flaxborough* (1972)— in the U.S. as *Kissing Covens, The Naked Nuns* (1975)— in the U.S. as *Six Nuns and a Shot-*

gun, One Man's Meat (1977) — in the U.S. as *It Shouldn't Happen to a Dog, Blue Murder* (1979), *Plaster Sinners* (1980), and *Whatever's Been Going on at Mumblesby?* (1982). ("Colin Watson (writer)").

To illustrate "tactful dealing" from the opening paragraphs of *Coffin, Scarcely Used*, together with a light humorous touch:

> Considering the undoubted prosperity of Mr. Carobleat's business establishment, the ship brokerage firm of Carobleat and Spades, its closing down almost simultaneously with the descent of its owner's coffin into a hole in Heston Lane Cemetery was but another sign that *gloria mundi* transits as hastily in Flaxborough as anywhere else [11].

The description of the "uninspiring" funeral with its tongue-in-cheek references to town councilors paying their respects out of duty to the "expressionless" widow has some parallels with Edmund Crispin's opening railway setting in *The Case of the Gilded Fly* with its blend of darker images set against human reactions.

Watson enjoyed puns. He is in good company with the other humorists Edmund Crispin, John Dickson Carr and Nancy Spain. The *gloria mundi* twist refers to the expression *Sic transit gloria mundi*, "Thus passes the glory of the world," attributed to Thomas à Kempis ("Sic transit gloria mundi"). Watson was only warming up, however. By the end of chapter one there is a second death, this time of Marcus Gwill: "His pale blue eyes like ice fragments beneath the unsympathetic cliff of his forehead, gazing coldly across Flaxborough from the extraordinary vantage point of the crossbar of an electricity pylon" (14). He has been electrocuted in what looks like an accident. The puns are appropriately bad or good depending upon the reader's sense of humor. Gwill is described as having been "very down to earth" (15), and later Inspector Purbright looks up at the tower and remarks: "What an odd perch for a newspaper proprietor…. Power without responsibility, I suppose" (27).

Inspector Purbright is the chief protagonist in the Flaxborough novels. His first appearance in *Coffin, Scarcely Used* has touches of Carr's Sir Henry Merrivale sitting unobserved in the darkened corner of a room as in *Night at the Mocking Widow*, and a physical appearance not unlike that of Edmund Crispin's Professor Gervase Fen:

> [An] expression of sympathy came from a dark corner of the room where a large, but unassuming-looking man in neutral shaded clothes had been keeping quite still during the editor's telephone conversation. He now turned into the light and revealed a bland, pleasant face beneath springy, corn-colored hair that not even relentless cropping could bring to conformity [14–15].

Gervase Fen is more slender in build but Purbright has acquired his hair. Purbright's sidekick Sergeant Love fits his surname: "Love watched presentable young females from behind his disguise of pink-faced single-mindedness…."

Purbright ... could never quite decide whether that cleanly shining feature properly belonged to a cherub or an idiot" (28–29).

It is interesting to see how writers characterize the disagreeable nature of the murder victim. Sometimes the information comes from a neutral source such as the press reports about Manderson's death in the first chapter of *Trent's Last Case*. Often a victim's unlikable traits are illustrated in flashback in sharp complementarity to their actions later in the novel. Usually one of the witnesses questioned by the investigator says it straight out as in the example below. Gwill is not likeable:

> "Did he have any other kind of enemies, do you know?"
> Malley pursed his lips. "Well ... put it this way. Nobody liked him. Does that help?"
> "Enormously," said Purbright. "I do like a big field."
> Love spoke. "But he had a circle of friends, surely?"
> "Oh, yes," said Malley. "Circle is the word."
> "Exclusive?"
> "Like the reptile house" [32].

There is a point that although what we read in these tales is contrived — fiction with sets of rules, clues and an investigation that sometimes leads to a chase and a sitting-room dénouement — a lot of crime methodology from the novels reflects what takes place in real life where, for example, murderer and victim often know each other (apart from random attacks in our large cities that appear to reflect different motives such as robbery or drug-fueled aggression or serial killers). Purbright observes this validity in real-life crime investigations when he says: "we can start from the sound assumption that people seldom get themselves murdered by complete strangers" (32).

In *Coffin, Scarcely Used*, apart from punning there is situation comedy as in the description of a waitress's body language: "The waitress drifted near, eyed them with sad disapproval, and retired to lean against the further wall like a martyr turned down by fastidious lions" (40–41). There is even a touch of slapstick that if developed would have rivaled Edmund Crispin: "Alderman Hockley's perpetration of the first-night drugging of the Amateur Operatic Society cast of *Rose Marie* (four of the Mounties had actually marched comatosely into the orchestra pit)" (44). The reserved and subtle nature of Colin Watson's writing does not rise to the insane heights as the best in Edmund Crispin or John Dickson Carr, but he comes close and is thoroughly engaging.

In a chapter for *Snobbery with Violence* titled "The Little World of Mayhem Parva," Colin Watson describes as a literary "school" the small English villages and country houses in which murders take place and that are settings for the tales by Golden Age crime writers serious alike (more or less) such as Agatha Christie and satirical such as Margery Allingham. Writing tongue-in-cheek, Watson says:

The setting for the crime stories by what we might call the Mayhem Parva school would be a cross between a village and a commuters' dormitory in the south of England, self-contained and largely self-sufficient. It would have a well-attended church, an inn with reasonable accommodation for itinerant detective-inspectors, a village institute, library and shops — including a chemist's where weed killer and hair dye might conveniently be bought. The district would be rural, but not uncompromisingly so — there would be a good bus service for the keeping of suspicious appointments in nearby towns.... One or more would get murdered; the rest would be suspected for awhile.... And then, the air cleared, everything would be set to continue as before [169–171].

The term "Mayhem Parva," evidently coined by Watson, means "little violence," my clumsy literal translation from the Anglo-French "to maim" and Latin for "little" or "small" (COD). Jeffery Ewener points out that it "is a fairly common suffix for English place names, and speaks to the sentimental English ear of spiritual peace, social order, and ancient privileges. (*See also* Peter Rozovsky's discussion in his web blog). Whether the violence is "little" is problematic, as many of these tales contain two or three corpses aside from the principal cadaver, and suspicious deaths often take place in the novelistic past before the main action. For Colin Watson this tradition is mythical, escapist, nostalgic, offering to the reader "relaxation, diversion, reassurance" (172). I would say it is also cathartic, as Watson states: "The identification and rendering harmless of the murderer at the very end of the book, somehow had the effect of cancelling out the death or deaths which had gone before. It was as if murder had been merely an engine that had set the story going and then been jettisoned" (173). This is what Watson does in his Flaxborough books where, as Ewener points out, there is a lot of sex and realism that I suppose is serious enough, except that Colin Watson composes his tales satirically.

Anthony Shaffer (1926–2001)

Anthony Joshua Shaffer was born on 15 May 1926 into a middle-class Jewish family of Liverpool (his father was an estate agent) and died on 6 November 2001 at the age of seventy-five. Anthony gained a degree in law at Trinity College, Oxford and practised as a barrister before entering into advertising, from which livelihood he graduated to that of a novelist, playwright and screenwriter. His twin brother Peter Shaffer was also a writer and dramatist who produced a mix of serious and comic screenplays such as *The Royal Hunt of the Sun* (1969), *Equus* (1977) and on the lighter side *Black Comedy* (1965). Anthony, however, developed more in a comic strain with five novels, six stage plays and ten screenplays. He also wrote two books of personal memoirs. Three of the novels are co-written, two with his brother Peter, *The Woman in the*

Wardrobe (1951), *How Doth the Little Crocodile?* (1952), and *Withered Murder* (1955), and, with Robin Hardy, *The Wicker Man* (1979).

There was nearly always a crossover between novel, stage play or screen-play, one work adapted to the other medium. *The Wicker Man* began as a film (1973). The six plays are *The Savage Parade* (1963), redone in 1987, *Sleuth* (1970) adapted for film in 1972, *Murderer* (1975), *Whodunnit* (1977), *Widow's Weeds* (1986), and *The Thing in the Wheelchair* (2001). Anthony Shaffer also adapted several of Agatha Christie's novels into screenplays, notably *Murder on the Orient Express* (1974), *Death on the Nile* (1978) and *Evil Under the Sun* (1982). ("Anthony Shaffer"). The following notes on the stage play *Whodunnit* illustrate nicely how the spirit of the farceurs of the Golden Age is carried on towards the present day.

Much the same elements as in the crime stories of the Golden Age appear in the play *Whodunnit: A Comedy Thriller*, which is a tribute to that period. There is reference to the Agatha Christie novel in which all the suspects join in dispatching the hated victim (this is *Murder on the Orient Express* that Shaffer adapted as a screenplay) and other intertextual allusions to the Christie character of Poirot and to John Dickson Carr and his Dr. Fell. Shaffer also alludes to his own play *Sleuth*. There is even a faint allusion to Edmund Crispin's character Broderick Thouless, composer of music scores for science fiction and horror movies, in a Shaffer casting of Rear Admiral Knatchbull Folliat who plays parts in B-grade thrillers and science fiction (as a robot, for example).

Whodunit ends with multiple unmaskings. Folliatt's true name is revealed and, along with every other cast member, he is found to be an out-of-work actor. Other elements include breaking through the fourth wall. One character directly addresses the audience in a distorted tape recording to reveal that he (she?) is the murderer, although the full revelation is left until the last pages of Act II. In a farcical stroke, it is the butler, thus bringing the cliché to life. Similarly, the audience is reminded more than once that they are watching a crime drama in the English tradition of a group of suspects in isolated country settings. This is of course a hallmark of the genre.

There is wordplay of a punning sort in which the blackmailer and victim Andreas Capodistriou from the Levant miscalls common English colloquialisms in a manner reminiscent of Mrs. Malaprop. For example, "She is the apostrophe of grace," "you are the apricot of my eye." These are my inventions because the copyright statement forbids even so much as the quotation of a phrase. It seems an excessive and ultimately self-defeating use of copyright, but perhaps standard for live theater. In a touch of political incorrectness the play's original title was *The Case of the Oily Levantine* ("Anthony Shaffer"). There appear to be inaccuracies. One reference associates catamites (the word is misspelled) with ship's captains (one of the characters is a rear admiral) with the fairy-tale line "a cat might look at a king/queen" but the connection appears dubious and may be invented by Shaffer. On the other hand, use of "fair suck of the sauce bottle" shows that the expression was not invented by a recent Australian prime minister, nor was it coined by Shaffer for it is recognized by *Wiktionary* and *Urban Dictionary* as an Australian colloquialism along with similar expressions such as "fair crack of the whip" or "fair suck of the sav" (saveloy = English pork sausage). The Wikipedia stub on *Whodunnit* has a useful plot summary.

Leslie Thomas (b.1931)

Leslie Thomas was born on 22 March 1931 in the Welsh city of Newport. When he was twelve years old (1943) he lost both parents and was brought up in one of the orphanages named for Dr. Barnardo. Thomas's first book, an autobiography titled *This Time Next Week* (1964), describes this period in his life. At eighteen in 1949 he was called up for military service and spent two years with the Royal Army Pay Corps, involved briefly in the Malayan Emergency (Communist uprising). In this period he started writing articles for English newspapers. Returning to England in 1951, he continued his journalistic career as a sub-editor and reporter, first for the North London paper he had worked for as a correspondent and then for the Exchange Telegraph Company and the *London Evening News*. From then on he wrote novels, beginning in 1966 with *The Virgin Soldiers* and continuing with an output of almost a novel a year to *Dover Beach* in 2005 when Thomas was seventy-four. According to the *Wikipedia* entry on Thomas, there are thirty novels all told with two autobiographies and three travel books. He is recognized for his contributions to literature for which he was awarded the Order of the British Empire (OBE) on 31 December 2004. Leslie Thomas is eighty-one at the time of writing.

Among Thomas's novels, four trace the career of Detective Constable "Dangerous" Davies: *Dangerous Davies: The Last Detective* (1976), *Dangerous in Love* (1987), *Dangerous by Moonlight* (1993), and *Dangerous Davies and the Lonely Heart* (1998) ("Leslie Thomas"). Perhaps because of their considerable appeal, all four novels have been adapted for film and television. The first came out in 1981 under the title *Dangerous Davies: The Last Detective* starring Bernard Cribbins (born 1928), described in a *Wikipedia* profile as a "musical comedian" who had parts in many television films, from the *Carry On* series to *Dr. Who*, *The Railway Children*, *The Avengers*, and a host of other very English productions. Although Cribbins is cast as Dangerous Davies, perhaps for his credentials in comedy, the film (and the book) has a more serious aspect than the later versions. More recently Peter Davison plays the part in the 2003–2006 television series *The Last Detective* (Granada 2008) with delectable Emma Amos in the role of Julie Davies, Dangerous's estranged wife with whom he becomes reconciled by the end of the series.

The character of Dangerous has traits similar to those of Simon Brett's Charles Paris (*see* below). As Thomas says in the first chapter (it has two paragraphs only):

> He was a drunk, lost, laughed at and frequently baffled; poor attributes for a detective. But he was patient too, and dogged. He was called Dangerous Davies (because he was said to be harmless) and was known in the London police as "The Last Detective" since he was never dispatched on any assignment unless it was very risky or there was no one else to send [7].

Leslie Thomas's first Dangerous novel is *Dangerous Davies: The Last Detective.* The film versions are mostly faithful to the novel, with some differences such as the greater and more sympathetic role played by his screen wife Emma Amos. After the first chapter, the plot moves through Davies' cemetery watch, courtroom scene, his trampling beneath the feet of fellow police, the first of many admissions to the hospital, and meeting with his drinking friend Mod (Modern Lewis) in the second chapter. A lot of the humor revolves around the relationship between Davies and Mod and the pranks they get up to when drunk. Chapter three introduces Inspector Vernon Yardbird (murderer), the case of missing person Celia Norris (victim), and a shady underworld figure Victor Ramscar. In subsequent chapters (there are twenty in all) we meet the landlady of the boarding house where Davies lives, Kitty the dog, various persons from Celia Norris's past, a scene in which a dustbin is thrown over Davies' head and he is beaten up and thrown into a canal (called by one reviewer funny but from my point of view not really so), a range of eccentric characters, the discovery of the cellar in which the skeleton of the girl is found, the rounding up of Ramscar and his gang, and the final confrontation with Yardbird.

As well as the situational comedy (mostly drunken nights and regular hospitalization after beatings) other touches of humor include a pun: "'Both tyres have gone down,' she said flatly" (178); a tasteless presentation to Davies: "a silver marmalade pot, plate and spoon" (268); also an allusion to the Sherlock Holmes characters that so many crime writers are impelled to make: "If I am to be your Dr. Watson [says Mod to Davies], I wish you could arrange for our investigations to be outside drinking hours" (48).

Simon Brett (b.1945)

Aged sixty-seven at the time of writing, Simon Brett is another producer of satirical crime novels that carry on the tradition of the Golden Age humorists. His first novel, *Cast, in Order of Disappearance* (1975) was written when he was thirty. Like others of his generation such as Anthony Shaffer, Brett's work spans several media. Aside from novels, some of the books are adapted for BBC Radio as well as television, and he writes for the live theater. This is similar to the activities of John Dickson Carr and Edmund Crispin who wrote for radio, film and television. Margery Allingham and Dorothy L. Sayers did not venture far into those media, and Nancy Spain participated in radio word game shows but not much else aside from book reviews.

The son of a chartered surveyor, Simon Brett was born on 28 October 1945 in Surrey at a place called Worcester Park and graduated through Oxford with first-class honors in English. He worked for BBC Radio and London Weekend Television but from the late 1970s took up serious writing. Currently he is president of the Detection Club. He lives in Sussex and is married with three children. Brett produced a number of comedies for the BBC, notably "the first ever episode of *The Hitchhiker's Guide to the Galaxy*." Comedy is his forte, "entertaining the reader through humour, eccentric characters, and intricate plot twists" in the tradition of the Golden Age he emulates ("Simon Brett"). He has a website in which he gives his autobiography complete with photographs from early and later childhood, university days, as Father Christmas, his wedding, and a number of photographic studies, some posed, others more casual such as sitting in his office or sleeping. He includes one of three cats, named Geoffrey.

Simon Brett's output is prolific. At a rough count his novels that begin with the Charles Paris series in 1975 come to seventeen, and there are six Mrs. Pargeter stories from 1986 onwards. Eleven novels are identified by location, the first of these, published in the year 2000, is set in "Fethering ... a fictitious village on England's south coast," with another village close by named Tarring. Brett also wrote eight plays, the first published in 1994 ("Simon Brett").

From the titles we see that Brett enjoys making puns, and many are alliterative as well, such as the Fethering novels *Death on the Downs* (2001), *Murder in the Museum* (2003), *The Stabbing in the Stables* (2006) or *Poisoning at the Pub* (2009). The Pargeter series has a mixture of punning and alliteration as in *Mrs., Presumed Dead* (1988) and *Mrs. Pargeter's Plot* (1996). The Charles Paris stories are a little more restrained with titles a little more appropriate to a crime tale, although they invite the reader to expect some humor, for instance: *A Comedian Dies* (1979), *Situation Tragedy* (1981) — a play on the better known term "situation comedy" — *Corporate Bodies* (1991) — a definite pun there — or *Dead Room Farce* (1998) ("Simon Brett").

Cast, in Order of Disappearance is structured thematically along the lines of the pantomime with such headings as "Cinderella Alone," "Prince Charming," "Enter the Funny Policeman," "The Ugly Sisters," or "King Rat." It demonstrates the pervasiveness of the older genres — fairy tales, fables and the like — in crime fiction. I draw attention to this elsewhere for another popular twentieth-century genre, that of science fiction and fantasy. Elements or motifs of the fairy story such as Čapek's "theme of obstacles, of questions, or of the tasks [linking] heroic deeds and adventures" ("Towards a Theory of Fairy-tales" 72) or "the setting of obstacles and vicissitudes, success or the happy ending" ("A Few Fairy-Tale Motifs" 74–82) appear just as malleable in detective novels and thrillers. Similarly, reflecting Brett's involvement in stagecraft and film, there are chapter titles such as "Speciality Act," "Interval," "Second Act Beginners," and "Slapstick Scene."

Cast, in Order of Disappearance is translatable into other media. It was serialized on BBC Radio 4 on 29 January 2010 with Bill Nighy in the part of Charles Paris ("Simon Brett"). One character Charles Paris takes to lunch might well be modeled upon Brett himself for moving from academia to a different occupation. The words are tongue in cheek: "Gerald had been a contemporary at Oxford, who had read Law and acted a little. He had been elected Treasurer of the Oxford University Dramatic Society and, as such, demonstrated the prime motive of his life — an unashamed love of money" (104).

Sociopolitical troubles of the time receive passing mention in "Disappearance," to help set the scene of Charles' investigations: "The offices around were empty and dead, street lights in the backwater thought unnecessary in the emergency" (39). A cab driver "with the predictability of all motorists over the last few weeks, commented on the petrol crisis, overcharged grossly, and drove off into the night" (80). As a reviewer for Amazon.com, Rich Milligan, writes: "The book is set in the winter of 1973–74 and it really does conjure up the 'winter of discontent,' the strikes, 3 day week, and the 10:30 TV watershed."

Charles Paris is a sort of anti-hero, a type defined by Chris Baldick as "a central character in a dramatic or narrative work who lacks the qualities of nobility and magnanimity expected of traditional heroes and heroines" (11). Such a hero is not new and goes back at least as far as Cervantes' *Don Quixote* (1605) says Baldick, but he or she is represented too in twentieth-century "modern" novels like James Joyce's *Ulysses* (1922) and appears as well in the theater of the absurd, as in Samuel Beckett's *Waiting for Godot* (1954). They inhabit a world "stripped of certainties, values, or even meaning" (Abrams 192). This is especially apt for post–World War II writers of crime/detective fiction. The anti-hero — who can also be fallible and in some instances an unreliable narrator — appears to become more commonplace in periods of traumatic cultural change and *fin de siècle* anxieties. Protagonists such as Crispin's Professor Gervase Fen and John Dickson Carr's Sir Henry Merrivale and Doctor Fell could be fallible in the tradition of Philip Trent in E. C. Bentley's novel, also more eccentric, but arguably they retain those "qualities of nobility and magnanimity" associated with heroes. The new breed of anti-heroes show more faults but continue to meet with the approval of readers.

Charles Paris, for instance, is described in the back-cover blurb as "a middle-aged actor who keeps going on booze and women, takes to detection, by assuming a variety of roles, among them that of a Scotland Yard Detective-

Sergeant, and the results are both comic and dramatic." We do not know who writes these back-cover promotions but, as noted before, it is often the author at the instigation of the publisher. Charles Paris has difficulties in his marriage and copes by going on a "blinder" (19), and difficulties in his profession where, in a cross-textual reference, his agent tells him, "You'll never get another job on *Doctor Who*" (20). He is forty-seven and, in chapter one, impotent when in bed with Jacqui, an old flame (15). But these faults are not insurmountable. Paris might have "an unhappily separated" relationship with his wife Frances, but it has lasted without divorce for more than thirty years ("Simon Brett"). As the *Wikipedia* entry says, he is a "moderately successful actor with a slight drinking problem who gets entangled in all sorts of crimes, and finds himself in the role of unwilling amateur detective."

His special skill, a motif of the novel, is that of disguise. This contrasts against his "unwillingness" and is also an occasion for Brett to comment upon crime writing: "his knowledge of blackmailer's habits ... was limited, all gleaned from detective novels" (49); "the days of the gifted amateur investigator were over. It was better to leave everything to the police, who with superior training and equipment must stand a greater chance of uncovering crime" (137). This is what novelists often do nowadays in those police procedurals. Charles Paris at one point feels "like the hero of some of the terrible thriller films he'd been in during the fifties" (80), and as the taxi carries him towards the home of suspected murderer Nigel Steen he loses his nerve. There is even a moment when evidence is destroyed, which is comparatively rare: "burning the vicious letter to Jacqui and the Sweet photographs had shown a regrettable lack of detective instinct" (174). Against these odds Charles Paris manages to rescue Jacqui in the face of Nigel Steen's gun and solve the case (184–185).

One of the Fethering novels, *Murder in the Museum* (2003), was written twenty-eight years after *Cast, in Order of Disappearance*. Along with *The Stabbing in the Stables* and I suspect others in the Fethering series, it demonstrates a greatly matured writing power. *Museum* and *Stables* are well constructed with a controlled humor of manners that shows Brett as a true legatee of the Golden Age. At the same time, however, Brett's work in another series, the Blotto and Twinks tales, is disappointing. But I am basing this opinion on having read only one novel from that series. *Blotto, Twinks and the Ex-King's Daughter* (2009) is a moderately silly *Prisoner of Zenda* parody. You can only get so much humorous mileage out of dimwitted English aristocrats like Blotto, his very clever sister Twinks, and middle European names like Vladimir and Schtoltz. It's virtually a one-joke novella of around 55,000 words and may have been dashed off as a shorter satirical piece in between the longer and more considered tales.

Murder in the Museum and *The Stabbing in the Stables*, on the other hand, I think exemplify some of Simon Brett's best writing. Both are substantial works, at around 111,000 words for the former and roughly 113,000 for the latter, but written as short chapters for easier consumption: forty-four chapters and forty-one respectively. This allows scope for an innovation that extends the Golden Age momentum to include psychological factors. I have noted that psychological detective/crime stories are a post–Golden Age development, often tied in closely with forensic and procedural methods as in P. D. James's Commander Dalgliesh and Cordelia Gray novels.

There are two protagonists in the Fethering novels, the amateur detectives Carole Seddon and Jude Nicol. They are a Holmes-Watson duo but in a very loose sense, for both women share equally in the detecting. This situation belongs to that trend towards psychological studies noted above, and rests in the brushing together of emotions between the two characters. Other aspects of this are relationships between suspects and, in the end, the psychology of the criminal(s) among them.

At fifty-five Jude Nicol is a full-bodied blonde with a past that includes close relationships with a variety of male lovers. She is described in hippy terms as liking to dress in voluminous and colorful tops, skirts and scarves. Carole Seddon's qualities are in contrast to those of Jude. Carole is more straight-laced, prefers a well-ordered home environment and is the introvert to Jude's extrovert. Her hair is gray and cut short. In *The Stabbing in the Stables*, "Carole Seddon suffered from the innate Puritanism of a middle-class southerner in her fifties, a system of values that had been dinned into her mind by timid parents in the post-war austerity of her upbringing" (3). Carole disapproves of Jude's more relaxed outlook on life, but she admires it as well. On her part, it is one of Jude's ploys to get Carole out of her comfort zone and so widen her friend's horizons. This relationship that appears to develop with each novel serves as a backstory to the main action of the plot, which is to uncover murderers and blackmailers.

The suspects Jude and Carole meet are an assortment of psychological characters, such as the hypocritical philanthropist Lord Beniston in *Murder in the Museum* (367–368) who likes to sit on the boards of charitable institutions where he has a minimum of duties and a maximum of social exposure that will one day bring in rewards such as a knighthood: "it had been agreed that, so long as his name appeared on the letterhead, he wouldn't have to attend any meetings; and third, he got free membership of the adjacent golf club." This is nice biting satire. Behind it lies a principle stated in one of the last pages: "At the beginning of the twenty-first century deviousness and cynicism were much more marketable commodities than faith and honesty" (369). The sentence comes after the ironic fate of the new museum: "In homage to the writer's new notoriety, it was then called 'The Bracketts Museum of Fakes and Fraudsters,' and contained the largest collection of confidence tricks and scams this side of the Atlantic" (368–369).

The plot revolves around rivalries between members of a Board of Trustees concerning the literary legacy of Esmond Chadleigh, a minor writer better known for a poem so good that it was frequently anthologized: the 1935 "Threnody for the Lost." It is difficult to guess the personage Simon Brett is drawing upon for this neat parody but it is reasonable and safe to see Esmond Chadleigh as a stock character. Many writers of the Golden Age, including most named in my list, produced works in different genres: novels, poetry including that for children, and critical essays. A lot of their work has slipped into obscurity, such as that of E. C. Bentley, A. A. Milne, even Dorothy L. Sayers, and are better known for a handful of their best work and not their entire oeuvre.

Members of the Board represent different types satirized by Simon Brett. There is Sheila Cartwright (first victim), formerly amateur administrator of the Bracketts Trust, who in chapter two walks in on the meeting of Trustees and takes over bare-facedly from the new Director Gina Locke. The other major woman rival is the American academic Marla Teichsbaum who is writing an unauthorized biography of Esmond Chadleigh. Graham Chadleigh-Bewes (second victim) is the great writer's grandson who as authorized biographer would produce a hagiography if he ever got round to it. He is an ineffectual character that prefers eating cake pressed upon him by doting Aunt Belinda in a quasi-mother-son relationship. Sheila Cartwright is shot dead by Aunt Belinda, who mistakes her for Teichsbaum. At the end of the novel the madwoman shoots her nephew as well. The family secret is a cover-up by their father Felix of the death of Graham Chadleigh, brother of the great writer Esmond. Rather than go to "the muddy holocaust of Passchendaele" (5), Graham commits suicide. Felix buries the body in the garden where the skeleton is dug up years later during preparations of the ground for a new museum in honor of Esmond the writer. A death before the narrative plot is a motif in several of the novels in my list.

Motifs creep in from other genres. Redolent of the thriller is "a cunningly hidden and complex Priest's hole" (101), in fact two priest's holes. The more obvious hidden room masks the presence of the other. It is in this latter room that Belinda Chadleigh traps Carole and Marla Teischbaum. Teischbaum, the confident and overbearing academic, goes to pieces in the confined space while Carole coolly sets about to discover the hidden pommel that opens the door from the inside. There are other touches of melodrama, in the shooting, for instance, of Sheila Cartwright: "Carole saw no lightning flash, but there was a sharp crack of what she took to be thunder. In front of her Sheila Cartwright shuddered and stood rigid for a moment. Then slowly, she toppled forward, face-down, on to the ground.... From the tall body on the ground came a guttural gurgling" (193). This is more apparent in the death of Graham Chadleigh-Bewes that has a touch of the grotesque: "He lay slumped back in his chair, redness spreading over his shirtfront. His eyes were wide with surprise, and there was a crumb of ginger cake on the corner of his mouth. In death, as he always had done in life, he looked slightly ridiculous" (349). The murderess "gave them a look of undisguised, cold-blooded fury" (348–349). This would be rather grim if it were not for Brett's satirical skill and psychological sketches.

Archival letters help solve the mystery while others provide light entertainment. A letter from someone nicknamed "Pickles" to Esmond Chadleigh ("Chadders") "looked like [and is] a pastiche of a schoolboy's letter home" (101). Physical sketches can be vivid. Another member of the Board, retired librarian George Ferris, "a short man whose curly hair and pepper-and-salt beard were a reminder of those Victorian pictures which still look like a face whichever way up they're held" (11), is likened to a Hobbit: "Jude found herself idly wondering whether, beneath the thick grey socks and stout brown walking shoes, there was hair on the top of George Ferris's feet" (269). Ferris is a poseur who misquotes Congreve as Byron: "Hell hath no fury like a woman scorn'd" (284). Academic practices attract light satire, for example, Jude becomes Laurence's "research assistant" (265), and crime writing, too: "If all murderers were as gentle as these men, she decided, there could be no more crime fiction" (53). In *The Stabbing in the Stables*: "I'm afraid it's only in crime fiction that the police share all the latest developments on a case with nosy local spinsters" (98), a clear allusion to Agatha Christie's characters. Again in the same novel Donal Geraghty refers to "a visit from the Fethering Miss Marple" (328).

Another form of humor lies in the describing of a character's sense for interior or personal decoration, well instanced in *Stables* by the description of the Brewis's décor that might be compared with a similar passage in Nancy Spain:

> No doubt when the room was finished, there would be even more pink flounces on the tartan curtains. Maybe more huge ceramic poodles would cluster round the fireplace, more turquoise teddy bears would sit on the silver lather sofas, more droopy stuffed clowns would dangle down from the light fittings. Perhaps another wall would be taken up by a huge plasma screen, and there might even be a second wrought-iron onyx-topped bar in another corner [307].

There are other touches such as the appearance of a writer's favorite stock description of a character's hairstyle as in Brett's liking for society women: "Sonia Dalrymple shook her perfectly coiffed blonde hair" (*Stables* 55), and Marla Teischbaum's "neatly sculpted hair" (*Museum* 122).

One literary allusion that is followed abruptly by an ironic development is a reference to the pathetic fallacy as Sheila Cartwright and Carole walk to the parking lot, moments before Sheila is shot: "Literary device Esmond used to use quite a lot. Him and the Romantic Poets. So you have the rain and wind echoing the storminess of the Emergency Trustees' Meeting" (192). Simon Brett makes frequent use of dialogue in this way to move the plot along. He also injects social comment into the narrative, and a love interest with insights into Jude's and Carole's psychology.

This is not depth psychology of the sort made popular in television crime dramas — the profiling of serial killers and so on — but "intuitive" thoughts of the kind that an observant woman might have. In this respect Simon Brett evidently is in close contact with his inner woman (the anima, for want of a better term). This is demonstrated through the thoughts and actions of Carole and Jude as well as the suspects. Graham Chadleigh-Bewes' childlike fixation on cake and his mutually dependent relationship with his aunt, or speculations about George Ferris's Hobbit nature are seen through the eyes of Jude and Carol. More to the point is the relationship between Carole and Jude that I suspect grows with each novel.

Some reviewers see the earlier novels weaker in conception and delivery but praise *Murder in the Museum*. An *Amazon.com* customer reviewer, M. J. Clark, says: "The plotting has tightened up a little since 'Torso' and 'Downs,' which is welcome, and Carole (and the reader) finally start to learn something of the history and inner life of Jude." Another reviewer, Clive A. H. Still, writes: "This is a more substantial book than many of the others in the Fethering series. Amateur detectives, Carole and Judy, each have an extra interest.... This is a good read, containing more strands and depth than most of the series but still filled with the usual warm humour." A third *Amazon* customer, Trevor S. says: "This particular novel continues to develop the two principal characters — though it manages to keep just enough back to make the reader want to read the next in the series to see what else can be disclosed there."

I have read only two of the Fethering tales but those reviews bear out what I suspect. There is a noticeable psychological development of the two main characters, of Jude *vis-à-vis* her relationship with Laurence in *Murder in the Museum* and, in *The Stabbing in the Stables* published three years after *Museum*, a lot of attention given to Carole's development, as in these examples:

> "She [Carole] could no more have gone into the café to use its facilities without making a purchase than she could have dismembered someone with a chainsaw" [101].

> "She [Carole] was surprised by the strength of her emotions. In the past she had had an incongruous relationship with Ted, and like most incongruous relationships it had been brief" [183].

> "Carole in her prim wet-blanket mode ... found her spoilsport pose weakening" [188].

In *The Stabbing in the Stables* Carole finds a greater self-confidence, remarked upon in Jude's thoughts: "She [Jude] was impressed by her friend's dominance since they had arrived at Cordham manor, particularly by the duplicitous way she had handled Yolanta Bewsis" (314). Aside from becoming a better amateur detective, Carole is led into the world of racecourse gambling — "Have you ever actually gambled, Carole?" (234) — another step in her individuation. Gambling is the social force whose etiquette is made a lot of in *Stables* whereas an aspect of the English prison system receives special attention in *Museum*.

Psychology, especially the quasi-Freudian variety, appears in other ways in *Stables*. In the case of teenage Imogen: "She channels most of her emotions through [the Pony Conker]. Displacement anxiety. The pony's easier to deal with than her parents' divorce" (282). On more shaky grounds I think is this summing up: "The theory of a connection between horse molestation and paedophilia was gaining credibility in academic circles" (351), but this is perhaps a satirical touch.

The love interest in *Murder in the Museum* has especial poignancy. Jude takes in Laurence Hawker, a run-down academic, chain smoker and heavy whisky drinker who is dying of lung cancer. The old love is reignited but it cannot be the same easy association with which it began years ago: "Jude had realized that she couldn't live with someone and not love them" (335). Laurence is a brilliant investigator who helps solve the mystery of the skeleton in the garden before he dies. While the focus seems to be more on Jude's personal attraction and her old lovers, Carole is not left out. She wonders about the relationship between Jude and Laurence and experiences frustration and resentment towards them, for "she couldn't define their level of closeness" (140). On her part, she has affection for Ted Crisp with whom she once had a brief affair, although in keeping with her nature: "Carole still had difficulty allowing herself to use the word 'affair' [but] ... glad still to be in contact with Ted" (208).

Further social issues are touched upon more than twice, so that they stand as important though minor indicators in the story, including religion and feminism. Roman Catholicism is anathema for a minor character, Mrs. Hidebourne, who is the source of letters studied by Laurence that help reveal the cover-up in the Chadleigh family. She says to Jude, "I am still sometimes appalled when I stop and think how much harm, how much total destruction, the Catholic Church must have caused in human sexual relationships.... [It] has made me daily more aware of what a pernicious creed it is" (308–309). Feminist issues appear more frequently as in George Ferris's clumsy pass at Marla Teischbaum (one of the best examples) while "enjoying his role of masculine reassurance" (274) and the resulting put-down when he gropes the woman's knee: "if I ever did go with a man, it wouldn't be some sawn-off, knee-high dork like you" (278). When a writer places confronting words or thoughts in the mouths and minds of the characters one is hard put to guess which attitudes belong to the writer and which are entered in as part of the fiction.

Into the Twenty-First Century

Today, several writers carry on the tradition. Simon Brett continues to navigate the stream of humor in crime fiction with at least eighty-three novels from 1986 to 2010, listed in his home page on the internet. At sixty-seven there are signs that he is slowing down. His latest Fethering novel, *The Shooting in the Shop*, came out in 2010. That series appears to be his chief interest aside from writing plays (for example, *Quirks* in 2009). However, the latest Mrs. Pargeter novel, *Mrs. Pargeter's Point of Honour*, was published in 1999, and the latest Charles Paris, *Dead Room Farce*, in 1998 ("Simon Brett"). Leslie Thomas' most recent work was published in 2005, the novel *Dover Beach*, and at eighty-one I would say he is slowing down although still strong.

Present-day crime/detective novels reflect the more serious stream of puzzle solving and forensic conversations over the autopsy slab and include humor more as comic relief than on its own terms. They have also a stronger international flavor and include such writers as the Sicilian Andrea Camilleri, beginning for Australian readers in 2004 with *The Shape of Water* (1994), and Shamini Flint's Inspector Singh tales set in Southeast Asia.

In Andrea Camilleri's Inspector Montalbano tales, the dialogue is at a cracking pace. The novels are clearly written with a view to the screen (Camilleri was a media studies lecturer). There is comic relief in the character of the bumbling officer Catarella as well as peaceful interludes over the eating of Sicilian seafood and Montalbano's relationships with women (not always peaceful, however), where there is a certain wit. But these are set against violent death, often in the criminal (Mafia) underworld. Camilleri's novels belong to what I call Italian noir or, as someone else put it, "Mediterranean noir," to which also belong the neatly crafted Commisario Brunetti novels of Donna Leon set in Venice.

A mix of old-fashioned detection with the police procedural and an eccentric investigator is found in Flint's books (2008, 2009, 2010, 2011) each set in a different country: Malaysia, Bali, Singapore, Cambodia. They tend to follow a similar plot structure and could do with variety. Their chief effort at humor is the protagonist's stoic bearing in the face of his nagging wife, and a fondness for rich food and consequent worries over his health.

There is an animal connection with humor, too, unusual in crime writing though well represented in science fiction and fantasy. It includes Spencer Quinn's Chet and Bernie mysteries (Chet is a dog) beginning with *dog on it* (2009) and follow-up novels with similarly punning titles (or should I say tales?). Bob Burke's *The Third Pig Detective Agency* (2009) is a burlesque in the noir tradition whose tough-guy detective is Harry Pigg, third of the "Three Little Pigs," who built a brick house "while my idiot brothers took the easy route and went for cowboy builders and cheap materials" (1). The small book is amusing for the overabundance of puns but is otherwise forgettable.

In Australia Kerry Greenwood's many novels, beginning with *Cocaine Blues* (1989), center upon the adventures of Phryne Fisher. Greenwood develops a cozy family atmosphere against the perils of the outside world. If anything, they have a touch of wit but little outright comedy. Their main humor comes from a subtle comedy of manners, recreating social life in Melbourne in the 1920s satirizing social class and religious differences (Catholics versus Protestants), the development of two romantic interests, and the characterization of two lovable larrikins Bert and Cec. The most endearing feature of Greenwood's novels is the way in which Phryne's world is constructed novel by novel into a family with a lady companion, two orphaned girls, a butler and his wife (the cook), Bert and Cec, and Phryne's Chinese lover Lin Chung. Greenwood cheerfully violates the rule of Van Dine, Knox and others that no Chinese are to feature in their tales.

There is in fact a strong leaning towards the thriller, and a touch of melodrama in the Fisher novels. As Sue Ryan-Fazilleau says, though she does not identify melodrama directly: "Greenwood has rewritten the Agatha Christie clue-puzzle by mixing it with other popular contemporary subgenres of crime fiction — the police procedural and the action thriller" (60). The dangers of the outside world are reflected in Bert and Cec's knowledge of Melbourne's underworld and their experience in the trenches of the First World War, murders and criminal gangs. Typically the novels have a main plot, that of Phryne's chief investigation, and a subplot in which a misdoing less extreme than homicide is resolved. The novels are uneven, something that is probably unavoidable with such a large oeuvre, with eighteen Phryne Fisher novels extant and a nineteenth on the way ("Kerry Greenwood").

Some unevenness is reflected too in the ABC television series *Miss Fisher's Mysteries* (2012) but with additional problems. At first I perceived the acting as sometimes wooden, the dialogue stilted, the pacing uneven. On a second viewing my criticisms seem unfair. Essie Davis (b. 1970) in the leading role is clearly the mainstay of the series, opposite Nathan Page who plays the part of Detective John (Jack) Robinson. Hugo Johnstone-Burt plays the part of Constable Hugh Collins opposite Phryne's lady companion Dorothy Williams or Dot played by Ashleigh Cummings. Together they represent the more obvious love interest. The less obvious is the underplayed relationship between Phryne and Detective Jack Robinson. Richard Bligh plays the eponymous role of Mr. Butler as Phryne Fisher's butler. Tammy MacIntosh, who has the part of the lesbian Doctor Mac as Phryne's friend and confidant, is accorded an entry in *Wikipedia*, albeit a stub. The villain is Murdoch Doyle played by Nicholas Bell. Aunt Prudence is played by Miriam Margolyes who at seventy-one has an extensive acting career behind her. There is almost a symmetrical balance in the casting of experienced actors and those of a younger generation and, through the exigencies of the script (and the books) a pairing off between

Phryne and Inspector Jack Robinson, Constable Collins and Dot, Bert and Cec. In all, the cast of *Miss Fisher's Mysteries* number eleven principals plus extras.

One vexed question is the revised plotting of *Miss Fisher's Mysteries.* There are two major changes in the casting, one that appears largely unaccountable and the other evidently due to a reworking of the plot in Greenwood's scripting. Readers who follow and enjoy the growth and consolidation of Phryne's "family" through the novels will be struck by the absence of Mr. Butler's wife Mrs. Butler, whose part in the novels is that of cook and housekeeper alongside her husband. A friend objected on seeing the television series: "They've killed off Mrs. Butler!" by introducing Mr. Butler as a widower.

The other omission/change in the plot is the identity of Phryne Fisher's long-term lover. In the novels this is Lin Chung. But the love interest in the television version is the developing relationship between Phryne and Inspector Robinson. Perhaps Greenwood decided to adhere to the Knox rule that no Chinese are allowed in detective fiction, a tongue-in-cheek broadside at the prevalence of these characters in the thrillers of Knox's day. Considering the wider avenue for melodrama and the obvious tribute to the thriller in Greenwood's Phryne Fisher stories, Lin Chung—who sustains the removal of an ear for his family's honor—would have been a good choice. Perhaps Australian television is not yet comfortable with major Chinese characters who become lovers on screen. On the other hand, the budding romance between Phryne and the inspector was one direction the novels might have taken. Its appearance in *Miss Fisher's Mysteries* might well have been born from that alternative suggested by the novels. It is something of a writer's dilemma to have two characters who might just as easily become the heroine's swain. All the same, it is interesting to see Greenwood's detective series brought to life on the screen and I am glad it has been done.

The shift towards forensic crime novels nowadays has not brought the older style of tale into obsolescence. What suggests that the time of the humorists is not yet over is the great number of British Broadcasting Commission adaptations for television of many Golden Age novels. If these media are any guide—television BBC series and others such as the Australian ABC and SBS, and the DVDs generated from them—crime tales with humor jostle shoulder to shoulder with the more serious stories. The English filmmakers are particularly good at using the country's natural and historical environments, within which traditionally so many of the detective/crime tales are set: picturesque country cottages, stately manor houses, looming castles, brooding woods, gloomy lakes, mossy streams, tidal estuaries, isolated peninsulas and islands, barren moors and treacherous quicksand.

CHAPTER **10**

Conclusion

A little to my surprise a strong tradition of humorous writing in crime fiction remains to this day exemplified in a short list of Golden Age writers and preferred works, virtually none of which I had read before taking up the project. E. C. Bentley started me off. *Trent's Last Case* was the first crime novel I read for this book, and I agree with the critics that he stimulated a lot of other writers to do the same. A. A. Milne's *The Red House Mystery* is something of a novelty, a slight romp upon which he never improved in the crime-writing genre. I read with delight his adult late-in-life novel *Chloe Marr*, not a crime tale. I admit to finding Edmund Crispin to my tastes although, as noted earlier, many readers find him irritating and not all his novels work for me. I like what I read of John Dickson Carr. I like too some of the novels of Nancy Spain, but think she should be read sparingly. Her work has remained neglected while other writers' tales are rediscovered after a period of neglect and their best works are back in print.

Transmission occurs when different writers take elements from their friends' works and by means of inspiration, parody, acknowledgment and innovation seek to improve upon their forerunners as well as contemporaries. Changes in approach, what Ned Polsky (1928–2000) calls a little misleadingly "obsolescence," are often influenced by events outside the world of fiction. Hence a World War or the rise of a national movement might attract satire in one instance or lead to a shift in subject matter: Nancy Spain in her use of lesbian and gay motifs and characters, for example, or Andrea Camilleri's satirical barbs at forensic investigators and corrupt politicians. Individual writers react differently to social and political anxieties. John Dickson Carr found post–World War II settings for his novels an almost insurmountable emotional barrier, while Bruce Montgomery writing as Edmund Crispin was more sanguine (although he too makes little direct mention of the war years).

In his sociological classic *Hustlers, Beats and Others* (1998) on the Village beat scene of 1960, Polsky touches upon the main threads of my theme when he implies that tradition and paradigm are closely related, although he does not use the word paradigm for the like-minded humorists described in the preceding chapters. He uses instead the word subculture:

> A particular group with its special way of doing things has *two or more genera-tions*, of course overlapping but nevertheless reasonably distinct, and the group's specially valued ways of perceiving, behaving, thinking, and feeling, including their embodiments in material objects (artifacts), are transmitted from one gener-ation to the next [his italics] [229].

In his choice of the words transmission and generation Polsky implicitly defines tradition.

For my purposes, the "subculture" is the loosely knit cohort of writers whose work is so influential that their two decades of activity brought in what is popularly called the Golden Age for detective/crime fiction. Their generations overlap and, individually, influence one another's work. That work (the novels and short stories, stage and radio plays, essays and commentaries) embodies ways of perceiving, thinking, feeling, and so on that are expressed not only in the works themselves but also in the creation for enjoyment of various "rules," sup-posedly to guide those works although they are in reality another contribution to the humorist/farceur tradition. Aside from the books themselves that count as material objects, we have such cheerfully macabre artifacts as the Detection Club's mascot "Eric the Skull," with whom various members, notably Dorothy L. Sayers, pose fondly for the camera (*see*, for example, Greene, plates 13 and 14 between pages 266 and 267). Houses and apartments are artifacts, too. The fictional address of Sherlock Holmes is mirrored/parodied in the abode of Margery Allingham's amateur detective and adventurer Albert Campion.

In a customer review for *The Animal Fable in Science Fiction and Fantasy*, K. Bunker considers the "fun stuff" in my approach to be the examination of "selected stories, novels, and authors in greater detail" while history and theory are treated more heavily and a little less to his taste. In *Humor in English Crime Fiction of the Golden Age*, I follow a similar pattern of review essays, playing down theoretical aspects while still considering them when necessary. I continue biographical and sociological sketches because arguably they are important for a better understanding of the authors and their subject matter.

As with the books and short stories in *Animal Fable*, I believe that descrip-tion is essential. The close reading is guided by distinctive elements in the works themselves. Hence for E. C. Bentley's *Trent's Last Case* there is the love interest worked out through metaphoric imagery and the psychological rela-tionship between Philip Trent and Mabel Manderson. Dorothy L. Sayers *Gaudy Night* shifts more towards puzzle solving with protagonists Harriet Vane and Lord Peter Wimsey, a love interest more subtle than in Bentley's novel, and an insightful satire on university life.

Elements of the thriller amble alongside serious detection for many of the later humorists. In A. A. Milne's *The Red House Mystery* the tropes are characteristic of the boys' adventure novel and the thriller mixed with detection. Something of the same applies as well to Margery Allingham's oeuvre, but with more attention to elements from the tradition of the thriller. John Dickson Carr combines elements of the supernatural and the thriller with serious detection that has lists and rules (Professor Fells' locked room typology), and slapstick that verges on the burlesque.

Edmund Crispin is notable for the way in which he constructs a mystery tale. His better novels, such as *The Case of the Gilded Fly*, follow a pattern redolent of the best in the subgenre: the presentation of characters with humor, violent death, investigation in which is uncovered one clue after another, a second death or more, discovery of the criminal, confrontation and resolution. At different points in such a framework there is often a chase scene reminiscent of the Keystone Cops, sometimes more than one as in *The Moving Toyshop*, or expanded over several chapters as in *The Glimpses of the Moon*. Chase and confrontation come straight from the thriller but are also a tradition in comedy.

Nancy Spain's novels of detection owe less to the thriller — although her work is often described in terms of that genre — than from pure farce and what one blurb calls high camp. Her tales are fast-paced, a little slapdash, and with each successive novel they grow darker.

Variations on these elements are found also for the writers to whom I give less space. Among the women of the Golden Age, Ngaio Marsh rests along the continuum with Dorothy L. Sayers for dense and subtly ironic detection tales. The wry humor of Sheila Pim places her a little further from Sayers and Marsh and closer to the satire and farce of Caryl Brahms and Gladys Mitchell. Michael Innes belongs to the Sayers/Marsh camp and Ronald Knox, of Innes's generation, writes a little further along the continuum away from dense seriousness to fallible investigators such as those in Milne's *Red House*. Colin Watson and Simon Brett carry on the tradition post–Golden Age.

In the literary world, as in academe, being well thought of by one's peers counts for a lot. A favorable review can affect a beginning writer's future both financially and inspirationally. Edmund Crispin's supportive critical reviews lent encouragement and confidence to two writers whose work is highly regarded today, P. D. James (b. 1920) and Ruth Rendell (b. 1930), both of whom began their writing careers in the 1960s ("P. D. James"; "Ruth Rendell"). Similarly, A. A. Milne put in a good word for John Dickson Carr and Nancy Spain. On the other hand, Milne had a run-in with Wodehouse when he accused him, a little unfairly, of treasonous broadcasts supporting the Nazis during Wodehouse's post-internment period in Germany ("A. A. Milne"). It is an unusual circumstance, for both men admired each other's work (Thwaite 443).

Disputes and personal enmities are common enough in the literary world (and in academe), as in Raymond Chandler's criticism of A. A. Milne, John Dickson Carr's tilt at Chandler, Nancy Spain's legal brush with Evelyn Waugh (whom she admired all the same), or Kingsley Amis's vexed friendship with Bruce Montgomery. We cannot really expect consistency towards one another among writers — they are fallible humans like us all, and several in my list were beset with psychological troubles — but, as well as dissension, the good fellow-feeling between many, especially in the Detection Club, seems exemplary.

I have not attempted a close one-to-one match between individual writers and the different types of humor and their effects as described in the first chapter, beyond picking out what appear to be their salient points. What the humorists seek is to surprise the reader by overturning expectations using a repertoire of stylistic conceits. I try to give a feel for the variety of techniques available to the humorists. Carnival with its adjective, the carnivalesque, implies riotous fun, ribaldry and the relaxation of taboos that paradoxically reinvigorate the social order (Bakhtin, Cervantes). Contrarily, humor (laughter) has an element of cruelty (Bergson, Baudelaire, Voltaire). Humor has a liberating effect but is concerned too with "comic contrast" through ugliness and caricature (Freud). It accords pleasure in wordplay: alliteration and, I suggest, the use of obscure words and literary allusions (Aristotle, Freud). Another contrast using different words is that of surprise and conformity to pattern (Lodge), hence humor is often if not always a mix of the unexpected with the familiar.

Defining works by their content is commonplace. Identifying the *effects* that any particular genre has upon its readers may be more useful. In crime fiction one effect is intellectual pleasure at solving (or attempting to solve) a puzzle, often taken seriously. Readers who like that sort of thing may be irritated by the less serious authors who appear to stray from that process. In this other subgenre, describable as that produced by the humorists or farceurs, the effect is to entertain through laughter although serious undertones remain.

In its contrasts between pure fun and seriousness, the comic can be unsettling. It may be cathartic but it also conveys serious ideas and often makes us stop to think. What I call facetiously the "jocularity scale" or continuum that includes wit, irony, satire, farce, parody, burlesque and slapstick is not a hierarchy, but this model charts a transition in modes from the subtle and low-key to the opposite extreme of the palpable and unruly, from wit to slapstick. Readers who prefer subtle, often ironic wit will place that mode uppermost, and those who go in for slapstick and burlesque will place those sorts of humor at the forefront, while satire will be preferred and so elevated in the minds of other readers.

Bibliography

This bibliography is divided into three parts: Print; Television and Film; Web. Where two dates are given, the first is the year of initial publication and the second, the year of the latest edition. Works are arranged by author and then chronologically by date of initial publication.

Print

Abrams, M. H. *A Glossary of Literary Terms*. Fort Worth, TX: Harcourt Brace Jovanovich, 1988.

_____, ed. *The Norton Anthology of English Literature*. New York: W. W. Norton, 1986.

Adams, Douglas. *The Hitchhiker's Guide to the Galaxy*. London: Pan, 1979/2009.

Allingham, Margery. *The Crime at Black Dudley*. New York: Felony & Mayhem, 1929/2006.

_____. *The Crime at Black Dudley*. 1929. In *The Margery Allingham Omnibus*, pp. 7–195. Harmondsworth, UK: Penguin, 1982.

_____. *Mystery Mile*. 1930. In *The Margery Allingham Omnibus*, pp. 197–384. Harmondsworth, UK: Penguin, 1982.

_____. *Mystery Mile*. London: Vintage Books, 1930/2004.

_____. *Look to the Lady*. 1931. In *The Margery Allingham Omnibus*, pp. 385–589. Harmondsworth: Penguin, 1982.

_____. *Look to the Lady*. New York: Felony & Mayhem Press, 1931/2006.

_____. *Sweet Danger*. London: Vintage Books, 1933/2004.

_____. *Mr. Campion and Others*. Harmondsworth: Penguin, 1939/1987.

_____. *The Tiger in the Smoke*. London: Vintage Books, 1952/2005.

_____. *The Mind Readers*. London: Vintage Books, 1965/2008.

Amis, Kingsley. *Lucky Jim*. London: Penguin, 1954.

Antony, Peter. *The Woman in the Wardrobe—A Lighthearted Detective Story*. Illus. Nicolas Bentley. 1951.

Appignanesi, Richard, and Chris Garratt. *Postmodernism for Beginners*. Cambridge: Icon Books, 1995.

Apuleius, Lucius. *The Transformations of Lucius: Otherwise Known as the Golden Ass*. Trans. Robert Graves. London: Penguin, 1950/1990.

Aristotle. *The Ethics of Aristotle: The Nicomachean Ethics Translated*. Trans. J. A. K. Thomson. Harmondsworth: Penguin, 1963.

_____. *Poetics*. Trans. Malcolm Heath. London: Penguin, 1996.

Armanno, Venero. "Antiquated Detectives No Match for a Gumshoe." Book review of *Talking About Detective Fiction* by P. D. James. *The Weekend Australian Review*, 30–31 Jan 2010, p. 21.

Bakhtin, Mikhail. *The Dialogic Imagination: Four Essays*. Ed. Michael Holquist. Trans. M. Holquist and Caryl Emerson. Austin: University of Texas Press, 1981.

_____. *Rabelais and His World*. Trans. Helen Iswolsky. Bloomington: Indiana University Press, 1984.

_____. *Speech Genres & Other Late Essays*. Ed. Caryl Emerson and Michael Holquist. Trans. Vern W. McGee. Austin: University of Texas Press, 1986/1996.

_____. "From the Prehistory of Novelistic Discourse." *Modern Criticism and Theory: A Reader*. Ed. David Lodge. London: Longman, 1988.

_____. From "Discourse in the Novel." *Modern Literary Theory: A Reader*. Eds. Philip Rice and Patricia Waugh, pp. 197–205. London: Edward Arnold, 1992.

Baldick, Chris. "Introduction (1995)." In *Trent's Last Case* by E. C. Bentley, pp. ix–xxii. Oxford: Oxford University Press, 1913.

_____. *The Concise Oxford Dictionary of Literary Terms*. Oxford: Oxford University Press, 1990.

_____. *The Oxford Dictionary of Literary Terms*. Oxford: Oxford University Press, 2008.

Baldick, Robert. *Dinner at Magny's*. Harmondsworth: Penguin, 1971.

Ballantyne, R. M. *The Coral Island: A Tale of the Pacific Ocean*. London and Glasgow: Blackie & Son, 1857.

"The Barber Who Killed the Monks." In *Pancatantra: The Book of Indian Folk Wisdom*, pp. 158–159. Trans. Patrick Olivelle. Oxford: Oxford University Press, 1997.

Barthes, Roland. *The Pleasure of the Text*. Trans. Richard Miller. Oxford: Basil Blackwell, 1990.

Baudelaire, Charles. "Of the Essence of Laughter." 1855. *Selected Writings on Art and Literature*, pp. 140–161. Trans. P.E. Charvet. London: Penguin, 1972/1992.

Bayliss, A. E. M., ed. "Introduction." *Plays of Adventure*, pp. 9–15. London: Harrap, 1938/1952.

Beckett, Samuel. *Waiting for Godot: A Tragicomedy in Two Acts*. London: Faber and Faber, 1956/1988.

Bentley, E. C. *Trent's Last Case*. Oxford: Oxford University Press, 1913/1995.

_____. *Trent's Last Case*. New York: Perennial Library Harper & Row, 1913/1978.

_____. *Trent Intervenes and Other Stories*. Cornwall: House of Stratus, 1938/2001.

_____. *Those Days*. London: Constable, 1940.

_____. *Dedication to John Buchan*. Aug 1949. *Elephant's Work: An Enigma*. New York: Alfred A. Knopf, 1950.

_____. *Elephant's Work: An Enigma*. New York: Alfred A. Knopf, 1950.

_____. *Clerihews Complete*. Illus. G. K. Chesterton, Victor Reinganum, Nicolas Bentley. London: Werner Laurie, 1951.

Bentley, E. C., with H. Warner Allen. *Trent's Own Case*. Cornwall: House of Stratus, 1936/2001.

Bentley, Nicolas. *A Version of the Truth*. London: Deutsch, 1960.

Bergson, Henri. *Laughter*. 1900. Comedy. Edited by W. Sypher, pp. 61–190. New York: Doubleday Anchor, 1956.

Berkeley, Anthony. *The Poisoned Chocolates Case*. London: Pan, 1929/1950.

Binyon, T. J. *Murder Will Out: The Detective in Fiction*. Oxford: Oxford University Press, 1989.

Blain, Virginia, Patricia Clements, and Isobel Grundy, eds. *The Feminist Companion to Literature in English*. London: Batsford, 1990.

Blamires, Cyprian. *World Fascism: A Historical Encyclopedia*, vol. 1. Santa Barbara, CA: ABC-CLIO, Inc., 2006. Cited in Wikipedia.

Bloom, Harold. *The Best Poems of the English Language: From Chaucer Through Robert Frost.* New York: Harper Perennial, 2004.

Bradbury, Malcolm. *Liar's Landscape: Collected Writing from a Storyteller's Life.* Oxford: Picador/PanMacmillan, 2006.

Brahms, Caryl, and S. J. Simon. *A Bullet in the Ballet.* London: Hogarth, 1937/1986.

Brecht, Bertolt. *The Threepenny Opera.* 1928.

Brett, Simon. *Cast, In Order of Disappearance: A Crime Novel.* San Jose: toExcel, 1975/2000.

_____. *Murder in the Museum: A Fethering Mystery.* London: Pan Books, 2003.

_____. *The Stabbing in the Stables: A Fethering Mystery.* London: Pan Books, 2006.

_____. *Blotto, Twinks and the Ex-King's Daughter.* London: Constable and Robinson, 2009/2010.

Briggs, Anthony. "Introduction." Tolstoy, Leo. *War and Peace.* London: Penguin, 1868–9/2007, pp. xiii–xx.

Browning, D. C. "Shakespeare's Tragedies." In *Shakespeare's Tragedies.* Everyman's Library No. 155, London: Dent, 1906/1956, pp. v–vi.

Bulwer Lytton, Edward. *Pelham: or, The Adventures of a Gentleman.* 1828.

Camilleri, Andrea. *The Shape of Water.* Trans. Stephen Sartarelli. London: Picador, 1994/2004.

Campbell, Joseph, ed. *The Portable Jung.* Trans. R. F. C. Hull. Harmondsworth: Penguin, 1971.

Čapek, Karel. "Holmesiana, or About Detective Stories." 1924. In *In Praise of Newspapers.* London: George Allen & Unwin, 1951, pp. 101–122.

_____. "A Few Fairy-Tale Motifs." 1931. In *In Praise of Newspapers.* London: George Allen & Unwin, 1951, pp. 74–82.

_____. "Towards a Theory of Fairy-Tales." 1931. In *In Praise of Newspapers.* London: George Allen & Unwin, 1951, pp. 49–73.

_____. *Tales from Two Pockets.* London: George Allen & Unwin, 1932.

_____. *War with the Newts.* Trans. Ewald Osers. London: George Allen and Unwin, 1936/1985.

Carpenter, Humphrey. *Geniuses Together: American Writers in Paris in the 1920s.* Boston: Houghton Mifflin, 1988.

Carr, E. H. *What Is History?* London: Penguin, 1961/2008.

Carr, John Dickson. "As We See It." *Uniontown Daily News Standard.* 4 May 1922. In "John D. Carr III on Realistic Writers in 1922." *John Dickson Carr: The Man Who Explained Miracles.* By Douglas G. Greene, pp. 454–455. New York: Otto Penzler, 1995.

_____. *The Blind Barber.* 1934. In *Four Complete Dr. Fell Mysteries*, pp. 1–177. New York: Avenel Books, 1988.

_____. *The Hollow Man.* London: Orion1935/1957.

_____. *In Spite of Thunder.* Harmondsworth: Penguin, 1935/1957.

_____. *The Crooked Hinge.* 1938. In *Four Complete Dr. Fell Mysteries*, pp. 349–519. New York: Avenel Books, 1988.

_____. *To Wake the Dead.* 1938. In *Four Complete Dr. Fell Mysteries*, pp. 181–345. New York: Avenel Books, 1988.

_____. *The Case of the Constant Suicides.* 1941. In *Four Complete Dr. Fell Mysteries*, pp. 523–660. New York: Avenel Books, 1988.

_____. "With Colt and Luger." *The New York Times Book Review.* 24 September 1950.

_____. "The Adventure of the Highgate Miracle." In *The Exploits of Sherlock Holmes.* By Adrian Conan Doyle and John Dickson Carr, pp. 80–110. London: John Murray, 1954.

_____. "The Adventure of the Wax Gamblers." In *The Exploits of Sherlock Holmes.* By Adrian Conan Doyle and John Dickson Carr, pp. 54–79. London: John Murray, 1954.

_____. Letter to David Higham. Jul 13, 1959. Cited in Greene, 519.

Cervantes (Miguel de Cervantes Saavedra). *Don Quixote.* Trans. Edith Grossman. London: Vintage Books, 2005/1605.

Chambers Biographical Dictionary. Edinburgh: W. & R. Chambers, 1993.

Chandler, Raymond. *The Little Sister*. London: Penguin, 1949/2005.

_____. "The Simple Art of Murder." 1950. In *The Simple Art of Murder*. New York: Vintage Books Random House, 1988.

_____. "Twelve Notes on the Mystery Story." In *Raymond Chandler: Later Novels and Other Writings*, p. 1007. New York: Library of America, 1995.

_____. *The Raymond Chandler Papers: Selected Letters and Non-Fiction, 1909–1959*. Eds. Tom Hiney and Frank MacShane. London: Hamish Hamilton, 2000.

Chaucer, Geoffrey. "The Prioress's Tale." In *The Canterbury Tales*. Trans. Nevill Coghill, pp. 169–176. London: Penguin, 1977.

Christie, Agatha. *Peril at End House*. New York: Dodd Mead and Company, 1932.

_____. *Agatha Christie 1920s Omnibus*. London: HarperCollins, 2006.

_____, et al. *The Floating Admiral*. London: HarperCollins, 1931/2011.

Clute, John, and Peter Nicholls, eds. *The Encyclopaedia of Science Fiction*. London: Orbit, 1993.

Cohen, J. M., and M. J. Cohen, eds. *The Penguin Dictionary of Quotations*. Harmondsworth: Penguin, 1960.

Coleridge, Samuel Taylor. "Biographia Literaria." In *The Norton Anthology of English Literature*. Ed. M. H. Abrams, pp. 397–398. New York: Norton, 1986.

Collins, Robert. *Concise French Dictionary*. Glasgow: HarperCollins, 1993.

Collins, Wilkie. *The Woman in White*. London: Vintage Random House, 1859–1860/2007.

Collis, Rose. *Lesbian Portraits*. London: M. Q. Publishers, 1997.

_____. *A Trouser-Wearing Character: The Life and Times of Nancy Spain*. London: Cassell, 1997.

Conan Doyle, Adrian, and John Dickson Carr. "The Adventure of the Gold Hunter." In *The Exploits of Sherlock Holmes*, pp. 30–53. London: John Murray, 1954.

_____. "The Adventure of the Highgate Miracle." In *The Exploits of Sherlock Holmes*, pp. 80–110. London: John Murray, 1954.

_____. "The Adventure of the Sealed Room." In *The Exploits of Sherlock Holmes*, pp. 135–163. London: John Murray, 1954.

_____. "The Adventure of the Seven Clocks." In *The Exploits of Sherlock Holmes*, pp. 1–29. London: John Murray, 1954.

_____. "The Adventure of the Wax Gamblers." In *The Exploits of Sherlock Holmes*, pp. 54–79. London: John Murray, 1954.

Conan Doyle, Arthur. "Silver Blaze." 1892. In *The Memoirs of Sherlock Holmes*. The Complete Sherlock Holmes Short Stories, pp. 305–333. London: John Murray, 1938/1952.

_____. *The Hound of the Baskervilles*. London: John Murray, 1902/1954.

_____. *The Conan Doyle Stories*. London: John Murray, 1929.

_____. *A Study in Scarlet*. In *The Complete Sherlock Holmes Long Stories*, pp. 1–139. London: John Murray, 1929/1954.

_____. "Thor Bridge." In *The Case-Book of Sherlock Holmes*, pp. 1215–1243. London: John Murray, 1938/1952.

Conrad, Joseph. *Heart of Darkness*. London: Penguin, 1902/1989.

Crispin, Edmund. *The Case of the Gilded Fly*. New York: Felony & Mayhem Press, 1944/2005.

_____. *Holy Disorders*. New York: Felony & Mayhem Press, 1945.

_____. *The Moving Toyshop*. London: Penguin, 1946/1988.

_____. *Swan Song*. New York: Felony & Mayhem Press, 1947.

_____. *Love Lies Bleeding*. New York: Felony & Mayhem Press, 1948.

_____. *Buried for Pleasure*. New York: Felony & Mayhem Press, 1949.

_____. *Frequent Hearses*. Harmondsworth, UK: Penguin, 1950/1982.

_____. *Sudden Vengeance*. New York: Felony & Mayhem Press, 1950.

_____. *The Long Divorce*. New York: Felony & Mayhem Press, 1951.

_____. "Foreword (1952)." In *Beware of the Trains*, p. 7. London: Penguin, 1953/1987.

_____. *Beware of the Trains*. London: Penguin, 1953/1987.

_____. *The Glimpses of the Moon*. New York: Felony & Mayhem Press, 1977/2012.

_____. *Fen Country*. Harmondsworth, UK: Penguin, 1979.

"Critique on John Dickson Carr." *National Review*. 8 Oct 1971.

Curran, John. *Agatha Christie's Secret Notebooks*, pp. 33. New York: HarperCollins, 2009.

Dane, Clemence. "At the Vicarage." In *The Floating Admiral*. By Agatha Christie et al., pp. 193–201, 303–305 London: HarperCollins, 1931/2011.

De Quincey, Thomas. *On Murder: Considered as One of the Fine Arts*. 1827. London: Oneworld Classics, 2009.

Dickens, Charles. *Sketches by Boz: Illustrative of Every-Day Life and Every-Day People*. London: Oxford University Press (The Oxford Illustrated Dickens), 1833–1836.

Dickson, Carter. *Skeleton in the Clock: A Sir Henry Merrivale Mystery*. New York: Belmont Tower, 1948.

_____. *Night at the Mocking Widow*. New York: Zebra, 1950.

Dunbar, Janet. *T. M. Barrie: The Man Behind the Image*. Boston: Houghton Mifflin, 1970.

Eco, Umberto. *The Name of the Rose*. Trans. William Weaver. London: Harvill Secker, 1983.

_____. "Casablanca: Cult Movies and Intertextual Collage." 1984. In *Faith in Fakes: Travels in Hyperreality*. Trans. William Weaver, pp. 197–210. London: Vintage, 1986.

_____. "Hugo, Hélas! The Poetics of Excess." In *Inventing the Enemy: And Other Occasional Writings*. Trans. Richard Dixon, pp. 97–125. London: Picador/Secker & Warburg, 2012.

_____. "I Am Edmond Dantès!" In *Inventing the Enemy: And Other Occasional Writings*. Trans. Richard Dixon, pp. 170–184. London: Picador/Secker & Warburg, 2012.

Eliot, T. S. Forum. *Monthly Criterion* (5 Jun 1927): 360.

Evans, Curtis. "Was Corrine's Murder Clued?" *The Detection Club and Fair Play, 1930–1953*. CADS Supplement Number 14 (2011).

_____. "T. S. Eliot, Detective Fiction Critic." *CADS: Crime and Detective Stories*, vol. 62 (Feb 2012): 3–8.

Field, Syd. *The Screen-Writer's Workbook*. New York: Bantam Doubleday Dell, 1984.

Forshaw, Barry. *The Rough Guide to Crime Fiction*. London: Rough Guides Ltd. (Penguin), 2007.

Fry, Stephen. *The Fry Chronicles: An Autobiography*. London: Michael Joseph (Penguin), 2010.

Gay, John. *The Beggar's Opera*. 1728. London: Penguin, 1986.

George, Elizabeth. "Introduction." 2003. In *In the Teeth of the Evidence*. By Dorothy L. Sayers, pp. vii–ix. London: Hodder & Stoughton, 1939/2003.

Gerrard, Nicci. "Foreword." In *The Adventures of Margery Allingham*. By Julia Jones, p. vii. Essex: Golden Duck, 1991/2009.

Godwin, William. *The Adventures of Caleb Williams*. 1794.

Gould, Julius, and William Kolb, eds. *A Dictionary of the Social Sciences*. London: Tavistock, 1964.

Grant, Michael. "Introduction." In *The Transformations of Lucius: Otherwise Known as the Golden Ass*. Lucius Apuleius. Trans. Robert Graves, pp. vii–xviii. London: Penguin, 1950/1990.

Grčić, Joseph. *Ethics and Political Theory*. Lanham, MD: University Press of America, Inc., 2000. Cited in Wikipedia.

Greene, Douglas. *John Dickson Carr: The Man Who Explained Miracles*. New York: Otto Penzler, 1995.

Greenwood, Kerry. *The Phryne Fisher Mysteries Volume One: Cocaine Blues and Flying Too High*. Brisbane: Pulp Fiction Press, 2003.

_____. *Dead Man's Chest*. Crow's Nest, NSW: Allen & Unwin, 2010.

Griffin, Roger, and Matthew Feldman, eds. *Fascism: Fascism and Culture*. London: Routledge, 2004. Cited in Wikipedia.

Haddawy, Husain, trans. *The Arabian Nights*. London: Norton.

Haggard, Henry Rider. *King Solomon's Mines*. London: Collins, 1885/1955.

Hawthorn, Jeremy. *Studying the Novel: An Introduction*. London: Edward Arnold, 1993.

Haycraft, Howard. *Murder for Pleasure: The Life and Times of the Detective Story*. New York: Carroll & Graf, 1941/1984.

Hennegan, Alison. "Introduction." 1993. In *Poison for Teacher*. By Nancy Spain, pp. ix–xvii. London: Virago Press, 1949/1004.

Herzel, Roger. "John Dickson Carr." In *Minor American Novelists*. Edited by Charles Alva Hoyt, pp. 67–80. Carbondale: Southern Illinois University Press, 1970.

Holme, Thea. "Introduction." In *Sketches by Boz: Illustrative of Every-Day Life and Every-Day People*. By Charles Dickens, pp. v–xi. London: Oxford University Press (The Oxford Illustrated Dickens), 1833–1836.

Holmes, Richard. *Sidetracks: Explorations of a Romantic Biographer*. London: HarperCollins, 2000.

Hope, Anthony. *The Prisoner of Zenda*. Oxford University Press, 1894/2009.

Hornung, E. W. *The Amateur Cracksman*. London: Atlantic Books, 1899/2008.

Hoyt, Charles Alva, ed. *Minor American Novelists*. Carbondale: Southern Illinois University Press, 1970.

Innes, Michael. *Death at the President's Lodging*. London: Penguin, 1936/1965. (Also known as *Seven Suspects*.)

_____. *Hamlet, Revenge!* London: Penguin, 1937.

Jacobs, Eric. *Kingsley Amis: A Biography*. London: Hodder & Stoughton, 1995.

James, Clive. "Raymond Chandler." *Reliable Essays: The Best of Clive James*, pp. 304–316. London: Picador, 2001.

_____. "The Sherlockologists." *Reliable Essays: The Best of Clive James*, pp. 293–303. London: Picador, 2001.

James, P. D. *Talking About Detective Fiction*. London: Faber and Faber, 2009.

Jerome, Jerome K. *Three Men in a Boat*. Stroud: Alan Sutton, 1889/1989.

Jones, Julia. *The Adventures of Margery Allingham*. Essex: Golden Duck, 1991/2009.

Joshi, S. T. *John Dickson Carr: A Critical Study*. Bowling Green, OH: Bowling Green State University Popular Press, 1990.

Joyce, James. *Ulysses*. Harmondsworth: Penguin, 1922/1960.

Keating, H. F. "The Classical Genre." In *The Crown Crime Companion: The Top 100 Mystery Novels of All Time*. Edited by Otto Penzler and Mickey Friedman, pp. 87–90. New York: Crown Trade Paperbacks, 1995.

Kermode, Frank, and John Hollander, eds. *The Oxford Anthology of English Literature: The Middle Ages Through the 18th Century*, Vols. I–II, Thomas Nashe (1567–1601), British poet. In Time of Pestilence (l. 15–20), 1973.

Kipling, Rudyard. *Kim*. Oxford: Oxford University Press, 1901/1987.

Knight, Stephen. *Form and Ideology in Crime Fiction*. Bloomington: Indiana University Press, 1980.

Knox, Ronald A. *The Viaduct Murder*. Merion Press, 1925.

_____. *Essays in Satire*. E. P. Dutton, 1930 (1928).

_____. "Thirty-Nine Articles of Doubt." In *The Floating Admiral*, by Agatha Christie, et al., pp. 129–164, 295–301. London: HarperCollins, 1931/2011.

Leitch, Thomas M. "E. C. Bentley." In *Dictionary of Literary Biography, Volume 7: British Mystery Writers, 1860–1919*. Edited by Bernard Benstock and Thomas F. Staley, pp. 23–29. Detroit: Gale, 1988.

Lodge, David. *20th Century Literary Criticism: A Reader*. London: Longman, 1972/1995.

_____. *Modern Criticism and Theory: A Reader*. London: Longman, 1988.

_____. "After Bakhtin." In *After Bakhtin: Essays on Fiction and Criticism*, pp. 87–99, 189–190. London: Routledge, 1990.

_____. "Milan Kundera, and the Idea of the Author in Modern Criticism." In *After Bakhtin: Essays on Fiction and Criticism*, pp. 154–167, 193. London: Routledge, 1990.

_____. *The Art of Fiction*. London: Penguin 1992.

_____, ed. "Introduction" (1992). In *Lucky Jim*, by Kingsley Amis, pp. v–xvii. London: Penguin, 1954.

_____. "Waugh's Comic Wasteland." In *Consciousness and the Novel: Connected Essays*, pp. 161–181. London: Secker & Warburg, 2002.

_____. "Afterword." Liar's Landscape: In *Collected Writing from a Storyteller's Life*, by Malcolm Bradbury, pp. 413–427. Oxford: Picador/PanMacmillan, 2006.

Magnusson, Magnus, ed. *Chambers Biographical Dictionary*. Edinburgh: Chambers, 1993.

Maron, Margaret. "The Cozy/Traditional Mystery." *The Crown Crime Companion: The Top 100 Mystery Novels of All Time*. Edited by Otto Penzler and Mickey Friedman, pp. 123–124. New York: Crown Trade Paperbacks, 1995.

Marsh, Ngaio. *Surfeit of Lampreys*. London: HarperCollins, 1941/1999.

Maugham, W. Somerset. "The Decline and Fall of the Detective Story." In *The Vagrant Mood*, pp. 76–101. London: Vintage Books, 1952/2001.

_____. "Mr Know-All." *Collected Short Stories Volume One*, pp. 343–349. London: Pan, 1975.

Mcdonald, Gregory. "Pebble, Pond, Perspective." *The Crown Crime Companion: The Top 100 Mystery Novels of All Time*. Edited by Otto Penzler and Mickey Friedman, pp. 135–138. New York: Crown Trade Paperbacks, 1995.

Mendelsohn, Michael J. "A(lan) A(lexander) Milne." In *Dictionary of Literary Biography*. Thomson Gale, 2005.

Milne, A. A. "Introduction" (Apr 1926). In *The Red House Mystery*. London: Vintage Books, 1922/ 2008.

_____. *The Fourth Wall: A Detective Story in Three Acts*. London: Samuel French, 1928.

_____. Letter to E. V. Lucas. Texas, 3 Oct 1933.

_____. "The General Takes Off His Helmet." In *The Queen's Book of the Red Cross*, 1939.

_____. *It's Too Late Now*. London: Methuen, 1939.

_____. *Chloe Marr*. London: Methuen, 1946.

_____. "Books and Writers." *Spectator*, 30 Jun 1950.

_____. *Winnie-The-Pooh: The Complete Collection of Stories and Poems*. London: Methuen, 2001.

Mitchell, Gladys. *The Saltmarsh Murders*. London: Gollancz, 1932.

_____. *When Last I Died*. London: Michael Joseph, 1941.

Murdoch, Walter. *Collected Essays*. Sydney: Angus & Robinson, 1940, 1941, 1945.

_____. "The Bloke." In *On Rabbits, Morality, Etc.: Selected Writings of Walter Murdock*. Edited by Imre Salusinszky, pp. 23–29. Crawley: UWA Publishing, 2011.

_____. "The Bloke." *Inquirer, the Weekend Australian*. Jul 2–3, 2011, p. 3.

Nicholls, Peter, and Cornel Robu. "Sense of Wonder." In *The Encyclopaedia of Science Fiction*. Edited by John Clute and Peter Nicholls, pp. 1083–1085. London: Orbit, 1993.

Norman, Sylvia. Review of *Four Days' Wonder*. *Spectator*. 3 Nov 1933.

Oleksiw, Susan P. *A Reader's Guide to the Classic British Mystery*. Mysterious Press, 1988.

Olivelle, Patrick. "Introduction." In *Pancatantra: The Book of Indian Folk Wisdom*, ix–xlv. Trans. Patrick Olivelle. Oxford: Oxford University Press, 1997.

Orwell, George. *The Road to Wigan Pier*. London: Penguin, 1937.

_____. "Raffles and Miss Blandish." Horizon, Oct 1944. In *The Penguin Essays of George Orwell*, pp. 257–268. London: Penguin, 1994.

_____. "In Defence of P. G. Wodehouse." *Windmill*, no. 2 (Jul 1945). *The Penguin Essays of George Orwell*, pp. 287–299. London: Penguin, 1994.

_____. "Good Bad Books." *Tribune*, 2 Nov 1945. In *The Penguin Essays of George Orwell*, pp. 318–321. London: Penguin, 1994.

_____. "Decline of the English Murder." Tribune, 15 Feb 1946. In *The Penguin Essays of George Orwell*, pp. 345–348. London: Penguin, 1994.

Panek, Leroy Lad. *Watteau's Shepherds: The Detective Novel in Britain, 1914–1940*. Ohio: Bowling Green State University Press, 1979.

_____. *An Introduction to the Detective Story*. Ohio: Bowling Green State University Popular Press, 1987.

Pancatantra: The Book of Indian Folk Wisdom. Trans. Patrick Olivelle. Oxford: Oxford University Press, 1997.

Parker, Dorothy. "Constant Reader." *New Yorker*, 12 Nov 1927.

Peacosk, Thomas Love. *Nightmare Abbey (1818) / Crotchet Castle (1831)*. London: Penguin Classics, 1986.

Pearson, Roger, trans. "Introduction." In *Candide and Other Stories*. Voltaire, pp. vii–xxxix. Oxford: Oxford University Press, 1990.

Penzler, Otto, and Friedman, Mickey, eds. *The Crown Crime Companion: The Top 100 Mystery Novels of All Time*. New York: Crown Trade Paperbacks, 1995.

Philpotts, Eden. *Saurus* (1938). Westport, CT: Hyperion Press, 1976, 1938.

Pim, Sheila. *Common or Garden Crime*. London: Hodder & Stoughton, 1945.

_____. *Creeping Venom: An Irish Gardening Mystery*. Boulder, CO: The Rue Morgue Press, 1946/2001.

_____. *A Brush with Death*. London: Hodder & Stoughton, 1950.

_____. *A Hive of Suspects*. London: Hodder & Stoughton, 1952.

_____. *Other People's Business*. London: Hodder & Stoughton, 1957.

_____. *The Sheltered Garden*. London: Hodder & Stoughton, 1964.

Poe, Edgar Allan. "The Fall of the House of Usher." *Burton's Gentleman's Magazine*. Philadelphia: Lea & Blanchard, 1839.

_____. "The Fall of the House of Usher" (1839). In *A Century of Creepy Stories*, pp. 957–974. London: Hutchinson, nd.

_____. "The Fall of the House of Usher" (1839). In *Tales of the Grotesque and Arabesque*. Philadelphia: Lea & Blanchard, 1840.

Polsky, Ned. "Thirty Years On." In *Hustlers, Beats, and Others*, pp. 201–247. New York: Lyons, 1998.

Porter, Dennis. *The Pursuit of Crime: Art and Ideology in Detective Fiction*. New Haven: Yale University Press, 1981.

Porter, Joyce. *Dover One*. New York: Foul Play Press, 1964/1989.

Pratchett, Terry. *The Colour of Magic*. London: Corgi, 1983.

Reade, Charles. *The Cloister and the Hearth*. London: Dent (Everyman's Library), 1861/1955.

Reynolds, Barbara. *Dorothy L. Sayers: Her Life and Soul*. New York: St. Martin's Griffin, 1993.

Ruskin, John. *Modern Painters*, vol. 3, part 4, chap. 12. London: Smith, Elder & Co, 1856.

_____. "Of the Pathetic Fallacy." In *The Norton Anthology of English Literature*. Edited by M. H. Abrams, pp. 1331–1333. New York: Norton, 1986.

Sayers, Dorothy L. "Introduction." In *Trent's Last Case*. E. C. Bentley, pp. x–xiii. New York: Harper & Row, 1913.

_____. *Great Short Stories of Detection, Mystery and Horror. Part I Detection and Mystery*. London: Victor Gollancz, 1928/1947.

_____. *The Unpleasantness at the Bellona Club*. London: Hodder & Stoughton, 1928/2003.

_____. *Strong Poison*. New York: HarperCollins, 1930/2006.

_____. "Aristotle on Detective Fiction" (1935). *Unpopular Opinions*. London: Victor Gollancz, 1946. (Lecture delivered at Oxford, 5 Mar 1935.)

_____. *Gaudy Night*. New York: HarperCollins, 1936/2006.

_____. *Busman's Honeymoon*. London: Hodder & Stoughton, 1937/2003.

_____. *In the Teeth of the Evidence*. London: Hodder & Stoughton, 1939/2003.

_____. *Lord Peter: The Complete Lord Peter Wimsey Stories*. New York: HarperCollins Perennial, 1972/2001.

Shaffer, Anthony. *Whodunnit: A Comedy Thriller*. New York: Samuel French, 1983.

Shakespeare, William. *Comedies*. Everyman's Library No. 153, London: Dent, 1906/1953.

_____. *Tragedies*. Everyman's Library No. 155, London: Dent, 1906/1956.

_____. *The Tragedy of Julius Cæsar. Shakespeare's Tragedies*. Everyman's Library No. 155, pp. 362–423. London: Dent, 1906/1956.

Shaw, Bruce. "The Tibetan 'Wheel of Life' Versus the Great Game in Kipling's Kim." *The Kipling Journal*, vol. 69.276 (1995): 12–21.

_____. *The Animal Fable in Science Fiction and Fantasy*. Jefferson: McFarland, 2010.

_____. "A Wave of Dark Brown Skirts: E. C. Bentley and Women." *CADS: Crime and Detective Stories*, edited by Geoff Bradley, vol. 62 (Feb 2012): 27–33.

Shelley, Mary. *Frankenstein or the Modern Prometheus*. London: Penguin, 1818/1992.

Sherrin, Ned. "Introduction" (1985). In *A Bullet in the Ballet*. Caryl Brahms and S. J. Simon, pp. i–viii. London: Hogarth, 1937/1986.

Simenon, Georges. The Hotel Majestic. Trans. David Watson. London: Penguin, 1942/1977.

Spain, Nancy. *Death Before Wicket*. London: Hutchinson, 1945.

_____. *Poison in Play*. London: Hutchinson, 1945.

_____. *Murder Bless It*. London: Hutchinson, 1948.

_____. *Death Goes on Skis*. London: Hutchinson, 1949.

_____. *Poison for Teacher*. London: Virago Press, 1949/2004.

_____. *Poison for the Teacher*. London: Hutchinson, 1949.

_____. *Cinderella Goes to the Morgue: An Entertainment*. London: Hutchinson, 1950.

_____. *R in the Month*. London: Hutchinson, 1950.

_____. *Not Wanted on Voyage*. London: Hutchinson, 1951.

_____. *Not Wanted on Voyage*. Harmondsworth, UK: Penguin, 1951/1956.

_____. *Out Damned Tot*. London: Hutchinson, 1952.

_____. *The Kat Strikes*. London: Hutchinson, 1955.

_____. *Why I'm Not a Millionaire: An Autobiography*. London: Hutchison, 1957.

_____. *Cinderella Goes to the Morgue: An Entertainment*. London: World Distributors, 1963.

_____. *A Funny Thing Happened on the Way*. London: Hutchinson, May 1964.

Smith, Alexander McCall. *The No. 1 Ladies' Detective Agency*. London: Abacus, 1998/2008.

Stirling, John, ed. *The Bible: Authorized Version*. London: The British & Foreign Bible Society, 1955.

Swinburne, Algernon Charles. "Appreciation (1886)." In *The Cloister and the Hearth*. Charles Reade, pp. v–ix. London: Dent (Everyman's Library), 1861/1955.

Swinnerton, Frank. *The Georgian Literary Scene*. Everyman's Library, London: Dent & Sons, 1938.

Symons, Julian. *Bloody Murder: From the Detective Story to the Crime Novel: A History*. Harmondsworth, UK: Penguin, 111985.

Sypher, W., ed. *Comedy*. New York: Doubleday Anchor, 1956, pp. 61–190.

Thomas, Leslie. *Dangerous Davies: The Last Detective*. London: Methuen, 1976.

_____. *Dangerous in Love*. London: Methuen, 1987.

_____. *Dangerous by Moonlight*. London: Methuen, 1993.

_____. *Dangerous Davies and the Lonely Heart*. London: Arrow/Random House, 1998.

Thomson, H. Douglas. *Masters of Mystery: A Study of the Detective Story*. London: Collins, 1931.

Thomson, J. A. K., trans. *The Ethics of Aristotle: The Nicomachean Ethics Translated*. Harmondsworth: Penguin, 1953/1963.

Thwaite, Ann. *A. A. Milne: His Life*. London: Faber and Faber, 1990.

Times Literary Supplement Review of Four Days' Wonder, n.d.

Todorov, Tzvetan. "The Typology of Detective Fiction." In *Modern Criticism and Theory: A Reader*. Edited by David Lodge, pp. 157–165. London: Longman, 1988.

Tolstoy, Leo. *War and Peace*. London: Penguin, 1868–9/2007.

Turner, E. S. *Boys Will Be Boys*. Harmondsworth: Penguin, 1948/1975.

Twain, Mark. *The Adventures of Huckleberry Finn*. London: Thomas Nelson, 1884.

_____. *The Adventures of Huckleberry Finn*. Harmondsworth: Penguin, 1884/1966.

_____. *The Adventures of Tom Sawyer*. London: Harrap, 1924/1953.

Voltaire. *Candide and Other Stories*. Oxford: Oxford University Press, 1990.

_____. *Zadig or Destiny: A Tale of the Orient, 1746–1747*. Oxford: Oxford University Press, 1990.

Watkins, Tony. "Introduction." In *The Prisoner of Zenda*. Anthony Hope, pp. vii–xxviii. Oxford: Oxford University Press, 1894/2009.

Watson, Colin. *Coffin Scarcely Used*. Lyons/Boulder: The Rue Morgue Press, 1958/2008.

_____. *Snobbery with Violence: English Crime Stories and Their Audience*. London: Eyre Methuen, 1971/1979.

Waugh, Evelyn. *Vile Bodies*. New York: Little, Brown and Company, 1930/1958.

Wilding, Michael. "For Writers, Crime Does Pay." *The Australian Literary Review*, vol. 6, no. 8 (Sep 2011): 22.

Wodehouse, P. G. *Leave It to Psmith*. London: Penguin, 1923/1988.

Wynne-Davies, Marion. *Bloomsbury Guide to English Literature*. London: Bloomsbury, 1989.

Television and Film

Allingham, Margery. "Dancers in Mourning." *Campion: The Complete Second Series*. BBC, 1990/2008.

_____. "Flowers for the Judge." *Campion: The Complete Second Series*. BBC, 1990/2008.

_____. "Mystery Mile." *Campion: The Complete Second Series*. BBC, 1990/2008.

_____. "Sweet Danger." *Campion: The Complete Second Series*. BBC, 1990/2008.

_____. "The Case of the Late Pig." *Campion: The Complete First Series*. BBC, 1996/2008.

_____. "Death of a Ghost." *Campion: The Complete First Series*. BBC, 1996/2008.

_____. "Look to the Lady." *Campion: The Complete First Series*. BBC, 1996/2008.

_____. "Police at the Funeral." *Campion: The Complete First Series*. BBC, 1996/2008.

Cousins. Film. Paramount, 1989.

The Mrs. Bradley Mysteries. BBC, 2007.

Sayers, Dorothy L. "Gaudy Night." *Dorothy L. Sayers Mysteries*, BBC, 1987/2002.

_____. "Have His Carcase." *Dorothy L. Sayers Mysteries*, BBC, 1987/2002.

_____. "Strong Poison." *Dorothy L. Sayers Mysteries*, BBC, 1987/2002.

Trent's Last Case. Film, Canal, Artwork, Optimum Releasing Ltd. 1953/2008.

Web

"A. A. Milne." Wikipedia. 19 Feb 2013. Web. 7 Mar 2013. http://en.wikipedia.org/wiki/A._A._Milne.

Ackroyd, Eric. "Cliff." *Myths-Dreams-Symbols: The Unconscious World of Dream*. ND. http://www.mythsdreamssymbols.com/dscliff.html.

"Ali Baba." Wikipedia. 7 Feb 2012. Web. 10 Feb 2012. http://en.wikipedia.org/wiki/Ali_Baba.

Amis, Kingsley. "The Art of the Impossible: *The Door to Doom*, by John Dickson Carr." *Times Literary Supplement*, 6 Jun 1981. Web. http://www.reocities.com/hacklehorn/carr/amis.htm.

"Anthony Berkeley Cox." Wikipedia. 1 Mar 2011. Web. 21 Mar 2011. http://en.wikipedia.org/wiki/Anthony_Berkeley_Cox.

"Anthony Shaffer (writer)." Wikipedia. 3 May 2012. Web. 21 Jun 2012. http://en.wikipedia.org/wiki/Anthony_Shaffer?oldid=0.

"Battle of Magersfontein." Wikipedia. 31 Jan 2012. Web. 20 Feb 2012. http://en.wikipedia.org/wiki/Battle_of_Magersfontein#cite_note-70.

"Bernard Cribbins." Wikipedia. 5 Jul 2012. Web. 31 Jul 2012. http://en.wikipedia.org/wiki/Bernard_Cribbins.

Blake, Nicholas. "Review of John Dickson Carr." *Spectator*. 17 Dec 1937. http://www.reocities.com/hacklehorn/carr/index.htm.

"The Book Browser: Around Melbourne Bookshops." 5 Oct 1946, *Argus*, p. 8. http://trove.nla.gov.au/ndp/del/article/22389529?searchTerm=The+Hermit+Convict.

Breen, Jon L. "Simon Brett and the Modern Whodunit." *Mystery Scene*. 2010. http://mysteryscenemag.com/index.php?option=com_content&view=article&id=2616:simon-brett-and-the-modern-whodunit&catid=38:profile&Itemid=191.

Brett, Simon. *Simon Brett Books*. Home page: Books. http://www.simonbrett.com/books/.

_____. *Simon Brett Books*. Home page: About. http://www.simonbrett.com/about/.

Brice-18. "Orson's In-Joke," Review. IMDb. 15 Feb 2008. http://www.imdb.com/user/ur6227819/comments.

Bruce Montgomery. 1990–2010. IMDb. http://www.imdb.com/name/nm0599736/.

Bunker, K. "An Interesting and Engaging Look at Animals in Science Fiction." Customer review, *Amazon.com*. 12 Jan 2013. www.amazon.com/Science-Fiction-Fantasy-Critical-Explorations/dp/0786447834/ref=sr_1_2?s=books&ie=UTF8&qid=1360880880&sr=1-2&keywords=The+animal+fable+in+science+fiction

"Burlesque." Wikipedia. 26 Aug 2011. Web. 30 Aug 2011. http://en.wikipedia.org/wiki/Burlesque.

"Capital Punishment in the United Kingdom." Wikipedia. 19 Jan 2013. Web. 22 Jan 2013. http://en.wikipedia.org/wiki/Capital_punishment_in_the_United_Kingdom.

"The Case of the Gilded Fly." Wikipedia. 2 Nov 2012. Web. 7 Mar 2013. http://en.wikipedia.org/wiki/The_Case_of_the_Gilded_Fly.

"Christianna Brand." Wikipedia. 5 Aug 2011. Web. 16 Aug 2011. http://en.wikipedia.org/wiki/Christianna_Brand.

"Cite." Wikipedia. http://en.wikipedia.org/wiki/Special:Cite.

Clark, Richard. "The History of Judicial Hanging in Britain, 1735–1964," 1995. Web. http://www.capitalpunishmentuk.org/biblio.html.

Clark, R. J. "Most Enjoyable of the Fethering Mysteries." Amazon.com Customer Review. 28 Nov 2010. http://www.amazon.co.uk/Murder-Museum-Fethering-Mysteries-Simon/dp/0330445286/ref=sr_1_1?ie=UTF8&s=books&qid=1232374164&sr=1-1.

Classic Crime Fiction. "Caryl Brahms — SJ Simon Bibliography." Web. http://www.classiccrimefiction.com/carylbrahms-sjsimon.htm.

Classic Crime Fiction. "Sheila Pim Bibliography." Web. http://www.classiccrimefiction.com/sheila-pim.htm.

Classic Mysteries. "Funny Mysteries 1." Web. http://www.classicmysteries.net/funny_mysteries/.

Classic Mysteries. "Funny Mysteries 2." Web. http://www.classicmysteries.net/funny_mysteries/page/2/.

Classic Mysteries. "Funny Mysteries 3." Web. http://www.classicmysteries.net/funny_mysteries/page/3/.

Classic Mysteries. "Funny Mysteries 4." Web. http://www.classicmysteries.net/funny_mysteries/page/4/.

Classic Mysteries. "Funny Mysteries 5." Web. http://www.classicmysteries.net/funny_mysteries/page/5/.

"Colin Watson (writer)." Wikipedia. 14 Nov 2012. Web. 7 Mar 2013. http://en.wikipedia.org/wiki/Colin_Watson_%28writer%29.

Collins, R. D. "Michael Innes — A Short Biography." *Classic Crime Fiction*, 2003. http://www.classiccrimefiction.com/innesbiog.htm.

Collins, Wilkie. "The Biter Bit." *The Atlantic Monthly*, 1858. Web. http://www.wilkie-collins.info/short_stories.htm.

"Commedia dell'Arte." Wikipedia. 29 Aug 2011. Web. 30 Aug 2011. http://en.wikipedia.org/wiki/Commedia_dell%27arte.

Contrasola. "Lesbian Portraits (14) Joan Werner Laurie and Nancy Spain—*She* Magazine." Blog, 28, 2010. [Extract from Rose Collis 1997]. Web. http://contrasola.blogspot.com/2010/10/lesbian-portrets-14-joan-werner-laurie.html?zx=9ceecfdd659fa095.

Crime Watch: News and Musings on New Zealand and International Crime/Thriller Writing. Web. http://kiwicrime.blogspot.com/2010/06/comedy-and-crime-divorce-or-potential.html.

"Dangerous Davies." Wikipedia. 24 Jun 2012. Web. 31 Jul 2012. http://en.wikipedia.org/wiki/Dangerous_Davies.

"Detection Club." Wikipedia. 24 Jun 2011. Web. 11 Aug 2011. http://en.wikipedia.org/wiki/Detection_Club.

"Detection Club." Wikipedia. 26 Feb 2013. Web. 7 Mar 2013. http://en.wikipedia.org/wiki/Category:Members_of_the_Detection_Club.

"Detective Fiction." Wikipedia. 16 Mar 2011. Web. 18 Mar 2011. http://en.wikipedia.org/wiki/Detective_fiction.

"Dives." Wikipedia. 9 Feb 2013. Web. 7 Mar 2013. http://en.wiktionary.org/w/index.php?title=dives&oldid=19496345.

"Dorothy L. Sayers." Wikipedia. 12 Mar 2013. Web. 12 Mar 2013. http://en.wikipedia.org/w/index.php?title=Dorothy_L._Sayers&oldid=540714754.

"Eden Phillpotts." Wikipedia. 19 Mar 2012. Web. 7 Apr 2012. http://en.wikipedia.org/wiki/Eden_Phillpotts.

"Edgar Allan Poe." Wikipedia. 4 Mar 2013. Web. 12 Mar 2013. http://en.wikipedia.org/wiki/Edgar_Allan_Poe.

"Edmund Crispin." Wikipedia. 28 Feb 2013. Web. 7 Mar 2013. http://en.wikipedia.org/wiki/Edmund_Crispin.

"Edmund Crispin, 1921–1978." *Literary Heritage West Midlands.* 1 Mar 2002. Web. 21 Apr 2008. http://www3.shropshire-cc.gov.uk/crispin.htm.

"Edward Bulwer-Lytton, 1st Baron Lytton." Wikipedia. 23 Jul 2012. Web. 14 Aug 2012. http://en.wikipedia.org/wiki/Edward_Bulwer-Lytton,_1st_Baron_Lytton#cite_note-Drabble2000pp147-4.

"Edward Gordon Craig." Wikipedia. 7 Apr 2011. Web. 7 Apr 2011. http://en.wikipedia.org/wiki/Edward_Gordon_Craig.

"Edwardian era." Wikipedia. 3 Aug 2011. Web. 9 Aug 2011. http://en.wikipedia.org/wiki/Edwardian_era.

Elms, Alan C. "Paul Myron Anthony Linebarger Biographical Summary." 2001–2008. http://www.ulmus.net/ace/csmith/linebargerbiography.html.

"Émile Gaboriau." Wikipedia. 22 Feb 2013. Web. 7 Mar 2013. http://en.wikipedia.org/wiki/%C3%89mile_Gaboriau.

Erickson, Hal. "Four Day's Wonder Plot Synopsis." allmovie, Rovi Corporation, 2010. http://www.allmovie.com/work/four-days-wonder-92197.

Evans, Curt J. "Two by Nancy Spain." http://mysteryfile.com/blog/?p=7630.

Ewener, Jeffery. "Secret Agent of the Absurd." *Mystery Magazine Web*, vol. 1.2 (Spring 2004). http://www.lifeloom.com/I4EwenerWatsonR.htm.

"Fasces." Wikipedia. 10 Jun 2012. Web. 24 Jun 2012. http://en.wikipedia.org/wiki/Fasces.

"Fascism." Wikipedia. 23 Jun 2012. Web. 24 Jun 2012. http://en.wikipedia.org/wiki/Fascism.

Fisher, L. R. "Poison for Teacher. (Lesbian Landmarks) (Paperback)." Amazon.com. 1 Jul 2010. http://www.amazon.co.uk/Poison-Teacher-Lesbian-Landmarks-Nancy/dp/1853817465/ref=sr_1_1?s=books&ie=UTF8&qid=1308017960&sr=1-1.

Foreman, Lewis. "Obituary: Geoffrey Bush." *The Independent.* 2 Mar 1998. http://www.independent.co.uk/news/obituaries/obituary-geoffrey-bush-1147950.html.

"Fourth Wall." Wikipedia. 21 May 2011. Web. 25 May 2011. http://en.wikipedia.org/wiki/Fourth_wall.

"Friedrich Schiller." Wikipedia. 19 Jun 2011. Web. 21 Jun 2011. http://en.wikipedia.org/wiki/ Friedrich_Schiller.

Fry, Stephen (director). *Bright Young Things*. Internet Movie Database, 2003. http://www. imdb.com/title/tt0325123/.

Fuller, Nicholas Lester. "Trent's Few Cases: The Detective Fiction of E. C. Bentley." 2004. http://www.geocities.com/hacklehorn/bentley/index.html (website no longer available).

gadetection (Wiki). *Phillpotts, Eden*. Ed. by PBworks. 2007. Web. http://gadetection.pb works.com/w/page/7931324/Phillpotts,%20Eden.

_____. "Van Dine's Twenty Rules for Writing Detective Stories," 2007. Web. http://gade tection.pbworks.com/Van-Dine%27s-Twenty-Rules-for-Writing-Detective-Stories.

"Genre Fiction." Wikipedia. 25 Mar 2012. Web. 14 Apr 2012. http://en.wikipedia.org/wiki/ Genre_fiction.

"The Girls of Radcliff Hall." Wikipedia. 19 May 2011. Web. 1 Jun 2011. http://en.wikipedia. org/wiki/The_Girls_of_Radcliff_Hall.

"G. K. Chesterton." Wikipedia. 5 Mar 2013. Web. 12 Mar 2013. http://en.wikipedia.org/w/ index.php?title=G._K._Chesterton&oldid=542209565.

"Gladys Mitchell." Wikipedia. 6 Apr 2011. Web. 20 Jun 2011. http://en.wikipedia.org/wiki/ Gladys_Mitchell.

Global Oneness. "Cliff." *Dream Interpretation Dictionary*, 2010. http://www.experience festival.com/a/Dream_Dictionary_Cliff/id/242570.

"Golden Age of Detective Fiction." Wikipedia. 19 Feb 2013. Web. 26 Feb 2013. http://en. wikipedia.org/wiki/Knox%27s_Commandments.

Greene, Douglas. "John Dickson Carr Locked Room Puzzle Mystery Author." MysteryNet. 1998. Web. http://www.mysterynet.com/books/testimony/carr/.

_____. "John Dickson Carr: Explaining the Inexplicable." MysteryNet. 2009. Web. http:// www.mysterynet.com/books/testimony/carr/.

_____, ed. *John Dickson Carr: The Door to Doom*. International Polygonics Ltd. September 1980/1991. Web. http://www.amazon.com/Door-Doom-Library-Crime-Classics/dp/1558 821023.

Grost, Michael E. *A Guide to Classic Mystery and Detection*. Web. http://mikegrost.com/clas sics.htm.

_____. "Margery Allingham." *A Guide to Classic Mystery and Detection*. Web. http://mike grost.com/allingh.htm#Allingham.

_____. "Ngaio Marsh." *A Guide to Classic Mystery and Detection*. Web. http://mikegrost.com/ ngmarsh.htm#Marsh.

_____. "Response to Hoch, Edward D. A 1001 MIDNIGHTS review: E. C. BENTLEY— *Trent's Last Case*." MysteryFile. Web. http://mysteryfile.com/blog/?p=1104.

Hacklehorn. *The Ministry of Miracles: The Detective Fiction of John Dickson Carr*. Dec 2004. http://www.reocities.com/hacklehorn/carr/index.htm.

_____. "John Dickson Carr Parodies." *Reocities*. 2009. http://www.reocities.com/hackle horn/carr/parodies.htm.

_____. "Scathing Attack on Celebrated Mystery Writer." *Reocities*. 2009. http://www.reoc ities.com/hacklehorn/carr/criticism.htm.

Hall, Jason. "The Stone House: A Gladys Mitchell Tribute site." *Gladys Mitchell*. 2000–2011. http://www.gladysmitchell.com/.

"Hermione Gingold." Wikipedia. 18 Aug 2011. Web. 31 Aug 2011. http://en.wikipedia.org/ wiki/Hermione_Gingold.

"Hilaire Belloc." *Wikipedia, the Free Encyclopedia*, 6 Mar 2013. Web. 7 Mar 2013. http:// en.wikipedia.org/wiki/Hilaire_Belloc.

Hoch, Edward D. "A 1001 MIDNIGHTS review: E. C. BENTLEY—*Trent's Last Case*." MysteryFile. http://mysteryfile.com/blog/?p=1104.

Hopwood, John. "Raymond Griffith," from *People with Bio Written by John C. Hopwood*, IMDb, 1990–2010. Web. http://www.imdb.com/name/nm0341586/bio.

"Imogen (Shakespeare)." Wikipedia. 4 Jan 2011. Web. 4 Apr 2011. http://en.wikipedia.org/wiki/Imogen_%28Shakespeare%29.

"Inklings." Wikipedia. 5 Jun 2012. Web. 16 Jul 2012. http://en.wikipedia.org/wiki/Inklings.

"The Inspector Alleyn Mysteries." Wikipedia. 1 Oct 2012. Web. 7 Mar 2013. http://en.wikipedia.org/wiki/The_Inspector_Alleyn_Mysteries.

"Ivor Novello Awards." Wikipedia. 27 Jun 2012. Web. 27 Jun 2012. http://en.wikipedia.org/wiki/Ivor_Novello_Awards.

"James Hepburn, 4th Earl of Bothwell." Wikipedia. 7 Mar 2013. Web. 7 Mar 2013. http://en.wikipedia.org/wiki/James_Hepburn,_4th_Earl_of_Bothwell.

Jaybee-3. "Silly Murder Mystery." New Jersey, 17 Feb 2002. Internet Movie Database (IMDb) 1990–2010. http://www.imdb.com/title/tt0027638/.

"Joan Werner Laurie." Wikipedia. 28 Apr 2011. Web. 29 May 2011. http://en.wikipedia.org/wiki/Joan_Werner_Laurie

"John Buchan, 1st Baron Tweedsmuir." Wikipedia. 22 Feb 2013. Web. 7 Mar 2013. http://en.wikipedia.org/wiki/John_Buchan,_1st_Baron_Tweedsmuir.

"John Dickson Carr." Wikipedia. 27 May 2011. Web. 6 Jun 2011. http://en.wikipedia.org/wiki/John_Dickson_Carr.

Jon. "Spain, Nancy." http://gadetection.pbworks.com/w/page/7931194/Murder,-Bless-It.

_____. "Spain, Nancy — Murder, Bless It (1948)." http://gadetection.pbworks.com/w/page/7931556/Spain,-Nancy.

"Josephine Bell." Wikipedia. 20 Nov 2010. Web. 20 Jun 2011. http://en.wikipedia.org/wiki/Josephine_Bell.

JP. "Cecil Beaton, the Randy Dandy of Photography & Fashion." *The Selvedge Yard: A Historical Record of Artistry, Anarchy, Alchemy & Authenticity*. Apr 18, 2009. Web. http://theselvedgeyard.wordpress.com/2009/04/18/cecil-beaton-the-randy-dandy-of-photography-fashion/.

"Joyce Cary." Wikipedia. 20 Jul 2011. Web. 22 Aug 2011. http://en.wikipedia.org/wiki/Joyce_Cary.

"Judge Dee." Wikipedia. 2 Feb 2011. Web. 18 Mar 2011. http://en.wikipedia.org/wiki/Judge_Dee.

"Kerry Greenwood." Wikipedia. 23 Jul 2012. Web. 8 Aug 2012. http://en.wikipedia.org/wiki/Kerry_Greenwood.

"Kilroy Was Here." Wikipedia. 17 Aug 2011. Web. 30 Aug 2011. http://en.wikipedia.org/wiki/MHRA_Style_Guide.

"Lemmy Caution." Wikipedia. 3 Jun 2012. Web. 3 Jul 2012. http://en.wikipedia.org/wiki/Lemmy_Caution.

"List of Years in Literature." Wikipedia. 9 Sep 2011. Web. 9 Sep 2011. http://en.wikipedia.org/wiki/List_of_years_in_literature#1970s.

Liukkonen, Petri, and Ari Pesonen. "J(ohn) D(ickson) Carr (1906–1977) — Pseudonyms Carr Dickson, Carter Dickson, Roger Fairbairn." *Books and Writers*. Kuusankosken kaupunginkirjasto, 2008. Web. http://www.kirjasto.sci.fi/jdcarr.htm.

_____. "Montgomery Edmund Crispin (1921–1978) — Pseudonym for Robert Bruce Montgomery Edmund Crispin (1921–1978)." *Books and Writers*. Kuusankosken kaupunginkirjasto, 2008. Web. http://www.kirjasto.sci.fi/crispin.htm.

"Love Lies Bleeding (novel)." Wikipedia. 2 Nov 2012. Web. 7 Mar 2013. http://en.wikipedia.org/wiki/Love_Lies_Bleeding_%28novel%29.

Lowe, Nick. "The Well-Tempered Plot Device." (Jul 1986). Ansible [Berkshire, Eng.] vol. 46. Web. http://news.ansible.co.uk/plotdev.html.

MacIntyre, F. Gwynplaine. "Whodunit Played for Laughs." IMDb. 3 Sep 2002. Web. http://www.imdb.com/title/tt0020513/.

Malcolmgsw. "Talk Talk Talk." *Birds of Prey* (1930). IMDb user review. 19 Jul 2010. http://www.imdb.com/title/tt0020694/.

Mander, Keith. "A.A. Milne." Just-Pooh.com, 1998–2010. Web. http://www.just-pooh.com/milne.html.

"Margery Allingham." Wikipedia. 17 Sep 2011. Web. 30 Oct 2011. http://en.wikipedia.org/wiki/Margery_Allingham.

"Marlowe Society." Wikipedia. 5 Dec 2012. Web. 7 Mar 2013. http://en.wikipedia.org/wiki/Marlowe_Society.

Medina, Drew. Digital artist. Cover photograph for the Felony & Mayhem 2012 edition of Edmund Crispin's *The Glimpses of the Moon*. http://drewzart.blogspot.com.au/p/my-blog-latest-work.html.

Milligan, Rich. "Cast, in Order of Disappearance (Charles Paris Mysteries)." Review. Amazon.com. 11 Sep 2005. Web. http://www.amazon.co.uk/Order-Disappearance-Charles-Mysteries-Paperback/dp/0595003397/ref=sr_1_3?ie=UTF8&s=books&qid=1232373792&sr=8–3.

MovieMail. "*Trent's Last Case*." 1996–2009. Web. http://www.moviemail-online.co.uk/film/dvd/Trents-Last-Case/.

"The Moving Toyshop." Wikipedia. 2 Nov 2012. Web. 7 Mar 2013. http://en.wikipedia.org/wiki/The_Moving_Toyshop.

"Murder Most English: A Flaxborough Chronicle, TV Series 1977." IMDb. http://www.imdb.com/title/tt1268707/.

"My Word!" Wikipedia. 25 Apr 2011. Web. 15 Jun 2011. http://en.wikipedia.org/wiki/My_Word!

"The Mysterious Affair at Styles." Wikipedia. 1 Mar 2013. Web. 7 Mar 2013. http://en.wikipedia.org/wiki/The_Mysterious_Affair_at_Styles.

"Nancy Spain." Wikipedia. 27 Jan 2011. Web. 19 Feb 2011. http://en.wikipedia.org/wiki/Nancy_Spain.

"Ned Sherrin." Wikipedia. May 2012. Web. 27 Jun 2012. http://en.wikipedia.org/wiki/Ned_Sherrin.

"New York Shirtwaist Strike of 1909." Wikipedia. 1 Mar 2013. Web. 7 Mar 2013. http://en.wikipedia.org/wiki/New_York_shirtwaist_strike_of_1909.

"Ngaio Marsh." Wikipedia. 28 Feb 2011. Web. 18 Mar 2011. http://en.wikipedia.org/wiki/Ngaio_Marsh.

"1950s." Wikipedia. Web. 11 Sep 2011. http://en.wikipedia.org/wiki/1950s.

"1940s." Wikipedia. 30 Aug 2011. Web. 11 Sep 2011. http://en.wikipedia.org/wiki/1940s.

"1970s." Wikipedia. 8 Sep 2011. Web. 9 Sep 2011. http://en.wikipedia.org/wiki/1970s#Literature.

"1960s." Wikipedia. 4 Sep 2011. Web. 11 Sep 2011. http://en.wikipedia.org/wiki/1960s.

"1930s." Wikipedia. 5 Sep 2011. Web. 11 Sep 2011. http://en.wikipedia.org/wiki/1930s.

"1920s." Wikipedia. 29 Aug 2011. Web. http://en.wikipedia.org/w/index.php?title=1920s&oldid=447292565.

"Noël Coward." Wikipedia. 18 Aug 2011. Web. 19 Aug 2011. http://en.wikipedia.org/wiki/Noel_Coward.

"Oxford University Dramatic Society." Wikipedia. 9 Feb 2013. Web. 7 Mar 2013. http://en.wikipedia.org/wiki/Oxford_University_Dramatic_Society.

"Panic of 1907." Wikipedia. 20 Feb 2013. Web. 7 Mar 2013. http://en.wikipedia.org/wiki/Panic_of_1907.

The Passing Tramp. "What 'Killed' Crispin? The Creative Life and Death of Bruce Montgomery/Edmund Crispin, Part Five. The Passing Tramp: Wandering Through the Mystery Genre, Book by Book." Sunday, 11 Dec 2011. http://thepassingtramp.blogspot.com.au/2011/12/what-killed-crispin-creative-life-and.html.

Patterson, Diana, and Stephen Davies. "Twenty Rules for Writing Detective Stories" (1928). Gaslight. http://gaslight.mtroyal.ab.ca/copyright.htm.

"P. D. James." Wikipedia. 26 Feb 2013. Web. 4 Mar 2013. http://en.wikipedia.org/wiki/
    P._D._James.
"The Perfect Alibi." 1930. Whosdatedwho, 2011. Web. http://www.whosdatedwho.com/tpx_
    809925/the-perfect-alibi/.
Pike, B. A. "In Praise of Gladys Mitchell." *The Armchair Detective*, vol. 9.4 (Oct 1976).
    http://www.gladysmitchell.com/.
Pike, Barry A. "Philip Youngman Carter." The Margery Allingham Society. c. 2009. Web.
    http://www.margeryallingham.org.uk/philip.htm.
Poe, Edgar Allan "The Murders in the Rue Morgue." *Graham's Magazine*. Philadelphia,
    Apr 1841. Wikipedia 23 Feb 2011. http://en.wikipedia.org/wiki/The_Murders_in_the_
    Rue_Morgue.
"The Poisoned Chocolates Case." Wikipedia. 18 Dec 2009. Web. 21 Mar 2011. http://en.
    wikipedia.org/wiki/The_Poisoned_Chocolates_Case.
"Quality Street (play)." Wikipedia. 9 Dec 2010. Web. 31 May 2011. http://en.wikipedia.
    org/wiki/Quality_Street_%28play%29.
Quan, Tracy. "Intoxicating in Her Tireless Appetite." In *The Honeypot of Alienation*. Web.
    http://www.tracyquan.net/gossip/the-honeypot-of-alienation-DB15.pdf.
"The Queen's Book of the Red Cross." Wikipedia. 13 Aug 2012. Web. 7 Mar 2013. http://
    en.wikipedia.org/wiki/The_Queen%27s_Book_of_the_Red_Cross.
Quinion, Michael. "Gas and Gaiters." World Wide Words. 24 Feb 2007, 1996–2010. http://
    www.worldwidewords.org/qa/qa-gas1.htm.
"Radclyffe Hall." Wikipedia. 3 Apr 2011. Web. 1 Jun 2011. http://en.wikipedia.org/wiki/Rad
    clyffe_Hall.
Radio Days. "My Word! (1956–1990)." Web. http://www.turnipnet.com/whirligig/radio/
    myword.htm.
"Rich Man and Lazarus." Wikipedia. 23 Feb 2013. Web. 7 Mar 2013. http://en.wikipedia.
    org/wiki/Rich_man_and_Lazarus.
"Robert van Gulik." Wikipedia. 22 Dec 2010. Web. 18 Mar 2011. http://en.wikipedia.org/
    wiki/Robert_van_Gulik.
"Roedean School." Wikipedia. 23 May 2011. Web. 31 May 2011. http://en.wikipedia.org/
    wiki/Roedean_School.
"Ronald Knox." Wikipedia. 14 Mar 2011. Web. 21 Mar 2011. http://en.wikipedia.org/wiki/
    Ronald_Knox.
Rozovsky, Peter. "Dry Humor in a Cold Climate." Detectives Beyond Borders. 2007. Web.
    http://detectivesbeyondborders.blogspot.com/.
_____. "The Little World of Mayhem Parva." Detectives Beyond Boundaries. 9 Jun 2007.
    Web. http://detectivesbeyondborders.blogspot.com.au/2007/06/little-world-of-mayhem-
    parva.html.
Rubio, Alexander G. "John Dickson Carr — Master of the Locked Room Mystery." Culture
    Section, Bits of News. 30 Nov 2006. Web. 2005–2007. http://www.bitsofnews.com/
    content/view/4441/42/.
Russell, Ray. *Guide to Supernatural Fiction*. Tartarus Press. 2 May 2008. Web. http://free
    pages.pavilion.net/tartarus/c29.htm.
"Ruth Rendell." Wikipedia. 2 Mar 2013. Web. 4 Mar 2013. http://en.wikipedia.org/wiki/
    Ruth_Rendell.
Ryan-Fazilleau, Sue. "Kerry Greenwood's 'Rewriting' of Agatha Christie." *Journal of the
    Association for the Study of Australian Literature*, vol. 7 (2007): 59–70. Web. http://www.
    nla.gov.au/openpublish/index.php/jasal/article/view/465/.
Salten, Felix. *Bambi: A Life in the Woods*. New York: Alladin, 1928/1998.
Sandles, Tim. "Legendary Dartmoor." 8 Sep 2009. Web. http://www.legendarydartmoor.co.
    uk/author_web.htm.
Schantz, Tom, and Enid Schantz. "Sheila Pim." Jan 2001. *Mystery Books from the Golden*

Age of Detective Fiction. Rue Morgue Press, 2004–2012. Web. http://ruemorguepress.com/authors/pim.html.

_____. "Introduction." Feb 2008. *Coffin Scarcely Used*. Colin Watson. Lyons/Boulder: The Rue Morgue Press, 1958/2008. http://ruemorguepress.com/authors/pim.html.

"Sephardi Jews." Wikipedia. 27 Jun 2012. Web. 27 Jun 2012. http://en.wikipedia.org/wiki/Sephardi.

Shelley's Bookshelf. "Review of *The Viaduct Murder*, by Ronald A. Knox." http://www.midwestbookreview.com/rbw/jun_02.htm#shelley.

Shortling, Grobius. "John Dickson Carr: Master of the Locked Room." Mysterylist.com, 1997–2005. Web. http://www.mysterylist.com/carr.htm.

_____. "Michael Innes: Sir John Appleby: Scotland Yard vs. Oxford Dona and Dotty Peers." Mysterylist.com, 2001. Web. http://www.mysterylist.com/innes.htm.

Shryane, Tony. "My Word!" *Ariel, the Staff Magazine of the BBC*, Jul 1958. http://www.turnipnet.com/whirligig/radio/myword.htm.

"Sic Transit Gloria Mundi." Wikipedia. 9 May 2012. Web. 25 Jul 2012. http://en.wikipedia.org/wiki/Sic_transit_gloria_mundi.

"Sir John Appleby." Wikipedia. 12 May 2012. Web. 17 Jul 2012. http://en.wikipedia.org/wiki/Sir_John_Appleby.

"S. J. Simon." Wikipedia. 13 Jun 2012. Web. 26 Jun 2012. http://en.wikipedia.org/wiki/S._J._Simon.

"Slapstick." Wikipedia. 20 Aug 2011. Web. 30 Aug 2011. http://en.wikipedia.org/wiki/Slapstick.

Smith, Patricia Juliana. "Messel, Oliver (1904–1978)." *Glbtq: An Encyclopedia of Gay, Lesbian, Bisexual, Transgender, and Queer Culture, 2002*. Web. http://www.glbtq.com/contributors/bio_58.html.

"Songs Without Words." Wikipedia. 26 Feb 2013. Web. 7 Mar 2013. http://en.wikipedia.org/wiki/Songs_without_Words.

"S. S. Van Dine." Wikipedia. 26 Feb 2013. Web. 7 Mar 2013. http://en.wikipedia.org/wiki/S._S._Van_Dine.

Sterling, Bruce. "Turkey City Lexicon — A Primer for SF Workshops." *Science Fiction and Fantasy Writers of America*. Web. http://www.sfwa.org/2009/06/turkey-city-lexicon-a-primer-for-sf-workshops/.

Still, Clive A. H. "One of the Best in the Series." Amazon.com. Customer Review, 9 Mar 2012. Web. http://www.amazon.co.uk/Murder-Museum-Fethering-Mysteries-Simon/dp/0330445286/ref=sr_1_1?ie=UTF8&s=books&qid=1232374164&sr=1–1.

Symphony No. 9 (Beethoven). Wikipedia. 22 Feb 2013. Web. 7 Mar 2013. http://en.wikipedia.org/wiki/Symphony_No._9_%28Beethoven%29.

"The Threepenny Opera." Wikipedia. 28 Aug 2011. Web. 31 Aug 2011. http://en.wikipedia.org/wiki/The_Threepenny_Opera.

"The Threepenny Opera (1931 film)." Wikipedia. Aug 2011. Web. 31 Aug 2011. http://en.wikipedia.org/wiki/The_Threepenny_Opera_%281931_film%29.

"Till Eulenspiegel." Wikipedia. 7 Feb 2011. Web. 28 Mar 2011. http://en.wikipedia.org/wiki/Till_Eulenspiegel.

Time. "Books: Now We Are Sex." Review of Chloe Marr, 2 Sep 1946. Web. 2010. http://www.time.com/time/magazine/article/0,9171,803972,00.html.

"Treaty of Versailles." Wikipedia. 6 Mar 2013. Web. 8 Mar 2013. http://en.wikipedia.org/wiki/Treaty_of_Versailles.

Trevoe, S. "Gentle Suburban Detective Story." Amazon.com. Customer Review, 23 Sep 2010. Web. http://www.amazon.co.uk/Murder-Museum-Fethering-Mysteries-Simon/dp/0330445286/ref=sr_1_1?ie=UTF8&s=books&qid=1232374164&sr=1–1.

Trippe, Caroline. "Murder and Humor: Oil and Water? The Tone of a Mystery." Crimespace. 28 Jun 2010. Web. http://crimespace.ning.com/forum/topics/murder-and-humor-oil-and-water.

"Tristan." Wikipedia. 27 Feb 2013. Web. 8 Mar 2013. http://en.wikipedia.org/wiki/Tristan.

"Tristan and Iseult." Wikipedia. 24 Feb 2013. Web. 8 Mar 2013. http://en.wikipedia.org/wiki/Tristan_and_Iseult.

"Tristan und Isolde." Wikipedia. 27 Feb 2013. Web. 8 Mar 2013. http://en.wikipedia.org/wiki/Tristan_und_Isolde.

"True Penny." Free Dictionary. http://www.thefreedictionary.com/True-penny.

"The Ugly Duckling (play)." Wikipedia. 13 Apr 2011. Web. 8 Mar 2013. http://en.wikipedia.org/wiki/The_Ugly_Duckling_%28play%29.

Van Dine, S. S. "Twenty Rules for Writing Detective Stories." *American Magazine* (Sep 1928). Web. 11 Jan 2000. http://gaslight.mtroyal.ab.ca/copyright.htm.

"Vanity." Wikipedia. 28 Feb 2013. Web. 8 Mar 2013. http://en.wikipedia.org/wiki/Vanity.

"Victor Gollancz Ltd." Wikipedia. 12 Jan 2013. Web. 25 Jan 2013. http://en.wikipedia.org/wiki/Victor_Gollancz_Ltd.

Vineyard, David L. "Review of E. C. Bentley —*Elephant's Work: An Enigma*." MysteryFile.com, 2009. http://mysteryfile.com/blog/?p=1101.

"W. Somerset Maugham Bibliography." Wikipedia. 30 Jul 2012. Web. 17 Sep 2012. http://en.wikipedia.org/w/index.php?title=Special:Cite&page=W._Somerset_Maugham_bibliography&id=504848352.

Watson, Colin. "Bump in the Night." Classic Mysteries, 6 Sep 2010. Web. http://www.classicmysteries.net/2010/09/bump-in-the-night.html.

_____. "Coffin Scarcely Used." Classic Mysteries, 8 Sep 2010. Web. http://www.classicmysteries.net/2010/09/looking-back-coffin-scarcely-used-and-mayhem-parva.html.

"The Well of Loneliness." Wikipedia. 31 May 2011. Web. 1 Jun 2011. http://en.wikipedia.org/wiki/The_Well_of_Loneliness.

Whittle, David. *Bruce Montgomery/Edmund Crispin: A Life in Music and Books*. Hampshire: Ashgate, 2007. Reprinted Gloucester: The Book Depository Ltd., 2011. http://www.bookdepository.co.uk/book/9780754634430/Bruce-MontgomeryEdmund-Crispin.

"Whodunnit (play)." Wikipedia. 13 Aug 2011. Web. 25 Jun 2012. http://en.wikipedia.org/wiki/Whodunnit_%28play%29.

Wood, Ralph. "Not Wanted on Voyage (1951)." Web. http://gadetection.pbworks.com/w/page/7931262/Not-Wanted-on-Voyage.

Wyatt, James. "Gervase Fen." MysteryList.com, Apr 2001. http://www.mysterylist.com/crispin.htm.

Young, Dave. The John Dickson Car Collector. JDCarr.com, 21 Apr, 2003. http://www.jdcarr.com/.

Zaslavsky, Robert. "Reviews of Stephen Knight, *Form and Ideology in Crime Fiction* (Bloomington: Indiana University Press, 1980. 202 pp.); Dennis Porter, *The Pursuit of Crime: Art and Ideology in Detective Fiction* (New Haven: Yale University Press, 1981. 267 pp.)." *College Literature*, vol. 10, no. 2 (Spring 1983): 204–208.

Index

chance/coincidence 1, 19–20, 22, 24, 26–27, 54, 69, 71, 75, 85, 101, 109, 120, 130, 162, 174, 180, 192, 202–203
Chandler, Raymond 10, 12, 37, 42, 46, 61, 81, 113, 147, 153, 194, 221, 266
change 9, 10, 11, 19, 12, 17, 32, 34, 35, 37, 38, 40, 43, 47, 53, 66, 69, 81, 103, 104, 106, 130, 158, 195, 203, 206, 216, 219, 236, 253, 262–263; *see also* social change
Chappel 96
characterization 10, 17, 38, 60, 63, 85, 91, 125, 135, 148, 156, 229, 261
characters: detestable 73, 85, 125, 164, 175–176, 190, 206, 233, 247, 249; minor 83, 85, 112, 161, 188, 232, 259; sympathetic 91, 152, 156, 221, 251; unsympathetic 85, 175, 229, 246
Charing Cross 51
Charity Ends at Home (Watson) 245
Charles Hopkins Theater, New York 88
Charminade 203
Chartered Surveyor 252
Charybdis (Crispin character) 191, 193; *see also* nicknames
Chase, James Hadley 177
Chaucer, Geoffrey 32–33
chemists 160, 201, 223, 248
Chesham Bois, Buckinghamshire 170
Chesterton, Gilbert K. 39, 42, 51–52, 54–55, 79, 127, 131, 146–147, 156, 160, 162–163, 189, 205, 238–239
Chesterton effect 206
Chet and Bernie mysteries (Quinn characters) 18, 260
Chew, Stanley (Spain character) 220
childhood 68, 93, 126, 130, 168, 209, 252
children 52, 54, 91, 121, 128, 134, 137, 146, 151, 165, 167, 204, 215–216, 218–219, 229, 231, 234, 236, 238, 252
children's tales 79–81, 90, 92, 115, 173, 256
The China Governess (Allingham) 100
Chinese 22, 28, 33, 261–262
chivalry 38, 68
Chloe Marr (Milne) 36, 79–80, 263
chloroform 115
chocolate 190, 191
Christ Church Choir School 126
Christchurch, England 127
Christchurch, New Zealand 134
Christianity 32, 120, 129, 131, 133, 178, 238
Christie, Agatha 6, 13, 36, 41–44, 46, 49, 60–61, 79–81, 95, 99, 115, 119, 134, 143, 152, 155, 180, 202, 231, 243, 247, 249, 257, 261
Christ's Birthday (Montgomery) 173
chronologies 180, 219, 245
Chung, Lin (Greenwood character) 261–262
church attendance 23, 56, 76, 144, 161, 171, 191, 239, 248
Churchill, Winston 160, 189
Cicely, Aunt (Carr character) 164
Le Cid (Corneille) 130

"Cinderella Alone" (Brett chapter heading) 252
Cinderella Goes to the Morgue (Spain) 26, 210, 213, 227, 231–234
ciphers/codes 23–25, 112, 132
circulating libraries 37, 40, 53
cities 39, 152, 188, 190, 208, 227, 247, 250
city-country divide 32, 227–228
civil rights 47
civilization 191
Clark, M. J. (reviewer) 258
Clark, Richard 74
class divisions 23, 32, 41–43, 53, 58, 99, 114, 158, 174, 191, 207–208, 210, 217, 228, 242, 244–245, 248, 255, 261
classic 25, 126, 168, 171, 221, 263; definition of 11, 40
Classic Crime Fiction 136, 138–139, 227
classifications/typologies 11, 15, 139, 162, 265
Cleaver gang (Allingham characters) 117
Cleaves, Clarice 148, 150–151, 153, 165–166, 210
Clements, Ann (Barbara Ann Montgomery) 4, 171, 199
Clemmie (Carr character) 166
clerihews 13, 52, 94, 216
Clerihews Complete (Bentley) 52
"The Clever Cockatoo" (Bentley) 57, 59
clew 36; *see also* clues; evidence
clichés 6, 18, 23, 25, 58–59, 69, 90, 99, 105, 140, 143, 161, 176, 197, 209, 220, 227, 231, 249; *see also* stock characters; stock phrases
cliff motif 29, 64, 67, 71–72, 133, 164
climax/climactic 18, 64, 107, 135, 163, 185, 187, 205–206, 226, 233–235; *see also* anti-climax
Climpson, Miss Katharine (Sayers character) 117
Clive (Crispin character) 179, 185
The Cloister and the Hearth (Reade) 162
close reading 2, 82, 264
closure 28, 106, 184
clothing 28, 70, 112, 120, 128, 152–153, 165–166, 175, 209, 219, 222, 228, 233, 246; mannish 128, 209, 219
Clotworthy, Mrs. (Crispin character) 204
Clouds of Witness (Sayers) 81, 129, 131
clowns 16, 168, 206, 257
Cluedo 83, 107
clues 6, 21–22, 24–25, 28, 36, 57–58, 65–66, 74, 76, 86, 87, 115, 154, 157–158, 161–164, 181, 195–196, 215, 224–226, 240, 247, 261, 265; *see also* evidence
Clues magazine 244
Clute, John, and Peter Nicholls 12, 202
Cocaine Blues (Greenwood) 261
Coffin, Scarcely Used (Watson) 48, 244–247
Cohen, J. M. 67
Colchester 93, 98
Cold War 46, 144
Cole, Barbara 209, 215

www.ingramcontent.com/pod-product-compliance
Lightning Source LLC
Chambersburg PA
CBHW021404110726
47901CB00008B/2057